Dear Reader,

Have you had your vacation yet? Even if you can't get away for a while, why not take the phone off the hook, banish your family and/or friends for an hour or two, and relax with a long cool drink and one (or all!) of this month's *Scarlet* novels?

Would you like a trip to London and the English countryside? Then let *The Marriage Contract* by Alexandra Jones be your guide. Maybe you want to visit the USA, so why not try Tina Leonard's *Secret Sins* and *A Gambling Man* from Jean Saunders? Or perhaps you'd like a trip back in time? Well, Stacy Brown's *The Errant Bride* can be your time machine. Of course, I enjoyed *all four* books and I hope you'll want to read them all too. So why not stretch that hour or two into three or four?

One of the aspects of my job which is both a joy and a challenge is getting the balance of books right on our schedules. So far, I've been lucky because each of our talented authors has produced a unique *Scarlet* novel for you. Do tell me, though, won't you, if you'd like to see more romantic suspense on our list, or some more sequels, or maybe more books with a sprinkling of humour?

Till next month,

Sally Cooper

SALLY COOPER,
Editor-in-Chief – *Scarlet*

About the Author

Stacy Brown graduated from McGill University with a Major in History. She worked in the publishing industry before quitting her job to try her hand at her first love – writing. Stacy has a beautiful baby girl and a wonderful husband who fill all her time when she's not thinking about her next romance novel.

With this, her first published novel, *The Errant Bride*, Stacy has brought a new and exciting voice to the *Scarlet* list and we know that readers will enjoy this book.

Other *Scarlet* titles available this month:

A GAMBLING MAN – Jean Saunders
SECRET SINS – Tina Leonard
THE MARRIAGE CONTRACT – Alexandra Jones

STACY BROWN

THE ERRANT BRIDE

Enquiries to:
Robinson Publishing Ltd
7 Kensington Church Court
London W8 4SP

First published in the UK by Scarlet, 1997

A copy of the British Library Cataloguing in
Publication data is available from the British Library

ISBN 1-85487-965-0

Printed and bound in the EC

10 9 8 7 6 5 4 3 2 1

CHAPTER 1

CHAPTER 1

England 1819

The dilapidated stagecoach bumped and swayed along the furrowed country road, its wheels creaking ominously. Inside the stuffy conveyance, Karina Simpson shifted uncomfortably on the hard, cramped seat to ease the numbness.

Seated next to her was the rather obnoxious and somewhat portly Mr James who dozed off repeatedly throughout the grueling journey. To her chagrin, he'd developed a marked preference for using her shoulder as a pillow. She was forced regularly to shove his unattractive, slightly balding head off her slender shoulder. On each occasion, he rallied, rewarding her efforts with a snort and a gruff, sleepy apology.

Her fellow crew of travelers fixed her with a stony look of disapproval. Turning her gaze to the window, she nudged ever closer against the conveyance wall. She told herself she was lucky to have a seat as this was the last coach from Liverpool to Hampshire.

1

Thus far, however, her arduous journey had presented more challenges than the uncomfortable seating arrangements.

Oh yes, her trip from Boston to England was pure delight! She was forced to wait several months to book safe passage as few passenger ships departed from Boston Harbor bound for England. After surviving what must be regarded as the roughest passage in history across the Atlantic for she was violently ill through most of it, she learned that this archaic, rundown stagecoach was the only available transport to Winchester.

Why was she surprised? Of late, her well-ordered life had deteriorated into total chaos. The last few months were like something out of a horrific nightmare. It had all started with her mother's illness, and culminated with the peculiar stipulation in her mother's will regarding Karina's legal guardian, Charles Dalton, the Duke of Overfield.

Karina's parents had been born in England, of course, but her mother had never mentioned any close friends. She knew nothing of the mysterious Dalton family. Surely, she thought, shifting her position on the narrow wooden seat in a vain attempt to reduce the stiffness, someone closer to Boston could have welcomed her into their home?

Perhaps it was just as well, she thought, as she gazed at the countryside passing by. She could not have remained in Boston, not with the haunting memories of her mother's untimely death. No, she was certain, as she swallowed the painful lump in her throat and held back the tears that threatened to fall, a fresh start was precisely what she needed.

The rickety old coach rumbled to a sharp halt dislodging several of its passengers from their precarious seats. And for once, Karina thought ruefully, she was glad the beefy Mr James sat at her side.

'Winchester!' the coachman shouted as he jumped down from his seat and flung open the coach door. ''Tis your stop, miss,' he told Karina with a nod in her direction.

Managing to extricate her rumpled skirt from beneath Mr James's rotund shape, she squeezed past his bulging appendages and climbed down from the overcrowded coach. The night air felt cool on her face. Taking a deep breath of the crisp air, she looked around and noticed, to her acute dismay, that she appeared to be in the middle of nowhere! What was more, she was the sole passenger disembarking at Winchester.

Even so, she thought rubbing her stiff limbs, she was pleased to have finally vacated her cramped position and that dreadfully hard seat.

The grumpy coachman dragged her abundance of trunks from the coach. Grunting his displeasure at their weight, he carelessly discarded them by the side of the road,

'I best be on me way, miss. I gotta keep to me schedule,' he added with a tip of his tattered cap.

'Do you normally leave people *here*?' Karina asked, her sapphire blue eyes widening incredulously. She had expected at least an inn or something. England certainly was a peculiar country, she thought with a frown. If this fork in the road passed for the coach stop, she would be loathe to visit the rest of Winchester.

'Aye,' he grunted in response and turned his back to leave her where she stood. 'T'ain't no more stagecoaches comin' 'ere tonight.'

'Oh,' Karina mumbled, biting her lower lip. 'Isn't it a bit . . . remote?' she asked hurrying after him. *And dark and desolate*, she thought with a shiver.

'Aye,' he muttered.

In an effort to delay his imminent departure further, she ventured to say, 'I am waiting for someone from Grantly Manor. Do you know of it?' After all, England was a comparatively small country.

'Grantly?' he inquired with a raised bushy brow.

Her face brightened. 'Yes. Do you know the Dalton family?'

The man shook his head.

'I am visiting from America,' she continued tentatively. 'Boston.'

He chortled and let his gaze roam over her velvet redingote and simple blue muslin dress with disdain, 'Aye, I guessed you was a foreigner, what with that accent o'yourn. Canno' say as I know anyone from th' Manor House tho'.'

'Oh,' she muttered, her heart sinking. Apparently, England was not as small as she had anticipated.

4

'Well,' she said with a sigh, 'that settles that. I suppose I shall remain here until someone comes for me.' Her voice was decidedly forlorn.

'I'm sure someone'll be comin' soon enough. I'll be sayin' goodnight to ye then miss.' Tipping his hat, he jumped on board the stagecoach and cracked his whip.

The team of horses responded to his gruff command and the old coach lurched forward. Clutching her precarious straw bonnet, Karina hastily stepped back from the road to avoid being trampled. As she watched the rickety coach disappear out of view a pang of fear stabbed at her heart.

Wandering over to her solitary pile of belongings, she tried to console herself. Of course, the coachman was right. Any moment now, the carriage would arrive to take her to Grantly. Satisfied, she perched on top of her trunks. And waited.

And waited.

And waited.

Drawing her collar around her neck, she sneezed. It seemed to be growing dark rapidly, and decidedly colder, she thought with a shiver. How long had she been here? It felt like hours. Opening her gold locket, she strained to read the black and white face of her timepiece, but the encroaching darkness made it impossible.

'There is no cause to be frightened,' she told herself as she took a deep fortifying breath of the cold night air, 'just because you are alone in the middle of England with no idea where the nearest town might be or when the conveyance from Grantly might show up!'

But, as she watched the creeping fog swirl around her ominously, realization dawned. Her shoulders slumped. No one from the elusive manor intended to fetch her tonight.

She could not very well pass the night on the side of the road. It was pitch black and the fog seemed to be thickening in every direction.

'This is positively awful!' she heard herself exclaim as she dug through her reticule for her embroidered lace handkerchief. 'Isn't it enough that I have traveled hundreds of miles, am exhausted, cold, and tired?'

Good heavens, but the English were extraordinary! She blew her dripping, ice-cold nose. Hadn't they the slightest notion that it was exceedingly rude, not to mention offputting, to leave a visitor sitting for hours in the damp cold, in a strange country, in the middle of the night?

Made of stern stuff, however, she was not easily daunted. Stuffing her crumpled hankie back into her reticule, she tried to wiggle her toes in her leather vamp boots. Her feet were numb, and she wasn't sure that she could still feel all her fingers.

Obviously, she could not stay on this frozen perch all night. If no one was coming to fetch her, she'd have to manage on her own. Getting to her feet, she appraised her bulky trunks. Dare she leave her belongings in the middle of the road, she wondered, chewing on her lip. No one would come by here, at least, not until daylight. And she carried the key to her trunks in her reticule. She could easily have them picked up in the morning.

Straightening her spine, she clutched her reticule tightly and started down the road with as much confidence as she could muster. After all, she thought, how far could the town be? In no time at all, she'd be resting comfortably in her new room at Grantly.

As she tramped down the dirt road, the billowing mist danced around her feet. Ice-cold fingers of night air clutched at her. She shivered and pulled her collar closer.

Where was this elusive town? The infernal fog swirled about her like a taunting ghost. She could see her breath, but precious little else. For all she knew, she was walking the wrong way.

She had not gone more than a mile when she heard a noise. It sounded like a horse. Yes, she thought, as the pounding thud of hooves echoed in her ears, it was definitely a horse and she realized with a pang of fear, it was galloping toward her!

She struggled to focus in the dense fog. But she could not make out a thing. Turning around frantically in a circle, her heart slammed into her ribs. It was impossible to determine from which direction the horse was approaching. Paralyzed with fear, she tried to focus. But in the pitch darkness, the sound seemed to be coming from different directions. At this point, the deafening sound of blood pounding

7

in her ears and the clamor of the approaching horse were indistinguishable.

The sound grew still louder. Ghastly images of being trampled beneath the great beast filled her mind. She had to get off the road. Her eyes darted in every direction. Which way? The cover of night made it difficult to determine where the dirt road ended and the grass began.

Swinging around she came abruptly face to face with an enormous black horse, rearing up on its hind legs. The white of his wild eyes glinted against the darkness and his raging breath clouded the cold night air. The rider wrestled with his mount, trying desperately to gain control of the massive beast.

Instinctively she threw her arms up to protect herself. She heard a scream. It was a bloodcurdling sound. Her throat went raw and she realized the cry had come from her own throat. And then she heard the rider yell something unintelligible. Suddenly, the ground was beneath her back, and she could scarcely draw a breath.

Throwing himself from the saddle, the rider approached the lifeless girl lying in the road. 'Hell!' he growled. Bending over her, he touched her chest and ascertained that she was breathing. 'Are you hurt?' he asked, his voice harsh.

Struggling to make sense of her situation, Karina opened her eyes and stared at the man looming above her. He was as dark as his horse and twice as ominous. She opened her mouth, but could not utter a sound. Or catch her breath for that matter.

8

In fact, she was having a great deal of trouble comprehending all that had happened.

'Are you in pain?' he snapped. 'Is anything broken?'

Karina stared blankly at him.

Grunting with irritation he examined her body. His large masterful hands seemed to touch her everywhere. Good heavens, she thought with a rush of embarrassment, they were all over her! The offensive man seemed to know her body better than she did. When he touched her right arm she suddenly found her voice and shrieked.

His hands fell from her body. 'So,' he said coldly, 'you have a voice. Can you move your arm?'

Karina attempted to move her arm and the throbbing pain spread. 'I don't think so,' she moaned. 'Ooh,' she said biting her lower lip. 'It hurts terribly!'

'You are damned stupid!' he spat out. 'What the hell were you doing? Trying to get yourself killed?'

'I . . . no I . . .' she stammered, struggling to rise, but the pain was overwhelming, 'was – ooh! Is it broken do you think?' she asked with a whimper.

He frowned. 'Could be. If you would stop holding it,' he muttered, 'I might have a chance to feel for broken bones.'

His touch was surprisingly gentle, given his rude manner. However, when he pressed on her forearm, feeling for the bone, she yelped in pain.

'Sorry,' he murmured, 'it is not broken, just badly bruised, I think.' He hesitated a moment, regarding

9

her pensively in the darkness. 'Can you stand?' he asked sharply.

'I — I think so,' she stammered feebly and struggled to push herself up into a sitting position, but she felt as weak as a new born colt. Before she knew what was happening, his arms were around her and he had swept her off the ground. It was most disconcerting to be held so closely by a man. Her face was pressed against his neck. She breathed in the strong, clean scent of him, and an odd jolt of pleasure coursed through her. The idea that the musky scent of a man mingled with brandy and tobacco should affect her so was quite alarming. And yet, it was also strangely exhilarating. Gracious! How unseemly, she thought, becoming quite flustered.

'Sir, please, I . . . this is not necessary . . . I believe I can walk, it is only my arm — '

But he ignored her protests, 'You are fortunate that my horse did not trample you to death,' he told her curtly. But his breath was like a warm caress on her temple. 'What the devil are you doing walking outside at this hour?'

Karina bristled. She did not have to explain her predicament to this atrocious man. Nor did she enjoy being carried in his arms. And the way his large hand splayed over her rib cage just below her breast was more than improper, not to mention profoundly disturbing. She felt a rush of heat spread through her and cleared her throat,

'I was trying to find shelter,' she shot back.

'In the middle of the road?' he snorted with derision.

If this was the way English gentlemen behaved she was certain to hate this country. 'I was *not* in the middle of the road!' she cried hotly.

'No? Then why, pray tell, is your arm aching?' he asked, looking down at his small but spirited burden.

'My arm,' she breathed, trying to calm her ebbing fury, 'is aching because of you! If you had not been riding so recklessly none of this would have happened. You should have paid attention to what you were doing and realized that there was someone along the road.'

'You were in the *middle* of the road,' he bit out, 'not on the side of it.'

Karina drew a deep calming breath, 'Sir,' she said coolly. 'It is dark and foggy. I recognized the impending danger and tried to avert it.'

'Tried, and failed, rather miserably, I'd say,' he muttered under his breath.

How dare he be flippant with her? This was all his fault! 'I should like to remind you that it was your monstrosity of a horse that struck *me* not the other way around!'

His eyes narrowed on her flushed face, 'Madam,' he said harshly, 'you seem to be in a very precarious situation at the moment.' Letting his dark eyes roam over her disheveled form, he added, 'I would strive to remember just who is assisting whom here.'

'I did not ask for your beast of a horse to run me down! And, for that matter, I have no desire to be

11

held in your offensive arms!' she countered hotly. 'Kindly release me, at once.'

'By all means.' He roughly set her feet on the ground.

She felt positively miserable. Her arm ached horribly, she was exhausted and dreadfully cold. Her stomach had started to grumble over the last quarter of a mile, reminding her that she had not eaten since morning. And this imbecilic man was probably wrong. Her arm had to be broken! Could anything hurt this much and not be broken? His medical knowledge was probably equal only to his charm.

'Can you ride?' he asked gruffly.

'Of course,' she retorted sharply.

He shook his head and reached out his arms to help her mount, but she shrugged him off.

'If you would please be so kind as to see me to the nearest inn. I promise to make it well worth your while,' she said over her shoulder, trying unsuccessfully to mount the horse. 'I should think two guineas would compensate you for your trouble.'

Good Lord, his horse was huge, at least eighteen hands! Without thinking she tried to pull herself up into the saddle. Agonizing pain shot through her arm. A cry escaped her lips and she fell helplessly backwards into a black abyss. Grunting with displeasure, he swore under his breath. 'Devil take it!' And then the strong capable arms were around her once more, gathering her close.

* * *

12

He was furious! He would already be arriving home later than he had planned. The blasted meeting in London had dragged on for hours to no avail. And to make matters worse, his mistress was strangely absent when he paid her a call, a fact he found mildly irritating. It was certainly true that he was growing bored with her, but the idea that she might share his *ennui* and avoid his visit annoyed him. It was one thing for him to dismiss her. Quite another for her to bed another man behind his back!

Now, this! He glanced down at the woman resting in his arms. The fiery little creature had felled his horse and spewed insults at him. He had a good mind to take the impudent baggage back to where he had found her and leave her there! His lips twisted with irritation. Damn and blast! He was somewhat responsible, he admitted to himself. Well, he'd take her to the Alewife Inn and gladly deposit her there. Good riddance!

By the time they reached the modest inn, his charge still had not roused. As he dismounted and carried her inside, her slender arm slid around his neck and she sighed, snuggling against him. He looked down at the woman in his arms. She was a pretty little thing he realized. His gaze ran over her heart-shaped faced, admiring the dainty upturned nose and appealing full mouth. Under different circumstances he'd be tempted to kiss that rosebud mouth, and perchance, taste the sweet nectar hidden behind those scathing lips. Not tonight, he told himself. He was late as it was.

As he entered the inn the door slammed shut behind him, and all eyes turned to stare at the large, impeccably dressed gentleman carrying a woman in his arms. The smoke-filled room dimly illuminated by the glow of firelight, fell deathly silent. The only sound was the crackling of the logs in the hearth.

'Do you have a room?' he asked the innkeeper.

At that, the men burst into gales of laughter, slamming their beer tankards on the wooden tables.

He eyed the rowdy occupants coolly. 'The girl needs a doctor,' he growled, turning back to the innkeeper, 'bring some smelling salts, she's fainted.'

The innkeeper motioned to his wife to bring the smelling salts, and hurried after the gentleman who was rapidly mounting the narrow wooden stairs.

'Milord,' the innkeeper called frantically. 'I run a respectable establishment. I'll not have you ravaging young innocents here!'

The gentleman stopped abruptly on the stairs and turned his piercing gaze on the scurrilous little man. 'Respectable by whose standards?' he asked icily, 'I am sure I can well afford a night's stay,' he added with a contemptuous gaze at the meager surroundings.

The innkeeper's greedy eyes took in the gentleman's fine clothing. The grey great coat with a velvet collar, polished Hessians, the white silk neck cloth, and the navy brocade waistcoat indicated a man of wealth and position. 'Aye. That you can,' he averred rubbing his grey stubbled chin. 'Come this way, milord.'

'Get me some brandy. And laudanum if you have it,' he snapped as he stalked into the tiny spartan room that passed for a bedchamber at the Alewife Inn.

It was clean, but that was all that could be said for it. The mattress, unless he was mistaken, was stuffed with old, dirty straw. And the wooden chair beside the sooty hearth was missing a leg. Placing his bundle gently on the bed, he called over his shoulder, 'Where are those blasted smelling salts?'

He lit the taper on the warped bedside table, and held it over the bed to examine the ungrateful little urchin. In the candlelight glow, he could see her clearly for the first time. As he suspected, she was very young and, she was more than pretty, she was beautiful. His flare of desire was not misplaced, he thought with a rueful smirk. It was hard to fathom such delicate pouty lips issuing a harsh word. His finger lightly caressed her soft cheek, noting the high cheekbones. Her skin was like smooth porcelain.

Obviously, this beauty was no peasant. His gaze flickered over her dress. The cut was simple, but, he observed, made from expensive fabric which indicated his initial impression of a waif wandering about in the middle of the night had been wrong. His eyes confirmed what his cursory examination of her body had told him. She had lovely curves and nicely rounded breasts. Her bonnet had fallen off revealing a mass of dark brown hair which was softly falling in curls around her face.

15

He found himself longing to look deeply into her eyes. They would be full of fire given what he knew of her temperament. Yes, he thought with a chuckle, this might prove to be quite an interesting evening.

The innkeeper's wife entered the room muttering to herself, 'Well, I never heard of anything . . . and at this time of night – ' she came to an abrupt halt beside the bed, 'milord?'

He tore his gaze from his enticing subject. 'Ah, Mrs Hutchins, you have brought the brandy, laudanum and smelling salts I see.' He lifted his charge's head and placed the smelling salts beneath her nose.

Karina came to immediately. She turned her head in an effort to avoid the foul odor. Removing the offending object, he gazed down at her, a slight smile tugging at his mouth. She looked adorable. Disheveled and disoriented, but infinitely more appealing than half the women of the ton.

'Here,' he said, thrusting a mug of brandy laced with a hefty dose of laudanum at her, 'drink this.'

Too confused to object, Karina took a sip. And choked, coughing nosily. The amber liquid seemed to burn a hole in her chest.

'All of it,' he ordered sternly as he pressed the mug to her lips.

Karina grimaced but she managed to swallow all of the vile liquid. Lying back she stared blankly at him. 'W-what happened?' she asked creasing her brow.

'You passed out,' he told her flatly. He crossed his arms over his chest and cocked an amused brow. 'I thought you said you could ride?'

Unamused, she eyed him coolly. He was responsible for her predicament! And she was in no mood for civility. For all she knew, he had broken her arm.

'I believe I agreed to compensate you for your trouble,' she said tartly. 'Although why I should pay you for the privilege of being run down by your horse, I am sure I don't know.'

His lips curled sinfully. This, he was going to enjoy. She was a vixen all right. He could not remember the last time he had been presented with such a challenge, or at least, one that held such sweet promise. Those alluring eyes of hers positively glinted with an invitation for pursuit.

'It was no trouble at all, I assure you,' he said smoothly. Boldly, he let his slow assessing gaze roam over her, deliberately lingering on the soft swell of her breasts before sliding downward over her slender waist and shapely hips.

Dropping her lashes, she flushed bright pink and quickly turned away to address Mrs Hutchins. 'Where am I?' she asked looking around the small sparsely decorated room.

The plump elderly woman approached the side of the bed, 'You're at the Alewife Inn, dearie,' Mrs Hutchins said, in a calm reassuring voice.

'I should like a physician, if you please,' Karina said primly. 'This rude, arrogant man may have broken my arm!' she snapped, fixing him with a frosty glare.

Mrs Hutchins's mouth dropped open and she gaped at him, 'Milord, is this true, did you break this poor girl's arm?' she asked. Horrified at the thought. This poor girl! She was managing just fine by his estimation. 'No. It is only a bruise. And it was my horse,' he muttered dryly, 'not I, who hit her.'

Karina glared at him.

'You'll not likely find a doctor who'll venture out on a night like this,' he imparted, leaning casually against the wall beside the bed.

Her furious gaze narrowed on his smug countenance. She was right about him, he was as monstrous as his damned horse! And twice as lethal. He looked precisely like a devil should. Full of mischief. He was a giant of a man. No wonder his horse was so intimidating. His wavy black hair was far too long to be respectable, curling at the back over his collar. And she did not like the way his dark eyes raked over her, it made her uncomfortable. Heavens! He had no business looking at her like that she thought, flushing to her roots. No gentleman would look at a lady as if she were a morsel of food soon to be devoured.

'You think not?' she snapped, her eyes flashing with temper.

'I know not,' he averred arrogantly. 'I am afraid you are stuck here for the night.'

'Whaat?' she gasped, panic welling up inside her. No lady would be seen at an inn with a strange man. It would ruin her reputation. Fully grasping the gravity of her predicament, she sat bolt upright in bed. This new life of hers was rapidly deteriorating into total mayhem. 'I cannot possibly stay here for the night!' she cried, struggling to rise. Grasping the bed post, she wobbled on her feet. She clutched her forehead with her fingers and tried to clear her addled brain. The brandy had gone straight to her head. She was unaccustomed to spirits and felt terribly dizzy. The effects of a hefty dose of brandy and extreme exhaustion on an empty stomach were deadly – she could barely form a coherent sentence let alone walk! But she must get to Grantly. Unfortunately, she felt as weak as a new born kitten and the pain in her arm had not subsided.

'No?' his deep resonant voice inquired silkily. 'Where do you think you are going?'

'I am leaving,' she said vehemently, trying unsuccessfully to curb her rising sense of panic, 'I – I cannot possibly spend the night here.'

'On foot?' his hated voice full of icy mockery. 'I think not. You may run into another midnight rider, one who might be,' his lips twitched wickedly, 'less understanding than I, shall we say?'

'But I must get to . . .' Her voice trailed off and she closed her eyes. The brandy was making her feel overly warm and dreadfully dizzy.

'In your present condition,' he informed her sternly, 'you're going nowhere.'

He judged the moment when she couldn't stand any longer. His strong arms encircled her and the floor slipped from under her feet as he swept her into his arms. She mumbled in limp protest before a black haze engulfed her.

My, Karina thought trying to clear her head, she felt terribly groggy. And her limbs seemed too heavy to move. On the verge of consciousness, she was unable to drag herself awake. Vaguely, she realized that her arm had ceased to throb. And she felt wonderful. She was having a lovely dream. Someone was caressing her. Gently rubbing her thighs, her hip, her waist, and lightly touching her breasts through the thin fabric of her chemise.

'Mmm,' she moaned and turned into the pleasant massaging. It felt good. Unbelievably good. Better than anything she'd ever experienced before. Not at all like a dream, she thought knitting her brow. And yet, it had to be. Unable to drag herself from a murky state of sleepiness, she sighed and snuggled closer, letting the delicious inexplicable sensations wash over her.

Gracious heaven! Brandy produced the most delightful effects. Tingling with the pleasure, she felt deliciously weak and languid. She was quivering with a strange excitement. Her nipples felt tight as if she were chilled to the bone. But she wasn't. Far from it! She was very nearly feverish.

A warm breath caressed her cheek. Too dazed to wonder at the origin she wriggled closer. Then warm, soft lips lightly touched her mouth.

This was no dream! It couldn't be. With little success, she struggled to drag herself from the realms of the netherworld. The effort seemed to exhaust her. She wasn't quite sure what was happening. But her mind was too fuzzy to reason it out. And she felt too wonderful to care.

Her lips parted with a sigh of pleasure and were met with a persistent, yet gentle warm caress. Moaning softly, she reached out her hand and felt the rough graze of stubble against her palm. It was a man's face. A man was lying next to her!

With a surge of panic, her eyes flew open, and she found herself looking into the sultriest pair of bedroom eyes she'd ever seen. For several moments her head swam with murky confusion. And then to her absolute horror, she saw quite clearly that the rogue who had nearly trampled her to death was also the source of that delicious warmth and spiraling pleasure. He was lying beside her. Bold as brass. His fine cambric shirt undone revealing black coarse hair that covered his broad muscular chest. His dark wavy hair fell loosely about his handsome face. He looked like an open invitation to sin.

All at once reality came crashing in on her. She sobered immediately and with a yelp of outrage she vaulted from the bed.

'You!' she screeched, her heart galloping in her chest. 'What are *you* doing in *my* bed?' she demanded to know, shivering from the cold. Apparently her dress had mysteriously vanished during

21

the night for her thin gauzy chemise was the only thing between her and his bold assessing gaze. She dragged the blanket from the bed in her wake and hastily tried to cover herself.

Casually reclining against the headboard, one arm draped over his knee, he looked supremely relaxed and annoyingly unruffled. If possible, under the humiliating circumstances, he looked mildly bored!

His lips curled sinfully as his deep silky voice told her, 'Sleeping. Until a beautiful young vixen awakened me, nestling her soft alluring body against mine.' He shrugged his shoulders nonchalantly. 'What else could I do, but reciprocate?' His voice was husky and deeply suggestive. And just as sinfully soft as his caress had been only moments before.

It was with great reluctance and practiced self-discipline that he lifted his mouth from hers. He had thoroughly enjoyed that tender kiss more than he would have guessed. Her uninhibited response excited him beyond belief. She was incredibly lovely. Yes, he thought, reflecting on her sexy sighs and eager, pliant body, she could teach a courtesan a thing or two about seduction.

How long had it been since he'd made love to a woman who knew the joys of slow sensual exploration? Too long. Who'd have thought it? The little baggage spitting daggers had turned into a highly desirable vixen. Damned good thing he hadn't run her down.

Karina's face turned crimson with shame. Good Lord! She'd let that rake touch her. And the way he'd touched her! It was shocking! But quite pleasant all the same, she realized. No. It was more than pleasant. It was incredibly good. But she wouldn't think of how his roaming hands felt against her burning skin. Nor how her breasts were peaking beneath the blanket right this minute! She must never think of it again. Not ever. At least, she thought biting her lip, not if she could help it.

He reached out a large, distinctly male hand – doubtless the very same hand that had boldly caressed her body – and patted the mattress. A sly grin curled the ends of his gorgeous mouth that had only moments before seared her flesh.

'Come back to bed, little vixen.' A wicked glint shone in his dark, hooded eyes. 'I am eager to sample more of your wares. Don't worry,' he added with a lazy, knowing smile. 'I'll make it worth your while.'

She gasped in shock and tucked the blanket beneath her chin. 'I will do no such thing!' she cried hotly. 'What do you take me for, sir, a common trollop?'

His heated gaze swept over her. 'Never common, surely.' His mouth curved into a mocking grin.

'G-get out of here right this minute!' she ranted furiously.

'Where do you suggest I go?' he asked cocking one ebony brow. 'This was the last room available in this establishment that narrowly passes for an inn.'

'You may go to the devil for all I care!' she cried. 'B-but go you will!' she shrieked.

With a careless shrug of his broad muscular shoulders, he lithely got to his feet. 'As you wish. But I think you should reconsider. It would be a shame to let a luscious little body like yours go to waste,' he said softly. His sultry gaze ran over her again, pausing on the soft swell of her rapidly rising and falling breasts and then back to her softly parted lips. 'You, my hotheaded little vixen,' he told her, 'were meant for pleasure.'

Her eyes widened with shock and she swallowed audibly. Never, in all her born days, had she imagined a man quite like him. Taking a step back, she caught her foot in the blanket and toppled, all arms and legs and indignation, to the floor.

His lips twitched with mirth. Clearing his throat, he raised the back of his hand to his mouth to conceal his smile.

'Allow me,' he drawled and reached down to scoop her off the floor.

'I require no assistance from the likes of you!' she muttered. Wrestling with the blanket that had somehow become wrapped too snugly around her hips, she struggled to rise to her feet.

Snatching the blanket over her bosom that was all but exposed by her sheer chemise, she raised her chin defiantly and fixed him with a quelling gaze, 'You, sir,' she told him breathlessly, 'will leave this room immediately. Or I

24

. . . shall scream. And I assure you, I am a capable screamer.'

'I am persuaded there is precious little you are not capable of, madam,' he informed her smoothly. With that he gathered his muddy Hessian boots and discarded waistcoat and left the room.

CHAPTER 2

The dawn found Karina pacing the small confines of her room. She had not slept, of course. Not a wink. She was thoroughly shaken by the harrowing night's events. And by what that unspeakable wretch had done to her. Or almost done.

A wave of panic assailed her as she reflected on just how close she'd come to becoming that rogue's unsuspecting victim. No, she admitted with a inward groan, she was not unsuspecting. On the contrary, she was his willing partner!

No wonder he jumped to the conclusion that her virtue was easy. Had the blackguard taken advantage of her, she could scarcely cry ravishment after the way she had clung to him. She'd behaved like a strumpet! Cupping her red cheeks with cold clammy hands, she groaned. What utter humiliation!

She was, it seemed, a wanton. That would certainly account for her behavior last evening. How would she ever explain passing the night with a strange man at a paltry inn somewhere in the middle of England?

She must escape this horrid little inn without delay. Fortunately, she would never lay eyes on the rakehell again. And as he did not know her name, he was unlikely to speak of what they had shared. Or hadn't shared, as the case may be.

Sinking down on the side of the lumpy, musty bed, she buried her face in her hands. England was a miserable country. Gentlemen simply did not spend the night in young ladies' beds in Boston. In fact, nothing out of the ordinary ever occurred in Boston. Certainly nothing as wickedly exciting as last night.

Karina hid in her squalid room until she was sure the despicable cad must have left the inn. Gingerly descending the creaky, old wooden staircase, she entered the paltry tavern. All eyes turned. It only took her a moment to comprehend the meaning of their consternation. Clearly, they suspected something untoward had gone on in the musty little room upstairs. And it had! Color rushed to her cheeks. Heavens, she thought dropping her head and quickly averting her gaze, she was fallen woman.

Who were they to judge her? Half of them were toothless. And the rest were in desperate need of a bath. Lifting her chin a fraction higher she marched over to Mrs Hutchins. And then she froze.

Not ten feet from her, the scoundrel lounged comfortably, munching on a hearty serving of sausage and eggs! He glanced over his shoulder as she entered the tavern. His slow brazen stare roved seductively over her. Had he no sense of propriety? When, finally, he raised his eyes to hers, he had the audacity to look faintly amused! Her face grew hot. And she hastily lowered her eyes. Clearing her throat she said, 'I must be on my way,' smiling tentatively at Mrs Hutchins. 'Is there someone who can take me to Grantly Manor?'

'Grantly?' Mrs Hutchins said and stole a curious glance in that annoying man's direction. A flicker of recognition crossed his dark hazel eyes. And he sat back, his lips curling wickedly. He was staring at her with the most peculiar expression on his face. As if there was something oddly humorous about her current predicament.

Humiliatingly conscious of his scrutiny, Karina frowned. 'Yes, Grantly Manor,' she snapped sharply. 'Is there someone who could take me? I am already dreadfully late,' she added shooting a hateful look at the despicable rogue.

'I happen to be going that way,' he said airily, 'I might be able to see my way to taking you there.' He set his knife and fork on the pewter plate. Her gaze fell to his long lean fingers, and she could not help recalling the feel of those hands on her flesh. They'd touched her everywhere! she thought, flushing a dull red.

The man had not an ounce of shame. If he thought for one moment she would accept a ride from him, he was sadly deluded. Balling her hands into angry fists, she told him in no uncertain terms, 'You, sir, are an incorrigible rogue. Quite possibly the rudest man I have had the misfortune to meet, and the very last person I would ever accompany anywhere!' she retorted hotly.

Mrs Hutchins gasped, 'Oh dearie, you mustn't speak to his lordship that way!'

Karina's eyes widened owlishly. 'His lordship!' she cried incredulously. This ill-bred man was a lord? 'If he is an example of the lords in this country I should hate to meet the King,' she muttered churlishly.

To her amazement, his lordship threw back his raven head and burst out laughing, 'Indeed you would. But the fact remains there is only one way you are going to Grantly. And,' he emphasized meaningfully as he got to his feet, 'it is with me.' A glint of amusement flickered in his wicked hazel eyes.

She gazed imploringly at the other measly tavern patrons. 'Surely one of you might be persuaded to help? I – I'd be happy to compensate you for your trouble . . .' Her voice trailed off and she gulped. The disgusting beatty-eyed men had leering down to a science!

'Oh aye, milady? In that case, we'd be more'n'appy to 'elp,' they replied in a ribald chorus eyeing her with lascivious pleasure.

Karina took a step back. What a perfectly ghastly circumstance. *He* was her only option?

Her life couldn't get much worse. Lost in the middle of England, she'd spent the night with a despicable rogue in her bed. And her reputation was very probably in tatters.

If sufficient damage had not already been done, she was in no position to refuse the cad. The other occupants at this charming little inn were far less appealing. Glancing at his lordship's arrogant expression, her lips pursed with displeasure. What else could she do? She had to accept his offer. And he knew it.

'Very well,' she said tightly. 'I accept your offer.'

He crossed his arms over his chest and a slow smile of triumph spread across his face. 'I thought you might reconsider,' he imparted dryly.

'I shall await you at the stables,' she told him sharply. Head held high, she stormed from the smoke-filled room into the chilling morning air.

He shook his head. Obviously, the little chit was accustomed to giving orders. And paying for services rendered! Was there no one the prim, and not so proper miss, didn't offer money to? Chuckling to himself, he tossed a few coins on the table and strode from the tavern.

'You must be chilled to the bone,' he said coming up behind her. 'Here, take my cloak.' He removed his great coat and tried to place it around her. But she stepped back in tacit refusal.

Craning her head back, she glared up at him. 'I want n-nothing m-more f-from you b-but a r-ride to Grantly,' she told him, her teeth chattering.

Shaking his head at her stubborn nature, he shrugged and threw his great coat around himself. He brought his massive beast of a horse from the stable. Karina was again impressed by the size and, unwillingly she admitted, the beauty of the animal. With the greatest of ease, his strong hands circled her small waist and he tossed her into the saddle. Hastily, she rearranged her skirts to cover her legs. Chuckling at her modesty, he mounted behind her. Clutching her hard against him, he kicked the great beast into a canter.

His arm felt like steel, digging into her ribs. 'You are holding me too tight,' she snapped.

'I do not want you to fall off,' he said, in a low voice. His breath was hot against her ear. 'You seem overly prone to accidents. I, for one, have had enough of your mishaps.'

She shivered convulsively. It was not from his overwhelming nearness or the warmth of his breath, she assured herself – she was cold. Nothing more.

'You're like ice,' he said, pressing his face against her cheek. Before she could object, he opened his coat and encased her in soft, welcoming warmth. His unwanted body heat seeped into her bones. She could feel his hard muscular thighs pressing against her own. She flushed crimson. What an appalling situation!

'I sincerely hope you know the way to Grantly,' she muttered churlishly and shifted her body in a futile attempt to avoid touching the hard muscular bulk of him.

He laughed. It was a deep throaty sound. 'Oh, I know it all right. Stay put,' he ordered inching her closer against him. 'Or would you rather freeze?' he asked with a modicum of mockery in his silky voice.

31

The warmth of his breath against her temple sent shivers through her. She *was* freezing. Her arm ached horribly and his proximity, however unwelcome, did bring a pleasant warmth. She closed her eyes and leaned her head back against his chest. Not much longer now she told herself, she would only have to suffer his embrace for a little while and then she'd be free of the rogue. Forever.

Her mortification would fade with time. Yes, she thought confidently, soon the fiasco would seem like a distant nightmare. The sooner she forgot the feel of his lips warm and wet against hers, the better.

Reining in his mount, he leaned down. His face grazed her cheek and her pulse skittered disconcertingly. 'That's Grantly,' he told her pointing just ahead through the mist.

Quickly averting her face, she leaned away from him. Gazing at the stone structure partially concealed by the early morning fog, she swallowed hard. The estate was enormous. It looked more like a castle than a house. Intimidated, she wondered if the occupants were as foreboding as this ominous structure.

She cringed inwardly just thinking about the impression she would make on her guardian, arriving at the crack of dawn. Her once stylish travel garb was horribly wrinkled and covered with mud. And she was riding astride on horseback with a strange man! Without a doubt, they would think her the most shocking sort of person. Even immoral, if the fiasco at the inn came to light.

She had always led an extremely well-ordered life, no calamity had ever befallen her in all of her eighteen years. Why now, when she was alone in a foreign country, mourning the death of her recently departed mother and about to meet her future family, did her life deteriorate into utter turmoil?

Damage control was essential. One thing was eminently clear; she must not be seen with this scandalous rogue.

His lordship dismounted and before she could stop him, his large hands slipped around her narrow waist and he helped her down.

'Are you going to be all right?' he asked in a voice as smooth as velvet. His strong, warm hands lingered around her waist, drawing her close. Too close. Her tattered skirts swirled intimately around his legs and she could feel his thumbs caressing her hips.

'Yes,' she muttered, too distracted by her troubled thoughts to notice the impropriety of their stance. She shivered in the chilly early morning air. He drew her closer against the hard length of him.

And then somehow, she was staring into his intense dark eyes. For an instant, she was mesmerized by the intriguing flecks of gold. Somewhere in the recesses of her mind, she thought, this is how it feels before man kisses a woman. Her heart slammed against her ribs. Realization flashed across her mind; he *is* going to kiss me! Oh no! Not again!

His hand reached up and lightly caressed her flushed cheek. How charming she was. And even more delightful to kiss. A man could get lost in those blue eyes. Nay, he could drown in them.

'I-I,' she stammered, licking her lips in an innocent yet enticing way, 'I . . . refuse to allow you to kiss me.'

His thumb ran down her cheek and along her jaw and smiled, 'Would you deny a starving man manna from heaven?'

Her stomach fluttered. She gazed into his dark smoldering eyes. 'W-what?' she whispered breathlessly, her eyes searching his face. Tipping her chin, his mouth descended on hers, capturing her lips in a fierce, passionate kiss. As his hot, wet, demanding mouth slanted over hers, her senses reeled. His arms tightened around her waist. With a groan of pleasure, he deepened the kiss. His hand slid up her back and caressed the softness of her silky hair.

His tongue thrust boldly into her mouth and panic seized her. Wildly, she pushed against his chest with her fists. When at last he released her, she rewarded his efforts with a hard slap across his cheek.

Breathless and weak, she took an awkward step back. She stared blankly at him, abashed at her body's willing response. Shocked by his ardor, she wiped the back of her hand across her mouth to remove his kiss. Trying to steady her breathing, she gasped breathlessly, her chest heaving with indignation, 'Why . . . you, sir, are no gentleman!'

He threw back his dark head and laughed. 'Just noticed that did you?' he asked, his golden eyes twinkling with mischief.

Drawing another deep steadying breath she snapped, 'Indeed not! You have shown yourself to be rogue and a blackguard from the first. I hope never to set eyes on the likes of you again!' Gathering up her torn, soiled skirts, she scampered away, depriving him of the opportunity to reply.

He watched her run away and smiled to himself. He hadn't planned on that kiss any more than he had intended to touch her delightful little body last night. The deuced room at the inn was freezing and the bed looked too enticing to resist. But he had no regrets. Not a single one. For all that, he thought rubbing his stinging cheek, it was well worth it.

Hurrying through the swirling fog toward the manor, she raced up the marble horseshoe shaped steps. Please God, she prayed as she lifted the brass knocker, let someone answer. Her eyelids fluttered shut and she rested her forehead against the enormous black lacquered door. But no answer came from within. Growing impatient, she pounded the door once more this time with her fist. The massive door creaked open and an old man with white hair stood before her, dressed in his nightshirt and robe. This she took to be the butler.

'I am Miss Simpson,' she rushed out breathlessly. The significance of her identity seemed lost on the stodgy old butler for he merely stared down his rather large nose at her with obvious disdain.

'I have come to live here, from America,' she continued impatiently as she nervously peered around the old curmudgeon. 'May I come in?'

He seemed reluctant to let the mud-spattered girl in, but he opened the door a little wider and told her to wait by the door.

Images of that impetuous rogue rushed to her mind while she stood there. Just thinking of him made her flush hot with embarrassment. How could she have stood there like a simpering dolt and let him kiss her? Again!

And last night! Her lashes fluttered shut and she suppressed a miserable groan. It must be the strain she was under. And the brandy he'd forced down her throat.

In ordinary circumstances, she would have successfully repelled his advances – regardless of the fact that he was by far the most handsome man she'd ever laid eyes on. Gracious heaven! The way he kissed. It was sinful! It must be for it was far more than just a light caress or a peck on the lips. His kiss was a mating of their mouths. She'd never realized kissing could be so intimate. But, then again, she'd never been kissed before. And her obviously inaccurate impressions were based on girlish gossip.

She quickly schooled her wayward thoughts, a light blush touching her cheeks at the realization that she had enjoyed the rogue's kiss. Very much. Perhaps too much.

Another grey-haired gentleman, also in his night-shirt and robe, but a bit younger, appeared.

'My dear girl, you look a fright. Please, come in, come in!'

As he ushered her further into the great hall, she offered lamely, 'I am Karina Simpson from Boston.'

'But of course you are. And I am the Duke of Overfield, but you must call me Uncle Charles. We received your letter, but you were not to arrive until the 20th. But no matter. Welcome, welcome, my dear!' he said eyeing her with concern. 'What on earth has happened to you? Have you had an accident?' he asked, his exacting gaze drifting over her with distress. 'Where is your baggage? How on earth did you get here and at this hour of the morning?' he asked, his expression turning grim.

'I – ' Karina began, but clamped her mouth shut. Her story was too fantastic. No one would believe it.

'Charles!' a woman's shrill voice called from the top of stairs, 'Is everything all right? Who on earth has the bad manners to arrive at this hour?' The chubby older woman, whom Karina guessed could only be the Duchess of Overfield, descended the stairs in a billowing white nightrobe with reams of lace, and a ruffled nightcap on her head.

'What is it Charles?' she asked clearly dismayed to see her husband standing with an indigent-looking young woman. 'Has some poor unfortunate had an accident?'

The duke frowned and cleared his throat, 'Er, no. My dear, this is Karina. Karina Simpson.'

The duchess' eyes widened beneath her lacy white cap, taking in Karina's tousled appearance, 'Heavens child! What has happened to you? You were not attacked were you? Oh Charles,' clutching her throat, 'the poor girl has been overcome by vagabonds!'

'No! I was not attacked by anyone,' Karina practically shouted, her normally calm reserved nature tested beyond all bounds. Her nerves were in shreds. Lowering her voice, she tried to explain, 'I was, er, that is to say . . . I . . . had an accident.'

'An accident! Oh dear me, what sort of accident?' the duchess cried, wide-eyed. 'In the middle of the night, it simply isn't safe for a young defenseless girl . . . dear me. Shocking, positively shocking. You must come in and have a brandy to calm yourself before you have an attack of the vapors,' she said as she escorted Karina into the library.

The duchess directed Karina to a winged-back chair, patting her hand as she helped her recline. 'Sit by the fire and tell us *everything*,' she said, her eyes wide with machination.

Shoving his hands in the pocket of his silk robe, the duke followed his wife and offered Karina a brandy. 'Yes, my dear,' he said handing her a large glass, 'please tell us all that has befallen you.'

Karina sipped the brandy and smiled at the plump duchess. She had a sweet face and Karina liked her instantly. Apparently, from her eager expression and probing eyes, disheveled young women seldom, if ever, appeared at Grantly. Particularly not ladies from Boston.

The duke, on the other hand, seemed to be genuinely worried. He had those piercing eyes just like . . . no, she thought squeezing her eyes shut, I will not think of that horrid man. But their heated embrace took root in her mind with unwanted clarity. She was still burning from his torrid kiss!

Drawing a calming breath she managed to relate the salient points of her adventure, making sure to omit the more sordid details. She neglected to mention the night at the inn. Or the rogue.

'You mean you walked all the way? Even after this wild horse struck you and ran off?' the duke asked, arching a suspicious grey brow.

Karina knew he did not believe her. The truth, however, was far too scandalous. If they knew she had spent the night at an inn, with a stranger whom she allowed to take shocking liberties, they'd form a very dim view of her character. And rightfully so! She couldn't quite believe it herself.

She took a gulp of brandy. And a sense of dread overtook her. What if she were to get caught in the lie? Her stomach sank. What then?

'Well, my dear, you must be exhausted,' the duchess remarked, completely satisfied with Karina's ludicrous story. 'One of the lads will go to fetch your trunks later. You must call me, Aunt Henrietta.'

Karina smiled with warmth. 'And you must all call me Kara, everyone in Boston used to.'

Aunt Henrietta sighed gleefully. 'We are so pleased you will be staying with us, even though we were not expecting you at this hour!' She chortled. 'Your room has already been prepared.'

The duke stared at Karina and he rubbed his chin thoughtfully. 'Do you require a doctor my dear?' he asked. 'Your arm may well be broken.'

Karina's eyes flashed wide. 'No! It's not broken. Just bruised, I can move it,' she declared, holding it up to show him. 'I-I examined it thoroughly myself and there are no broken bones.' More to the point, she'd already been examined by that lascivious rake. To her dismay, she found herself wondering just how many women's bodies he'd fondled in his lifetime.

'What a resourceful girl you are!' the duchess exclaimed, clapping her pudgy hands together. 'I should never have thought of that.'

You will never know how resourceful, Karina thought ruefully.

'No,' the duke said pensively, 'nor would I.'

Karina felt wretched. What a dreadful beginning to her new life. But she had precious little choice in the matter. If her guardian ever caught wind of the appalling truth she would be ruined!

The library doors swung open and the duke turned around, 'Ah, Alex! Why don't you join us? We've had an unexpected visitor,' the duke said, eyeing Karina with an odd curiosity. 'I would like to introduce my son.'

Karina rose from the chair and pinned a bright smile on her dirt-smudged face. She looked up and her breath caught in her throat. With a soft gasp of horror her head reeled. And her fingers clutched at the back of the chair.

She stood there, blank, amazed and very shaken. It was *him*! And he hadn't wasted any time changing into his night shirt and robe. Of all the rotten luck! The duke's son! What a predicament!

'A pleasure,' he murmured, his eyes glittering with devilment as he took her left hand and pressed it warmly to his lips.

She could feel the color drain from her face. Her heart pounded furiously in her chest and a loud ringing sounded in her ears. The room started to spin and grow dark.

'She is going to faint,' his hated voice pronounced.

And she did.

Kara opened her eyes and squinted against the sunlight pouring in the two large casement windows. Dazed and confused, she looked around trying to get her bearings. This was apparently her bedroom.

The furniture was crafted from walnut, with rich designs of fruit and flowers. Her bed was gigantic! Three people could have slept comfortably in it. The canopy above her was fashioned in rose-colored fabric that formed an intricate design in the center. The wall paper was an elaborate floral design of rose, blue, and green. It was a quite magnificent room and a world away from what she'd had in

Boston. A pang of sorrow tugged at her heart but she shook it off. Her mother would want her to begin a new life.

Spying a breakfast tray beside the bed, she gave in to the grumbling in her stomach. She was famished. Pushing back the bed coverings she hopped out of bed. Catching a glimpse of herself in the cheval-glass, she burst out laughing. The duchess's nightgown dwarfed her! The lace cuffs hung over her hands, and the ruffles revealed a bit too much cleavage. Who undressed me? She wondered and sank down on the side of the bed. Last night! The sordid events of the day before flooded her mind and she buried her face in her hands with a groan.

Her self-recriminations were cut mercifully short by sheer panic. Had *he* told them? She got to her feet and began to pace around the room chewing on her thumb nail. She would feign total ignorance of his accusations; to admit her conduct would be fatal. She raked her hand through her horribly knotted hair and sighed, utterly miserable.

Clearly, the only sensible person in this household was the duchess. She had believed Karina's story without batting an eye. Biting into a piece of toast, Kara sank down in the large chair beside the breakfast tray.

A knock sounded at the door and Aunt Henrietta peered in, 'Ah, so you are awake, my dear.'

Kara smiled and nodded her head. 'Please come in. I fear I am a bit of a nuisance,' she said staring into her teacup. 'It was very kind of you to take in a stray kitten like me.'

'Lud no. My dear gel, your father was Charles's oldest and dearest friend,' Aunt Henrietta said plopping down on the edge of the bed. She patted Kara's hand with her warm pudgy hand.

Kara looked astounded and shoved her teacup back on the silver tray. 'What do you mean, oldest and dearest friends? I'd never even heard of your family until two months ago. My mother never even so much as mentioned your name to me.'

Aunt Henrietta's hand flew to her mouth and she paled slightly, 'I cannot think why Charles should speak so highly of your father and you not know of their association. I – I am sure it was an oversight. Nothing more.'

'My father died when I was very young. I know so very little about him. When did he meet Uncle Charles?' Kara asked anxiously.

Aunt Henrietta sighed. 'Well, my dear, I can tell you only what little I know. Charles told me a few things before you came to live with us. I don't suppose,' she said eyeing Kara nervously, 'there would be any harm in my telling you. As I understand it, your father was the only son of Lord Eden, Duke of Ravenwood. They shared that. You see, Charles's brother died when he was young and he was an only child. Apparently, the Daltons and the Edens spent every summer together. Their fathers were best of friends. It was natural that the boys would form a lasting attachment. I believe they attended Oxford together, and remained close during the war. Your father had, er, an unfortunate accident, as you must know, when you were very, very young. Heartbroken, your poor dear mother fled to America. She had an aunt or something there I do believe.'

'Cousin Victoria,' Kara supplied. 'She passed away a few years ago. But my name is Simpson, not Eden.'

Aunt Henrietta's eyes widened and her hand flew to her mouth. Getting abruptly to her feet, she stammered, 'Well, ah, y-your mother must have changed it when she went to America.' She was flustered by the comment. 'It is of little consequence,' she said dismissing the topic with a wave of her beefy arm. 'Tea is served at four o'clock in the green salon.' With that she hurried from the room in a sea of purple taffeta.

Kara furrowed her brow in thought. She did not know what to make of this strange development.

After enjoying a luxurious bath and dawdling in her room for several hours, Kara descended the stairs for tea. The manor was exquisitely decorated. Large paintings lined the marble stairway, some depicting men on horses which she, for obvious reasons, quickly bypassed. But others appeared to be Dalton ancestors, and she pored over the portraits with interest.

In the light of day, the once ominous front hallway looked bright and cheerful. As her satin slippers padded against the black and white marble floor toward what she guessed was the green salon, she noticed that the duchess was inordinately fond of large floral arrangements.

Collecting her wits, she took a deep breath and opened the door. There was no reason for her to be beset with nerves, just because the duke's son was an insufferable cad! And she'd spent the night with him.

Uncle Charles got to his feet. 'Ah, my dear Karina,' he said, taking her hand and guiding her to the green and white striped sofa. 'How lovely you look. You are well rested, I trust?'

Kara smiled with warmth. 'Yes, thank you. You are very kind. I must apologize, but I fear last night's escapades left me quite exhausted.'

'Nonsense! We are like family. Be at ease,' Uncle Charles told her patting her hand affectionately.

Kara smiled and accepted a piping hot cup of tea. How could such a charming, kind man have such a repellent son? She heard a deep throaty chuckle from across the room and raised her eyes.

Alex was reclining with characteristic arrogance on the window ledge sipping his tea. Kara's lips pursed with displeasure. He cut a fine figure of a man. If possible, the cur looked even more handsome this morning. And the way his fawn-colored pantaloons, white shirt, and yellow brocade waistcoat clung to him left nothing to anyone's imagination. His lips lifted slightly as if he knew what she was thinking, and he inclined his head to acknowledge the compliment. Color crept into her cheeks and she quickly looked away.

He got up from the window and sauntered, for that was the best word to describe it, across the room to pour himself some more tea. Careful to avoid his gaze, Kara lowered her eyes to her lap.

She was immeasurably relieved. He'd obviously not recounted any of the sordid aspects of last night's abysmal ordeal. At least in this matter, he'd been circumspect. But for how long could she rely on his discretion? Somehow, she just knew blackmail would not be beneath such a libertine.

It was best to ignore the cocky rascal. Of course, that proved a bit difficult when he sprawled beside her on the sofa. He was sitting far too close to her to be considered decent. Politely listening to the duchess's mundane conversation about the weather, Kara shifted on the sofa. Try as she might, she could not move away from the despicable man. The more she eased into a smaller spot the more he seemed to expand. Either the sofa was inordinately narrow, or the man was a giant.

Each time she scooted away he inched his way closer. The feel of his body pressed against hers was terribly disconcerting. His muscular thigh was pressed against hers and the warmth of his body seeped through her thin pink muslin morning gown. She felt uncomfortably warm. She tried, to no avail to ignore his proximity and concentrate on the conversation.

'How is your arm Karina?' Aunt Henrietta asked, gently lifting the lace of Kara's gown to view the wound. She frowned. 'Charles, I still think it looks rather bad.'

'It's fine, thank you,' Kara replied demurely and clasped her teacup on the saucer to cease its shaking. Shifting her weight to the edge of the striped sofa, she cleared her throat and hastily changed the subject.

'I would love to see the manor,' she said brightly.

Enthralled with the vision before him, Alex muttered languidly, 'Would you now?'

Kara directed a cool polite gaze toward him. And he smiled at her. His gaze was far too sultry. She knew where this was leading and wanted no part of it. She tossed him a frosty look which was meant to quell his interest, but had the opposite effect.

She was charming, Alex thought. So sweet and demure. No inkling of the minx she had been last evening. Yes, she was the prettiest thing he'd seen in some time. His gaze lingered on her mouth. And he wondered what it would be like to kiss that rosebud mouth more thoroughly. As if she'd read his thoughts, a stain of pink touched her cheeks and she lowered her lashes.

'I am sure one of the servants could show me the grounds,' she said stiffly and eased toward the end of the sofa. But there was no place for her to go, her hip was grinding into the arm of the sofa as it was!

'I wouldn't hear of it,' he said flashing her a waggish grin. 'I'd be happy to take you.' His heated gaze drifted over the tight bodice of her gown.

Kara flushed hot. The conceit of the man! Did he think she was so besotted with him that she would accept his offer, unable to resist his lordship's charming companionship?

'No.' She snapped the word. 'I believe you presume too much sir, I do not require any of your services,' she said coolly.

'But my dear,' Aunt Henrietta exclaimed, stupefied. 'Alex would be more than happy to show you the estate. Wouldn't you Alex?'

A lazy grin formed on his lips. 'Mm, yes, more than happy,' he said in a voice that felt like a caress.

Kara glared at him. Were there no bounds to this maddening man's presumptuousness? Those dark wicked eyes of his indolently relished her perturbation. And that smile was surely suggestive enough to make a seasoned harlot blush.

'Perhaps,' she said stiffly. 'I might be persuaded to accept your offer.'

'Yes,' the duke agreed. 'Alex knows this property better than anyone. He grew up here, you know.'

Alex lifted his teacup. 'I look forward to . . . taking you,' he said meeting Kara's eye over the rim.

Flushing to her roots, Kara quickly looked away. He was a devil! Clearing her throat, she turned to Uncle Charles and said, 'I understand you and my father were great friends.'

The duke looked surprised. 'Indeed? What gave you that idea?' he asked, his tone turning dour.

Aunt Henrietta's teacup rattled nosily against her saucer and she glanced nervously at her husband. Seeing his frown, her pudgy hand steadied the rattling cup and she set it down with a loud clank on the table. Anxiously biting her lip, she said meekly, 'I'm afraid it's my fault Charles. I let it slip this morning. I – I didn't mean to – '

'No matter,' the duke remarked waving his hand in a dismissive manner.

'I didn't see the harm in it, Charles,' Aunt Henrietta rushed out. 'After all she was bound to find out sometime.'

'We'll talk no more of it,' the duke snapped, effectively silencing his babbling wife.

Aunt Henrietta paled considerably. 'No, of course not. I shouldn't have spoken,' she muttered bowing her head in submission.

'No matter, my dear. How about that tour?' the duke asked his son with a meaningful glance.

'Sounds like an excellent idea to me.' Alex quickly rose to his feet. 'Shall we?' he asked offering Kara his arm.

Kara shot him a quelling look and kept her hands at her side. Rising from the sofa, she glanced from Aunt Henrietta's stricken face to Uncle Charles's taut features and frowned. What a singular household! Why shouldn't she know about her father? 'I hope I haven't spoken out of turn,' she said with contrition.

Uncle Charles forced a smile. 'Of course not, my dear. You must tell me what you think of Grantly after you've seen it,' he said opening the door and practically pushing her into the hallway.

She smiled wanly and nodded her head. But she couldn't shake the uncomfortable feeling that they were all keeping something from her.

CHAPTER 3

Alex took Kara's arm and slipped it through his as they walked across the expanse of green lawn that led to the famous Grantly gardens.

'Unhand me, sir,' she whispered fiercely.

But he held her fast. 'I feel compelled,' he whispered against her ear, 'to remain close by. You seem to have a rather disagreeable habit of fainting.'

Kara stiffened, and dismissed his remark by ignoring it.

'Tell me,' he said in a low soft voice that sent currents of unwanted pleasure through her. 'Is it just me, or do you faint around all men?' he asked, his voice all silk and seduction.

Her large blue eyes flashed with anger. 'Certainly not,' she countered hotly.

He grinned at her. It was an insufferable, knowing grin. 'Ah. Shall we begin our tour with the stables?' he asked arching a mocking brow.

'I have no wish to remain in your company a moment longer than is necessary,' she hissed under her breath and snatched her arm free.

He pulled a frown. 'Perhaps the stables are not the best place to start. You really don't have much horse sense.'

'On the contrary,' she retorted crisply. 'I happen to be an experienced horse woman.'

'Really?' he asked dubiously. 'Then I suppose it's near-death collisions that trouble you?'

She stopped in her tracks and whirled about to face him. 'Sir,' she snapped, 'You are the most rag-mannered man I have ever met. How you have the gall to face me after your outrageous conduct last night. I do not know.'

He chuckled softly. 'No one was more surprised than I to learn your identity, believe me,' he drawled. 'Your conduct last evening gave me an entirely different impression to be sure.'

'My conduct!' she gritted.

'Don't worry, your secret is perfectly safe with me.' One side of his mouth lifted. 'I wouldn't dream of telling my father how you swooned in my arms. That, my sweet,' he said leaning one large, broad shoulder against the enormous elm tree, 'will be our little secret.'

'Oh, you are despicable!' she growled. 'And I did not swoon.' But, of course, she knew she had, and that disturbing fact continued to baffle her. 'Have you no compunction whatsoever?'

'What for?' he asked crossing his arms over his chest, 'I enjoyed every minute of it. And I would never diminish what little pleasure we shared with regret,' he told her gazing amusedly into her indignant fiery blue eyes.

'Pleasure,' she croaked. 'You are nothing but an irresponsible rake. Apparently you do not care about your reputation,' she said tartly.

He drew his brows together. 'Reputation?' he echoed in mock confusion. 'What reputation might that be?'

'I would be curious to learn with how many damsels in distress you've frequented inns,' she hissed.

'Normally,' he quipped sarcastically, 'when I see a changeling in the middle of the road I chalk it up to excess drink or fog, but in your case, I had the misfortune to be taken under your spell.'

'Oh, I am flattered,' she muttered acidly, 'but I fear, vastly unamused. What you seem to take lightly, I regard as precious. Now kindly take yourself off. I am sure you have some pressing matter to attend to. Pray, do not let me detain you.' She turned her back on him and marched across the sprawling green lawn toward the house.

Alex shook his head and laughed as he watched her long, angry, purposeful strides. He doubted that there was another girl in the world quite like her. And he wanted her more than he had wanted any other woman in a very long time. Most women allowed themselves to be kissed. Either that, or they were over-eager, showering him with slobbering kisses.

Not Kara. She had savored the experience. And she had enjoyed it on both occasions. Of that he was quite sure, regardless of her protestations to the contrary. He had kissed enough women to recognize the difference.

Admiring the sway of the bewitching little wanton's hips, he admitted with a sigh, that it was a very auspicious beginning indeed. His only regret was that he did not, as a rule, seduce young innocents – regardless of how great the temptation.

Upon her return to the manor, Kara found Uncle Charles waiting for her in the marbled foyer. 'Was the estate not to your liking?' he asked with surprise.

'Oh, no, your grace, Grantly is lovely,' she rushed out. *It's your son I despise.* 'I am still a bit shaken after my experience last night, I-I thought I might rest some more before dinner.'

'Sensible,' he replied inclining his head. 'May I say, that you are the spitting image of your mother? It struck me this morning when I first saw you, but even more now. Your mannerisms, everything about you, it is remarkable.'

Kara's face fell. A spasm of sadness tugged at her heart as she remembered her lovely mother. She had successfully pushed that pain away, but now it returned with a vengeance.

The duke's forehead creased in a frown. 'I am sorry, my dear, if I have caused you to feel melancholy,' he said noticing her sudden sadness.

Kara smiled faintly and sighed. 'You haven't. It is just that sometimes it is difficult,' she admitted woefully. 'I had no idea that you knew my mother or my father until this morning when Aunt Henrietta mentioned you'd grown up with my father. Were you best friends? I never heard the Dalton name before my mother . . .' she swallowed, 'I mean, except when the will was read.'

'Henrietta mentioned all that did she?' He sighed with displeasure. 'What precisely did she tell you?' he asked, his eyes narrowing on her face.

Kara shrugged. 'Not much, just that you and father were great friends. One thing puzzles me, however, why did my mother change our name to Simpson?'

His lids drifted downward. 'Henrietta tends to exaggerate,' he muttered.

'I see. Then you and my father weren't good friends, after all?' Kara asked pointedly.

He shook his head at her cunning nature and smiled. 'Ah well,' he said on a sigh, 'I suppose there is no harm in your knowing. Yes. We were very good friends. I had known your father since we were boys, we grew up together. It was all a very long time ago and of no importance now.' He gazed out the window, his eyes glazed over as if he were reliving that time. 'Your father would be proud of you, my dear.'

'What was he like?' she asked barely able to conceal her excitement.

The duke stared at her for a moment, apparently surprised by the question. 'He was my closest ally,' he said. His tone was sober. 'I owe him my life. I have sworn to protect and care for you.'

Kara frowned. What a bizarre thing to say. At this moment, the only 'protection' she needed was from his son! 'Protect me?' she said a gurgle of laughter escaping her throat. 'From what?'

The duke's eyes pensively searched her face, but he made no reply. Feeling awkward with the silence, Kara looked away, turning her gaze out the window. 'Is my father's family living here? In England?' she asked.

'No,' he said sharply, 'you are his last remaining family member.'

Her startled eyes flew to his and she stared at him, taken aback by his curt manner. 'I didn't realize. I know so little of my father and there is so much I long to discover. Tell me about him?'

He shrugged. 'There is nothing to tell. He loved you and your mother dearly. That is all you need to know. Don't go poking your nose into things better forgotten,' he told her roughly. 'It will only bring heartache and misery.'

Stunned, Kara stared wide-eyed at the harsh man before her. 'I didn't mean to upset you, Uncle,' she mumbled softly.

His features softened and he smiled at her. Taking her left arm he pulled it through his and patted her hand affectionately. 'You could never offend my dear. Never. Let's leave the past alone, shall we?'

Thoroughly confused, but not daring to push him further, she smiled wistfully and allowed him to escort her to the great hall, claiming an eagerness to see his art collection.

To her acute dismay, Kara was forced to accept Alex's escort into dinner. She'd managed to avoid the insufferable cad for the remainder of the day, but a confrontation was inevitable.

As soon as the two were out of earshot, he said in a silky voice, 'So, you think I'm wicked, do you?'

'You know I think you are a rogue. Certainly no gentleman would speak to a lady so brazenly as you did this afternoon,' she hissed under her breath.

'I should like to remind you that had I not been a gentleman, last evening could have ended quite differently,' he breathed against her ear.

Kara stiffened and clenched her jaw. 'I don't see how,' she bit out.

'As I recall,' he murmured, his lips twitching ever so slightly, 'you were more than willing to continue our romantic interlude. I must admit your behavior verged on wanton.'

Her cheeks burned red with angry shame. 'I was not at all myself,' she whispered fiercely. 'I-it was the brandy. A-and the strain of the evening.'

He chuckled softly against her ear. If she knew about the laudanum she'd have his head for sure. Best keep that pertinent piece of information to himself. 'I am afraid you are utterly transparent,' he said in that bedroom voice of his. 'Do not trouble to deny your flagrant attraction to me.'

'Ooh, I loathe you!'

'Quiet dear heart. Is it your intention to cause a scandal everywhere you go?'

They reached the dining room and Alex politely pulled out Kara's chair. 'If you were not such an unscrupulous scoundrel,' she grated, 'there would be no chance of scandal!'

'Ah, yes, but then I wouldn't enjoy the benefit of your attention, now would I?'

She suppressed the urge to slap his egotistical face. 'I am persuaded that you sir, are completely beyond redemption,' she muttered under her breath.

Pushing her chair in, he leaned down and whispered in her ear, 'Do try to keep a civil tongue in that pretty little head of yours. I would not want to slip and mention last night. I have a strange feeling that others would take a rather dim view of your conduct.' His breath swept over her neck sending a delightful little shiver down her back.

Straightening her spine, Kara clenched her jaw. He was the lowest, most detestable person she had ever met. She could not think of words vile enough to describe him. She might have known he would wait for a moment such as this to blackmail her.

The duchess took her seat beside Kara. 'My dear child,' she inquired 'are you all right? You look a bit flushed. Is your arm paining you overmuch?'

Kara lowered her lashes, shutting out Alex's smug, arrogant grin. 'I am fine.'

Alex cocked a dubious brow. 'No ill effects from last evening?' he asked silkily.

She scowled at him, 'Nothing I am not already over,' she assured him coolly. 'Fortunately, I suffered no lasting effects from my ordeal. None whatsoever.'

His eyes flickered over her flushed face. 'I would not be so sure about that,' he said, a mocking smile curling his lips.

'Alex is entirely correct,' Aunt Henrietta remarked, 'these harrowing experiences can often have lasting effects.'

His smile widened. 'Quite often, I do believe.'

Kara glowered at him. And his eyes glinted with amusement.

The duke frowned at their almost hostile exchange. 'Karina, I sincerely hope you are finding everything here to you liking,' he said, briefly glancing in his son's direction. 'And that you are comfortable in your new home.'

'I am persuaded that England is a most singular country, Uncle. Indeed, I've experienced more bizarre mishaps in the past two days than in an entire lifetime in Boston,' she added fixing her icy stare on the smug cad across the table. 'Verily,' she added on a sigh, 'a girl needs a gallant protector, I am so pleased mother chose you.'

'I collect the poor gel is right, Charles,' Aunt Henrietta chimed in. 'When I reflect on her harrowing trip,' she added with a shudder, 'I feel positively overset.'

'Think no more of it, dearest,' the duke said patting his wife's pudgy hand. 'Kara is safe now.'

That's what you think! Kara thought, eyeing the hateful rogue across the table with disdain. A slow smile spread across Alex's face as his heated gaze moved from her eyes to her full mouth. Her face turned scarlet and she stabbed her pheasant with her fork, mentally defaming Alex's character.

Dinner was a dreadful affair Uncle Charles and Alex exchanged political opinions while the women sat quietly by. Kara was seething. In her mind, she recounted the things Alex had said and done to her. And she felt herself grow warm.

'Stupid fool,' she heard someone say in a voice that sounded remarkably like her own.

'Did you have something to contribute?' Alex asked his voice heavy with irritation.

She had spoken out loud! All eyes were on her. Aunt Henrietta looked mortified. Uncle Charles's expression could best be described as troubled.

Kara swallowed, abashed by her rude outburst, she stuttered, 'I . . . no.'

'I thought not,' Alex said, his eyes glinting coolly into hers.

Good. Kara thought, let him think I meant to insult him. I am only sorry I didn't utter a more forceful expletive.

At the end of what proved to be a perfectly hideous dinner, Kara scurried up the red carpeted stairs to the safe refuge of her room.

After tossing and turning for several hours, she decided to curl up with a good book – anything to keep her mind off the disturbing recent turn of events. Between that scoundrel's haunting dark eyes and the peculiar news of her father, her mind was whirling. Donning her wool wrap, she slipped from her room. Taper in hand, she descended the dark stairway in search of the library.

Bare foot, she scurried across the cold marble floor and crept into the library. The fire, still ablaze in the fireplace, cast a flickering light on the extensive collection of books lining the walls from floor to ceiling. Above the mantel was an enormous life-sized portrait of a woman. Raising the taper higher, Kara looked up and noticed that the woman was not the duchess.

How odd, she thought and drew closer to the magnificent portrait bound in a heavy gold frame. The lady – whoever she was – was a striking creature garbed in a scarlet velvet gown. She looked somehow familiar, the same Dalton black hair.

'She's my mother,' a deep, distinctly male voice that was horrifyingly familiar remarked from behind.

Kara jumped and spun around to face Alex. He was draped, for that was the best way to describe his indolent position, across the winged-back chair before the fire. With a brandy snifter in one hand and one strong muscular leg encased in tight buckskins hooked over the side of the chair, he looked sinfully provocative.

Kara carefully averted her gaze from his billowing white cambric shirt which was undone, revealing a mass of raven hair and tempting bronze skin.

'I . . . you startled me,' she stammered with a hard swallow.

'So it would seem,' he said laconically. His dark hooded gaze slowly and seductively slid over the length of her.

Kara curled her toes beneath her robe and squirmed uncomfortably. 'How can she be your mother? I thought Aunt Henrietta – ' she offered lamely.

'Was my mother?' he asked lazily swinging one shiny black Hessian-booted foot. She nodded. 'She is my step-mother,' he explained, a smile tugging at his lips. 'I never knew my real mother. My father rescued her from the guillotine during the French Revolution.'

'Oh, how romantic,' she said gazing at the portrait.

Alex shot her a sideways glance. Did she have any idea how intoxicatingly innocent she was? Standing there in her bare feet, ruffled white flannel nightgown and crooked nightcap, she looked about twelve. He must be depraved for he'd never seen such an enticing sight.

'He brought her to England and made her his wife.' He dragged his gaze from hers and motioned toward the portrait, 'She died a year later in childbirth.'

'Oh, I am sorry,' she said softly.

He held her gaze for a long moment before he looked back at the painting, 'You have no need to be, I never knew her.'

'Surely you must have missed her?'

He shrugged and looked away. 'How can you miss someone you've never known?'

'It's easy,' she said quietly. She had never known her father. And yet, she'd spent a lifetime imagining what he would have been like. She missed him dreadfully.

'My father remarried when I was twelve. I never had a mother. Nor a father for that matter. He was always off some place or other when I was young. So, I had the run of Grantly. Perhaps that accounts for my wicked ways.' A mischievous smile formed on his lips and he downed his glass of brandy in one gulp.

'You must have led a very lonely childhood.'

He shrugged and got to his feet. 'I had various distractions. Not the least of which was an excellent tutor and a stable full of the best horseflesh in England. Now that you know all about me, suppose you tell me what you came down here for?' he asked slipping the taper from her unresisting hand.

His voice, like his smile, was dark and suggestive. And she was suddenly uncomfortably conscious that she was wearing a very thin nightgown. Her fingers clutched at her wrap drawing it closer. 'I couldn't sleep – '

'Thinking of me, were you?' he asked, a wicked gleam sparkling in his dark sultry eyes.

'No. Of course not,' she snapped blushing right down to her toes. 'I – I came to get a book.' She backed away from him. His gaze flickered over the rapid rise and fall of her breasts beneath her nightgown and she felt her breasts peak.

He smiled indulgently at her and let his finger lightly run over her jaw. 'And you found me,' he murmured softly, his dark penetrating gaze holding her captive. 'How nice.' He moved closer and she stumbled backward.

To her dismay, she backed into the book shelf. She gulped. His eyes followed the smooth line of her creamy throat. Any closer and she'd be pressed against that formidable brawny male body of his. Her heart pounded erratically in her chest at the mere thought.

'I – I think I should be getting back to bed,' she said nervously licking her lips and trying to calm the fluttering of her heart. 'I'm suddenly quite tired,' she rushed out breathlessly. She could feel the warmth of his breath on her cheek. This was quite alarming, she realized, as he dipped his raven head and said in a throaty whisper, 'Perhaps if you were to kiss me goodnight, I might be persuaded to let you go.' His mouth was dangerously close to hers.

Her heart leapt to her throat. 'I – I'd rather not,' she cried and ducked beneath his arm. Scurrying for the door she flew from the room, the echo of his hated laughter ringing in her ears.

The following morning Kara breezed into the breakfast room. And stopped dead in her tracks. The subject of her disturbing dreams was seated at the breakfast table. Hovering on the threshold, she debated whether she could sneak away without him taking note. Quietly turning around, she tip-toed back toward the door.

'Leaving so soon?' his hated voice drawled. 'Cook will be terribly disappointed. She's gone to a great deal of trouble. It would be such a shame to let all this good food go to waste.'

Straightening her spine, Kara swung around to face him. She marched over to the table and stiffly took her seat.

The austere butler filled Kara's cup with coffee, and stood by the sideboard awaiting further instructions.

'Thank you, Collins. We will serve ourselves,' Alex said.

'As you wish, milord.' Collins said with a bow. With that he departed, closing the large double doors behind him.

'Shall we?' Alex asked, gesturing toward the sideboard brimming with mouth-watering creations. Kara had lost her appetite at seeing him. Her stomach was churning fiercely. But she inclined her head in polite agreement and got up to serve herself.

He followed a bit too close for comfort. The impertinence of the man was boundless!

In an effort to escape his nerve-racking proximity, she thoughtlessly heaped food onto her plate and hastily returned to the table.

'Hungry, are you?' he asked amusedly.

Ignoring him, Kara diverted her gaze and toyed with the massive quantity of food on her plate. Sharing his company was one thing, but conversation was quite another.

'I am delighted we are alone,' he said in low seductive tone.

Her head shot up.

'Relax, I have no intentions of kissing you,' he told her with a roguish grin, 'at least . . . not for the moment.'

For the moment! Color rushed to her face and she lowered her lashes. Addressing his cravat she managed to find her voice, 'Sir, you are under a misapprehension if you think for one moment – '

His lips curved faintly. 'I think,' he pronounced, leaning forward across the table to take her hand in his, 'that you are the most exquisitely beautiful woman I have ever seen.'

Her blue eyes widened in disbelief. Tracing the palm of her hand with his thumb, he continued, 'You are also deeply passionate.' His mouth curled slightly. 'And that is a quality I admire.'

She snatched her hand away. 'Sir! You go too far! You are beyond impudent!'

He did not seem excessively perturbed. Instead, he leaned back in his chair, crossed his arms, and studied her flushed face. 'And from your vast experience, how should I behave?' he asked cocking an ebony brow.

She eyed him coolly. 'I have no intentions of continuing this discussion. Your conduct is scandalous. I believe you take pleasure in trying to shock me,' she said curtly.

'Now, why should I want to do that?'

'I don't know,' she sputtered. 'I suppose it is because you delight in tormenting me.'

'I take pleasure in a great many things,' he assured her with a suggestive smile, 'but tormenting you is not one of them.'

'You are despicable.'

'You did not seem to mind being improper, the other night,' he said with a wicked grin.

She turned a deeper shade of red. 'You know you took unfair advantage!' she spat out. 'I-I was not at all myself.'

'Be that as it may. I will grant only that I kissed you. I have yet to take advantage of you.'

She opened her mouth to utter a scathing rejoinder, but the doors to the breakfast room swung open and Uncle Charles strode in. 'Good morning,' he exclaimed brightly. Taking his seat at the head of the table, he frowned.

'Is something amiss?' he asked noting Kara's mulish expression. 'The food not to your liking?'

'No,' Kara replied avoiding his gaze as she slurped her coffee and contemplated murder. 'The food is fine.'

Alex smiled. It was an arrogant self-satisfied smile that made Kara want to slap his smug face.

The duke furrowed his brow in confusion before turning his attention to his eggs. An ominous quiet hung in the air. Finally, unable to endure the awkward silence, Kara cleared her throat and spoke up,

'Uncle Charles, I am dying to hear all about your exploits in France.'

The duke choked on his coffee. 'I beg your pardon?'

'Alex told me how you rescued your first wife. That was gallant!'

Uncle Charles shot an accusatory glance at his son. Alex raised his hand in self-defense. 'I assure you, I only mentioned your swashbuckling rescue of my mother.'

'Greatly exaggerated I'll warrant. My dear Kara, Alex has a flare for the dramatic. You mustn't believe everything you hear.'

She was not going to argue with any criticism of Alex. However, there was something more than mere modesty in her uncle's reaction. He was uncomfortable. Intrigued, she asked, 'Did my father go to France with you?'

He lowered his gaze to his plate. 'Er, no.'

Uncle Charles was a perfectly dreadful liar. She knew immediately that her father had been in France. Why all the secrecy? What difference did it make? What a peculiar, cryptic household.

The duke sat back from his untouched breakfast and checked the time on his pocket watch. Rising from his chair he said grimly, 'May I have a word in the study, Alex?'

Alex bowed his black head in tacit assent and followed his father from the breakfast room. Kara breathed a sigh of relief and picked up her fork. At last she could eat something without her stomach tying into knots.

After breakfast, Kara was informed that Aunt Henrietta was laid up in bed with a miserable headache, so she decided to explore the estate on her own. Wandering down the long marbled hall she recognized the entrance to the library on her right, and the afternoon parlor where the family had shared tea the day before on the left. But where did the door directly ahead lead?

Drawing closer, she heard voices from within. It was Uncle Charles and Alex. Obviously, this was the study. She was about to turn away to investigate another closed door when she distinctly heard her name. She moved closer to the study and pressed her ear against the door, straining to hear the conversation.

'She knows nothing,' Alex was saying.

'No, but she is not stupid!' Uncle Charles sniped. 'Between your idle boasting and Henrietta's foolish slip of the tongue, she's bound to suspect. It was not wise of you to mention France.'

'It was a completely harmless comment. Anyone might have told her. All she'd have to do is inquire about the portrait. Anyway, it is a common enough tale. What can she determine from your actions in France?'

'She can determine her father's involvement! Which I may remind you she very nearly did.'

'All that is in the past now.'

'Just the same, I do not want her to know anything about it! It is not a risk I'm prepared to take, are you?'

Alex sighed heavily. 'Come father, she of all people must certainly have the right to know.'

Kara heard someone clear their throat rather boisterously from behind. Abruptly straightening from her snooping position, she whirled about and came face to face with the staunch butler, Collins. Her mortification knew no bounds.

'May I be of assistance?' Collins asked in a dry condescending tone.

Flustered, Kara shook her head, 'No, I . . . was just . . . er – '

'Eavesdropping?' he supplied.

Her face turned beet red. 'I needed to . . . that is, I wondered where . . . this, um, door leads,' she stammered. 'You see, I was exploring the estate.'

'Yes, I see. That's the study.'

'Ah. Yes. The study. Well, then,' she said taking a deep breath. 'That solves that. Thank you. I'll just continue my exploring now,' she offered lamely.

'If that is your pleasure, Miss Karina.'

'Oh, ah, Collins,' she added hesitantly, 'I would prefer that you do not mention this little . . . incident,' she said wrinkling up her nose.

'Shall I tell his grace you were looking for him?' he asked.

'N-no,' she rushed out. 'That won't be necessary. Thank you.'

Gathering her skirts, she hurried upstairs and prayed Collins would keep silent about her gross indiscretion. It was bad enough to get caught by the butler, but if her uncle knew it could prove more than a trifle embarrassing.

Once safely ensconced in her bedroom she reflected on the bizarre conversation she'd overheard. It was all rather perplexing, she thought flinging herself into the rose-colored velvet chair beside the bed.

What had her father been involved in that was so ghastly Uncle Charles chose to keep it from her? The two were obviously embroiled in something. But why had Kara never heard of the Daltons? Uncle Charles had said he knew her mother and was apparently a close friend. Their lives were clearly interwoven.

Curiosity ate at her. She had to know more about her father. As his daughter, she deserved to know. Hadn't Alex said she had the right to know? Dear Lord, she thought getting to her feet with a weary sigh, was she actually agreeing with *him*? She cringed at the thought and pulled back the heavy rose-colored drapes to gaze at the courtyard down below.

Alex was there. His raven hair blowing recklessly in the wind as he reined in Goliath, who pranced excitedly beneath the bit while his master spoke to the stable boy. Good, she thought, the rogue is leaving.

He was appropriately dressed – except for the stark white of his shirt and neckcloth, he was all in black. What perfect garb for the spawn of the devil, she mused. She chose to ignore the fact that he also looked magnificently elegant. His jet-black hair and chiseled profile created an irresistible picture of masculinity. As usual, the sight of his lordship sent her pulse racing uncontrollably. He looked up at the manor suddenly and, to her absolute horror, caught sight of her in the window. He had the audacity to smile at her. And wave!

Kara gasped and hastily stepped back from the window, humiliated to the core. He'd seen her! It was one thing to ogle the man from a safe distance, but it was quite another to be discovered. How would she ever live it down?

CHAPTER 4

Alex was positively vexed! He had ridden Goliath hard, until he was frothing at the bit, to make an appointment with Sir Gilbert, only to find that Gilbert had been unavoidably detained.

Helping himself to some of Gilbert's fine French brandy, he tried to wait patiently. His thoughts wandered to Kara and a slow smile crept across his face. She was quite a handful. Undeniably the most passionate woman he had ever met.

Yes, he thought with a wolfish smile as he savoured his brandy. He was looking forward to their next encounter. If the past was a precursor to the future, it was going to be sublime ecstasy. It had taken all his self-control to tear himself away from pursuing the highly desirable little hellion and come to London. And for what? He thought bitterly. Gilbert had better have an update on the Bouchard case.

The sly fox Bouchard had outwitted Alex once too often. But, this time Alex felt confident he would catch the blackguard. After all, there were only so many places a traitor could hide. The ports were being watched and Bouchard wasn't foolish enough to attempt another escape to France.

For three long years Bouchard had evaded Alex. He was a clever opponent, fooling Alex by masquerading as Lord Robert Collins, defender of the realm. Alex chafed at the painful memory.

Shifting uncomfortably in his chair, he reflected on the close friendship the two had once shared. All the while Bouchard was conveying details of the British offensive, which Alex unwittingly divulged to Napoleon's forces. He would never be able to forgive himself for the loss of British lives he unknowingly caused.

He swallowed the remainder of his brandy in one gulp and helped himself to another. His hands began to perspire just thinking of that traitor Bouchard, or whatever the devil he called himself these days. For the first time in Alex's life he was hungry to kill a man.

'Ah, Dalton,' Sir Gilbert said closing the door behind him. 'Sorry to have kept you waiting.'

Alex whipped around to face him. 'What news?' he asked anxiously.

Gilbert walked over to the drinks table and poured himself a brandy. 'Nothing about Bouchard, if that is what you're hoping.'

'What the devil is so urgent then?' Alex growled.

Slamming the crystal decanter on the table, Gilbert replied coolly, 'Try to remember this office functions as more than a vehicle to satisfy your revenge. Bouchard is one of many problems. There will be time enough for him later. It is best that you keep your mind focused on our present task.'

Alex's jaw tightened. 'And what might that be?' he ground out.

Gilbert sat down behind his desk and motioned for Alex to be seated. Laggardly, Alex acquiesced.

'You are, of course, familiar with the Treaty of Paris,' Gilbert remarked rifling through the papers on his desk.

Alex nodded.

'Then you also know how tenuous the agreement is.'

'How tenuous can it be?' Alex snorted in derision. 'Aren't you forgetting the little general is safely tucked away in the South Atlantic?'

'That may be, but we have much to lose if the peace does not last. The members of the Quadruple Alliance are determined to maintain peace.'

'I cannot credit your concern. Napoleon has had his last hundred days.'

Undaunted by Alex's skepticism, Gilbert went on. 'As you know, England has an interest in Louis XVIII remaining King.'

Alex sighed heavily, the King of France, in his opinion, was a coxcomb controlled by Talleyrand. 'Louis's throne is safe.'

'Yes. But Napoleon's March invasion cannot be overlooked.'

'And the Royalists launched their White Terror against Bonapartists,' Alex said with a tired nod.

'You'll never get me to believe that the French would welcome any of his supporters. They are all listening to him dictate his autobiography on St Helena.'

'Privately, I concur with your impressions. However, publicly, I must take these concerns seriously. Don't forget the unrest at home. Anyone wishing to upset the balance of power might use the economic troubles to their advantage.'

Alex tugged at his cravat. He was not unaware of the economic depression. The unemployment rate was startling and many people were disgruntled, eager for William Cobbett's notion of parliamentary reform.

'What do you want me to do? Go to France and ask for the few remaining instigators to confess?' He shook his head. 'Honestly, Gilbert this is a waste of time! France is dominated by moderates who support the Duke of Richelieu and his policies. I refuse to believe that anyone in France would desire another war.'

'Nonetheless,' Gilbert snapped with irritation, 'you will make some inquiries. The social and economic deterioration of England would benefit those who oppose the Corn Law. Let's not forget that dreadful Peterloo Massacre.'

Alex was not likely to forget. Several hundred people had been injured, some even killed, at a rally supporting the repeal of the Corn Law and parliamentary reform.

'Who knows where this radical agitation will take us.' Gilbert sat back in his chair and steepled his hands beneath his chin. 'Unless of course,' he said pointedly, 'you would prefer I assign another agent?'

Alex bristled. 'No,' he said tightly, fixing Gilbert with a frosty look. 'I can manage it. When do I leave for France?'

'You don't.'

Alex frowned.

'On your advice, I've enlisted Daniel Rutherford. He is already investigating any possible link.'

Alex smirked. He could well imagine what his good friend Daniel was investigating – and it was not a conspiracy!

'The plot, if there is one, may be developing at home.'

Alex's brow darkened and he leaned forward. 'By whom? And for what purpose?' he demanded sharply.

A slow smile spread across Sir Gilbert's face. 'That is what you must find out.'

'Kara,' Uncle Charles called to her from the doorway of his private study, 'May I see you?'

Kara's smile faded as she entered the room, for the duke's expression was stern.

'Please be seated,' he said stiffly.

As she sat down on the brown leather winged-back chair she observed a man standing in front of the fireplace and frowned. Judging from the way he was dressed she guessed him to be from the village.

'Do you recognize this man?' Uncle Charles asked her. His tone was cool.

Furrowing her brow in confusion she looked at the man. 'No,' she replied shaking her head and wondering why on earth Uncle Charles would ask her such a question.

'You have never seen him before in your life?' he prodded with a questioning look.

Her eyes narrowed in confusion and she glanced once more at the shabbily clad man. 'No,' she said eyeing her uncle with curiosity. 'Never.'

'She's the one your grace,' the man exclaimed wringing his tattered hat between his grimy paws. 'I seen her with him at my inn. He took her right upstairs he did. Impatient he was for a room – '

'That is enough!' The duke roared, 'I will not have these accusations leveled against Miss Simpson in my own house.'

Panic seized her. Her heart pounded so hard that at any minute she expected it to burst from her chest. He had seen her at the inn with Alex! The room whirled. She was going to be sick, right there on the spot. No. She couldn't be sick not in front of Uncle Charles. Taking deep breaths, she tried to calm herself. He could prove nothing.

'I ain't doing no accusing!' the beastly man cried. ''Tis the truth! My wife and I run a reputable establishment. I told him so that night. I can prove it, I can. Other people seen 'em too. Ask 'em if you don't believe me.'

'My son, the Marquis of Overfield has been notified of your allegations. He should be arriving home this evening. If you are attempting to slander my family or Miss Simpson's good name, you will wish you had never been born,' the duke assured him in a deadly voice.

'All I'm asking for is what is due me. His lordship gave me wife five pounds to keep quiet and I just want me share.'

'Then I suggest you ask your wife for it. Now, get out!' the duke bellowed in disgust.

As if on cue, Collins opened the door and gruffly escorted the offensive man from the room.

Kara could not look Uncle Charles in the eye. What was she going to do? Lie! a small voice whispered in her brain. It's the only way out. But she couldn't. What if that abhorrent little man brought witnesses? What would she do then? She had to tell the truth. Goodness! she thought resting her weary head on her palm, what an unholy mess! She waited nervously for the impending interrogation. But, it never came. Instead, Uncle Charles sat calmly behind his desk waiting for her to speak.

'I . . . don't know what to say Uncle,' she said with a nervous swallow. Her throat felt like flint.

'I will hear what Alex has to say about the matter. Then we will decide what has to be done,' he said curtly and bent his head to resume his work.

Shakily getting to her feet, she approached the desk, her legs wobbling horribly. 'Uncle, I . . .'

Without so much as a glance in her direction he said in a chilling voice, 'Go to your room. We will discuss this matter later.'

If he had slapped her she could not have felt more hurt.

'Yes,' she said quietly and managed somehow to walk to the door. Clutching the door knob for support she hesitated at the threshold, 'Uncle you do not believe that . . . I – ' she stuttered with a hard gulp.

He continued with his work as if nothing out of the ordinary had passed between them. 'I believe that a serious judgement error has been made.' Looking up, he told her sternly, 'Say nothing of this to anyone. Particularly not Henrietta.'

She nodded and hastily fled from the room. Reaching the solace of her bedroom she flung herself on her enormous bed and burst into tears. No one person deserved such bad fortune in one lifetime. What had she done to warrant this rash of ill fate?

When Kara opened her eyes the room was dark. She must have cried herself to sleep. Reality came crashing down on her and a sense of dread enveloped her.

A knock sounded at the door and she jumped. 'W-who is it?' she asked in a pathetic, small voice.

The maid, Violet, called to her through the door, 'His grace an' his lordship are waitin' for you in the library, miss.'

'I will be down directly,' Kara managed to reply. Dragging her limp body off the bed, she stumbled over to her dresser.

Gazing in the mirror she recognized her face, but not the red puffy eyes and disheveled hair. Hastily, she bathed her face with a cool cloth and brushed her tangled hair in an effort to repair some of the damage.

Descending the stairs on shaky legs, she felt like the heroine she once saw in a play in Boston who went courageously to her death sentencing. But she did not feel brave; she felt sick. Any moment now, she was going to be violently ill, she just knew it.

She was guilty of nothing, she told herself, rallying for the fight. She took a deep breath and summoned all her courage. Head held high, she opened the library door.

The room was dimly lit and the curtains ominously drawn. Confronted with her uncle and Alex her mettle vanished. And nausea overtook her. So much for fortitude, she thought ruefully. Where was her grit when she needed it most?

Alex was standing by the fireplace his booted foot resting on the fire grate, one hand leaning on the mantel and the other in the pocket of his fawn-colored britches. He was the epitome of sleek masculinity mingled with compelling brawn, the sum total of which was profoundly disturbing to her pulse. Even now in a crisis, he looked disgustingly elegant. How could she consider the rogue handsome at a time like this? she wondered, mentally cursing her foolish heart for racing at the sight of him.

Intently studying the flames, he did not look up as she entered. The expression he wore was grim. It must be serious for she had never seen him look coolly unamused before.

Uncle Charles addressed her from across the room. 'Alex has told me everything,' he said with a defeated sigh. 'I knew you were prevaricating that first night.' Rubbing his temples, he shook his grey head in dismay, 'But I confess, I had not imagined this.'

Kara's stomach sank. Heavens. Not everything! Her eyes darted to Alex's somber face. She prayed he had not imparted *every* detail of the sordid tale. It was bad enough to be ensconced at an inn with a stranger, but to kiss him was atrociously bad breeding. And to spend the night! That was positively shocking.

Managing to find her voice she said, 'Then you know that horrible man's insinuations are lies.'

'I knew that all the time. I think it is safe to say you are chaste, my dear. The question now, is what to do.'

'Perhaps if you paid him as he requested – ' she began, but Alex interrupted her, 'I refuse to pay that good-for-nothing a farthing,' he snapped.

'Why so reluctant now?' she asked archly. 'It was you who started the whole thing by paying his wife five pounds.'

Alex's head snapped up and he glared at her, his dark eyes flashing dangerously. 'Well, little miss,' he said through his teeth, 'if you had not been parading around in the middle of the road on a pitch dark night this would never have happened.'

'Parading around!' she screeched. 'Your giant beast collided with me. I am lucky to be alive.'

Alex's mouth tightened in a thin line of anger. 'It was you who insisted on being taken to the inn!'

'Well, I certainly did not expect you to carry me in and demand a room as if I were . . . were a trollop! But I suppose,' she said putting her hands on her hips, 'you spend so much time with strumpets you don't know the difference!'

The muscle in his cheek throbbed dangerously. 'If memory serves,' he murmured sarcastically, 'it was you who offered me payment for services rendered, not the other way around. You seem to have conveniently forgotten that you fainted in my arms. What would you have preferred me to do?' he asked looming over her.

'Anything would have been preferable to your spending the night in my bed,' she spat out, craning her head back to glare at him.

'You did not seem to mind that night,' he countered smoothly. 'Afterwards when I kissed you. You came alive in my arms.'

Before she could control the impulse, her hand snaked out and she slapped him hard across the face. The loud smack echoed through the library. Stunned, she stood motionless.

A red mark formed on his cheek where her blow had struck. He stared down at her, his dark stormy eyes burning into her flashing blue orbs.

'Well,' the duke breathed, 'I see we have quite a situation on our hands.'

Acutely ashamed, she lowered her gaze. She was not normally a violent person. The insufferable cad seemed to bring out her worst side.

Alex stalked across the room to pour himself a much needed drink. Gulping it down he said icily, 'Quite.'

Nervously sweeping a hand through her hair, Kara perched on the edge of the winged-back chair beside the fireplace.

'My dear,' Uncle Charles said, 'like it or not, you have been compromised. There is only one way to resolve this – '

'Marry me,' Alex interjected bluntly.

'Whhaat!' she shrieked, jumping to her feet. 'Are you mad?' she gasped her luminous blue eyes widening in shocked disbelief.

'The prospect of a hoyden for a bride does not thrill me either,' he told her harshly.

'I'm afraid Alex is right,' Uncle Charles remarked. 'It is the only way.'

She shook her head wildly and cried. 'It is not the only way! I will not marry you!'

Alex met her hostile gaze with equal enmity. 'Yes, you will,' he countered firmly.

Her fiery blue eyes narrowed on his face. 'You cannot force me to marry you,' she said hotly.

'Can't I just?' he fired back, his eyes glinting dangerously.

'No scandal has ever threatened this family,' Uncle Charles warned sternly, 'I will not tolerate one now. I have no intentions of paying that man. Blackmail only leads to more blackmail. He'll be back with some of his friends no doubt.'

She gazed at Uncle Charles, a look of complete incredulity on her face. 'But, you said yourself that it was all lies. You know he spoke falsely. What difference do other people's opinions make?' she asked, her voice shrill with desperation.

'You cannot be serious?' Uncle Charles replied, utterly dismayed, 'You must comprehend the gravity of spending the night at an inn with a man who is not your husband.'

She stamped her foot. 'I did not spend the night!' she cried frantically.

'You are splitting hairs,' Alex snorted with irritation.

'Nothing happened!' she screeched, 'you must tell him nothing untoward occurred. You know I am innocent of any wrong doing. That is all that should be important.'

Alex shook his head. 'It is a matter of honor, Kara,' he imparted briskly.

'Honor!' she scoffed. 'Whose? Yours? That is ridiculous! My virtue is still intact, that should be an end of it.'

'By a hairsbreadth,' Alex muttered.

Her cheeks burned at the memory of how close she'd come to bedding a complete stranger at a decrepit old inn. She bit her lip and sank down on the sofa. This was not happening. It could not be. This was all one long wretched, abhorrent nightmare. Soon, very soon, she would wake and find herself back in Boston with her mother.

'Think of what you are saying, Kara,' Uncle Charles urged. 'Compromised is compromised. We must do the honorable thing. It is the only way to avoid total disgrace.'

'Stop saying that!' she cried covering her ears.

'It is my duty to marry you,' Alex averred with more sincerity than she would have given him credit for. 'Whether you like it or not, the fact remains, you are ruined. I cannot bring further disgrace upon my family or you. I must offer you the protection of my name.'

Her heart felt heavy in her chest. She could feel herself being dragged into this arrangement. 'If you knew this calumny would result, why did you take me to the inn and spend the night in my room?' she beseeched.

Alex let out a strangled oath. 'We've been through all this,' he snapped with irritation. 'You asked me to take you there. Based on your impertinent manner,' he grumbled with discomfort, 'well, I naturally assumed you were a common girl. What else should I have done, left you where you lay?'

'Oh, yes. It is very clear to me now,' she ranted breathlessly. 'It would have been perfectly acceptable to carry me up the stairs and bed down with me if I had been a lowly wench. Tell me, my lord,' she asked, her voice dripping with venom. 'How much money does it usually take to avoid that kind of scandal?'

'Perhaps you would have fared better with the other guests,' he growled, his eyes glinting with anger. 'If memory serves, they seemed to like you quite well.'

'Perhaps I would have,' she tossed back. 'It certainly could be no worse than this!'

'You think not?' he arched a sardonic brow.

'Obviously, your sense of honor does not necessitate that you marry every woman whose virtue you jeopardize. Or you'd be a bigamist, as well as a libertine,' she snapped with contempt.

'If you do not comport yourself as a lady you do not deserve to be treated like one,' Alex snarled.

'Alex!' the duke censured. 'I've heard enough for one evening,' he rose from his chair and walked around to the front of his desk. 'Now,' he began stoically, 'I will have to procure a special license. That should not present too great a problem as I am personally acquainted with the Archbishop of Canterbury.'

'Uncle, heed me well,' Kara said, breathless with indignation. 'I will not marry that-that miscreant!' she cried, glaring at Alex scornfully.

'*That* happens to be my son, the Marquis of Overfield, Lord Alexander Charles Edward Dalton. You *will* soon be the next marchioness. Or you shall remain in your room on bread and water until such time as you come to your senses.'

'Anything would be preferable to marriage with him!'

Uncle Charles smiled at her coolly. 'You have such lovely hair, Kara,' he said in a lethal tone, 'it would be a shame to lose it.'

Her mouth parted on a soft cry of horror and she stared at the suddenly harsh man standing before her in shocked dismay.

'Father!' Alex admonished sharply.

The duke silenced Alex with a raised hand. 'Do not underestimate me, my dear,' he told her harshly. His determined gaze fixed on her pale stricken face. 'I am not a stern man, but I shall be obeyed in this matter. Your father and mother entrusted you to my care. It is my obligation to oversee your future. As your legal guardian, I would be remiss if I permitted your reputation to be tarnished.'

'Neither of you are thinking of my well-being!' she cried. 'It is your precious family name that you are protecting. I declare. Uncle Charles, you are the most selfish man I have ever known! You have deceived me from the start about my father and now . . . now you wish to force me into marrying your son. I have the right to find happiness. To marry for love and in my own time – '

'Love!' Alex exclaimed and shook his head. 'I'm afraid you've read too many books dear heart. Love is for poets and fools,' he said, his voice dripping with sarcasm.

'I suppose,' she snapped angrily, 'you think your precious honor is all that matters? Are my feelings of no import?'

'Honor is far superior to your insipid notion of love,' Alex said gruffly.

'Spoken like a bounder,' she grated.

'Silence!' Uncle Charles thundered. 'You two will have the rest of your lives to quarrel.' He regarded Kara for a moment, his eyes cold and implacable. 'I am truly distressed you have such a disparaging image of me. Let me assure you, you have severely misapprehended the situation.' He glanced from Kara to Alex and said brusquely, 'Be that as it may, we must take the appropriate actions to remedy this appalling situation. Your father, Harry, would never forgive me if I allowed this allegation to spread. I must confess, I cannot fully comprehend your aversion to this marriage. But you two will marry!'

Hot tears rolled unchecked down her cheeks. 'Never! I will not marry him!' she ranted fleeing from the room.

'Kara!' Alex called after her and made to give chase, but the duke grabbed him by the arm.

'Let her be! She has been through a great deal of late. She needs time. She'll come around.'

Alex shook his head and raked his hand through his raven hair. Would she? Lord she was hostile! The little baggage was stronger than she looked too. He rubbed his cheek that was still smarting from her blow.

Other women would be thrilled at the prospect of marriage to one of the wealthiest peers in the realm. Not Kara. His unpredictable American enchantress was brimming with fire and ice. Damn the chit!

Didn't she know it was an honor to become a marchioness? Why didn't she dwell on that instead of harping on about empty-headed notions of love? What a damnable mess! He could throttled Hutchins!

Alex had always prided himself on seldom, if ever, considering marriage. On those rare occasions, however, the woman he envisioned was a pliant subject whom he facilely controlled. Not a little hoyden like Kara.

Initially, when he received his father's note he too had been livid. But he reasoned his father's resolution undeniably had merit. Particularly when he envisaged the impending blissful nights of passionate lovemaking.

By the time he arrived at Grantly, he was thoroughly delighted with his father's solution. He imagined Kara would resist at first. When understanding dawned that she would become Lady Dalton, she would naturally melt in his arms. He was gravely mistaken.

Taming her shrewish nature would require all his attention. His lips curled slightly. He'd change her attitude toward him. It was quite a challenge to make a woman fall in love with him. He'd never tackled anything like this before. But then, he'd never met a woman like Kara before. She had more spirit than most, and twice as much intelligence which pleased him, oddly enough.

Kara would be happy as his wife. Eventually. He'd see to it. And what fun the seduction promised to be!

This awkward circumstance was hardly ideal, however. Quite an inauspicious beginning to a marriage. One did not ideally become affianced to prevent dishonor. Naturally, it would have been better to woo her prior to their union. But this arrangement was not completely unsatisfactory.

'Quite a woman, eh?' Uncle Charles said interrupting Alex's thoughts.

Alex snorted scornfully.

The duke smiled. 'I'd watch my back if I were you. She's got a temper like her father's. You've met your match, my boy!' he remarked, clapping Alex on the shoulder 'Tell me what *exactly* did you do to her to make her disgust you so?'

Alex scowled. 'I am glad you find my predicament so entertaining. I, on the other hand, find it most unpalatable.' With that, he stormed out of the library slamming the door behind him.

The duke sat back rubbing his neck. This was going to be a stimulating match. He only hoped he could survive the fireworks!

The following morning Kara was summoned to the blue salon. She opened the door and almost made an about face when she saw his lordship standing at the window. With his booted feet slightly apart and his hands clasped behind his back, he looked supremely relaxed and completely in control. While she, on the other hand, had dark circles under her eyes, induced by a long, sleepless night.

As he turned around to face her, bestowing a devastatingly handsome smile, she wondered if the damnable rogue had ever looked rumpled in his entire life.

'Ah, Kara. Good morning. I trust you slept well?' he asked with a warm smile.

She met his smile with cool disdain. 'Do you think that likely, my lord?' she asked in a clipped tone.

He laughed softly. 'I had hoped,' he said dryly.

Lifting her chin mutinously, she squared her narrow shoulders and said, her tone like ice, 'My resolve has not weakened, if that is what you are hoping for. I will not be forced into this marriage.'

He winced and rubbed the tension from his neck. 'You may have no choice. I'm afraid father is as good as his word. Trust me. He is implacable once his mind is made up.' He reached out a hand and gently touched her silky dark hair. 'It's quite lovely,' he breathed examining the rich color and soft texture. 'I wouldn't like to see you lose it. Once we are married you'll be under my protection. If anyone dare lay a hand on you, they will answer to me.'

'How very reassuring, my lord,' she said, her voice heavy with sarcasm. 'But who pray tell will protect me from you?'

His lips pursed with displeasure.

'Losing my hair might be preferable to a life of drudgery with you,' she said tightly.

He shook his head and dropped his hand to his side. 'That is just what you'll have if you continue on your present course. Banishment. Or the rod. Believe me, father has a formidable temper and a stubborn nature. One way or the other, he will bend you to his will.'

She gasped in horror. The duke was indeed a harsh, proud man. 'But you cannot want to marry me,' she cried in desperation.

'What I want is beside the point. Whatever else you may think of me, I won't subject you to total disgrace. I am trying to save you, Kara,' he said gently. 'Not destroy you.'

'Then tell me you have brought me here to say you've come to your senses and decided against our ridiculous marriage,' she said softly.

'I cannot.'

'Ah,' she said with a deep sigh of regret. 'One can always hope.'

He grimaced. Hell! She wasn't making this any easier. He was actually nervous, which was a novelty in itself. He prided himself on being in control at all times and this agitation was a new and unwelcome feeling. It simply would not do. 'Kara, I realize you are upset and with good reason. But believe me when I tell you our only course of action is to – '

'Make the best of an appallingly bad situation?' she suggested, her voice heavy with mockery.

He slanted her a dark look and cleared his throat. 'Allow me to speak freely – '

Taking a seat on the blue velvet Grecian style sofa, she asked coolly, 'Have I any choice in the matter?'

This was a bad idea. The woman had the most disconcerting effect on him. She was just a woman,

93

perhaps more attractive than most. Why then was his natural aplomb disturbed? His manner toward women was usually detached, but he felt a deep abiding need to make amends. After all, she was soon to be his wife. Some semblance of peace must be established.

'I wish to apologize most sincerely.'

'Apologize?' she repeated duly. Her blazing azure gaze locked with his. 'For which gross transgression? Nearly trampling on me with your horse? Spending the night with me at an inn and taking scandalous liberties while I was under the influence of spirits? Or kissing me without the benefit of invitation, or for that matter, permission?' she asked tersely.

He drew in his breath sharply. She was a hoyden! Not one woman in twenty would have dared give him that reply. They'd be pleased he deigned to offer an apology and leave it at that. After they'd gratefully accepted, of course. He struggled to suppress his rising anger. 'I am willing to make amends for all my offenses,' he assured her, his jaw set.

'And how exactly do you propose to do that?' she asked tartly.

He smiled then, his anger fading for the moment. She'd played into his hands. 'Why,' he said, one end of his mouth curling, 'by making you happy, how else?'

The arrogance of the man was beyond comprehension. 'Do you honestly believe there is anything you could do that would make me happy?' she asked, incredulously.

His dark hooded gaze moved over her body. 'I think there are a great many things,' he assured her with a wolfish grin.

She stiffened and lowered her lashes. 'Then you are sadly mistaken,' she told him crisply.

'Am I?' he asked cocking a brow. 'I think not.' His hands were caressing her arms in a circular motion that was strangely relaxing. Very pleasant actually, she realized with a tingling rush of pleasure. Lifting her chin with a long finger, he gazed deeply into her eyes. 'You claim to long for love and happiness. But I wonder if you are willing to work for it?' he asked softly.

'With you? A notorious rake and a peerless cad?' She shook her head. 'No. I think not.'

'There are certain advantages to wedding a rake,' he told her smoothly, his eyes glittering wickedly. 'You might be persuaded to enjoy some of the benefits.'

Color crept into her cheeks. And she realized on some horrid base level she was intrigued by his offer. The memory of his kisses had not faded. Nor could she seem to forget the feel of his hands searing her flesh. She found herself wondering, to her absolute dismay, if all men offered such pleasures, or if such talents were reserved for rakes. She turned her face away. 'I think you are too frivolous, my lord, for us to ever share anything of value.'

He chuckled softly. 'Passion is no small thing. Do not underestimate it. And there will be children.'

Her head snapped up. 'Is that all you think of? A moment's pleasure and an heir to carry on your exalted position?' she asked sharply.

He shrugged an elegant shoulder and gently caressed her cheek with the back of his hand. She quivered in response to his touch and he smiled. 'One or two other things enter my mind from time to time,' he drawled.

It was just a game to him. Her life was disintegrating before her eyes and it amused him! She swatted his hand away.

'Damn you, sir!' she cried, glaring at him. 'What right have you to call yourself an honorable gentleman? You have not one decent bone in your body. My life may seem puny and insignificant to you,' she grated breathlessly, 'but it has great meaning to me. Through your own carelessness, you have destroyed my chance for happiness. And now you expect me to graciously comply when you throw me a crumb of hope to nibble on!'

His brow darkened. He was no longer amused. 'What an outrageous hellion you are! How dare you question my honor and fling insults at my head?'

'I not only question it,' she countered hotly, 'I rightfully scorn it.'

'The devil you say,' he growled and reached for her, jerking her hard against him. In a futile effort to resist him, she pressed her palms against his chest.

'Shall I prove to you how fragile your resolve is, my chaste little wanton?' he asked, his breath warm on her face. She squeezed her eyes shut and shook her head.

His mouth descended on hers, taking her lips in a brutal kiss. A tiny sound escaped her throat as his tongue forced her lips apart and ravaged the soft recesses of her mouth. His open mouth, hot, wet and demanding, slanted passionately over hers. Arms of steel enfolded her while his hands caressed her back and the sides of her breasts.

With a helpless whimper, she gave in to his savage kiss. And her arms crept around his neck. And she kissed him back.

He tore his lips from hers and stared down at her. His breathing was labored as he said, '*That* is what we share. Dare you deny your attraction to me now?'

Pushing away from him, she stumbled backwards. 'You are beneath contempt!' she said gasping for air. 'I will never share anything with you! You are a heartless cur who uses women for momentary diversion. Understand this, if we marry it will only be under the threat of violence, not because I harbor an ounce of regard for you!'

Tears of shame and indignation pricked her eyes for she had fallen prey yet again to his devilish charm. Her pride, however, would not allow him to see her cry. Head held high, she departed the room.

Alex walked over to the window and gazed out at the grey sky. 'Perhaps not as heartless as you believe,' he said on a sigh, rubbing his chin thoughtfully.

CHAPTER 5

As the carriage made its way to the church, Kara felt like she was being led to Newgate prison. She had been sentenced to life with the rogue, Alex. It was a cruel punishment. She did not deserve to be treated so unjustly. If she ever saw Mr Hutchins again she would surely murder him.

'Your wedding is quite a spectacle,' Aunt Henrietta enthused, her chubby face etching a smile, 'it is not every day the marquis takes a bride.' She squeezed Kara's hand affectionately. Kara sighed dolefully and looked away.

Uncle Charles greeted the somber bride at the back of the church, 'Angelic! My dear, you look simply breathtaking. I know my first wife and your dear departed parents are smiling down upon us this day.'

Kara's lips thinned with displeasure. She sincerely doubted that. Nevertheless, she tried to remain placid and look dignified in her ivory lace satin gown.

Her legs felt weak, however. And the church seemed horribly stuffy. She found it difficult to draw breath. As she heard the music begin, she suddenly realized *I am actually going through with this!*

Her heart thudded in her chest as Uncle Charles led her down the endless marble aisle. She could still run away, she thought frantically. There is still time! She wasn't married yet.

Darting a frantic glance around the enormous church, her eyes spied the nearest exit. Unfortunately she'd reached the altar. The warmth of Alex's hand closed over her quivering, ice-cold fingers trapping her at his side.

She tried to pull her hand away, but he tightened his grip. His eyes darkened and he shot her a lethal glance. Flashing him a desperate look, she tried to loose her hand. But he pinioned her to his side, his eyes glinting dangerously into hers. It was as if he had read her thoughts, and was determined to make her his wife. Shoulders slumped and head hung, she admitted defeat.

As the vicar droned on, she felt completely detached from the ceremony. Acutely aware of Alex's overpowering, manly presence beside her, she looked down and saw that his large hand still held her much smaller one in his inescapable grip. Evidently, he was not taking any chances with his skittish bride.

She heard herself speaking in a barely audible voice, 'I, Karina Elizabeth Simpson . . .' Then she heard Alex speak. His deep, resonant voice was forceful as he swore to love, cherish and honor her all the days of his life.

Numbly, she watched as he clasped her left hand and gently slid the gold wedding ring on her third finger. Then his hand slid beneath her chin and he tilted her face to receive his kiss. The momentous kiss that would seal her fate.

As he bent his head to her mouth, his dark orbs bore into her terrified blue depths and he smiled slightly. It was a kind, reassuring smile, but did little to lessen her distress. The feel of his lips tenderly caressing her own sent shivers through her. Damn her treacherous body! She was helpless to resist. With a tiny sigh of surrender, she gave in to the insistent, yet gentle caress of his warm, soft lips and she kissed him back.

Alex fully intended his kiss to be perfunctory, but her soft lips were too inviting. He felt her quiver. Felt her hands clutch his arms. Never known to refuse such sweet temptation, he accepted the invitation her trembling lips offered and he deepened the kiss as her lips parted sweetly beneath his.

The vicar cleared his throat. When at last Alex pulled away, Kara was breathless. He stared at her flushed face, a dark and unreadable expression marring his handsome face. Taking her arm, he escorted her briskly to the back of the church.

The ride home from the church began in taciturn silence. Kara sat across from the man who was her husband, gazing out of the window. She could feel his dark, penetrating stare, but continued to look out the window pretending to be interested in the countryside.

Alex was indeed studying his bride. She was an infuriating blend of seductress and hoyden! He would like to take her over his knee for that stunt in the church. She was far too spirited and independent. Did she actually think she could leave him at the altar? Or was she hoping to humiliate him before his guests? She was stubborn and rebellious. He demanded a submissive wife. And by God he would have one! It didn't help matters, however, that with every kiss he was drawn more and more under her spell. He was equally shaken by their kiss in the church.

'Did you think to leave so soon, my beloved?' he asked, his voice dripping with sarcasm.

Kara turned from the window to glare at him. 'It is no secret that I detest you,' she snapped, 'I made it patently clear that I had no wish to wed you.'

'Nor I you,' he said cruelly. He was fabricating, of course. He wanted this vixen more with every passing minute. And it irked him. He was unaccustomed to unrequited desire. Or for that matter, unfulfilled lust.

He leaned forward. His eyes narrowing angrily on her pale, pinched face, 'Be that as it may, we are man and wife. You, my sweet, will act the part, particularly in public. I will brook no disobedience from you.'

'My lord,' she gritted, her blue eyes ablaze with fury. 'I should think you'd have realized it is my most fervent desire never see you again.'

'Is that so?' he asked raising a dubious brow. Sitting back he crossed his arms and inspected his lovely wife from head to toe, his sensual gaze clinging to her revealing lace bodice. She shifted uncomfortably beneath his stare. His lips curled into a mocking smile. 'Your kiss tells me differently.'

'You are gravely mistaken, my lord,' she imparted crisply. 'I detest you.'

'And you are a brazen liar, my sweet,' he said chuckling to himself. 'But it pleases me to play this little game with you. For the moment.'

'I may be forced to endure your frequent mauling. But pleasure, for me, will never enter into it. Not with a man like you,' she said curtly and turned her attention back to the window.

'And just what would you know about a man like me, hmm?' he asked, a smug grin on his lips. It gave him great pleasure to goad his prim and proper little wanton.

'Enough to know I could never come to love you,' she said coolly.

He tossed back his raven head and laughed. 'Well, then it is a good thing it is not love I'm after.'

The carriage came to a halt and the gold and blue liveried footman opened the door. Alex jumped down. Holding out his arms to her, he grinned, 'Come my dear, show me those charming ankles I remember so well.'

Tossing him an angry frown, she hesitantly placed her hands on his muscular arms, being sure to avoid contact with his broad, well-formed chest. Flustered by his strong hands around her waist, she carefully averted her face. Effortlessly, he swept her from the gilded carriage and drew her close against him.

'There now, isn't this cozy?' he asked, his eyes twinkling with mirth. 'Seems vaguely familiar, does it not?' His lips were twitching unbearably.

Her temper flared and she pushed against his rock hard chest. 'Beyond a doubt, you are the most insolent man I ever had the misfortune to – '

'Marry?' he cut in. 'Truly, my sweet,' he sighed in a bored tone, 'you must endeavor to conduct yourself in a more graceful manner, as befits your new station as my wife.'

She eyed him with cool disdain. 'My lord,' she snapped, chafing against his possessive grip, 'is it your wish to brand me, or suffocate me?'

A slow smile spread across his handsome face. 'I have no need to brand what is already mine,' he said, a wicked gleam shining in those devilish eyes. She glared at him, her fiery blue orbs spitting fire.

'Come, dearest,' he said, amused at her enraged face, 'let us celebrate our blissful nuptials and greet our anxious guests.'

'It is not necessary for you to hold me so close,' she bristled.

'My little vixen,' he murmured, as he whisked her past scores of well wishers, 'is a bit flighty. I would not care to lose her.' His warm breath on her ear sent unwanted shivers down her back.

Clenching her jaw, she tried to ignore his overwhelmingly masculine presence at her side. Even hating him, as she was certain she did, she was uncontrollably affected by him. It was pathetic. She seemed utterly helpless.

Alex traced his index finger along her forearm. He could see the green and yellow coloration through the lace of her gown, 'Are you completely recovered from your accident?'

His touch was far too soft and seductive for her liking. She suppressed the desire to snatch her hand away. 'Y-yes. My arm is feeling much better,' she stammered, nervously licking her lips.

He smiled, his dark eyes, gleaming like the very devil, as he watched the flicker of her tongue over her inviting lips.

'I am so glad. Shall we dance?'

Before she had the opportunity to refuse, his arm went around her waist and he led her onto the dance floor. Much to Kara's dismay it was a waltz. His hand seemed to sear her flesh right through her gown.

The glittering ballroom was indeed spectacular. If it had been any other occasion she would have enjoyed herself immensely. Stealing a covert glance at her husband, she was struck once again by his annoying good looks. He was holding her much closer than propriety allowed. All too aware of his clean manly scent, she averted her gaze and pretended, as they floated around the dance floor, to be interested in the floral arrangements.

'Dear heart,' he whispered, his dark sultry gaze mocking her. 'The waltz is for lovers.'

'We are not lovers,' she snapped, her blue eyes sparkling with rage. 'Ours is a marriage of convenience, or have you forgotten?'

'I have not forgotten,' he said staring deeply into her eyes. 'But why not make the best of an unpalatable situation?'

She stiffened and looked away. 'Spoken like a true bounder,' she mumbled under her breath. 'It was remiss of me, my lord, to forget your penchant for the endless pursuit of pleasure. I quite forgot what a wretch you are.'

He chuckled and whirled her past the crowd of interested spectators. 'You are quite adorable when you are angry,' he told her. His voice was all silk and seduction. 'But then, I have yet to have the pleasure of seeing you smile at me.'

She fixed him with a chilling gaze. 'Nor are you likely to.'

'No?' he asked cocking a skeptical brow. 'Would you smile, little vixen if you succeeded in reforming my rakish ways and I pledged my eternal devotion and fidelity?'

'Don't be absurd,' she muttered forcing a smile to her lips as they floated past Uncle Charles on the sidelines. 'I have no desire to reform you. Nor do I think it a worth while endeavor.'

'Oh, yes you do. Every woman believes in the reformation of a rake.'

Her lips pursed with displeasure. 'I suppose

you've known enough women to judge,' she said harshly.

'You could you know, if you put your mind to it,' he assured her in a dark sultry voice guaranteed to send her pulse racing. 'There is precious little that luscious little body of yours couldn't wheedle out of a man.'

Her face grew hot. And she turned away unable to meet his eyes. 'You are entirely too familiar, my lord,' she whispered fiercely.

'Quite true,' he agreed, with an impervious smile. 'The result of a wild undisciplined childhood, no doubt. But I am not sorry for it. And neither are you.'

She tried to pull away, but he would have none of it. His fingers dug into her flesh and he swept her around the dance floor as if she were a mere featherweight in his masterful embrace.

'Careful, my little vixen,' he warned. 'No scenes on our wedding day, surely?'

'You are beyond the pale, my lord,' she said with contempt.

'Do you think so?' he asked amusedly as he moved her effortlessly around the dance floor. 'I wonder how much you crave this illusive love your poets write about?' His sensuous mouth quirked unforgivably.

Her blue eyes glinted with anger. 'Do not mock me,' she hissed. 'If your life of carnal delights is superior to deep and abiding love, then by all means indulge yourself, my lord. But pray, leave me alone!'

107

'If you weren't such a tempting little morsel, I'd do just that. Which is it to be, will you teach me respectable ways? Or shall I corrupt you, do you suppose?'

She opened her mouth to issue a scathing retort, but the music stopped and the waltz came to an end. His hand closed over her elbow and he escorted her off the dance floor. 'Shall we greet our eager guests, dearest?' he asked in a voice that brooked no disagreement. He'd closed the previous topic of discussion purposefully and persuasively. She had no choice but to acquiesce.

Glancing at his errant bride Alex wasn't quite sure what he felt, except an overwhelming desire to indulge in a delightfully intriguing challenge. That he could tumble her into bed, he had no doubt. But could he seduce her into loving him? he wondered idly. Now that would be the greater challenge.

The thought of having to face a deluge of gawking guests overwhelmed Kara and she felt her knees go weak. 'I thought this was to be an intimate affair,' she mumbled to herself as she looked around at the veritable crush of guests.

'It is,' he drawled, purposely misunderstanding her comment. 'Our marriage is going to be extremely intimate, I assure you,' his voice was like a velvet caress. And his blatant insinuation unnerved her. He must be mad if he thought for one moment she would welcome him in her bed. Or perhaps he would not wait for an invitation? Her lips twisted with displeasure. How like a rogue to take what he wanted! Well, if he thought she'd fall prey to his seduction ever again, he was sadly mistaken.

The droves of guests began their inspection of the new Marchioness of Overfield. Alex was only too happy to commence with the introductions, 'Sir Gilbert White, Lord Pool, may I introduce my wife, Lady Dalton.'

The two gentlemen bowed, and kissed her hand. Sir Gilbert was an attractive older man with silver hair and piercing blue eyes. Lord Pool, on the other hand, could best be described as corpulent and salacious. She disliked him instantly.

'Now I know why Alex was in such a hurry to wed you,' the portly Lord Pool prattled, eyeing her like a delicious dessert. 'May I say you are the most radiant bride I have ever seen.'

She inclined her head and replied politely, 'I think you must not have attended very many weddings or else, my lord, you wish something from me.'

Sir Gilbert burst out laughing, 'Charming, positively charming. Alex you are a lucky man!'

Alex nodded, 'I like to think so,' he said eyeing the obnoxious Lord Pool with displeasure.

'Did you know that Alex was a war hero?' Lord Pool inquired, arching a bushy red brow and slapping his rotund belly. Kara's eyes widened and she glanced at Alex. Somehow her rakish husband did not fit her image of a hero. 'No. I had no idea. In what war?'

'Oh, my dear,' he chortled patting her hand with his sweaty paw. 'What a charming little American you are. So sheltered from the ways of the world. Allow me to tell you, it was the Napoleonic War, of course. Damn good man your husband. Saw a lot of action on the Peninsular. He's been decorated several times.'

'Really,' Kara mumbled in amazement. Perhaps there was more to this notorious rake than she thought.

'Ah, yes! I don't know what our office would do without him,' Lord Pool said, his eyes ogling her tight bodice.

'He has served his King and country loyally for many years. Like his father – '

'Would you care for something to eat, my dear?' Alex interjected, his hand clamping over her elbow.

Kara reluctantly accepted the rough command and bid the gentlemen a hasty farewell. What had Lord Pool meant by 'our office'? she continued to wonder as her husband led her briskly toward the dinning room.

Aunt Henrietta greeted them with a warm smile and a plate brimming with food. 'Well, my dears,' she crooned, her blonde ringlets bobbing on either side of her pudgy flushed face. 'The reception seems to be a tremendous success, as I knew it would be. Everyone adores your wife Alex,' she exclaimed, munching on a slice of duck.

'Not nearly as much as I,' he drawled, eyeing Kara with unbridled hunger. He was trying to shock her, Kara knew, but she could not control the slight blush that crept into her cheeks. She dearly wished he would stop ravishing her with his eyes. It was most disconcerting. Almost as disturbing as her wildly skittering pulse.

Alex tore his gaze from his comely bride and examined his pocket watch. Damn, it was only ten o'clock. It could be several more hours before they could retire to luxuriate in marital bliss. What he wouldn't give to bury himself deep inside her right here and now! He had to stop thinking of their love making. He would never last the evening at this rate.

Sir Gilbert interrupted his reverie,

'May I have a word, Dalton? In private,' he added meaningfully.

Alex nodded grimly and turned to his bride.

'Kara, my darling,' he said, acting the solicitous bridegroom.

'Yes, my lord?' she jeered, annoyed with her fluttering heart.

He smiled apologetically, 'Something has come up. I must leave you I'm afraid for a while. I'll see you later tonight.'

'Oh no, Alex. Not on your wedding day! That is the limit. The absolute limit!' Aunt Henrietta cried, throwing her sausage-like arms up in the air in distress.

'What has happened?' Kara asked in confusion. 'Is it Sir Gilbert? Is something wrong?'

Alex's eyes narrowed on her face. She was extremely perceptive. In future, he was going to have to be more prudent. He did not want her mercurial quick mind suspecting.

His lips curled into a smile. 'It is always nice to have such an attentive and fervent bride. I am truly blessed,' he said smoothly and brought her hands to his lips. Turning them over, he kissed her palms. 'Never fear, I would not presume to keep my enthusiastic bride waiting on her wedding night,' he said meeting her gaze as he pressed his lips to the sensitive flesh on her right wrist.

Tiny shivers crawled up her arm and she snatched her hand away as if she had been scalded. 'Take as long as you need. I assure you I shall be fast asleep when you return.'

'In that case, my love,' he hastened to add, his voice like silk, 'it will be my distinct pleasure to awaken you.'

Her cheeks flooded with color and she quickly looked away. Bowing to take his leave, Alex chuckled softly and left to attend his meeting with Sir Gilbert.

Kara was immensely relieved that he was gone. But she was also exceedingly anxious. She had no intention of submitting to him – tonight or any other night. Agreeing to this farce of a marriage was one thing, but *that* was something entirely different! She could not possibly make love to a man she barely knew and certainly did not love. He'd simply have to understand her reservations and respect her wishes. Wouldn't he?

* * *

When at last Kara was able to escape the crowded reception and creep up the stairs to her new sleeping quarters, she was exhausted and her head was splitting. Sighing, she leaned back against the door and surveyed the room. So, this was his lordship's chamber.

The first bedroom which she took to be hers, was slightly smaller than her previous room. The wood was dark mahogany, and the color scheme was blue, not rose. She disliked it heartily.

The connecting door was slightly ajar. Why not? she thought as she pushed the door open. Her husband's room was much larger than hers which annoyed her instantly. Nothing but the best for the marquis! The room was decidedly masculine with a deep, rich burgundy canopy and drapes. The bed, she noticed was enormous and quickly glanced away. She did not want to think about what might go on there.

A second door caught her eye. Upon further inspection, she saw that it led from the master bedroom into a small study. Judging from the dent in the comfortable brown leather chair, Alex spent a great deal of time here. Papers were strewn all over the desk. Obviously, he had recently been at work.

These are his private rooms, it is unethical to read someone's personal papers, she told herself. But she was his wife, she reasoned and gave into the temptation to rifle through his desk.

Shuffling through the papers, she tried to make head or tail of his scribbled notes. There seemed to

113

be a list of people's names in one column and possible connections in the other, all of which signified nothing of importance to her. She noticed the words Bow Street Runners were circled and furrowed her brow. Who, or what were they?

She sorted through the other scattered papers. The notes he'd scribbled on how to proceed with 'the current London investigation' caught her eye. Apparently, the Bow Street Runners were investigators. What was Alex up to? And why should one of England's wealthiest marquises want to investigate anyone?

'I beg ya pardon milady.'

Startled, Kara gasped and jumped from the desk. She released her breath and fanned her hand over heart. 'Oh, Violet, it's you. You frightened me to death.'

She realized the picture she presented, being caught rifling through her husband's things, and cleared her throat. 'I . . . thought . . . I was alone,' she stammered lamely.

Violet bobbed a curtsy and said, 'Th' duchess thought ya might be needin' assistance, milady.'

Kara smiled. 'Yes, that was thoughtful. Thank you.' Returning the piece of paper she was holding to the desk, she quickly brushed past the maid and went into her room.

'His lordship could barely keep his eyes off ya,' Violet remarked as she brushed out Kara's luxurious dark hair. 'Everyone was sayin' so. There'll be lil' uns 'fore ya know it.'

Does anyone in this house ever think of anything else? Kara wondered with a frown. Slipping the nightgown Violet offered her over her head, Kara caught sight of her reflection in the mirror and froze in a stunned tableau. The gown was completely sheer!

Even Aunt Henrietta was in on the conspiracy. 'I would like my other nightgown if you please,' Kara said curtly.

Violet looked perplexed, 'Beg ya pardon milady? Th' duchess told me 'tis the one fer tonight.'

She felt like a mare being sent to the Grantly stud farm. 'Nevertheless, I would like my other nightgown. I will freeze in this!'

Violet giggled. 'Not with his lordship to keep ya warm,' she said with a knowing wink.

Kara eyes widened. 'That will be quite enough. You may go. I will manage on my own.'

Shrugging, Violet bobbed a curtsy and left, closing the door after her.

Kara was livid. What did Alex think? She would fall into his arms like some simpering idiot? Of course, the fact that she had done just that on previous occasions was irrelevant. She would rather die than stand before his probing gaze in this gossamer-thin gown! Just thinking of his slow seductive gaze roaming over her naked form made her grow hot.

She'd made up her mind. Theirs would be a marriage of convenience. She simply could not bring herself to share the bed of England's premier rake. If he did not like it, he could seek his pleasures elsewhere.

Contented with her solution, she retrieved her white flannel nightgown from the armoire, and quickly donned it. Buttoning it up to her chin, she climbed into bed and blew out the candles.

Downstairs in the library, Alex was eager to get the blasted meeting over with. He had waited long enough for his bride and his appetite was sorely whetted. That imbecile Lord Pool was objecting to some point Sir Gilbert was making.

'What I take exception to Pool, is you practically giving away the nature of my work,' Alex quipped nastily. 'You know what I do is confidential and only a handful of people are privy to the details. My bride is not one of them.'

Lord Pool's mouth dropped open, 'I say, that was uncalled for Dalton.'

'Enough bickering gentlemen,' Sir Gilbert interrupted slanting a frown in Alex's direction.

'May we get to the point of this urgent meeting?' Alex demanded. 'My bride awaits me.'

'Certainly,' Daniel Rutherford interjected, grinning wolfishly. 'We all know how impatient Alex is to join his enticing new bride.'

The entire group broke into laughter. Alex frowned. Apparently, he was the only one not amused. He found the joke in poor taste. Normally, he enjoyed his friend Daniel's sense of humor, but tonight it perturbed him for some reason.

116

'I say, where did you meet her?' Lord Pool piped up trying to quell his mirth.

Alex had heard about enough from Pool. 'In the middle of the road,' he spat out.

Lord Pool laughed nervously, 'Such a wit, Dalton, such a wit.'

'The reason I called this emergency meeting,' Sir Gilbert spoke up, 'is that we believe there may be a connection between Bouchard and the insurrectionists.'

'Why would he bother with such an elaborate ruse?' Alex asked.

Gilbert shrugged. 'Who knows? I thought you would be pleased, Alex. After all, you are obsessed with the man.'

Alex frowned with irritation. He had good reason for his obsession. And Gilbert knew it. 'I'll pursue this lead upon my return to London. We can meet next week,' Alex said rising from his chair. 'Daniel, I will need your assistance now that you are returned from France.'

Daniel nodded his assent and got to his feet. 'The customary romantic month-long honeymoon in the country is out I see,' he quipped dryly.

Alex smirked and nodded his head. 'So it would appear.' Looking at his pocket watch he saw it was nearly one o'clock.

Sir Gilbert slapped Alex on the back. 'Gentlemen, we have kept this groom from his bride long enough.'

* * *

Alex climbed the stairs two at time. Devil take it! He was behaving like a young stag on his first romantic adventure. He opened the sitting room door, and heard the clock in the study chime the hour.

Judging from the pitch black room, his vivacious young bride had not waited up for him. Letting out a strangled oath, he fumbled for a match and lit the taper on the table.

He strolled into Kara's bedroom. The embers were still smoldering in the fireplace, partially illuminating the room. Standing over her, he watched her sleeping. He felt a strange tightening in his chest. His wife! She was incredibly lovely. The soft candlelight revealed her dark, rich hair fanned over the white pillow. Her rosebud lips practically invited his kiss. The soft sound of her breathing mingled with the gentle rise and fall of her breasts beneath the satin coverlet, made his heart beat faster. It was good she had some time to rest for he intended to keep her up for the rest of the night.

It was too late to bother with his valet, so he sauntered into his room to undress. He was entirely satisfied with the arrangement, he thought as he tugged at his neckcloth. She certainly was a fiery wench. But to his surprise, that delighted him far more than he would have thought.

Besides, he reasoned, after tonight she would settle down. He might even get her with child. All women calmed down when they were with child. Didn't they? Of course they did.

* * *

When Kara heard the door open, sheer panic assailed her. She had been tossing and turning for hours. She hoped that her pretense of sleep had fooled him. He wouldn't wake her, would he? Oh no! He might, hadn't he said as much? Aunt Henrietta's words echoed in her brain. A woman must submit to the marriage act and give in to her husband's demands. Well, not this woman!

She knew exactly what she would tell him if he pressed her. She had had ample time to rehearse her speech over the last few wakeful hours. Still, the image of Alex listening to her tell him was quite a different matter.

She heard him enter the room and place the candle on the bedside table. The mattress dipped under his great bulk as he sat down on the bed and leaned over her. The next thing she knew his lips warm and demanding, were on hers. And he was kissing her, gently urging her to respond. Gracious! He did not waste any time did he? Pushing him away she sat up.

He smiled down at her and her heart skipped a beat. 'Hello darling.'

In the flickering light, his dark eyes were ablaze with passion. He looked more handsome than Kara thought possible. Her pulse skidded unbearably. Clad in his silk brocade dressing robe which was laid part way open displaying thick black hair covering his massive chest, he looked gorgeous.

He placed his hand over hers. Instinctively she looked at it. It was a very large hand. Alarm ripped through her. Oh dear, she thought biting her lip, she had not considered his size. He was a very powerful man.

Tipping her chin up he smiled at her. She supposed it was meant to be a reassuring smile, but it made her even more nervous. He rubbed her jaw with the pad of his thumb.

Oh no! This is how I lost control last time. Tearing her gaze away, she took a deep breath.

'Don't be frightened. I won't hurt you,' he whispered kissing her neck.

'I am not frightened of you,' she managed to get out. Goodness! What a predicament! She wished he'd stop touching her. This was more difficult than she had imagined.

'No,' he breathed, 'then why are you trembling?' he murmured, kissing the sensitive skin behind her ear.

Oh dear, that felt incredibly good. 'I . . . I . . . am not,' she stuttered, stealing herself against the pleasure of his touch.

He smiled against her mouth. 'Aren't you?' he breathed. 'It's all right. I think I know.' His hands were lightly caressing her shoulders.

Pressing her palm against his chest, she pushed away from him. With a hard swallow she said, in a voice that sounded horribly shaky even to her own ears, 'N-no, you don't. I have come to a decision.'

'Mmm,' he mumbled pressing his lips against her temple, her eyelids, her cheek and finally kissing the side of her mouth.

Turning her face away, she launched into her well-practised speech, 'Yes, I have. I am not . . .' Her eyes fluttered shut and she tried to concentrate on her all-important speech instead of the warmth of his breath and the feel of his soft supple lips on her neck. 'I cannot think . . . when you do that,' she mumbled shoving her palms against his shoulders.

'Go on, Kara I am listening,' he said softly as he moved closer and nuzzled her neck. 'What is it you wish to say to me?' he asked in a husky voice.

She was losing all composure. And most of her train of thought. She leaned back even further into the pillows and said breathlessly, 'I don't like it when you kiss me like that. I wish you wouldn't.'

'I see, is that all?' he asked nibbling at her earlobe with his teeth.

'No, I . . . you,' she stuttered. 'My lord,' she rushed out slamming her fists against his shoulders. That got his attention. He blinked and stared down at her in confusion.

'There is something I must tell you,' she told him twisting the sheets between her fingers.

Placing his hands on either side of her, he leaned down, his face only inches from hers. 'It can wait,' he whispered against her mouth and dipped his head to kiss her inviting lips.

'No!' she cried pressing her fingertips over his lips. 'I'm afraid, it can't.'

Covering her hand with the warmth of his, he kissed her fingertips laving her soft skin with his tongue.

Dear heaven! If she allowed this sweet torture to continue much longer, she'd have no use for her speech!

Snatching her hand away, she cleared her throat. 'I-I have come to a decision,' she told her lap. 'About our, er, relationship. I don't want one. I mean, I don't want to . . . to, well, to be intimate with you.' There, she thought with a surge of relief. It was out. She'd said it. Now he'd go away. And she could finally sleep in peace.

But Alex had no intention of leaving. 'I see,' he replied tonelessly. This was a rather new experience for him. Never in all his twenty-six years had a female spurned his advances. And so he chalked up this particular rejection to a case of wedding night nerves.

'Good. Then you understand and you won't press me,' she said primly.

His lips curled without amusement. 'I understand that you do not want to be, how did you put it, intimate?'

She nodded her head.

'But I'm afraid I can't leave,' he assured her silkily.

'Can't?' she echoed duly. Can't or won't? She sat bolt upright in bed. 'What do you mean, can't?' she asked her eyes narrowing.

'I mean, that you are my wife. And under the law, you are my chattel to do with as I please. And it is my desire to make love to you. Tonight.'

Stunned, she opened her mouth and then shut it again. Naturally, she assumed that when she told him how she felt he would respect her wishes and leave. She was sure that this type of arrangement existed, she had heard people whisper about it at parties in Boston. Regardless, of what custom dictated, she was not submitting to him.

'Kara,' he said, gently brushing her cheek with his palm, 'it is not unusual for you to be afraid. But I promise you there is nothing to worry about. All brides are nervous, I would not want you to be any other way. I'll be very gentle.'

His condescending tone rankled her to the core. Oh, he would, would he! The temerity of the man was boundless. Precisely how many women tumbled into his bed believing that ridiculous poppycock? she wondered irritably.

'I am sure your intentions are good and kind,' she informed him coldly. 'But I do not want you!'

He stared at her agog. 'Are you actually refusing me?' he asked dubiously.

Clearing her throat, her legs wriggled uncomfortably beneath the sheets. She was well aware that refusing one's husband was simply not done. Aunt Henrietta would be have an attack of the vapors if she knew about this conversation. Not to mention what the good vicar would say. But their situation was different. She had been forced to marry Alex. And she did not love him.

'Many marriages are in name only,' she told the coverlet. 'You are not in love with me. And I would need to, well, know the man I am intimate with better – '

'You could have fooled me,' he snorted with derision. 'You had no difficulty with a perfect stranger at a dingy little inn not so long ago.'

Must he continually remind her of that ghastly night? It was difficult enough to quell the rampant memories without him throwing them in her face.

'It was the brandy,' she replied, her blush deepening considerably. 'I was not at all myself.'

His lips twitched with irritation. The audacity of the little vixen amazed him. And the idea of slipping his wife a healthy dose of laudanum had definite merit. Such a pity he didn't think of it earlier.

'Did it ever dawn on you that I might not agree to your little arrangement?' he asked, his voice like steel cloaked in velvet.

Her head shot up. And she looked at him, her eyes wide with amazement. 'I-I don't see why you'd care.'

'No, you wouldn't,' he muttered with sarcasm.

He got up. Shoving his hands in the pocket of his robe, he wandered over to the fireplace and stared at the dying embers. Dragging his hand through his hair he sighed.

'Lord, save me from frightened virgins,' he muttered with an inward groan. He had married an inept child.

Heaven knows what stories she had heard about marriage. Glancing at her over his shoulder, he almost felt sorry for her. Almost.

On the other hand, he had never been so incensed! The little imp was flatly denying him his rights! Sitting in the middle of the bed, dictating their marital accord, in her virginal white nightgown which was not designed to be the least bit provocative, but sure as hell was having an effect on him!

'I'll fight you all the way,' she assured him, her chin jutting defiantly.

'It is my right as your husband, you do realize?' he remarked crossing his arms over his well-made chest.

'I'll scream,' she told him firmly.

His handsome face contorted into an angry scowl. 'What the devil are you talking about?'

No matter how much he wanted to make love to her, or how angry he was, he would never force himself on her. Although at this moment, it would serve the little hellion right if he gave in to his desire and ripped that ridiculous nightgown off and made love to her, forcing her to his will. But he knew he never would, regardless of the provocation. He loathed men at his club who bragged about abusing their wives. The mere thought was repugnant to him. However, he'd thoroughly enjoy taking her over his knee and giving her a royal spanking.

'I've no desire for frightened virgins or child brides. I'd rather have an alluring woman in my bed. So you, and your precious virtue, are quite safe,' he said cruelly. 'I will require an heir at some point in the future,' he continued. 'But that can wait. I give you fair warning, however, I am not a patient man. I don't intend to wait forever.'

With that, he left, slamming the door to his bedroom behind him.

Kara had never been so insulted! She was not a child. Throwing herself down on her back, she told herself she was well rid of him. Once a rake always a rake. Let him seek his pleasures elsewhere. As he undoubtedly would.

CHAPTER 6

Kara opened her eyes, and judged by the offending sunlight peeking through the velvet drapes, that it was morning. The second day of her married life. Goodness, she was married! And to him! A man she neither liked nor knew particularly well. And whose sole offer to make amends for this dreadful mess was to pleasure her in bed. Surely she deserved more? Like love and commitment.

She glanced over at the breakfast tray. Apparently, it had been there for some time for the once hot chocolate was now cold and congealed. Observing the door to the beast's room was closed she wondered if he was still sleeping.

The effrontery of the man, to expect that she would share his bed. Under the circumstances, it was unthinkable. She wondered if she'd ever have the fortitude to go to such a man even if he promised untold sensual delights. It was all far too humiliating to contemplate. Although the memory of his searing kisses and expertly caressing hands tempted her more than she would have liked to admit.

Why should anything change? Her life could continue exactly as before. Who was she fooling? In one fateful day her entire life had changed irrevocably.

It was ghastly! This was going to be more complicated than she had originally thought. He could take himself off to London, which he probably intended to do. She need never see him, except perhaps on the odd public occasion.

She closed her eyes and groaned. She certainly was making a fine mess of her life. Last night ranked as one of the worst evenings to date. Based on her recent record, however, she was confident that if she gave it time, another disaster would befall her shortly. Misfortune seemed to have plagued her since her arrival in this Godforsaken country!

Springing out of bed she hurried to wash and donned her black riding habit. Just because she was trapped in a loveless marriage with a devilish rake, she was not about to mope. A brisk morning ride was just the thing to lift her spirits.

Waiting for the stable boy, Tom, to saddle the dapple grey, Kara heard a horse gallop into the courtyard behind her. And froze.

'Walk him Tom. He'll need it,' her husband's deep resonant voice commanded.

Biting her lip, she groaned inwardly. The very last person she wished to be confronted with first thing this morning was her rakehell of a husband.

She could feel him staring at her. His eyes nearly bore a hole in her back. Taking a deep breath she turned around and raised her defiant blue eyes to his. He was clad in a loose white cambric shirt that clung to his perspiration-soaked chest. And the brown buckskins he was wearing must have been painted on his muscular thighs. His breathing was unsteady and the handsome face looked flushed. He'd obviously ridden Goliath relentlessly.

Kara's heart skipped a beat. Did he have to be so incredibly attractive all the time?

He wiped the back of his forearm across his damp forehead. And his gaze slid over her from the top of her riding hat to the tips of her riding boots. She squirmed uncomfortably under his intense scrutiny.

'You might be interested to learn that I'm leaving for London,' he told her coolly.

Kara's head shot up. Obviously, he had no plans to take her to London. He wouldn't humiliate her by leaving the morning after the wedding? Or would he? 'So soon?' she asked, forlorn.

He cocked a raven brow. 'Disappointed? I rather thought you'd be glad to be rid of me,' he muttered tersely. 'At least, that was the impression I received last night. Changed your mind, have you?' he asked, his devilish eyes cruelly mocking her.

'Certainly not!' she snapped. What difference did it make that her husband intended to leave her behind to ruminate in the country? She liked ruminating quite well. And was very good at it.

He took a step closer. And despite her desire to appear calm and collected, her eyes widened and she hastily stepped back. My, he was quite impressive towering over her, she thought and swallowed with difficulty.

His lips curled wickedly. 'It is not too late, you know,' he said softly, his face perilously close to hers. She stiffened and lowered her lashes.

'I might be persuaded to take you with me, provided you were willing to be my wife in truth. Think of all the parties you'll be missing. I know an expert dressmaker who'd create an exquisite wardrobe especially for you. And of course,' he added, his eyes gleaming wickedly. There are the balls. London is quite exciting at this time of year.'

Her heart flopped around in her chest. 'I've no doubt,' she managed to reply. 'But I am afraid you are confusing me with someone else,' she added tartly, brushing past him toward her mount.

One corner of his mouth lifted slightly in a crooked smile. 'Oh?' he asked following after her. 'How so?'

Struggling to mount the horse, she informed him coolly, 'I am not one of your mistresses to be bought with a few trinkets and pretty clothes.'

He chuckled. It was a deep throaty sound that served to unnerve her further. Before she knew what was happening, his hands slipped around her waist and he tossed her into the saddle.

'Perhaps not,' he said smiling at her efforts to straighten her skirts and cover her lovely bare legs.

'If you don't mind the quiet country life, I'm sure I'll be able to find suitable distractions.'

Gathering the reins, she told him sharply, 'Of that, I have no doubt. Good day, my lord,' she muttered and urged her horse into a canter.

'I am going to London first thing tomorrow morning,' Alex announced several hours later at the solemn dinner table. 'I have pressing business to attend to. It simply cannot wait, I'm afraid.'

Aunt Henrietta's soup spoon paused in mid-air. 'Alex, you are incorrigible,' she cried. 'You cannot mean to say – '

Alex flashed a winning smile. 'I am afraid I must. I truly wish that I did not have to depart so quickly after the wedding,' he said with a sigh. 'But I have some affairs which require my undivided attention.'

Uncle Charles nodded his head. 'Well,' he said cheerfully. 'I am sure Kara would love to see London. So much to do this time of year.'

'I'm afraid that is not possible,' Alex answered smoothly, his lean fingers caressing the stem of his wine glass. 'I'd be far too busy with my personal affairs to entertain a new bride.'

'I could spare Henrietta for a few weeks until Kara is settled,' Uncle Charles offered amicably.

Alex pulled a mock frown. 'What? And force my poor new bride to endure the boring social deluge? Being ferried from party to party without a thought to rest and relaxation?' He shook his head. 'I wouldn't think of it. What Kara needs is a nice stay in the country, where the air is fresh and her time completely her own without any interruptions.' He glanced in his irate bride's direction, a tiny smile tugging at his lips.

'Well, I don't know what to say,' Aunt Henrietta muttered, shaking her head with disapproval. 'It is most irregular. Have you nothing to say about this, Kara?'

Kara shook her head and pretended to be engrossed with the meager contents of her plate. If she could have crawled under the table, she gladly would have. Either that, or reach across the table and slap that amused smirk off her husband's face.

'There is simply no way around it,' Alex went on to explain with characteristic charm. 'Kara understands, I have explained the situation to her. Is that not so my love?' he asked, his lips quirking hatefully.

Kara's furious gaze collided with his. Oh, she'd love to scratch his eyes out! 'But of course, dearest,' she imparted with a tight smile. 'I consider myself among the luckiest of brides to have such a kind and thoughtful husband,' she added with derision.

He inclined his glossy dark head. 'And so you should, my sweet.' His lips continued to twitch with amusement.

'Pray, do not concern yourself, Aunt,' Kara said blithely, her frigid gaze impaling her amused husband. 'I shall be perfectly content here.'

Yes, Alex thought smiling into Kara's enraged face, a few weeks alone in the country ought to suffice.

Being cooped up at Grantly was exactly what she needed to tame her hotheadedness. Besides, under the circumstances, having her bedroom right next to his was a temptation he could do nicely without.

He was thankful this Bouchard business had prevented his planning a honeymoon. Being secluded with that highly desirable virago for weeks would be pure hell! Let her remain in the country until sheer boredom settled in.

Impertinent little chit was dashed annoying. His desire for her had not ebbed, however. If possible her rejection had served only to heighten his desire. In his perverse way, he wanted her even more. It would not be long, though, before she was warm and willing in his arms. And he could wait, for a little while.

The following week a spindly legged gentleman arrived from London. He was Alex's solicitor, Sir Harry Cheney. Kara greeted him in the rose salon. 'Good afternoon,' Sir Harry said politely bowing to the new Lady Dalton. 'His lordship is desolate he could not present you with these in person,' he remarked adjusting his wire rimmed spectacles on the edge of his enormous snout.

He paused before opening a large black velvet box from his carrying case. Cherishing the box, as though its contents were extremely fragile, 'May I assure you that these are the very finest sapphires? I selected them myself after a thoroughly exhaustive search,' he said opening the lid to the case.

Kara was stunned. 'You selected them!' she cried, her face full of incredulity.

The wretch had not even picked out the jewelry he sought to use to win her affections! So, he thought he could buy her affection with gifts? At least, she thought ruefully, she ranked on a par with the rest of his kept women. Well, she would not be bought. Crossing her arms over her bosom, she directed her frosty gaze beyond the solicitor's confused face.

'Was there anything else his lordship wished you to deliver?' she asked with cool disdain. She did not so much as glance at the sparkling blue stones.

Flustered. Sir Harry gulped and tugged at his collar which seemed to be strangling him. He cleared his throat and said, 'Allow me to assure you that these are flawless, the finest necklace and earrings money can buy. Indeed, in all of London there are none finer. His lordship insisted on the very best. And as in all tasks, I followed his instructions to the letter.'

Waving her hand in a dismissing fashion she instructed nonchalantly, 'You may leave his lordship's . . . gift on the table.' Smiling prettily at his stricken face, she clasped his bony elbow and showed him the door.

'Thank you for coming all this way. I am sure that you have excellent taste. And I thank you for your thoughtfulness in my regard.' So saying, she opened the door.

Clutching his black portmanteau to his chest he swallowed. 'I–it is nothing. I have represented this family for several years and I am only too happy to be of service,' he gulped, a smile stretching over his elongated face.

Kara smiled and extended her hand in farewell. Clumsily juggling his cumbersome baggage, he managed a handshake and quickly disappeared.

Taking a deep breath, Kara went back into the parlor. She wandered over to where the black velvet box lay, eyeing it with curiosity. Giving in to her feminine side, she opened the box.

Her breath caught in her throat. They were exquisite! She had never seen their like. They must have cost a fortune. She sank down on the settee and snapped the box shut.

Chewing thoughtfully on her bottom lip, she wished she could summon the nerve to refuse the gift. But she knew that was out of the question. Even she did not quite have the courage to refuse her husband's wedding present.

But the rogue was not going to buy her with jewels. Angrily, she slammed the box back on the table. She might have to accept the odious offering. But that did not mean she had to wear the jewels.

The snake would not ingratiate himself so easily. Even with sapphires beyond price, she vowed scowling at the offending box. She could not help wondering, however, what her husband was doing in London. And more precisely what beautiful women he was spending time with at the moment.

Alex stopped off at White's Club. But he did not stay long. His mood was strangely tempestuous. He played a few rounds of commerce with Daniel and drank a liberal quantity of brandy, but his heart wasn't in it. His mind kept wandering back to a dark haired enchantress.

Lord, the girl had got under his skin! He seemed to think of her constantly. What the devil was the matter with him? He could barely concentrate on the game for wondering how the little vixen was enjoying her banishment in the country. And if his little hellion of a bride liked the sapphires he'd sent. Of course she did. Every woman loved jewels. Didn't they? His lips curled with pleasure as he contemplated the desirable vixen lavishing him with gratitude when he saw her next.

The choice of her wedding present had been easy. Sapphires were the exact color of those gorgeous sparkling eyes that haunted his consciousness with surprising persistence.

Alex looked down at his hand and realized he was losing miserably at cards. He threw in his hand and left the club.

Still feeling restless, he decided to pay a visit to his mistress, Jenny Carrington. He'd put off the inevitable long enough. News of his recent nuptials must have reached her keen ears by now. And he ought to formally put an end to their association. No matter what his feelings for her, she deserved to receive the news in person.

Besides, he thought as he climbed into his carriage and signaled his driver to take him to the usual address on Chelsea Road, he was entitled to an explanation of her recent absences. Although he had no proof of her infidelity, he believed the grasping creature capable of almost anything.

Their liaison had lasted only three months. During that time, he had frequented the quaint, yet adequate town house he'd purchased for her, exclusively. It annoyed him that she could have deceived him. Faithlessness in women disgusted him.

As he opened the front door of the small red brick establishment and stood in the narrow front hall, his gaze fell to the umbrella stand. A black walking stick, which was obviously not his, protruded from the blue and white porcelain container. The soft gurgle of feminine laughter that reached his ears followed by a low distinctly masculine growl, confirmed his earlier suspicions. So, he thought tugging off his gloves and removing his curly brimmed beaver hat, she'd deceived him.

Curiosity got the best of him. Rather than turning on his heel and sending her a scathing rejection by messenger, he mounted the stairs that led to the bedroom he'd once used to satisfy his carnal desires. And the woman he had once found irresistible.

He threw open the door and leaned his shoulder against the door jamb. His indolent gaze swept over the bed and the two startled and completely naked occupants.

He recognized his replacement immediately. The blond haired skinny man was none other than Lord Robert Rodale, the new Viscount Rodale.

'A viscount,' Alex drawled, his gaze like his tone was distinctly mocking, 'Jenny, your tastes have changed. Is a marquis now too rich for your blood? Don't bother to get up on my account,' he said with a flash of perfectly straight white teeth at the cowering viscount.

'My Lord, I-I can explain,' the viscount stammered, scrambling to cover his scrawny white body.

'Truth to tell,' Alex admitted with a sigh. 'I don't give a damn about your explanations.' He turned a lazy eye to his now ex-mistress, 'How long, my dear?'

'Two months,' she told him. Her lower lip trembling. 'It was not my fault, Alex. You left me alone all the time What was I supposed to do? I got horribly bored.'

'Mmm. Yes. I can well imagine,' Alex drawled out.

'Are you going to call him out?' Jenny asked nervously clutching the sheet over her small flat breasts.

Alex let his gaze slide over her pale skin and white-blonde hair. Had he ever actually found her attractive?

'For what?' he asked, utterly revolted. 'You, my dear, are hardly worth a man's life, no matter how foolish he happens to be. Unless of course,' he added his voice like ice, 'you were suggesting Rodale challenge my honor?'

'N-no, Dalton I-I wouldn't dare,' the viscount quaked.

'Robbie's offered to marry me,' Jenny muttered raising her chin a notch. Alex arched a dubious brow. 'Has he now?'

'A-as soon as my mother gives me permission,' the cowering whelp stuttered.

Alex drawled derisively. 'But of course.'

Jenny bit her lip. 'Well, why shouldn't he? You never loved me,' she muttered.

Alex's brows shot up. 'Loved you,' he echoed in surprise, his lip curling with contempt. 'My dear girl, you never even satisfied me.' He shifted his laconic gaze to the despicable viscount. 'You owe me two months' expenses. I expect payment tomorrow.' The viscount nodded his head vigorously.

'Just a word of advice, sir,' Alex remarked coolly. 'Don't ever bed another man's mistress. It simply isn't done. And may well cost you dearly. Pathetic though it may be, I've a suspicion you value your life.' He turned his back on the revolting scene and strode from the room.

Hurrying down the stairs in disgust, he left the town house for the last time, closing the door with a resounding slam.

Reaching the street, he bade his driver goodnight. A walk in the fresh air would do him good. After that sordid little scene, he needed to clear his head.

He was well rid of Jenny. He had not been her first lover. Nor was he her last. Obviously.

They had shared a mutually convenient arrangement, nothing more. Most of the men in his circle enjoyed similar circumstances. So why was he feeling as if he needed to bathe?

This evening's confrontation revolted him thoroughly. He couldn't think why. Why should he care? He harbored no deep feelings for Jenny. She had simply served a purpose in his life. He'd never led her to believe otherwise. It was one thing to give your mistress the congé and know that there'd be others to take your place, but quite another to meet your replacement using the very same bed you had once lain in! It didn't sit well.

Hell, he thought shaking his head as he walked along the dark, deserted street, what would Kara think if she knew? She'd be profoundly repulsed by the scene he'd just witnessed. He was deeply offended himself!

He suddenly felt embarrassed. It was a new and startling sensation for the marquis. The idea of having his name linked with the likes of Jenny and her vile viscount was repugnant.

Yet, he was hardly in a position to judge the other couple. How many similar situations had he enjoyed? For the first time in his life, he was ashamed and thoroughly disgusted with himself. What *was* happening to him?

His only hope was that the viscount would be discreet. He did not want to read about this in the morning papers. More importantly, he did not want anyone at Grantly to hear of it. Particularly not Kara.

★ ★ ★

140

Despite all her best efforts to occupy her time, Kara was restless. She'd explored the grounds thoroughly and committed each wing of the mammoth estate to memory.

To say that Uncle Charles and Aunt Henrietta were not exactly stimulating company was an understatement. As with most older couples they'd settled into a comfortable routine which seldom if ever included interesting dialogue. Finally, Uncle Charles took pity on Kara and offered her the use of his private study.

'I've a selection of novels that may interest you, my dear,' he told her over breakfast, 'by writers like Fielding, Austen, Richardson, and Radcliffe, to name just a few. If you are of a mind to read them, you may use my private study.'

Kara face brightened. 'Oh, yes, please, I'd love to.' At last, something besides Plato and Aristotle to fill the long hours of sheer boredom.

'Bored, are you?' he asked.

'Dreadfully,' she replied and then caught herself. 'I mean . . .' she stuttered flushing bright red.

Uncle Charles smiled and winked at her, 'You'll find some of Lord Byron's poetry as well, if you dare,' he said in a low voice careful not to be overheard by the duchess.

Kara smiled and nodded her head, 'I shall only sneak a peek at Byron after I've finished reading Pope.'

'What is that you say, my dear?' Aunt Henrietta asked leaning her robust form against the table to hear Kara's whispering.

'I was saying that I thoroughly enjoyed Coleridge. Though I must confess a dislike for Wordsworth.'

Aunt Henrietta blanched. 'Dear me, child I hope you are not turning into a bluestocking. Alex would never stand for an educated wife.'

'Oh, I don't know,' Uncle Charles remarked wiping his mouth with his napkin. 'He might enjoy the challenge.'

Kara hid her smile and hurried through her breakfast eager to submerge herself the study's treasures. She didn't care what Alex preferred. She couldn't wait to delve into a good book!

Directly after breakfast Kara disappeared into the study. Well, she thought gazing up at the rows of leather-bound novels behind the desk, if she started now she might be able to occupy herself at least until the end of the month. She'd heard a great deal about Mrs Radcliffe's *The Mystery of Udolpho*. But she wanted something a bit more exciting to counter her severe boredom. Mary Shelley's *Frankenstein* caught her eye, but she quickly moved on. From all that she'd heard about the controversial novel, she wasn't sure she could read such a gruesome tale without having nightmares for months!

Spying Henry Fielding's novel *Amelia* on the top shelf, she reached up towards it. But her arm proved hopelessly too short. Even standing on her tip toes, her fingers barely grazed the binding. In her haste to secure a stool, she knocked the blotter from the desk, spewing papers and books in every direction.

Frowning, she crouched down to gather the scattered items from the floor.

She was busily rearranging the documents on the desk when she noticed one of the books she'd accidentally knocked on the floor was a ledger of some kind. Bending down to close the book, an entry under the name of Simpson caught her attention. Curious, she turned the page. What she saw written there took her breath away.

All sense of guilt for ransacking her uncle's desk vanished. The entries in the little black book were transfers of funds to Boston from England. Flipping through the pages, she found a yellowed envelope protruding from the back of the book. It was from Boston, Massachusetts.

Setting the open ledger on the desk, she unfolded the creased paper with shaky hands. The letter was from her mother to Uncle Charles! And it was dated two months prior to her mother's death.

'*My dearest Charles,*' Karina read aloud to herself. '*My condition, I am sorry, to say has worsened. I know now that my illness is terminal. The doctor confirmed my fears yesterday.*

'*I have not told Karina. I do not want her upset. It is best this way. At first, I was devastated to be leaving my beautiful daughter behind, but I know she is in good hands; your capable hands. As Harry left me to you; so I now leave Karina to you. I know I will never really be gone from her; some part of me will always be with her, as a part of Harry has always remained with me.*

'*The danger in England, I pray, is passed. It has been fifteen years. And I trust you to protect my precious Kara from all possible harm. How can one cling to a vendetta for so long? I would not send Kara to you if I thought you would not forfeit your own life to save her.*

'*I am confident that my little darling will love England. How I miss it! But I have been content in America. I am at peace and resigned to my fate. I know that I will finally rejoin Harry after so many years. As you have sworn to protect me, I know you will tend to my daughter after I am gone.*'

Dropping the letter, Kara realized her face was wet with tears. Her mother had known for months that she was going die. Yet, she had said nothing. All that time she knew. And kept it from her daughter. Apparently, that was not the only thing she'd kept from Kara.

She hated to think of her own mother or, for that matter, Uncle Charles as devious. There must be a reason why they chose to keep this from her. Clearly, her mother had been fond of the duke. And it was obvious he had supported them all those years in Boston. She'd naturally assumed they were living on her father's inheritance. If her mother trusted Uncle Charles, then Kara should as well.

Still, this recent development was unsettling. She had been raised to be forthright and honest. If she wanted to know something, she asked. Her instinct was, as she folded the letter and dried her face, to confront Uncle Charles and make him tell her the truth.

But that would never work. He'd blatantly lied to her. Repeatedly. And he was decidedly tight lipped about her father in general. Just because she was frantic to know the truth did not necessitate his cooperation.

Hugging her arms around her waist, she paced the room turning the recent development over in her mind. The sketchy details of her father's past, Uncle Charles's reaction to Aunt Henrietta's apparent slip of the tongue, his open hostility when she pressed him for details about her father. And then there was Uncle Charles's peculiar conversation with Alex that she'd overheard. He was undoubtedly keeping a number of things from her. Important things. And if that letter was any indication, potentially dangerous things.

Her animosity against the duke increased tenfold as the startling revelation took hold. What right did he have to keep her in the dark? If something sinister had occurred involving her father she should know about it. Her mother had known about it. It hurt Kara deeply to learn that the conspiracy had included her dear mother.

What danger had existed in England fifteen years ago? And what was the vendetta her mother's letter referred to? Why, oh why, would no one tell her anything about her father?

She toyed with the idea of pumping poor Aunt Henrietta for more information, but thought better of it. At this juncture, she probably knew little more than Kara. Besides, the likelihood of the duchess keeping her secret safe from Uncle Charles was nil.

There was only one thing to do – uncover the truth for herself. She must connive her way to London. Using her own money left over from the journey to this horrid little country, she'd hire one of those Runners mentioned in Alex's notes. After all, she had a right to know the truth. Drying her eyes, she took a deep breath and set her mind on formulating a plan.

CHAPTER 7

When Alex descended the stairs of his stylish London town house the next morning he found Fowler, his butler waiting impatiently to speak to him.

'Begging your pardon, my lord, but there is a, er, gentleman here to see you.'

'Does this gentleman have a name?' Alex asked, an easy smile playing on his lips.

Fowler cleared his throat. 'He is, er, from the city, my lord,' he whispered with disdain.

Intrigued, Alex arched a brow. 'Ah. Well then, you'd best show him into the library.'

Curious to met this peculiar stranger, Alex sauntered into the library. Reclining behind his large mahogany desk, he crossed his booted legs on top of the desk and rubbed the tension from his neck.

Six weeks! And not a blasted clue about this supposed radical plot. Not a single lead. It was deuced annoying. He was probably on a wild goose chase. And he was growing impatient. He needed some assistance; locating all the disgruntled ex-patriots singlehandedly in London was a formidable task even for him.

The library door opened and a shabbily dressed older man sheepishly entered the room. Clearly intimidated by his surroundings, the grubby, stout man shifted nervously from one foot to the other.

'You wished to see me?' Alex asked eyeing his visitor with curiosity.

'Aye, guv'ner,' the man replied with a nod of his balding head.

'Well?' Alex prodded, steepling his hands over his chest.

'I 'eard ya was at the docks day 'fore yesterday.'

'So were a great many other people,' Alex said with a shrug, 'get to the point.'

'I knows what yer lookin' for.'

Alex leaned forward. 'And what might that be?' he asked, his eyes narrowing on the man's dirty, wrinkled face.

'Them that's started ol' th' trouble. Plannin' those uprisin's is what.'

Alex had already infiltrated the group of radicals who were instigating riots in reaction to the government's inability to stimulate the economy. Their demands, however, were for parliamentary reforms, not destruction of the country, nor a resumption of the war.

'What makes you think I'm looking for anyone?' he asked studying the indigent before him with a keen eye.

'There 'as been talk 'bout ya askin' questions. Them's that nervous they don't want ya snooping 'bout.'

News travels fast. Alex hesitated for a moment. 'Let's say that you are right,' he conceded slowly. 'Why tell me this?'

''Cause me thinks ya might 'ave a guinea or two fer some information.'

'If the information is worth it,' Alex affirmed with a nod.

'There is a group o' men who's got no work. At the docks most o' the time.'

'So?'

'These men are lookin' fer someone to blame fer their empty bellies, that's what. Then comes this gentleman. I got somethin' fer ya, says he. Now they meet regular like. An' I asks meself, what's that all 'bout? I heard 'em plannin' treason. Aye, it was treason, it was.'

'And how do you come to know all this?' Alex asked suspiciously.

The man shrugged his tattered shoulders. 'I 'eard 'em talkin'.'

It was certainly true that the cessation of the war had not brought prosperity, but economic hardship. Could these discontented masses be behind this plot? Alex dismissed the thought almost as quickly as it entered his head.

'This man whom you said organized this group. What did he look like?'

'Ordinary. But me thinks he's a nob.'

'Why?' Alex asked, knitting his brow. 'What makes you say that?'

'Th' way he carries 'imself. Like a nob.'

Alex sat back. 'This may be of use to me. What is your name?'

'Me name's 'arper, Billy 'arper.'

Alex smiled. 'Where can I find you Billy Harper, if I need to?'

''Ere and there. At the docks mostly.'

Alex reached into his pocket and tossed the poor soul a guinea, 'I want you to keep your eyes and ears open. Should this information be valuable, there may be more money in it for you.'

Billy bit down on the coin. 'Thank ya, guv,' he replied pocketing the money.

'I am sure you can see yourself out.'

Securing his scruffy cap on his balding head, he nodded, 'Aye, guv'ner.'

A second later, Fowler entered the library. 'Shall we be expecting other . . . persons like him do you think, my lord?' he asked tugging at his collar.

Alex laughed, amused by his stodgy old butler's snobbery. 'No. I shouldn't think so.'

'I am relieved to hear it, my lord,' Fowler said as he bowed and left the room.

Alex got up from his desk and walked over to the window. Who was this instigator? Was there a link between these meetings and this farcical plot? No, it was too easy. It couldn't be. Or could it?

It was certainly Bouchard's style. But if it was Bouchard, why go to all this trouble? Where the hell was he? And more importantly, what was his game? For if Alex knew anything about Bouchard, he knew he loved to play games.

The room was completely dark except for the shards of sunlight streaming through the old torn curtain. It smelled damp and musty. Several layers of dust covered the paltry furniture.

'The trap is set guv'ner.'

'Good,' the man sitting in the shadows replied. 'You've done well, Billy. You are sure he will follow? And he believes the plot is real? I want to rid myself of this pest once and for all.'

'Aye. I set th' trap. He believed me, all right. I seen 'im attend lots o' meetin's askin' questions.'

'Mmmm. Then enticing him should be easier than I thought. He is by nature an impatient man. And I am very good at trying his patience,' he smiled. 'He will act without thinking and then we'll have him.'

'Beggin' ya pardon sir, but what 'appens when 'tis all over?'

'Your work has been satisfactory, Billy. If you continue to please me, your reward will be great.'

'Thank ya sir,' Billy said and clumsily made his way out of the dingy shack.

When he had gone, a short dark haired man stepped out from the shadows. 'Bouchard,' he said anxiously, '*Tout se passe selon les prévisions?* All is going according to plan, *non*?'

'*Oui, bien sûr*, but of course, everything is going just as I envisioned it,' Bouchard replied rising from his seat behind the desk. 'Philippe, I hear that my nemesis has taken a wife. Do you know who she is?' he asked, an evil smile curling his lips.

'*Non.*'

'Eden's daughter.'

'Ah,' Philippe said with a sigh of delight. 'At long last. I'd almost given up hope. *Ca c'est bon!*'

'Did I not tell you I would help you avenge your father's death on the English?'

Philippe nodded his head. '*Tiens.* When do I kill her?' he asked, his eyes glowing with excitement.

Shrugging his shoulders, Bouchard snorted, 'That is your affair Philippe, not mine.'

'But you promised – '

Bouchard raised his hand to silence him. 'When the time comes, you may do what you like about the girl. I want him first. I grow tired of his constant pursuit. He is like an itch that I cannot scratch. Do you know what it is like to know a man so well that you can predict his every thought?'

Philippe shook his head violently. '*Non, mais je suis* – '

'Enough! You may seek your revenge for your father's death *after* I have finished with Dalton.'

'I have waited so long for this. I feared I would never make them pay. It is good fortune that he has married the daughter of my father's murderer, *n'est pas? Peut-être*, we use her to lure him?'

'*Non*, I do not want his death to raise suspicion. If he dies investigating this ridiculous insurrectionist plot, no one will ask questions. I do not care when or

152

how you kill the girl. Torture her, if you like. Just let me deal with Dalton first.'

'I was deprived of the pleasure of killing Eden's wife, but I will enjoy watching his daughter die. *Promis-moi*, you will think about my idea? We could torture your enemy with the death of his beloved. And then I would not have to wait so long for my revenge. Yes?' he asked rubbing his hands together in anticipation.

'*Oui*. I will think about your suggestion.' Bouchard said with a bored yawn.

'*Bon! Merci mon ami!*' Philippe replied beaming from ear to ear.

As Philippe slipped from the decrepit shack, Bouchard laughed and shook his head. 'You are quite mad, *mon petit* Philippe. But for now, you serve my purposes very well.'

Alex anxiously paced back and forth before the fireplace in his London library while Daniel reclined comfortably in a leather chair calmly imbibing a glass of port.

'I tell you Daniel, my patience is wearing thin. We are not getting anywhere. If I have to dress up like an indigent slob one more night and roam the streets looking for clues – '

'Relax. We know Bouchard is behind it, at least, that should make you happy. You've been after him for three years. We can safely assume that he knows we are on to him.'

'So?' Alex growled. 'Where exactly does that leave us?'

Daniel rolled his eyes heavenward. 'He has to make a move sometime.'

Alex resumed his agitated pacing. 'I am tired of waiting!' he roared. 'We have not uncovered one shred of evidence to support this absurd notion of a plot to undermine the government.'

'I don't believe in it any more than you do,' Daniel said sharply.

'All these meetings we have attended disclosed only one thing: there are a great many discontented people roaming the streets of London,' Alex muttered with irritation.

'What we need to discern is why?' Daniel interjected thoughtfully, 'what's in it for Bouchard?'

'Don't you think I know that!' Alex gritted, 'I think he is leading us on a merry chase and enjoying every minute of it.'

Daniel slammed his glass on the table and got to his feet, 'Devil take it man! What the hell is the matter with you? I own, ever since you got married, you have been an absolute bear. Why don't you haul that lovely bride of yours up here and get her with child. Maybe that will improve your nasty disposition.'

'When I need your advice on how to handle my wife, I'll ask for it!' Alex snarled.

Daniel inclined his head and crossed the room to take his leave. 'Trouble is,' he tossed over his shoulder, 'you can't leave her out of it.' He shut the door, leaving his cantankerous friend to brood.

Alex scowled at Daniel's back. He was right, of course. Alex had thought abandoning Kara in the country was exactly what she needed. She was entirely too headstrong. Much to his chagrin, however, he found himself unable to rid his mind of her, most especially the way she smelled. The silkiness of her hair. And the feel of her soft lips beneath his.

Good grief! He wasn't actually missing the little chit, was he? Alex, pining after a woman? He shook his head. It was just because she was, for the moment, out of his reach that made him want her with burning fervor. Unrequited lust was a powerful emotion, he'd discovered.

Of course, he knew he would never have been able to pursue Bouchard with his inquisitive bride in London. It was better that she remain in the country lest she become suspicious of his nightly trampings all over London. He wondered if Sir Gilbert had any idea of the sacrifices Alex made for King and country.

This absurd situation was driving him mad, however. He felt like a pent up tiger. Sexual frustration was entirely new to him. And celibacy was completely unnatural! He couldn't credit that it was self-imposed. What had got into him of late? The Alex of old would have frolicked with half of the courtesans in London by now. And easily forgotten the silly wench.

Perhaps it was that ghastly interview with Jenny and her despicable viscount that had turned his stomach. Or worse yet, he might feel in some dark recess of his heart that it was wrong to break his marital vows.

Hell! He wasn't getting morals at his ripe old age was he? Perish the thought. No. It was quite simple. He wanted Kara. And only Kara. No other woman would do.

Kara sat back on the soft velvet swab seats and tried to enjoy the ride to London. Contemplating seeing Alex again put her stomach in knots. It was imperative that she keep her head clear and take the situation in hand. At the moment, it was crucial that she unlock the key to her father's past, no matter what the consequences.

She arrived with an exhausted Aunt Henrietta and a tetchy Violet in tow, at approximately three o'clock in the afternoon. The Dalton town house, naturally, was located on the very fashionable Upper Brook Street in London and the outside was richly decorated complete with marble steps and stone pillars.

A disgruntled Fowler opened the door and inspected the unannounced visitors from head to toe. He not been informed that his lordship was expecting guests.

Kara tugged off her gloves. 'Tell his lordship that his wife has arrived,' she said with a good deal more authority than she felt.

Bowing stiffly, Fowler left to inform his lordship of his wife's untimely arrival.

Smiling wanly at the duchess's incessant muttering, Kara twisted her soft kid gloves in her hands and braced herself for Alex's reaction to her blatant disobedience. She did not have long to wait.

His lordship materialized a few moments later. Dressed in grey pantaloons that fitted far too well and a light blue embroidered satin waistcoat, he looked the picture of suave sophistication. The effect was not lost on her. To her chagrin, her heart thumped like a wild thing against her rib cage.

Kissing his step-mother on her round chubby cheek, he bid her a warm welcome. And then he turned the full force of his devastating gaze on his wife.

'Well, well, well,' he drawled crossing his arms over his formidable chest. 'If it isn't the Lady Dalton.'

Bracing herself for a fight, Kara straightened her spine and met his indolent hooded gaze with aplomb.

'Forgive me, my dears,' Aunt Henrietta bemoaned fanning her flushed face with her lacy handkerchief, 'but I simply must rest before dinner.'

'Of course. Fowler will show you to your room,' Alex said amicably, his faintly amused gaze never leaving Kara's face. Alex shook his head and watched the duchess ascend the stairs cackling to poor Violet about the arduous journey. Then he turned his devastating grin in Kara's direction causing her pulse to throb erratically.

'Shall we adjourn to the library, my love?' he suggested. 'After all, we've so much to discuss,' he added with a warm smile that made her heart turn over.

'As you wish, my lord,' she said stiffly.

'Such sweet music to my ears,' he said his lips curling wickedly. 'If only it were true.'

Ignoring his gibe, she lowered her gaze and tried to ignore the skittering of her pulse as she followed him down the narrow carpeted hall to the library.

'So,' he drawled, leaning against the library's double doors. 'You've come.' Those dark bedroom eyes of his took her in with keen interest. 'Have you finally decided to become my wife in truth?' he asked letting his warm gaze wander over her lovely face and the shapely figure he remembered and liked so well.

A slight blush touched her cheek. But she met his sensual regard and lifted her chin mutinously. 'Certainly not,' she said defiantly. 'I decided to see London for myself.'

He chuckled softly. 'Country not to your liking, dearest? Or have you been missing me?' he asked, his lips curling unbearably. 'How long has it been now?'

She smiled at him without warmth. 'I have admirably endured the humiliation of being discarded in the country for six weeks whilst you, no doubt, have been cavorting with ladies all over London.'

'And with whom have I been cavorting, pray tell?' he asked lifting an ebony brow.

'How should I know?' she snapped. 'And I scarcely care.'

'I see,' he remarked shoving away from the door. 'Just as long as I don't bother you with my lustful carnal desires, you don't mind if I bed down with as many women as I fancy. Is that it?'

She lowered her gaze to her lap. 'Must you be so crude?'

'Was I being crude?' he asked, faking surprise. 'Please accept my most sincere apologies.' He sketched her a mocking bow.

Her lips thinned with displeasure and she looked away.

'Come, Kara,' he said with a winning smile, 'you should consider yourself fortunate to have such a knowledgeable, concerned husband looking out for your interests.'

'And his,' she muttered.

'Why not both our interests?' he asked, his voice low and suggestive.

She fixed him with a chilling glance. 'My reasons for coming to London do not concern you,' she assured him evenly. 'Please do not let my presence inconvenience your . . . habits.'

He sighed. 'Such a generous bride,' he said dryly. 'I'd quite forgotten how blessed I am.'

Removing her straw bonnet, she brushed her dark curls back from her forehead.

'You need not put yourself out on my account, my lord,' she informed him coolly, 'I shall manage quite nicely on my own.'

'I am sure you will,' he said with a slight smile. 'But I haven't got a mistress at present. Nor do I plan to take one. So you needn't worry on that score.'

She looked up at him sharply. Her face was a portrait of disbelief.

'Surprised?' he asked with a hint of mockery in his deep voice. 'Do you doubt that a rake is capable of reform? Or are you worried that I might press you to do your how would you phrase it? Ah, yes, I believe the term you used was, duty?'

Bristling at his gibe, she shot him a frosty gaze. 'I assure you, my lord, I do not care where you seek your comfort.'

'Yes, I know as long as it is not in your bed,' he amended with a cool smile.

'When the time comes,' she told him curtly. 'I shall fulfil my obligation to the Dalton family line, my lord, have no fear.'

He cringed. Obligation! He had something far more pleasurable in mind.

'That comes as an enormous relief to me,' he said, his voice laced with derision. 'And when might that fateful day be? Soon do you think? Or shall I continue to covet you from a distance?'

She shot him a quelling glance. 'I am sure I do not know.'

'You wound me to the core,' he said clutching at his breast. She frowned at him with displeasure. And he laughed good naturedly.

'Well.' He dropped into the winged-back chair beside the fireplace. 'You obviously haven't been pining after me in the country, a fact that I lament most grievously,' he added with heavy sarcasm. 'So why have you decided to come to London?'

She was not about to explain her alarming discovery to him. She knew without asking where his loyalty lay. She'd uncover the truth all by herself, thank you very much.

'I was given to understand London offered a whole host of activities not the least of which is sightseeing,' she said airily.

'Ah, how gratifying to learn my wife finds architecture more stimulating than my company.'

She licked her lips in a most endearing fashion and shifted uncomfortably on the brown velvet sofa.

'My lord,' she said, now in earnest appeal, 'I wish for us to share some measure of civility.'

He shook his head. 'As long as you hold yourself from me, that eventuality is slim,' he assured her.

She sighed and lowered her lashes. 'Then it appears there will be dissension between us.'

He inclined his head. 'If that is your preference,' he said getting to his feet. 'But you may regret your decision to come to London, my sweet.' His dark eyes twinkled with mischief.

She met his haughty gaze. 'I doubt it, my lord,' she countered, her mien aloof.

Resting his elbow on the mantle, he grinned at her. 'There are only three bedrooms.'

'Yes. I am aware of that, Aunt Henrietta told me,' she replied primly. 'You may sleep in your study.'

The smile slid from his face. 'The hell I will!' he growled. 'I fully intend to sleep in my own bed, madam.'

'Very well,' she said calmly as she smoothed the wrinkles from her navy muslin gown, 'I will stay with Aunt in her room.'

'Over my dead body!' he thundered. 'You, madam, will share my room or return to Grantly. I, for one, have no intentions of airing our marital discord in public.'

Her eyes flashed with temper. 'I suppose, you collect all those weeks you left me to rot in the country went unnoticed?' she fired back. 'And let's not forget the piles of correspondence from my lovesick husband.'

'So,' he murmured softly, his sensual mouth twisting with pleasure. 'You did miss me, after all.'

'You flatter yourself, my lord.'

His face grew dark. 'It comes down to this, dear heart. Just how badly do you want to remain in London?'

'That is blackmail!' she cried, jumping to her feet.

'Not quite,' he bit out.

'Very well,' she gritted and snatched her straw bonnet off the sofa. 'It seems I have no choice. I will sleep in your bed. But that is all,' she challenged. 'I have no intentions of granting liberties to a virtual stranger. Particularly one I do not like.'

'We shall see,' he replied with a nauseatingly arrogant smile.

Her furious gaze narrowed on his smug face. 'My lord,' she said, her tone like ice, 'if you are under the delusion that you will seduce me, you are gravely mistaken.'

'Am I?' he asked, his lips twitching with mirth. 'I think not.'

Oh! He was insufferable! 'As you say,' she muttered slapping her gloves angrily against her leg, 'we shall see.'

He sketched a mock bow. 'I look forward to entering . . . the fray with baited breath,' he drawled out with a knowing smile.

'Ooohh!' she screeched, her hands balled into fists at her side. 'If I were not a lady, my lord, I'd issue the retort you surely deserve!'

He threw back his head and laughed. 'I believe you would.'

She tossed him a look full of hate and stormed from the room muttering under her breath.

His shoulders shook with mirth. She was quite a woman. He'd wondered just how long it would be before his fiery little vixen rebeled. It was quite improper for his willful bride to take it upon herself to just show up without so much as a by your leave. Nonetheless, he was delighted. His charming bride had missed him enough to follow him all the way to London.

Perhaps it was time to try a new approach. After all, he did not want a hellion for a bride. Time apart had done nothing to quell his raging desire. If possible, he wanted her more.

Maybe if he wooed her like any other woman, their marriage would progress naturally? Yes, that was it. He would charm her. After all, what woman could resist his charms? It would not be long before she was writhing in ecstasy beneath him. And he could finally satisfy this savage hunger.

Kara stormed upstairs. His lordship's bedroom seemed to have his stamp all over it. With the East India Company flourishing, Chinese dragon bed hangings were apparently all the rage. Kara found the creatures less than appealing for bedroom decor, but wholly appropriate symbols for the man downstairs!

Not wishing to reflect further on her wolfish husband, she walked over to the window and pushed the red and gold velvet drapes aside to gaze down at the bustling street below. She must commence her detective work as soon as possible. She'd penned a letter of inquiry from the country and arranged an appointment on Bow Street. First thing tomorrow morning, she would visit the Runners. And with any luck, the puzzle would start to come together. The only question was how to slip out without being noticed by her husband?

Aunt Henrietta's idle chatter dominated the dinner hour for which Kara was immensely grateful. That is, until Henrietta's merry prattling turned to the subject of Kara's new wardrobe.

'It was so generous of you, Alex to make an appointment for Kara. Have you chosen a famous dressmaker? French, no doubt. But of course, you have.'

Alex shot his step-mother a queer look.

Kara shifted uneasily on her chair and cleared her throat. 'Aunt,' she rushed out. 'I'm sure Alex does not wish to discuss such a mundane topic.'

'On the contrary,' Alex remarked eyeing Kara suspiciously. 'I am very interested. Pray, continue.'

Kara's shoulders slumped and she cringed inwardly.

Aunt Henrietta's plump face beamed. 'I was certain he wouldn't mind sharing his plans. After all, child, you deserve nothing but the best! And Alex is a man who knows what a woman likes,' she crooned with a knowing wink.

'You flatter me,' Alex countered smoothly. 'Precisely what are you referring to?' he asked taking a sip of an excellent white bordeaux.

'Why, your generous offer to purchase a new wardrobe for your new bride, of course,' she chortled munching on her sauteed tomatoes. 'You must recall. It was all in your letter.'

Alex sat back and dabbed his mouth with a white linen napkin. 'And what letter might that be?'

Toying with the sole on her plate, Kara quickly averted her gaze and bowed her head, wishing the floor would swallow her whole.

Aunt Henrietta shot him a wry glance. 'Alex, I shall be very cross with you for teasing me,' she replied waving a pudgy digit at him across the table. 'The letter you sent Kara asking her to join you here. You must recollect your invitation?'

His pensive gaze lingered on Kara's downturned head. So, she'd connived her way to London by inventing an invitation from him. Well, well, well, this was indeed an interesting development. One with decided possibilities.

'Ah, yes, *that* letter,' he said, a slow smile spreading across his face.

Kara released the breath she'd been holding. Thank goodness he hadn't given her away.

'Yes, I remember now,' he said enjoying Kara's discomfort immensely. 'Let me see, I believe I insisted on undertaking the project personally.'

Kara's head shot up and her eyes widened with horror. 'Oh, no. There was nothing of that nature in the letter, my lord,' she hastened to assure him.

'No? Then it must have been an oversight on my part,' he flashed her a winning smile.

'Not at all,' Kara said quickly. 'I wouldn't dream of bothering you with such a trivial matter.'

'Trivial?' His lips twitching with amusement. 'My dear girl, the design of my wife's wardrobe is hardly trivial. Why, all of London will judge you by the cut and quality of your clothes. And believe me when I say, I shall see to it that your delightful figure is shown in the best light. We shall visit the most famous French dressmaker in all of London in the morning. Madame Jourdan will provide the most exquisite gowns money can buy.'

Kara's eyes glinted with irritation. He'd cornered her. And he knew it. 'That is not necessary,' she insisted, her fury mounting.

'But of course it is. It will be my greatest pleasure to accompany you first thing tomorrow morning,' he said, his eyes brimming with mirth. 'You will find that I am a generous man. With my affections as well as with money.' He reached out and covered her hand with his, his eyes staring deeply into hers. All the while the pad of his finger traced her palm sending delicious tingles of pleasure all through her. 'There is so much I long to give you, my dear, if only you'd let me,' he told her in that sexy bedroom voice of his.

Kara's cheeks flushed a dull red and her lashes fluttered downward. She slipped her hand from beneath his. 'You are too kind to be sure, my lord,' she mumbled, furious with herself for letting him manipulate her into this ridiculous outing. How was she ever going to make her appointment with the Runner?

CHAPTER 8

The next morning Kara awoke to find Violet pulling open the drapes. She sat up in bed and yawned. Then, she remembered where she was – in her husband's bed! Stiffening self-consciously, she darted a glance at the pillow beside her expecting to encounter his amused grin. But instead, she found herself staring blankly at an unruffled white pillow. Surely, he had not been out all night? Had he?

Mentally shaking herself, she wondered what was the matter with her? By rights she should be relieved that he'd chosen not to sleep with her. But instead, she was busy conjuring up images of Alex wrapped in a passionate embrace with some strange woman. He was a playboy, certainly not worthy of her concern, she told herself. Why then, did she feel so lousy?

The door to the dressing room opened and the object of her consternation sauntered in. He looked like hell, unshaven, disheveled and exhausted. From frolicking with his mistress, no doubt, Kara thought with irritation. Once a heel always a heel. She could not help but notice, though, that even after a night of rascality, he was remarkably attractive.

He filled the white porcelain basin with water from the pitcher and splashed his face. Tearing off his shirt, he opened his armoire and reached for a clean one.

Startled at seeing his half naked body, Kara gaped at him, unable to tear her gaze away. He was formidable with his shirt on, but his bare chest was broader than she had imagined and her eyes feasted hungrily on his well-made chest. His stomach muscles rippled down to his narrow waist. And the black hair that covered his chest tapered into a thin line which made her wonder exactly where it ended.

With a sigh of appreciation she bit her lip. She'd never seen a man in dishabille, especially not one built like Alex! He was quite magnificent. And the effect was decidedly unsettling.

'Had an edifying look?' he asked, his lips curling with amusement as he toweled his face dry.

Mortified at being caught admiring her husband, her face went scarlet.

'Do you rakes never sleep?' she asked in a caustic tone.

He made no reply. He was too busy admiring the curve of her lovely throat and the gentle rise and fall of her round soft breasts.

'Dare I hope you are jealous, my love?' he asked crossing his arms over his magnificent chest.

'On the contrary,' she spat out, tossing back the covers and hopping out of bed. 'I am disgusted.'

He shook his head mockingly and leaned one broad shoulder against the bed post. 'You know, you are quite beautiful fresh out of bed.'

She felt herself flush a deeper shade of red. 'I suppose I should take that as a compliment from a cad like you who has no doubt seen countless women under similar circumstances,' she snapped angrily.

His heated gazed slid over her white flannel nightgown and he smiled. 'You may take that as a statement of fact,' he assured her and shoved away from the bed post to summon his valet. He hesitated on the threshold and he tossed over his shoulder, 'Do hurry dearest, we don't want to keep Madame Jourdan waiting. You know how eager I am to outfit you,' he added his dark eyes mocking her.

She glared at him murderously. She was tempted to ask exactly where he'd been all night, but held her tongue.

Why should she care? As long as he didn't bother her with his attentions, she should be relieved. Shouldn't she? Besides, she had other fish to fry. Starting with her investigation.

Scurrying over to the escritoire, she penned a note to the Bow Street office requesting her morning appointment be changed to this afternoon. Unless she heard to the contrary, she would arrive at three o'clock to enlist their assistance in a very urgent matter.

As the Dalton carriage stopped outside the exclusive Bond Street shop and the two disembarked, Kara glanced up at her husband's face. He was scowling.

'Is something wrong?' she asked and looked over to see what had caused his perturbation. There was an ominous looking black carriage with darkened windows parked directly opposite the shop.

'What?' he asked distractedly. 'No.' He hastily escorted Kara into the shop. 'Forgive me, dearest. It is nothing,' he assured her with a smile that made her tingle right down to her toes. Stealing a glance over her shoulder at the odd conveyance, she wondered at its significance.

As usual, Madame Jourdan was very excited to be serving the Marquis of Overfield. She was a middle aged woman with even features. Her vibrant magenta dress with black lace edging was indicative of her flamboyant nature.

'*Vous êtes trés belle, chérie*,' she told Kara. And then to Alex, 'She is young, *monsieur*,' she remarked looking at Kara with a critical gaze.

Alex cleared his throat. 'She is also *my wife*,' he told Madame meaningfully.

The woman looked startled, but she quickly recovered herself. 'Oh, *c'est parfait! Trés bien*! We will take very special care with your bride, *monsieur*, to be sure.'

Alex expelled a deep breath and smiled reassuringly at Kara. Thank heavens for Madame Jourdan's tact! It simply would not do for Kara to learn how many other woman he'd outfitted.

Although, he thought, as he dropped into the red velvet chair that he'd reclined in countless times before, today was different. He was looking forward to devoting several hours to making Kara happy. He enjoyed her company more than that of any woman in a long, long time. He couldn't decide which charmed him more, her feisty spirit or her guileless innocence.

As the fabrics were displayed and the styles discussed Kara's titillation grew. Alex helped her choose several blue, pink, and lavender muslin fabrics, along with some richer crimson and midnight blue velvet riding habits. And then there were several white gowns in a variety of different patterns. He selected some soft pastel velvets for stylish spencers to wear over the gowns.

Alex was very particular about the style and cut of gowns. He'd apparently put a great deal of thought into exactly how Kara should dress and what colors suited her best.

In spite of herself, Kara was flattered by his attention. At first she was scandalized by the skimpy bodices and the lack of stays. But when Madame assured her that all women wore such shocking gowns, she reluctantly gave in.

It was all the rage, according to Madame Jourdan, to wet the chemise under these daring gowns to heighten the effect, but Kara felt half naked as it was and adamantly refused. Alex laughed at her shyness and called her a little puritan. But his smile, like his gaze was warm, and she delighted in his teasing.

When Kara finally departed from the shop, her hair was styled in the latest fashion, she was clad in a baby blue empire style gown, light blue velvet spencer and blue kid slippers to match. She felt absolutely beautiful. Of course, it had nothing to do with the admiration shining in her husband's eyes, she told herself. But she knew that was a lie.

Laden down with boxes, the footman made his way precariously to the carriage. Kara rested her head against the back of the velvet seat and sighed.

'Happy?' Alex asked, oddly touched by her spontaneous enthusiasm to an ordinary occurrence. He was surprised and pleased by her guileless nature. He'd never met a woman who wasn't calculating and grasping. It was a pleasant change.

She turned her head to look at him and smiled. She was very happy. Everything was going according to plan. The dreaded shopping spree had turned into a splendid experience. He had successfully lifted her poor spirits. And she eagerly awaited her afternoon appointment on Bow Street.

'Yes, thank you. It was a lovely morning. Although I fear you purchased far too many gowns and spent an exorbitant amount, my lord.'

Reaching out his hand, he traced the delicate line of her jaw with his finger. It was a harmless gesture of affection that he'd extended to other woman and dismissed as inconsequential. But it was somehow different with this woman who was his wife.

173

'Don't be ridiculous,' he said in a voice like velvet. 'I can well afford it, dearest. And besides, I enjoyed it. It pleases me to please you,' he told her, his eyes glowing with a sincerity that surprised even him.

For a moment, she was lost in his incredible hazel eyes. Rousing herself, she looked away and cleared her throat. 'Thank you,' she said awkwardly, 'I am pleased with the day.'

Not half as pleased as I, he thought smiling to himself.

Upon their return to the town house, Aunt Henrietta commandeered Kara. Gabbing about the newest styles, she dragged Kara up the stairs. Kara shot a furtive glance in Alex's direction, before she was spirited away. He flashed a sympathetic smile and went into the library to pour himself a stiff drink.

He was exhausted! He couldn't remember the last time he'd had a decent night's sleep. Slumping into the chair before the fire, he downed the port and propped his weary legs on the ottoman.

He was, it seemed, being followed. He suspected the black carriage belonged to Bouchard or one of his henchmen paid to do his dirty work. It was an excellent sign. If Bouchard was shadowing him, then it confirmed that Alex was his target. All he had to do was wait for Bouchard to make his next move. Yawning hugely, Alex closed his eyes and dozed off.

Several hours later Fowler knocked on the door

rousing Alex from his slumber, 'My lord,' he said, handing him an invitation on a silver plate.

Alex yawned, 'Thank you, Fowler.' Taking the card, he asked, 'Is Lady Dalton still upstairs?'

Fowler frowned, 'No, my lord, the Lady Dalton has gone out.'

Alex sat up, his brow darkening. 'Gone out? Did she say where?'

'No my lord. I was under the impression that you had sanctioned her outing.'

Alex raked his hand through his raven hair. 'How long ago did she leave?'

'Approximately one hour ago. Should I have delayed her?'

'No, that is fine,' Alex said distracted by his thoughts. 'Thank you, Fowler. Send Lady Dalton to see me as soon as she returns.'

'Very well, my lord,' Fowler said with a bow as he closed the door.

Turning the card over in his hand, Alex contemplated where his impetuous bride could have gone. Looking down at the white card, he tore it open. It was an invitation to a ball.

He was about to refuse when he thought, why not? Kara had not seen much society. And it would give her the opportunity to do what every woman wanted – show off her elegant new wardrobe. He signaled Fowler and penned his acceptance.

Kara successfully slipped out of the town house. But she was agitated. What if she discovered something sinister in her father's past? Maybe it was better to leave things as they were. Uncle Charles was adamant that she learn nothing. The truth must be ghastly!

As the hackney wound its way through the crowded London streets a sense of dread enveloped her. This may well be a terrible idea. But there was no turning back now for the cab had arrived at Covent Garden.

Stepping down, she hastily paid the driver. Surveying the area, outside the Bow Street office, she identified what had to be prostitutes – no one dressed like that during the day except fallen women! She hastened her gait.

Taking a deep breath, she knocked on the door, and looked about her nervously. The door opened and she was faced with a rather slovenly man.

Kara hesitated, hoping he would not be the one assigned to her case. 'I was given to understand that this is where I might find the er, ah, Runners who could assist me?'

'That depends miss,' he said, as his wide smile displayed several rotten teeth, 'on what you be needing.'

She cringed and unconsciously leaned back. 'Well, I need someone to do some investigative work. I suppose you have colleagues who do that sort of thing?'

He snorted in agreement, scratched his head, and motioned for her to come inside. As she entered a small, but clean office, Kara glanced around warily.

Pulling out a well-used handkerchief, the man blew his nose and spat. He shoved the handkerchief back into his torn pantaloons pocket.

Kara sat down in front of the desk and cleared her throat, 'Do you work for someone, who, ah, does the sort of thing I need?'

'Aye,' he said taking his seat behind the desk.

Kara was positive she heard what sounded like flatulence as he sat down. The noisome odor reached her nostrils and she wrinkled up her nose with disgust. Like the man, the smell was positively rank.

'Sir, I would like to meet with, ah, another Runner if I could,' she muttered searching her reticule for her handkerchief. 'Perhaps one of the Fielding brothers. I was given to understand they founded this office.'

'They're too busy with important cases at the moment. I will just take down the facts. Dependin' on the gravity of your situation, I can do some investigatin'. Now, have you lost something of value?' he asked.

Leaning across the desk, his fetid breath invaded her senses. She sat back and clutched the scented hankie to her nose.

'Jewels, furs, or mayhap a favorite pet?' he prodded, his eyes dancing with anticipation.

Kara shook her head. 'No. I need someone to look into my father's past. He died fifteen years ago and I need to know about more about his life. What he did before his death, things like that.'

The man belched and reclined in his chair, scratching his voluminous belly beneath his scarlet waistcoat.

'Oh, aye. Well, I can have one o' the boys take a look into it or I could handle it for you myself.'

Kara blanched. 'Yes, well. I think a colleague would be best. Can I meet with one of your associates now . . . I mean, immediately.'

'Can you pay?'

'Naturally,' she said primly. 'But I would like to deal directly with the gentleman in question before that issue is discussed.'

'Fair 'nough. I can take the case.'

'Is there no one else?' she demanded to know.

'I'm all there is at the moment. As you can see, the office is deserted 'cept for me. Busy time o' year, this is.'

Kara swallowed. 'Oh. I see. Very well, then,' she said on a sigh. 'If there is no one else.'

Scratching his cheek, he paused, looking Kara over to assess her ability to pay, ''T'will be fifty guineas.'

That was highway robbery! Judging from the looks of the man she'd be lucky if she got a shilling's worth out of him. 'Twenty,' Kara countered firmly.

'Thirty,' the man haggled.

'Twenty-five and not a shilling more,' she stated crisply.

He frowned and scratched his scruffy face. 'Twenty-five 'tis then.'

Shifting uncomfortably in the hard wooden chair, she cleared her throat. 'I am sure you are capable at your job, but I feel this case requires someone who could move about relatively unnoticed.'

'Like I says. I am all there is at the moment. But I have contacts in high places, don't you fret none,' he told her with a knowing wink. 'I'll find out what you wants to know 'bout your father.'

'I must insist that my case remain confidential. Mr er.'

'Briston, name's Briston.'

'Can your guarantee success, Mr Briston?'

'Oh aye. Now you just leave it all up to me. Tell me all you know 'bout your father.'

Kara explained all the details she could recall.

'So, you father's name was Eden, eh?'

'Yes.'

'He died fifteen years ago?'

'He did. And I want to know why he sent my mother and me away. And why our name was changed to Simpson. As I mentioned already, I am fairly certain that my father rescued French aristocrats during the Revolution. You might start there. When do you think you will have some leads?' she asked, anxiously twisting her linen handkerchief between her fingers.

'Hard to say. I'll contact you when I do.'

The idea of this repulsive man coming to the town house on Upper Brook Street was definitely out of the question. 'No! It would be better if we set up prearranged meeting times.'

'Spies' stuff, eh?' he asked raising a bushy brow. 'All right. Say, in a fortnight outside St James's Palace. I'll be there 'round two.'

She rose unceremoniously from her chair. Eyeing his outstretched hand with displeasure she rejected the notion of shaking his grubby paw to seal their arrangement. Briston dropped his hand and hastily showed her the door.

'I need half now and half later,' he muttered rocking on his heels.

'I shall give you five guineas now, and each time you impart some useful information, I shall provide you with another instalment,' she told him primly.

His face fell. 'That only leaves me five weeks! That ain't me normal way.'

'Take it or leave it. What say you?' she asked him with a steely gaze.

He cawed, but in the end he accepted her money and her terms.

Entering the house on Upper Brook Street, Kara was relieved to find no one waiting at the door ready to pounce on her with questions concerning her whereabouts. Evidently, she had not been missed. Or so she thought.

'His lordship wishes to see you my lady. In the library,' Fowler announced.

Kara's heart leaped to her throat. 'Has he been asking for me?' she croaked, as she handed Fowler her new bonnet and smoothed her hair.

'He merely inquired of your whereabouts my lady.'

Kara nodded and hurried down the hallway. Taking a deep calming breath, she tapped on the library door. They'd passed such a pleasant morning together, what could possibly go wrong now?

Hearing his deep voice bid her enter, her pulse quickened and she opened the door. He was relaxing before the fire with a book. Lord, he was stunning. She was trembling just looking at him! Would she ever adjust to his good looks and stop this cursed quivering?

'You wished to see me?' she asked with a painful swallow.

Alex sat up and snapped his book shut. 'Where the devil have you been?' he demanded to know.

Wringing her hands, she muttered nervously, 'I, ah, went out for a ride. I-I don't know much about London so we took a bit of a tour.'

His lips twisted with irritation. 'This is not the country, Kara. You cannot disappear for hours without someone worrying. If you want a tour, I'll take you. I do not want you traipsing all over London with your maid. Is that understood?'

Kara quickly averted her eyes. She could well imagine his reaction if he learned Violet had been left behind.

'I assure you, I am quite capable of taking care of myself,' she imparted coolly.

'In Boston perhaps, but not here. Anything could have happened to you. Father would have my head on a silver platter if you came to any harm,' he muttered with a sigh.

Arching a dainty brow, she asked pointedly, 'And what harm might that be?'

Meeting her gaze, his eyes narrowed on her face and stared at her for a long moment. 'Why thieves and vagabonds abound in London, don't you know?' he mocked with a lazy smile.

She fervently wished she had the nerve to call his bluff. 'Is that so?' she replied with wide eyed innocence. Taking a seat across from him, she endeavored to make polite conversation.

'Did you pass a pleasant afternoon?' she asked tentatively.

Alex smirked. 'Not particularly. Oh, I almost forgot to tell you, we've been invited to a ball. And I've accepted.'

'Oh,' she said placidly.

Alex was amazed by her nonchalance. What woman did not want to attend a ball? They lived for those frivolous events, didn't they?

'Kara,' he said, leaning forward, 'why so glum?' he asked gazing deeply into her eyes. 'I thought you would enjoy it. I certainly would not have accepted if I thought you would blanch at the mere idea.'

She melted. When he was kind and caring like this, it was hard to believe he was a heartless rogue. How she dearly wished this ambrosial rapport would last! Then she could trust him and tell him everything about her detective work. But it was too soon, she reminded herself. She could not afford to confide in anyone. Not yet. If she told Alex the truth, he'd go straight to Uncle Charles and that would be the end of her investigation.

'Well,' she said flippantly. 'I would not want to do anything wrong. After all, I am an uncouth American.'

'Kara, you are the Marchioness of Overfield. Nothing will go awry. They will adore you.' He almost said, 'as I do' but quelled the idea. Empty expressions weren't appropriate with Kara. 'I would never have taken you for a coward,' he teased.

She looked at him sharply and opened her mouth to rebuke him, but smiled instead. 'I must admit, I am a little frightened. Everything here is so different. I feel so terribly alone. I have no one . . .' her voice trailed off and she lowered her gaze to the floor. She could hardly confess to her own husband that she had no one to confide in.

Alex felt like a complete swine, his sweet innocent bride was opening her heart to him. Perhaps he should have been more sensitive to her predicament. Maybe he was a licentious beast? No. The situation was not entirely his fault. This was one of the few times they'd exchanged a complaisant word.

'Kara,' he said taking her hands in his. 'It is normal for you to feel lost and a bit lonely. You have been through quite an ordeal. England is new to you. But I promise you will learn to like your new home.'

'I am sure I will, my lord,' she muttered stiffly.

Alex's gaze slid appreciatively over her face. Her cheeks were a lovely shade of rose, and her voluminous dark hair was piled high with a few locks spilling down her back. At this moment she was a stimulating combination of a guileless child and a provocative woman. He raised her hands to his lips and kissed each palm. 'Believe me when I say that I will do everything in my power to make sure of your happiness,' he said staring deeply into her clear blue eyes.

She sighed and looked away. 'Please don't,' she said, pulling her hands free.

Alex blinked. 'Don't what?'

'Don't treat me like, well, like your next conquest.'

Pricked by her remark, he asked coolly, 'And how should I treat you?'

'Oh, I don't know. I wish we could be friends.' Her luminous blue eyes gazed imploringly at him. 'Good friends.'

He frowned slightly. 'I suppose you will be suggesting that I entertain brotherly feelings for you next?'

Her face fell. 'Don't you want to be friends?' she asked, dejected.

Friends! Alex raked his hand through his hair and debated what approach to take. She was a naive child he told himself. He wanted a lot more than friendship from this delectable little vixen. But friendship was as good a place as any to start. 'Kara, I am your husband.'

She glanced at him sharply. 'Aren't husbands and wives friends?'

He hesitated for a moment utterly lost in her brilliant blue eyes. 'I suppose some are.'

'Well, given that this marriage was thrust upon us both, don't you wish to find some common ground?'

He smiled at that remark. They already shared common ground. One he was very familiar with. And liked quite well. He reached out and gently smoothed a strand of hair behind her ear,

'You are really quite beautiful, do you know that?' he murmured softly.

Kara shook her head. She did not think she was pretty in the least. This was just another rakish ploy. But it was wonderful to hear him call her beautiful, particularly when he sounded so sincere.

His eyes turned dark green, limpid with desire. And she could not tear her gaze away. She knew he wanted to kiss her. Absentmindedly, she wet her lips.

That was all the invitation he needed. He smiled and leaned closer.

'Such a lovely habit you have, my love,' he said caressing her cheek with his palm. He slid his hand behind her neck and dipped his head. 'So inviting,' he murmured against her lips. He felt her tremble, and smiled before his lips covered hers. Reminding himself to go slowly, he gentled the kiss and wrapped his arms around her lovely quivering body, drawing her close against him.

While Kara found his kisses undeniably enjoyable, she could not relax. This was not at all what she had in mind. Besides, something had been nagging at her all day. Where had he been last night? If in fact he had no mistress, then with whom did he spend the night?

She broke the kiss and turned her head. 'I was wondering,' she mumbled to the portrait of Wellington on the wall, 'where you were last night?' she asked.

Taken aback by the question Alex stared at her blankly for a moment. Then he got to his feet and walked over to the drinks table.

'I was at my club,' he said not meeting her gaze. 'Where did you think I was?' he asked pouring himself a glass of sherry.

A stab of pain shot through her heart and she looked away. It was obvious he was lying. So much for trust, she thought ruefully. But what did it matter? She certainly expected nothing less from him. And she truly did not feel she had any hold on the man. But for some perverse reason, it hurt to imagine her husband in the arms of another woman.

Tired and grimy from her day of sleuthing, she got to her feet and excused herself, claiming a miserable headache.

Swearing under his breath, Alex downed the sherry in one gulp. He'd mismanaged that badly. But what else could he do? His work was secret. And that meant deceiving those closest to him. Cursing the oath he'd made to the Crown, he vowed to make it up to her. Somehow.

Reaching the solace of her room, Kara called for a hot bath. Happily climbing into the steaming copper tub, she let the hot water seep into her tired bones. Wetting her hair, she lathered the sweet smelling lavender soap, humming to herself. Ducking under the water, she came up gasping for air. She reached out her hand and groped for a towel on the table beside the tub.

A towel was placed in her outstretched hand. 'Thank you Violet,' she said as she matted her face dry.

'You are entirely welcome,' a deep sexy voice that was definitely not Violet's replied. 'I assure you, the pleasure was entirely mine.'

It was Alex! She practically leaped from the tub, but remembering her nudity, she quickly sank beneath the water in a failed effort to shield herself from his heated gaze. He was standing beside the tub staring at her. His eyes were far too dark and seductive for her liking.

'Do you mind, my lord?' she snapped, instinctively moving her arms to cover her bare breasts.

'Not at all,' he drawled, his bold gaze searing her naked, glistening skin.

'Exactly how long have you been here?' she demanded hotly.

'Long enough,' he replied, with a wicked grin. Dragging his scorching gaze from her enormous blue orbs, wet black lashes and rosy lips, he took in every inch of her naked form, the soft curving breasts she tried desperately to hide, her narrow waist and her softly rounded hips. His eyes lingered over her womanhood.

Her cheeks burned beneath his sensual perusal. 'How dare you come in here while I'm bathing?' she ranted breathlessly. 'Get out!' she yelped, pulling her knees up against her chest, and wrapping her arms around them, all the while glaring at him.

His wicked eyes continued their brazen assessment of her bare flesh and his smile broadened.

'Excellent idea, a bath before dinner. Perhaps, I'll join you,' he said tugging at the folds of his intricately tied silk cravat.

'You will not!' she cried in utter frustration for he had not moved an inch. Nor did he look inclined to follow her edict any time soon.

'I insist you leave right this minute! I would like to finish my bath in private, if you don't mind,' she fumed, still hugging her knees tightly to her chest.

He shrugged and dropped his cravat on the bed. 'But of course,' he said rolling up the sleeves of his fine white linen shirt. 'It would be my very great pleasure to assist you,' he continued, reaching for the lavender scented soap.

'That will not be necessary,' she sputtered swatting at his hand. Unwittingly offering him an excellent view of her round creamy breasts. He ignored her protests and began to lather her back, his masterful hands moving in a circular massaging motion, caressing her taut body.

This was intolerable! 'Will you get out!' she screeched. She'd never been so humiliated in her life. And the very worst part was that it felt wonderful!

'Relax, Kara,' he whispered in a voice like velvet. His large soapy hands caressed her shoulders, 'you are extremely tense. This is a simple task a husband may perform for his wife. And it is enjoyable, is it not?'

His hands traveled down to her breasts and caressed the portion exposed above the water. She was about to complain, when he altered his direction, shifting his caress to her waist, sliding his hands over her hips, up her back and then to the sides of her breasts.

Goodness, she thought flushing to the roots of her hair, it was much more than enjoyable. But he was entirely too close. And the way he was touching her. It was shocking. Worse, it was positively sinful!

'*Oh, yes* – I mean no! Get out right this minute,' she cried helplessly. He was a loathsome cad, she tried to remind herself. But her resolve was weakening by the moment. And she was far more affected by his sensual assault than she wanted to be.

He chuckled softly and cupped his hands to fill them with water. Trickling the warm water down her back, he rinsed her soft lathered body.

Touching Kara was driving Alex wild. Slowly, his hands covered her breasts. But she made no move to stop him. His lips brushed a kiss against the back of her neck. She sighed. And he kissed her again, nuzzling her neck.

Shivers ran down her spine as his warm breath tickled her neck and his teeth nibbled at her earlobe. His hands continued their love play, making her breasts harden with desire. He kissed her ear, her temple, her cheek, dragging his lips across her face in search of her mouth.

All she had to do was turn her face to feel his lips on hers. In the recesses of her mind, she knew she should pull away, she should not succumb to his overtures. But she was helpless. With a whimper of defeat, she turned her head and welcomed his hot, wet, demanding mouth.

With a groan of pleasure, his warm lips came down possessively on hers. Instinctively, she parted her lips. And his mouth moved hard against hers, bruising her soft pliant lips with his fierce need. His fingers tangled in her hair holding her captive. Sliding her arms around his neck, she returned his kiss with equal craving.

Tearing his mouth from hers, he whispered, 'Oh, . . . Kara! I ache for you.' His voice was raw with emotion.

She wasn't particularly interested in talking at the moment. Not with the delectable prospect of kissing

Alex. Propelled into that wonderful sensual world where rational thought no longer existed, she only knew that she wanted him to touch her and feel his lips on hers again.

Pulling his neck down she parted her lips in eager anticipation of another searing kiss. He met her demand, his mouth covering hers in a passionate kiss. His hands strayed from her soft supple breasts to stroke her waist and abdomen savoring the soft curves of her womanly body as his lips devoured her sweetness with unbridled craving.

With a groan of pleasure, he crushed her to him and he kissed her passionately, violently, as if he could not get enough of her. Hungrily, open mouthed, she kissed him back. His tongue slipped inside, taking full possession of her sweet warmth. And his hands slid down her back pressing her tightly against him as his tongue drove into her mouth and slowly withdrew and then plunged again and again; mimicking the age old erotic ritual of lovemaking and making her dizzy with excitement.

Alex was vaguely aware that a knock had sounded at the door. He toyed with idea of ignoring it. But whoever it was, was very insistent. With a growl of irritation and deepest regret, he tore his mouth away from her delectable rosy lips and crossed the room to issue a scathing comment to the fool with such awful timing.

He yanked open the door and barked at whoever, 'What the devil do you want?'

Violet shrank back in horror. 'M-my lord,' she stammered cowering in the face of his fierce expression. 'I just came to 'elp milady with 'er bath. Please, my lord, don't beat me,' she stammered perilously close to tears.

Alex frowned at the maid shrinking with fear.

A splash of water followed by a gurgle of nervous laughter echoed from behind. He swung around to find Kara had slipped from the tub and cocooned herself in a towel, which he supposed she thought concealed her delightful little body adequately. But it only emphasized her shapely hips and round bosom.

'It's all right, Violet,' she said, too embarrassed to dart a glance at her husband. 'His lordship will not eat you. Come in.'

Violet slipped past Alex eyeing him with obvious trepidation. He frowned slightly and dragged his hand through his hair.

Kara clutched the towel to her bosom and shivered. Why didn't he leave?

He met her eyes across the room and burst out laughing.

How dare he laugh at her! 'Should I thank you for your assistance, my lord?' she asked her eyes brazenly meeting his torrid gaze.

He smiled at her, his eyes dancing wickedly. 'The pleasure was all mine, my lady,' he told her with a knowing grin.

A blush touched her cheeks and she lowered her lashes. 'I'm sure Violet will be able to help me dress for dinner,' she said glancing coyly at him from beneath half-closed lashes.

When he had gone, Kara sighed and bit her lip. The pleasure had not been entirely his. Not at all!

CHAPTER 9

Early the next morning, as the sun was just peeking through the clouds, Kara donned her crimson velvet riding habit and quietly descended the stairs. Eager to explore Hyde Park where, Aunt Henrietta had explained, all the fashionable ladies went riding, but never galloped, Kara was ready to shock Londoners for she fully intended to work off some of this tension by giving her mount full rein. She was about to escape the silent household when her husband's deep silky voice sent her pulse racing.

'A morning ride is just the thing to get the blood running don't you think?'

Turning on her heel, Kara fixed him with a frosty gaze. 'I suppose it all depends on how one spent the evening,' she said tightly.

Despite the fact that he'd been out all night doing Lord knows what to heaven knows whom, her foolish heart hammered against her ribs at the sight of him. Elegantly clad in tight black pantaloons, white linen shirt, a burgundy brocade waistcoat and a grey velvet coat, she wondered how he always managed to look so disgustingly stunning.

Completely unruffled, he merely smiled at her wrathful face and tucked her hand in his arm. 'And how did you sleep? Well, I trust?'

'As well as can be expected under the circumstances,' she muttered tersely. 'Unlike you, my lord,' she added with contempt, 'I am not accustomed to sleeping in a strange bed.'

He let his searing gaze wander over her hectic face.

'Such a pity you did not mention this ailment earlier, my dear. I would have been only too happy to acquaint you with that particular bed.'

Clamping her jaw shut, she pursed her lips with displeasure. 'I believe you said something about a ride, my lord? Pray, do not let me detain you.'

He bent his perfectly groomed black head, 'But of course,' he said, his amused eyes glinting into her fiery blue orbs, 'it will be my pleasure to spend the day with you. I am sure you will be pleased to learn I have cleared my schedule for the next few weeks.'

Kara's eyes widened in disbelief. That was the very last thing she wanted! How would she be able to pursue her investigation? 'Oh no!' she rushed out. 'You mustn't alter your busy schedule to accommodate me. I shall get along very well by myself.'

'Nonsense, I wouldn't hear of it. What sort of a husband would I be if I left my poor wife to her own devices in London of all places?'

Utterly dumbfounded, she gaped at him. 'B-but you cannot want to spend time with me?' she protested wildly. 'I-I mean, you'll be bored.'

'Me? Bored in the presence of my wife? I hardly think that likely. After all, my dear, we have so much to learn about one another, do we not?'

Kara chewed on her lip. 'Well, I suppose so. But I wouldn't want to put you out. As you may recall, my arrival here was not heralded. You must have a million things to do.'

'What could be more important than spending time with my bride?'

Kara blinked in amazement. 'What indeed,' she whispered in defeat.

'I've decided to devote all my time to pleasing you, my dear. Do you think it possible?' he asked, his eyes gazing longingly into hers.

She swallowed and his gaze flickered over her face, settling on her softly parted lips.

'I should imagine whatever you put your mind to, you'll manage quite admirably, my lord,' she told him breathlessly.

A slow seductive smile spread across his face and she felt herself grow warm. Flustered, she bowed her head and tried to loose her hand from his possession, but he would have none of it.

'Then I shall make your happiness my one goal,' he said in a soft caressing tone as he lifted her hand to his lips and kissed the delicate spot on her wrist just above her glove.

Try as she might Kara could not elude her

husband. He was as good as his word. He'd promised to be a kind and thoughtful husband, and he was, and more!

For the past two weeks he'd barely left her side. And to her absolute horror she found herself enjoying his company. She even looked forward to their early morning rides through Hyde Park which had become their usual habit. And each afternoon they took a long, romantic walk through Green Park.

Her husband lived up to his reputation, entertaining her with amusing anecdotes about Beau Brummel and friends. As an affectionate, caring husband, he was flawless. And the envy of all the women in London.

Of course, there was nothing new about that! Try as she might to resist his undeniable charm, however, Kara knew she must face facts – she was falling for her husband. Why should that come as a surprise? He was after all a rake who doubtless knew exactly the right words to melt the coldest of hearts.

All the same, she found it difficult to believe his tender touch and caring kisses were empty attempts to manipulate her into bed. In some small way, he must care for her. Either that, or he was a practiced actor. And she was a prize fool.

Dare she believe in him when he had such an atrocious record? He was a skilled seducer and more than likely, she was naive chit to trust him! But she could not help herself.

His nocturnal disappearances became more and more painful to bear. How could he act the kind, considerate husband by day and turn into a roving rake by night? Had he not an ounce of regard for her feelings?

Kara grappled with this problem for days, but no satisfactory solution presented itself. Unless she chose to become his wife in truth, and profess her growing affection, she was powerless. Given his callous attitude toward love, though, she wasn't willing to risk exposing her deepest feelings to her seemingly heartless husband.

The following afternoon when Kara and Aunt Henrietta returned from a shopping expedition, Alex greeted them in the hallway.

'Did you enjoy yourself?' he asked. Taking Kara's hand in his, he kissed the back of her hand and let his gaze sweep appreciatively over her tight bodice.

'Yes,' she said, a pretty blush coloring her cheeks. 'Thank you. I have never seen such a selection of hats, nor so many feathers,' she replied with a gurgle of laughter.

He looked amused. 'I am glad. Do you think you could stand another outing this afternoon?'

'Oh, Alex, you haven't accepted another invitation have you?' Aunt Henrietta asked, appalled. 'The poor child will be exhausted.'

'I am afraid I have,' he replied not a bit sorry. 'Can I help it if I've married a raving beauty and am eager to show her off, mother?' he asked, his gaze never leaving Kara's face.

'You are incorrigible, my lord. And by rights I should be very cross with you for accepting an invitation without consulting me first,' Kara laughed.

'Do you mind?' he asked caressing her cheek with his palm.

Lost in his gorgeous eyes, she sighed and shook her head.

A few hours later, the Dalton carriage came to a halt outside Lady Austin's town house. As Alex helped Kara disembark, the sky darkened and torrential rain burst forth.

He set Kara down from the carriage quickly. 'Let's hurry or you'll be soaked,' he said trying to shield her pink satin gown from the wind and rain.

Laughing good naturedly, the two drowned rats hastened up the steps and rang the bell. A rather staunch butler appeared and opened the door. Stamping his feet, Alex brushed the rain drops from his great coat. He graciously assisted Kara with her soaked bonnet and velvet pelisse. The butler reluctantly accepted their wet things and led them to the parlor.

As usual the room was swarming with all the important members of the ton. A strikingly beautiful red-head made her way through the crowd toward Kara and Alex.

'Alexander, darling, where have you been?' she crooned. Extending her gloved hand to Alex, she smiled.

'Hello Elizabeth,' Alex replied, dutifully bowing to kiss her hand.

Kara hated this woman on sight. Whoever she was, she was far too attentive. No one smiled like that naturally. She looked as if her perfect face might crack, and Kara found herself hoping it would.

'I heard that you got leg shackled, but I just could not believe it. What on earth possessed you?' Elizabeth preened. 'It can't be love, Alexander, you are simply not the type. I heard she was a little slip of a thing. Quiet, and horribly shy. An American of all things! Tell me it is not so. You have not married an uncouth colonial?'

Seething with anger, Kara stood silently at her husband's side. If he was annoyed with this vapid creature, he did not show it. Clearing his throat, he made the formal introductions, 'My dear, may I present Lady Elizabeth Townsend?'

Kara inclined her head and smiled sweetly at the vapid, hateful woman.

'How sweet you are,' Elizabeth said, her insipid voice laced with condescension. 'Why, you are just a child. Is this your first time in London?'

'Kara recently came up from the country,' Alex supplied with a smooth smile.

'Oh, but of course she has,' Elizabeth remarked eyeing Kara's damp frock.

By the end of the annoying conversation Kara abhorred Elizabeth. She did not know how much more of this woman's company she could tolerate.

Turning away from the doting creature, she surveyed the crowded room. Her spirits plummeted further as she caught sight of a gaudily dressed elderly woman with a mangy white pooch in hand gliding across the room. She was coming right for Kara! That was all she needed.

'Alex, how lovely to see you. How is your father?' the ornate fossil asked as, completely ignoring Kara she spirited Alex over to the settee.

Left to her own devices Kara sighed heavily, meandered towards the corner of the room and stood awkwardly against the wall. Out of acute boredom, she began to admire the enormous floral arrangement beside her, trying to remember the genus and species of the exotic flowers.

'Quite dull,' a friendly voice remarked from behind her.

Kara turned around and saw that the voice belonged to a kind faced young woman.

'Positively humdrum,' she replied with a smile.

'You must be Lady Dalton. I am Vanessa Holmes,' she declared extending a warm hand.

Kara was vastly relieved to have finally found a sociable person among the tonnish elite. 'Yes, I am Karina Sim-Dalton,' she replied flustered by her *faux pas*.

Vanessa chuckled, 'It is difficult to get used to, isn't? Although I imagine Alex makes it a whole lot easier,' she added with a conspiratorial smile. 'You are very lucky, you know. Catching a notorious rake like Alex. How ever did you manage it?'

Kara smiled wanly, her gaze following the predatorial Elizabeth Townsend around the room.

'Oh, we just happened to run into each other.' Literally!

'I must say, I am surprised Alex did not take you off for an extended honeymoon.'

'You know my husband?' Kara asked in an attempt to change the topic. She did not want to discuss the circumstances surrounding their hasty marriage.

'Not in the way *you* think,' she with a laugh. 'My husband does, or used to move in the same circles.'

Kara frowned. What way did she mean?

'They say,' Vanessa whispered, nodding at Lady Townsend who was slinking around the room ready to pounce on Alex, 'she wanted Alex, but you got in the way. I am glad you saved him from her talons. They were quite an item a few years back. But then again your husband broke most of the hearts in London.'

Kara looked away. So, they'd been lovers. Of course, she'd guessed it when they were introduced. It was decidedly unpleasant to have her suspicions confirmed. Hearing about her husband's past indiscretions turned her stomach.

Only this morning she'd noticed a striking brunette in Hyde Park eyeing her husband. And she'd felt certain the woman had known Alex. Of course, she consoled herself with the idea that she'd imagined their silent exchange. But now she knew her suspicions were correct. Watching the red-headed goddess seduce him with her insipid charm, Kara's heart sank.

Had she actually imagined these past weeks of quiet conversation and serene walks meant anything to her rakehell of a husband? How could an innocent like her compete with such gorgeous sophistication? This was what he was used to. And it was what he wanted. Excitement, wit and beauty. She offered none of those things. And would never fit into his world.

'Of course,' Vanessa was saying, 'I doubt Alex ever had much interest in her. Not his type. Though that would not stop her.'

'Excuse me,' Kara mumbled, hastily departing the room. What she needed right now was a good cry.

Desperate to find a door that might lead to a quiet room where she could seek refuge, her eyes scanned the long empty hallway. On her third try, she found a quaint sitting room. Falling into a chair, she miserably held her head in her hands. As the over-whelming sense of self pity overtook her and two enormous tears trickled down her cheeks, a white linen handkerchief suddenly appeared and danced enticingly back and forth in front of her face.

'If you wanted to leave you might have said so,' a deep male voice drawled from behind her.

Kara jumped at the sound of her husband's voice. She snatched the dangling handkerchief from mid-air and tried to avert her wet face from his piercing gaze. 'H-how did you find me?' she sniffled.

He shrugged his elegant shoulders. 'It wasn't terribly difficult. I had a hunch I might find you here. I am relieved, however, to find you alone,' he said mildly as he dropped into the chair opposite her. 'I'll grant you that Lady Austin is a dead bore, but her tea parties have never been known to cause weeping,' he remarked lightly as he crossed his booted feet on the marble table.

Kara sniffled, but did not enlighten him as to the reason for her tears.

He frowned. 'Was it *that* boring for you, then?' he asked peering at her tear-stained face.

Shaking her head, she looked away.

'Then why are you crying?' he asked.

She shrugged her shoulders and sniffled.

Alex sat forward. 'Come now, dearest,' he coaxed gently. 'Tell me what has happened?' he reached out and covered her hand with his own.

She squeezed her eyes shut, 'I wish you wouldn't use meaningless endearments.'

Stung by her rebuke, he released her hand. 'A moment ago you were chatting gaily with Lady Holmes. And now you are hopelessly down-hearted. Has someone insulted you?'

Kara lifted her teary eyes to his. She was surprised that he had taken notice of her departure or to whom she was speaking. She was under the impression that he had been neglecting her.

'No,' she said shaking her head. 'Lady Holmes was . . . pleasant. Quite informative, I must say,' she muttered tersely.

'Was she indeed?' he drawled in a bored tone. 'And what did she say that caused you such distress?'

Given the fact that she refused her husband her bed, Kara knew she had no right to be angry with him for seeking his pleasure where he may. And she knew she had no right to hold him accountable for his past indiscretions. He was no saint. What he had done prior to their marriage shouldn't matter. It was the here and now that was important. But she couldn't help it. It hurt.

'Pray do not concern yourself with my inconsequential feelings,' she said flippantly. 'I am sure Lady Townsend must be missing you by now. Verily, my lord, I collect you practically fell all over her.'

He stared at her, a look of complete surprise on his face. 'You're jealous,' he whispered incredulously, flattered to his core.

'I am not,' she snapped. Recognizing the mendacity in her words even as she spoke. 'Whom you choose to associate with about town with is your affair. I had hoped, however, you'd have the common decency not to humiliate me in public.'

'And how have I humiliated you?' he asked, his dark hazel gaze skewering her blotchy face.

'Brandishing your latest paramour in your bride's face is anything but tactful,' she said softly, her shoulders drooping.

'For your information, I haven't flaunted anyone in your face, since the day we met.'

She looked up sharply. 'I don't believe you.'

'Kara,' Alex sighed impatiently, 'given that it is you whom I would most like to bed, I will most definitely require your involvement and yours alone.'

A mantle of red crept over her cheeks and she retorted archly, 'Then perhaps you might explain where you disappear to each night after dinner?'

The corners of his lips lifted ever so slightly. 'I cannot quite figure you out, my dear,' he said, his eyes glittering beneath their heavy lids. 'Are you angry because I haven't joined you in bed? Or because you suspect I am unfaithful?'

Vaulting to her feet, she pinioned him with an icy stare. 'I assure you, I do not concern myself either way.'

A flicker of disappointment crossed his face, but was instantly replaced with his usual laconic expression. 'Of course, my dear, how stupid of me,' he said in a mocking tone. 'I should have remembered you harbor no feelings for me whatsoever.'

Instantly contrite, Kara stammered, 'No I – '

He chuckled softly and shook his head at her poor harassed face.

'Come,' he commanded as he stood up and offered her his hand. 'We shall take our leave. I hope you realize,' he added with a warm smile, 'we are developing a scandalous reputation for invariably leaving our engagements early.'

Kara smiled faintly and placed her hand in his. He squeezed her small hand encouragingly as he led her back into the lion's den.

Was he in earnest? She wondered. Or was this attempt at honesty just another frivolous way to cover up his infidelity? She couldn't be sure. But her foolish heart desperately wanted to believe in him.

As expected, immediately after dinner that night, Alex explained that he would be going out for the evening. 'Kara, my darling, will you see me to the door?' he asked with a sultry smile.

It was the same ritual he engaged in every night. Tonight, however, she had a mind to refuse him. His affection must be a facade. It had to be. He didn't really care for her. Not in the slightest. Why else would he sneak out each night to pleasure himself in another woman's bed?

She longed to tell him to go to the devil. Glancing at Aunt Henrietta's interested chubby face, however, Kara thought better of confronting her husband publicly. Tomorrow, on their morning ride, she'd demand a full explanation.

'Do not bother to wait up for me, dearest,' he said donning his great coat and beaver hat. 'I fear I shall be quite late returning home. These deuced card games last well into the dawn.'

Crossing her arms over her chest, she muttered under her breath, 'I wouldn't dream of it.'

He smiled at her and shook his head. 'Trust me,' he said cupping her cheek with his palm and gazing warmly into her eyes. 'You have no need to be jealous. I swear it,' he whispered softly.

Those damned eyes of his tore at her heart. And for a moment she almost believed him. But, then she caught herself. How many heart broken women had heard those same words? Jerking her head back, her blue eyes glinting with rage, she snapped, 'And who says I'm jealous?'

He chuckled softly and arched an ebony brow. 'What else could account for your lovely blush, dearest?' he murmured running his finger over her flushed cheek. His dipped his head to kiss her mouth. But she turned her face and his lips brushed against her cheek.

'Pray, do not treat me like a mindless child, my lord. We both know you are an unconscionable cad.'

He winced and his eyes turned cold. 'How well you know me, my love. And in such a short period of time,' he said mockingly.

His remark stung. She struggled to cover the hurt written all over her face as she told him icily, 'Go, if you must, but do not patronize me. That is too much to bear,' she added, her voice sounding horribly small. To her utter humiliation, she had to bite back the tears that threatened to fall. Good grief! What was the matter with her? She was turning into the most horrid watering pot.

He sighed and pulled on his gloves. 'Believe what you like. Given my reputation, I can hardly blame you if you think the worst.' With that he disappeared down the marble steps and the dark night eclipsed his tall figure.

Chastising herself for being an incurable romantic and a complete idiot, Kara hugged her arms around her waist and wandered into the library where Aunt Henrietta was attending to her fancy work.

Sensing Kara's concern Aunt Henrietta chortled, 'Men frequently go to their clubs, my dear.'

'Or their mistresses,' Kara mumbled, gazing thoughtfully into the fire.

'Gracious no, child! Alex would not be so uncouth.'

Kara laughed hollowly and sat down, 'He might.'

Aunt Henrietta shook her head. 'You are wrong. I have it on good authority he discarded Jenny Carrington directly after your wedding,' she added with a conspiratorial smile. 'So you need not fear his infidelity.'

Kara blinked. For a seemingly disinterested woman, Aunt Henrietta was remarkably informed. 'I see,' Kara mumbled. She wasn't sure which was worse, thinking he kept a mistress, and committing all manner of intimate acts with her, or actually knowing her name. 'How . . . reassuring,' she muttered.

'You mustn't blame Alex for his wild nature. He cannot help it, I expect.'

'Can't he?' Kara asked sharply.

'What can you expect from a child who never had any parents to speak of?' Aunt Henrietta asked on a sigh. 'Charles wasn't prepared to take on a son after his wife died. He was devastated by the loss. I think in some small way, he blamed the child. So, he hired nannies and tutors and ignored the child for the most part.'

Kara gasped. 'That's atrocious,' she exclaimed. 'How could Uncle Charles be so heartless?' But remembering his implacable attitude toward her inquiries and her forced marriage, she found it easy to imagine such a man abandoning a child he could not handle.

'Poor Alex,' she whispered, her heart breaking for the small child who had never known his parents. Or worse, felt forsaken by his father.

'You cannot imagine what it was like for Alex when his father decided he wanted a son again. The boy hardly knew his father. And Charles can be such an austere, stern man. It is hardly a surprise Alex rebelled.'

'It must have been terrible,' Kara said softly. 'But just because Alex had a difficult childhood, doesn't give him the right to cavort with women all over London.'

'Is that what he is doing?' Aunt Henrietta asked admiring her fancy work.

'Well . . . where else could he be?' she sputtered.

Aunt Henrietta shrugged her beefy shoulders. 'Perhaps you should ask him.'

Kara got to her feet. 'I have,' she said fingering the mantle. 'And he claims to be at his club.'

'Then, he is at his club. Just because a man is guilty of one offense does not automatically mean he has committed another.'

Kara tossed a dubious look over her shoulder at her gullible aunt.

'You know, my dear, you might consider trusting your husband rather than judging him. Besides,' she said with a knowing grin, 'it is common knowledge that reformed rakes make the very best husbands.'

Kara sneered. Obviously there were exceptions to the old adage.

Aunt Henrietta reached out and squeezed Kara's hand, 'You and Alex have a real chance for happiness, my dear. Do not throw it away over some petty jealousy.'

Kara nodded her head and left the room. How real was their chance at happiness? she wondered as she mounted the stairs to her solitary bed. If Aunt Henrietta's information was reliable, then Alex did not have a mistress. So where was he sneaking off to every night? Whatever he was doing, Kara was fairly certain he wasn't passing each night in gaming hells.

The night of the infamous ball arrived sooner than Kara would have liked. The gown she wore was made of white silk with tiny pearls sewn into the tight bodice and sleeves that puffed slightly at the shoulder and then narrowed tightly down her arm. Violet piled Kara's locks high on her head with several loose ringlets falling freely down her back.

A bundle of nerves, Kara descended the stairs to find Alex waiting for her. She tried to ignore the fact that he looked magnificently elegant. His jet black hair and chiseled profile created an irresistible picture of masculinity. As usual, encountering his lordship made her pulse race. And her stomach was nearly bursting with butterflies.

As if he had sensed her presence, Alex looked up and did a double take. Kara smiled, inwardly pleased with her effect on him.

His hungry eyes raked her over, from the top of her dark silky hair, over her breasts and hips, down to her white satin slippers, and then settled on the soft enticing swell of her breasts. He reached out and his hand closed over hers, drawing her close. 'You look positively radiant, my love,' he told her with a searing smile as his admiring gaze fell on her beautiful flushed face.

She was strangely elated by the stir her gown created. And she realized to her surprise, that she had hoped he would be pleased with her appearance.

'Exquisite,' he murmured, bringing her hand to his lips. His warm gaze locked with hers and her heart skipped a beat.

When they were settled comfortably in the carriage, he remarked offhandedly, 'You are not wearing the sapphires.'

'No,' she replied turning her attention to the window. The man had a genius for ruining perfectly pleasant occasions.

'Why not?' he asked. 'Were they not to your liking?'

'It may come as a surprise to you, my lord,' she told him primly. 'But I want nothing from your solicitor.'

'I see.' After a rather lengthy silence, he said, 'It may interest you to know that I asked my ever faithful solicitor to bring me several settings from which to make my final decision.'

Her head whipped around. '*You* selected them yourself?' she croaked. 'But I thought . . .' She wanted to crawl under the seat. It seemed she was constantly underestimating this unpredictable husband of hers.

He smiled slightly. 'Give me some credit, dearest. There are some things that are simply not done. I am curious, however, why it matters to you. I mean, why should you care one way or the other?' he asked fighting back a smile.

'Well . . . I . . . I don't care,' she snapped hotly.

'Ah.' He nodded his head. But she just knew those damned eyes of his were laughing at her.

The enormous ballroom was swarming with elite members of London's fashionable ton. As the butler announced, 'the Marquis and Marchioness of Overfield,' all four hundred eyes turned to inspect the Lady Dalton. Kara's stomach turned over.

'I'm going to be sick,' she whispered under her breath. Alex gathered her close to his side and assured her under his breath, pinning a bright smile to his lips, 'No. You are not.' Escorting her down the marble horseshoe shaped staircase, he

213

bowed to several familiar faces and quickly directed his wife to the side of the dazzling ballroom.

'Is there something wrong with my gown?' she asked in a heated under breath. 'I fear it is too revealing, my lord.'

'Not at all,' he assured her patting her hand encouragingly.

'Then why is everyone staring at me as if I had an enormous pimple?' she whispered fiercely.

He chuckled softly. 'It is because you are the most beautiful creature they have ever beheld, my dear.'

Kara shot him a dubious look. And he smiled at her. Stopping a passing footman, he retrieved two glass of bubbling champagne from the silver tray.

'Here drink this,' he said thrusting the chilled champagne into her shaking hand. 'It will settle your nerves.'

Taking a calming sip, she gazed about the room and hoped, despite the inner turmoil she felt, that she looked serene.

A large strong hand closed implacably over her wrist and her eyes widened in surprise. But her husband merely smiled amicably,

'Come,' he said escorting her from the over-crowded glittering ballroom. 'I've just the thing to help you relax.'

The music faded into the distance and the clamor of voices dimmed to a dull roar as the two slipped through the gilded doors into a deserted hallway.

'Where are you taking me?' she asked looking around her at the magnificent mansion.

He stopped short in the middle of the marbled hall. 'Here,' he replied, as he pulled her into his arms.

'What are you doing?' she asked in confusion.

His lips curled into a wolfish grin. 'I'm helping you relax my dear,' he told her in a deep silky voice.

She saw the devilish look in his eyes and recognized his sensual, languid expression. His dark hooded gaze moved over her flushed face and settled on her inviting rosebud mouth. *He is going to kiss me. Right here, in the hallway*! she thought with a surge of panic.

'Alex,' she cried struggling against his embrace, 'Are you mad? You can't possibly think to . . . anyone might see us!'

Glancing around him, he agreed, 'Mmmm. Yes. Quite right. Over here,' he commanded, dragging her beneath the white marble staircase. He leaned over her with one arm against the wall and the other tracing the delicate curve of her jaw line.

Her senses reeled. 'I-I . . . don't think – '

'Oh good, don't,' he said, in a low voice that sounded like velvet.

She swallowed and looked down at his gleaming white shirt, in an attempt to regain her poise. These tight quarters were having a disastrous effect on her. Her heart was racing and she felt hot all over; worst of all she absolutely could not think straight. It was, she admitted, a wonderful feeling!

He slipped his finger beneath her chin and tilted her face to receive his kiss. She looked at him, her eyes searching his face.

'I-I . . . don't want you to kiss me,' she protested, swallowing hard and taking a deep breath.

'Liar,' he murmured as his mouth descended on hers, taking her lips in a sensuous assault. His hungry lips gently stroked hers. Giving in to his burning kiss, she parted her lips. Her arms went around his neck and she stood on her tip-toes, fitting herself closely against the hard length of him. His steely arms enfolded her, caressing her back and sides, as his mouth passionately devoured hers.

Suddenly, Alex pulled his lips from hers and stared down at her, his dark hazel eyes brimming with passion. His breathing was becoming as quick as hers. Lord, how he wanted this woman! But now was not the time or the place. With a groan of regret, he crushed her against his chest and held her fast.

Kara's cheek was pressed against his crisp white shirt front and she could hear his heart pounding in his chest. Closing her eyes, she smiled slightly, pleased that he was equally affected by their heated embrace.

'I thought you said you did not want me to kiss you?' he teased.

'I didn't,' she whispered still in awe of how he could make her feel.

'You could have fooled me,' he drawled out. Her innocence delighted him! She was nothing like the jaded women of his acquaintance. And it was quite refreshing.

He smiled down at her. 'I am not complaining,' he said brushing her flushed cheek with the back of his hand. 'But the next time you decide to come alive in my arms let's make sure we are at home, shall we?'

Blushing to the roots of her hair, she nodded her head.

'We'd better join the party,' he told her huskily, 'or they'll be wondering what has happened to us.' His roguish grin made her flush even hotter. He politely offered his arm and she placed her trembling hand on it.

As they slipped into the noisy ballroom, Lord Rutherford waved to Alex and cannoned his way through the throng to join them.

'Kara,' Alex said sliding his arm possessively around her waist, 'you remember Daniel Rutherford.'

Lord Rutherford flashed a warm smile and dipped his blond head. 'Good evening, Kara,' he said pressing a kiss on her outstretched hand. 'You grow more lovely each time we meet, my lady.'

Kara smiled. 'You are very gracious, my lord.'

He shook his head, 'I am many things, my lady, but never gracious.'

'Fustian, my lord. I've little doubt you've charmed many a woman senseless.'

Daniel laughed. 'Your wife is delightful, Alex.'

Alex did not like the way Daniel was looking at his wife. He was smiling too damned much. And his laugh was too intimate. It grated on Alex's nerves.

'May I have this dance?' Daniel asked bowing over Kara's hand. Kara glanced at her husband. He

217

had planned on dancing the first quadrille with Kara himself. Frowning with displeasure, he stiffly inclined his head. Kara graciously accepted Lord Rutherford's hand and he guided her to the dance floor.

'I was wondering when Alex would come to his senses,' Daniel said as they reached the dance floor. 'I cannot conceive why he would ever be so daft as to deposit a wife, as lovely as you, in the country.'

Kara blushed prettily. 'On the contrary,' she said with a smile, 'I thoroughly enjoy rusticating, my lord.'

Daniel laughed. 'And are doubtless very good at it.'

'But of course,' she assured him.

'If I were married to you, madam, I would scarce let you out of my sight,' he murmured.

'Ah, but you are not married to me, my lord. And it is a very good thing too.'

'A lamentable fact, my lady,' he said bowing over her hand with a kiss.

Watching from the sidelines, Alex was growing angrier by the minute. Daniel was an outrageous flirt. And right about now, Alex would like nothing better than to plant his fist right in his friend's face.

Daniel escorted Kara back to Alex. By this time, Alex was seething with jealousy.

'Enjoy it, did you?' he bit out, his dark eyes flashing with temper.

Her smile collided with his blistering gaze and her face fell. 'I . . . yes,' Kara stammered uncomfortably, wondering what in the world had come over her husband. A moment ago he was kissing her. And now he looked ready to commit murder.

'Tell me,' he quipped, his voice full of sarcasm. 'I am afraid I've forgotten, is it strictly necessary to whisper in your partner's ear during a quadrille?'

Daniel smiled at his friend and accepted a glass of champagne. 'Indeed it is. Particularly when one is dancing with such a delightful partner.'

'She has a delightful everything else too,' Alex muttered viciously. 'Doubtless, you did not fail to notice. And I'll thank you, in future, to keep your hands, and your eyes, to yourself,' he growled downing the remainder of his champagne.

Daniel paled considerably. 'I say, that was not generously done. You are insulting in the extreme. And do your wife a great disservice. When you've come to your senses,' he said stiffly, 'I'm sure we will both be happy to accept your apology.' Bowing graciously over Kara's hand, he disappeared into the crowd.

'I sincerely hope your neanderthal performance is at an end,' Kara hissed under her breath. 'Have you quite finished humiliating me? Or shall I brace myself for more ridiculous accusations?'

'If you hadn't been brazenly flirting with him – '

Her eyes widened owlishly. 'Whaat?' she sputtered almost choking on her champagne.

'Do you dare deny it?' he ground out, his expression turning murderous. 'I watched you, fluttering those dark lashes of yours and blushing prettily at

219

his banter. You will not look at another man that way ever again. Is that understood?'

She stamped her slippered foot on the marble floor in frustration. 'No. It is not understood,' she hissed. 'I shall look at any man, in any way I choose.'

'The hell you will,' he growled.

'I am sure I have never witnessed such a foolish display of petty jealously in my entire life. You are ridiculous! I should think you'd know your best friend, if not your wife, better than to jump to such an outrageous conclusion. You are acting like a jealous school boy.'

'I am not jealous,' he bit out.

'No?' she asked lifting a delicate brow. 'Then what else, pray tell, could inspire a grown man to behave so stupidly?'

Alex glared at her for a long charged moment. Dragging his hand through his hair, he sighed. Good grief! He *was* jealous! And of his own friend! It was a startling revelation and he felt very foolish. Jealousy was a totally new emotion for him. He'd never felt possessive of a woman in his life. And yet, the mere idea of another man admiring his wife sent him into a lather. What was wrong with him?

'Kara, I – ' He fully intended to apologize for his over-reaction when a rather stout elderly woman, spying at them through her spectacles, approached through the crowd. Clutching Kara by the arm, he whispered in her ear, 'Brace yourself.'

'Alexander Dalton are you going to introduce your American wife to me or not?' she demanded.

Rolling his eyes heavenward, Alex let out a heavy sigh. 'If you like, Aunt Eugenia,' he said tightly. He turned to Kara, his eyes conveying his displeasure. 'May I introduce my father's sister Lady Eugenia Carter.'

Kara forced a cordial expression onto her face. 'How do you do?' she asked politely.

Lady Carter raised her quizzing glass and inspected Kara like an insect. 'You are not at all what I thought you'd be,' she muttered.

Fidgeting beneath Lady Carter's exacting gaze, Kara murmured, 'Really?' What was the old bat expecting? Someone more attractive no doubt, with more sophistication than a provincial Bostonian. Well, too bad.

'Too refined and gentile. Can you handle this ruffian?' she barked, gesturing toward Alex.

Alex chafed at her remark. 'Aunt, I assure you I am not the boy you remember. No frogs in my pockets,' he remarked dryly.

Lady Carter grunted. 'Well, you have played around long enough. I am glad you have finally settled down. What I want to know is when will you give me some grandnieces and nephews?'

Kara choked on her champagne. Alex frowned and patted her on the back, 'Are you all right?'

'Yes, I am fine. Thank you.' But her face told a different story entirely.

'He hasn't got you with child already, has he?'

Lady Carter demanded eyeing Kara's abdomen with interest. Kara wished the marble floor would open up and engulf her.

'No,' Alex snapped irritably. 'I have not.'

Lady Carter's eyes narrowed with scorn. 'When a husband is positive his wife is not with child, something is definitely amiss. You will come to see me, my dear. Thursday afternoon for luncheon. You,' she said addressing Alex, 'will attend as well.'

'That would be lovely,' Kara murmured finding her voice at last. 'I am sure we shall both be pleased to accept.'

Lady Carter scrutinized the couple once again and hurramphed before she whirled about in a black wave of lace and tunneled through the crowd to seek out new prey.

'Blunt isn't she?' Alex sighed, as he took another sip of champagne.

'Rather,' Kara muttered unable to meet his eye. Lady Carter was the most ill-bred person she had ever had the misfortune to meet. Between Alex's ridiculous behavior and Lady Carter's rude insinuations, the evening was rapidly deteriorating into yet another calamity.

Kara was mystified. Prior to arriving in this blasted country, she had been successful in society. But tonight had all the markings of a crashing catastrophe.

'She's a meddling old cow,' Alex imparted briskly. 'If you had not so graciously accepted her invitation, we would be well rid of her meddling.'

Kara glared at him. 'And what should I have said?' she snapped with irritation.

'No, would have sufficed very nicely I should think,' he drawled.

'Why thank you, my lord! I'll remember that the next time one of your obnoxious relatives corners me. Now, if you will kindly excuse me, I need some air.' With that she turned on her heel and plowed through the crush of people toward the nearest exit.

Stealing out onto the balcony, she gazed up at the stars twinkling like diamonds in the night sky and sighed. How dare he criticize her after behaving like a possessive fool? He was the one who insisted they attend this ghastly affair.

'*Bonsoir, madame,*' a dark ominous voice said from the shadows.

Kara jumped and whirled about to confront a short, dark haired, obviously French man.

'*Monsieur,*' she replied inclining her head politely. Fully aware that being alone on a secluded balcony with a strange gentleman who was not your husband was most improper, she made to return to the ballroom, but his question drew her up short.

'You are Eden's daughter, *n'est pas?*'

Kara froze. He knew her father? Could he be one of the people her father had helped to escape from the French Terror? She turned back to face him, 'You knew my father?' she asked tentatively.

'*Oui,*' he nodded, taking a step closer.

Kara frowned. The man looked too young to be an intended victim of the guillotine. 'When? I mean, how? Did he help your family too?'

He smiled with derision. 'I knew him fifteen years ago. When you were only *une enfant*.'

'Then you were a friend of his?' she asked eagerly.

'*Oui*, I knew him quite well,' he affirmed regarding her from beneath dark lashes.

She furrowed her brow. 'But you must have been just a boy at the time. How is it that you came to know my father?'

'He was,' he said with a chilling smile, 'shall we say, acquainted with *mon père*.'

'I am afraid, *monsieur*, I am at a loss. You seem to know of me, but I do not know your name. How could you know that I am his daughter?

'It is not important,' he said with a snarl, his tone suddenly harsh and impatient.

Kara stepped back. What a singular man. Her eyes narrowed suspiciously on his twisted face.

Something about him was suspect. Standing in the shadows like that, he looked almost demonic. Inexplicably scared, her eyes darted toward the door.

As if sensing her trepidation he smiled, altering his manner,

'*Chérie*, forgive me, it was not my intent to be so cryptic. It is just that there is danger here for me. As you know, your father's work was confidential. I would not want anyone to overhear us.'

Kara hesitated. 'But that is just it, *monsieur*, I do not know very much about my father's work. No more can I comprehend your reference to danger. How could our innocuous conversation possibly endanger you?'

'Forgive me, *chérie*, I meant no offense. I thought you would welcome an old acquaintance of your father,' he said turning to take his leave.

Against her better judgement, she stopped him, 'No wait. Please, *monsieur*, I beg your pardon. I am interested to know any friend of my father's. There are so few people who can tell me anything about him.'

He turned back to face her, watching her beneath heavy eyelids.

'I would be most honored to inform you in any way I can. Perhaps,' he said, his lips twitching. 'We can meet again? Tomorrow?'

Weighing his offer carefully, she bit her lip. The man was a link to her father's past. But his peculiar demeanor made her wary. He *was* odd.

She was about to agree to the clandestine meeting, when she heard Alex calling her name. Presumably, the Frenchman did as well because, before she could reply, the strange little man vaulted over the stone balcony and disappeared into the dark gardens.

Kara stared after him in astonishment. What a curious man. She was seriously questioning her judgement in speaking to the stranger in the first place, when Alex came up behind her.

'There you are. I've been searching everywhere for you. It is very bad form to go darting off at one of these blasted events.'

She was too distressed by the bizarre Frenchman to reply. A shiver wracked her bones.

Alex put his arm around her. 'You are like ice,' he remarked. 'It is chilly out here. Come back inside.'

Thankful for the timely exit, she gladly acquiesced and returned to the swarming ballroom.

In the bright light of the ballroom, Alex knew immediately that something had disturbed her for she looked white as a ghost.

'Are you feeling all right?' he asked eyeing her pale face with concern.

'I'll be fine,' she said with a wan smile. 'But I would like to go home, if you don't mind.'

'We've only just arrived. They won't be serving dinner for hours yet.' He lifted her chin with his finger and examined her face with a critical eye and shook his head. 'Something has disturbed you, Kara. What is it?'

She shook her head, not daring to divulge her strange meeting. 'Don't be ridiculous,' she said blithely. 'I have a headache. Nothing more.'

Alex's insecurities rushed to the forefront of his mind, clouding his ability to reason. 'You met someone on the balcony?' he said roughly.

Trust him to imagine the worst! Unfortunately, her transparent face reflected the truth. She had met someone. But he was hardly her paramour.

What a fool he was to let her out of his sight for a moment. She wasn't prepared for the prowling wolves of the ton dressed in gentlemen's clothing. 'Who was the cad?' he growled.

Several people had turned around to observe the spectacle. 'Alex please,' Kara whispered under her breath. 'You are causing a scene.'

'I'll do more than that if you do not tell me his deuced name,' he hissed.

Shaking her head she whispered fiercely, 'You don't understand.'

'I understand,' he growled, 'And I warn you, I will not be cuckolded. Especially when I am not even permitted to touch you.'

Her mouth dropped open. Just like a scoundrel to assume she'd had a midnight tryst on the balcony!

'You are leaping to ridiculous conclusions,' she snapped.

He knew she was lying. And it rankled him beyond belief. Devil take it! The little baggage was ripe for a rake's picking. Didn't he know it!

Taking her by the hand, he dragged her through the crowd toward the door. Helplessly trotting along after him, she issued hasty apologies to the astounded onlookers.

Marching her down the marble steps, he virtually threw her into the carriage awaiting at the curb and she scrambled to right herself on the velvet swab seats.

He climbed in after her, slamming the door in his wake. He fixed her with a furious gaze. Devil take it! While he was living like a monk, the little chit was enjoying herself to the hilt!

'I have played the wag long enough,' he ground

out. 'I have no intentions of remaining celibate while you play the coquette.'

'Play the coquette? Are you mad?' she gasped. 'How dare you drag me through a crowded ballroom and toss me in a carriage like a-a disobedient child! I don't think I've ever endured such humiliation in all my days.'

'No?' he asked arching an ominous brow.

She glared at him. 'You are indeed a scoundrel.'

He leaned over her, his face dark and menacing. 'I know you met someone this evening. I need a name, Kara.'

'Well,' she panted, leaning away from his savage expression. 'You will be severely disappointed, my lord, for I have none.'

'In that case,' he told her in a deadly voice, 'I'll draw my own conclusions. There are a few well known Corinthians who prey on unsuspecting innocents, particularly young widows, or hopelessly miserable wives. I shall call each one of them out.'

Her eyes went wide. 'That is absurd! I tell you, I met no one.'

'And I say you are a poor liar,' he bit out. 'Think of all the blood you'll have on your hands!'

Good lord, he was serious. 'Do you truly intend to go through with this folly?'

He shrugged an indifferent shoulder. 'That all depends.'

'On what?' she asked breathlessly.

'On you. What is it to be, Kara? Senseless

bloodshed at dawn? Or a simple confession? The choice is yours. I think it only fair to warn you, however,' he said with an icy smile. 'I'm an excellent shot.'

CHAPTER 10

'You may retire for the evening, Fowler,' Alex said, curtly dismissing him.

Fowler glanced at the beleaguered Kara and muttered an obedient, 'Very good, my lord.'

Taking the taper from the table Alex took Kara by the arm and led her upstairs to his private study. Opening the door, he waited for her to enter, his eyes following her as she walked over to the fireplace where she warmed her ice-cold hands. He couldn't believe the innocent beauty before him was capable of deception. And yet, she'd met someone on the balcony, of that he was sure.

Setting the taper down, he came up behind her. He was so close, she could feel his breath on her neck, but he made no move to touch her.

'Look at me.' When she made no move to obey him, he took her by the shoulders and turned her around to face him. 'You haven't given me your answer.'

Petulantly, she averted her gaze. Tipping her chin, he gazed into her stormy blue eyes. His intense gaze seemed to penetrate her soul.

'What is it to be?' he asked her quietly.

She sighed and looked away, 'Very well, my lord, since I don't wish to see innocent men shot down in their prime, you leave me little choice,' she said bitterly. 'It seems I must tell you.'

'Very sensible,' he nodded curtly. 'Now, give me the blackguard's name.'

'I don't know his name. It is true, I met a man. But not in the manner you suggest,' she assured him coolly. 'Ordinarily, I wouldn't have spoken to him. But when he said he knew my father, I was intrigued. I desperately want to learn more about my father. You cannot imagine what it is like not knowing.'

Alex drew his brows together in consternation. 'This man claims to have known your father?'

'Yes, I tried to explain in the carriage, but you were bent on believing the worst.'

Alex frowned, he did not appreciate being reminded of his quick temper. 'What was his name?'

She shrugged her shoulders, 'I have no idea. He ran off when he heard you approach.'

'Ran off?' he asked, his brow darkening.

'It was most peculiar,' she said thoughtfully.

Alex looked baffled. 'You say you don't know his name? But you spoke to him?'

'Well, he spoke to me. He must have followed me when I went out for some air. Strange,' she said recalling the peculiar foreigner, 'he knew I was Eden's daughter. He called me that.'

'Eden?' Alex echoed duly.

'Yes, that was my father's real surname.'

'And how would you know that?' he asked sharply.

She dismissed his question with a wave of her hand. 'It is not important. The Frenchman said – '

'Frenchman?' Alex snapped, grabbing her by the arms. 'You met a Frenchman tonight?'

Bouchard! Could it be? Was he pursuing Kara? Hell! Alex had no idea Bouchard knew who Kara's father was. Or for that matter, that he was involved with the War Office. Perhaps he didn't. Maybe he was bluffing, trying to gain her trust? Would the devil use Kara to get to Alex?

'Yes, he was French,' she averred, confused by Alex's concern.

'Describe him,' he said roughly.

She blinked in surprise. 'I don't know,' she stammered.

He shook her harshly. 'Try!'

She stared at him for a moment before she answered. 'Well, he was dark haired, with a moustache. I am not certain what color his eyes were, he stayed in the shadows much of the time. Alex, what is all this about? Do you know this man?' she asked her eyes searching his troubled countenance.

Bouchard used disguises. It could well have been him. 'How tall was he?' Alex snapped.

'I honestly don't know. I did not dance with him,' she imparted sarcastically. 'Contrary to what you may believe, I did not kiss him, either.'

'It's important, Kara,' he said, his fingers digging painfully into her arms.

Kara drew her brows together. 'Yes,' she winced at his fierce grip. 'I can see that. He was short. At least, shorter than you.'

'How did he say he knew your father?'

She shrugged. 'He didn't, really. He just said that he was an old acquaintance. He mentioned something about his father knowing mine, which must have been when he was a boy.'

'Did he touch you, Kara?' Alex growled. 'Or suggest another meeting somewhere, perhaps more secluded?'

She nodded her head. 'He said we could meet again and he would tell me more about my father and his work.'

Hell! He hoped to get her alone. 'What the devil did he mean by that I wonder?' Alex muttered almost to himself.

'I have no idea. But whatever it was, it must have been dangerous.'

His eyes narrowed on her face. 'What makes you say that?'

'Well, for one thing, my father obviously helped Uncle Charles during the Revolution, which was a dangerous business. And for another, that peculiar little Frenchman, whoever he was, was extremely cautious. Almost afraid he would be discovered discussing my father.'

Alex swore under his breath. 'I don't want you in the middle of this,' he told her sternly.

'Middle of what?' she asked perplexed.

'Never mind that now. I forbid you to see this

man ever again. You are not to go out alone. You are to be escorted at all times. Is that understood? I will brook no insubordination from you.'

She opened her mouth to object, but Alex deprived her of the opportunity. Drawing her against him, he wrapped his arms around her and held her tightly. Heavens, he thought groaning inwardly, if it was Bouchard, Alex had come close to losing Kara tonight.

Then his mouth covered hers and he kissed her with slow deliberation, savoring the sweetness of her lips. He kissed her cheek and then her eyelids, 'Kara,' he whispered hoarsely, holding her close and kissing the top of her head, 'it is for your own safety. Do not disobey me in this. You must give me your solemn word. You will not go out alone.'

'Alex, what is this all about? Why are you so concerned? Please, tell me. I know nothing about my family's past. Living in Boston, none of that seemed to matter. But now, being here, with my mother gone, I am desperate to learn the truth. Everywhere I turn I'm confronted with obstacles. Please, you must help me.'

He sighed and crushed her to him. He was still a bit shaken at how close he'd come to losing her tonight. And he was worried. Kara's safety may be at stake. If this mysterious Frenchman wasn't Bouchard, he was probably working for him. Lord knows how many co-conspirators the blackguard had.

If Bouchard was hoping to ensnare Alex by manipulating Kara, Alex would personally see to it that the devil pay dearly for the attempt. Just the same, it irked him that Bouchard had gained the upper hand. The mere idea of any harm coming to Kara made Alex shudder. He must ensure her protection any way he could. And the easiest way was to keep her as much in the dark as possible.

'All right. If I promise to look into your father's past, will you promise me that you will not disobey my wishes?' he asked softly, his lips brushing against her temple.

Her enormous blue eyes, artless and serene, searched his face. 'But there is already a great deal you know,' she insisted softly. 'I know Uncle Charles is keeping things from me. Please, Alex.'

Caressing her cheek with his palm, he assured her gently, 'Kara, father is only trying to protect you.'

Her eyes flashed with temper. 'But I have the right to know, you said so yourself!'

'And when did I say that?'

'At Grantly. I overheard you. Actually,' she admitted bowing her head in shame. 'I, um, listened at the door to Uncle Charles's study.'

'You did what?' Alex was utterly astounded – not to mention concerned. How often had he been the object of this lamentable habit?

She bit her lip. 'I know it was deceitful. But is it worse than purposely concealing details about my father's past?' she asked gruffly.

Alex sighed, 'Kara, I must honor my father's dictates in this matter. I have given my word.'
She opened her mouth to protest but he pressed

his finger to her lips. 'But,' he sighed, 'I will see what can be done.'

Relief rushed through her, for the first time since arriving in this cursed country she felt safe. As if she belonged somewhere. Come what may, Alex would protect her. It was a good feeling. Very soon, with his help, she'd get to the bottom of this and solve the enigma of her life.

Tilting her chin, he smiled at her upturned face. 'I will have your word. Your solemn pledge, you will not go out of this house alone.'

She hesitated for a moment, she truly didn't want to deceive him. But she knew he would never condone her meeting with a Runner. And she was not about to forfeit her appointment with Mr Briston. She'd waited too long and worked too hard for the information. Besides, her husband knew more than he was telling, that much was obvious. Crossing her fingers, she said on a sigh, 'Oh, all right.'

'You will never speak to this man or arrange to see him again,' he strictly enjoined her.

'I won't,' she conceded willingly. 'I never want to lay eyes on that queer little man ever again,' she shivered.

She felt the tension ease from his body. He cupped her face between his hands. His tender hazel eyes stared deeply into her brilliant blue depths,

'You must trust me, Kara. It is for your own good.'

236

Slowly, his lips descended on hers. His mouth slanted over hers, gently brushing back and forth urging her soft, pliant lips to part beneath his. And to his delight, her soft, trembling lips parted and she opened for him, welcoming his probing tongue as he drove in and out of the soft recesses of her mouth.

She whimpered with pleasure, giving in to her burning need for closeness. She needed him, desperately. Her arms clasped his hard muscular body pressing closer against him. With trembling hands she caressed his beautiful body, running them over his muscular chest, arms, broad back and clutching at the nape of his neck.

When his hands moved to caress her shoulders and ease her gown off, she offered no protest. He dragged his mouth from her lips and kissed her cheek. His lips moved to her ear and he nibbled her lobe. She moaned and turned her head, inviting his exploration. His hot tongue moved to her neck.

His hands tugged at her gauze chemise, freeing her plump, round breasts. And he drew in his breath with pleasure.

'Oh, but you are lovely.'

Tenderly cupping her breasts in his hands, he stroked the rosy buds with his thumb.

Kara's eyelids fluttered opened and she gasped in surprised excitement. He watched her wild, uninhibited response and his chest tightened. Dipping his head, his mouth captured her nipple gently drawing the swollen peak into his mouth, laving the sensitive pebble with his tongue until she moaned with pleasure and arched against him begging for more.

'Oh, Alex,' she whimpered as the delectable sensations washed over her. She never wanted him to stop giving her this exquisite pleasure.

He eased her down onto the carpet before the blazing fire, and she went willingly, clinging to him and kissing his face, his neck. Her fingers tore open his shirt and she kissed his bare chest.

Rolling her onto her back, he leaned over her. She looked up into his eyes, which were teeming with desire and her heart skipped a beat. Reaching out her hand, she traced her fingertips over his lips. He kissed her fingers. Taking her hand in his, he kissed her palm and her wrist sending the most glorious sensations through her.

'Oh, Kara,' he whispered in a husky voice. 'My beautiful, wonderful, Kara. How I want you,' he murmured as his hand slid under the hem of her filmy chemise and caressed the inside of her thighs.

She was tingling again and it was wonderful. And she knew what she'd been trying her hardest to deny – she loved him. Desperately.

'Kara,' he whispered, 'you are wonderful.' His voice was ragged with passion as his hand covered her creamy peaked globes and squeezed gently. Slowly, he undressed her, planting small kisses all over her body. And she writhed mindlessly under his roaming lips and tongue like a wild thing. Quickly slipping free of his britches and discarding his shirt, he stretched out beside her.

Leaning up on his elbow he gazed down at her in her naked glory.

'My darling, you are more beautiful than anything I could imagine,' he breathed. He dipped his head and his mouth closed over each of her ripe, full breasts in turn, sucking and teasing the pink mounds until she mewed with pleasure.

Lifting his head from her sweet bounty, his lips captured hers once more kissing her deeply, hungrily, as if he could not get enough of her. His hand slid up her thigh and she tilted her hips offering his roving, torturing hand freer access.

When he was sure she was ready for him, he pulled his mouth away. Kara was breathless, clutching at him, desperate for more. He rolled on top of her enveloping her naked body with his. He moved between her legs and gently nudged her thighs apart.

She stiffened, suddenly becoming afraid of what was to come. Alex sensed her panic and his mouth descended possessively over hers in a passionate kiss that drugged her senses and dispelled her fear.

Reveling in the sublime feel of his erotic kisses, she could feel the blood pulsating through her body. And was alive with pleasure. His mouth devoured hers, his tongue plunging deep inside her mouth. His hot, sinewy, naked flesh pressed against her sending shivers of raw pleasure all through her. She ran her hands over his muscular shoulders. He was so wonderfully virile. Caressing his broad back, she pulled him closer to her, as if she could not get enough of him.

Alex was more than ready to plunge deep inside her snug, wet passage.

'Kara, my love,' he whispered close to her ear, he sounded strangely out of breath. 'My sweet. How do you feel?' He was hanging on to his control by a thread. 'Are you ready for me, my love?' His hand slid between her legs and his long, lean fingers teased her slick, wet petals of feminine flesh.

'Oh, yes,' Her voice, was a tiny whisper of mystification. 'Alex, yes!'

He kissed her again, inhaling the sweet smell of her skin as his mouth moved down her neck. He kissed the soft skin behind her ear, sending shivers all through her body.

'Oh, Alex,' she murmured breathlessly and realized his prophecy had come true. They shared passion. She was on fire with desire. But it was more than that, so much more, they were in love. She loved him, with all her heart. And he must love her. Could anyone share such intimacy with someone they did not love?

Her natural uninhibited response drove him to the edge of his tenuous control.

'Kara, open for me,' he whispered. His heart slammed into his ribs, his need to possess her almost unbearable. Groaning with pleasure he nudged into her soft, welcoming wetness. The hard feel of him seeking entrance brought Kara abruptly back to reality. Panicking, she went rigid beneath him.

What was happening here? She'd experienced his intense passion and knew he was deeply moved. But she wanted to be absolutely certain of his devotion before they made love. And she wasn't sure of anything, except for the fact that her husband was an excellent lover.

How could she be such a fool? She'd vowed not to let him seduce her. But like a lovesick dolt, without any guarantees, she tumbled into his arms at his practiced beckoning. And on the study floor, no less! She did not even know where or with whom her husband was spending his nights! She had Aunt Henrietta's assurances, but absolutely nothing from him.

Oh, he wanted her. He had clearly demonstrated that, but did that mean he loved her? He'd never actually said the words. And he obviously had done this many times before with his mistresses, but he didn't love *her*. Was Kara simply another conquest? Or did he feel something more for her? She had to know.

'Alex,' she said breathlessly, alarm evident in her soft voice.

He was trying to be gentle, to go slowly, but he could not control his own rampant desire. He had to possess her completely. Taking her face in his hands, he looked into her beautiful blue eyes, 'Easy, Kara. I'll be gentle, my love, I promise. Relax and let me love you,' he said, his voice rough with passion.

'No! Please. I cannot do this,' she whispered in desperation.

His hands gripped her soft hips. 'Yes . . . you can, my love,' he coaxed breathlessly as he pushed against her soft, moist flesh seeking the entrance he desperately needed.

She shook her head. 'No. Alex, please. Not this way. Not with all these lies between us. Please. Stop!' she cried as two tears spilled over her dark inky lashes and trickled down her cheeks.

Dazed by passion, it took a few moments for her words to sink in. He shook his head as if to clear his mind. Staring down at her lovely face in the firelight, he smiled tenderly.

'Oh, my sweet, you mustn't be afraid,' he kissed her, burying his hands in her luxurious dark tendrils. 'I'll be very careful. And I'll make it as easy for you as I can,' he whispered kissing the tears from her cheek. 'I've rushed you, taking you like a rutting stag on the floor when you deserve a soft bed. I'm sorry,' he said kissing her temple, her eyelids and then her mouth, 'it is just that I want you so damned much. I am impatient when I should go slowly with you. Forgive me, my love. But I cannot help myself.'

'It's not that,' she sobbed, shaking her head.

'What then?' he asked bracing himself on his forearms and smoothing the hair from her tear stained face.

'Don't you understand?' she cried. 'I can't do this. Not without something more . . . something lasting between us.'

He smiled at her, his eyes dark with desire.

'I know you want me, Kara,' he whispered and bent down to take her rosy, swollen lips in a lingering kiss. 'And heaven knows, I want you,' he groaned.

Gazing at his passion-flushed face, she wanted to scream, but you don't love me! She shook her head. 'It's not enough for me. I'm sorry.'

He dipped his head to kiss her mouth, but she turned her face away.

'*Please* . . . Alex, don't.'

Alex stared at her in utter disbelief. He wanted this woman more than the air he breathed. And she was rejecting him.

For the first time in his life, he was unable to seduce a woman. And it didn't sit well. But Kara wasn't just any woman. She was the only woman in the world he wanted to distraction. With a deep sigh of regret, he moved off her and got to his feet. Snatching his britches off the floor he pulled them on.

'I won't press you again,' he told her gruffly and left the room, angrily slamming the door.

Kara buried her face in her hands and wept. Against her better judgement she'd fallen helplessly in love with her rakehell of a husband.

The following morning, Alex settled down at his library desk and penned a missive to his father. He was concerned about the identity of this elusive Frenchman. What if it was not Bouchard? Could this man be the one his father feared? No. It was too preposterous. Too much time had passed. Or had it? Whether the French-man was a threat from the past or not, the duke should be kept abreast of the situation, particularly Kara's rising curiosity.

Signaling Fowler, he instructed him to send the missive. 'Oh, and Fowler,' he said to the butler's hunched back. 'Ask her ladyship to join me in the morning room.'

'Yes, my lord.'

Sooner or later Alex knew he had to face her. And it might as well be sooner. He owed her an apology for last night. Never in his life had he pounced on a woman and forced her into lovemaking. He cringed as he recalled his clumsy attempt at seduction like some untried school boy. Good grief! His lack of control was utterly appalling.

Normally, he took his time with these things. He'd probably scared her. Where the devil was his finesse when he needed it? Never had he experienced such mind altering desire. And he didn't like it one bit.

Hell! He'd practically begged her to make love to him! And he'd barely been able to contain himself, when she'd rejected his advances. That was a bitter pill to swallow!

As Kara entered the morning room, she wondered if Alex had gone out for their customary ride without her this morning. Feigning a miserable headache, she'd hidden beneath the covers for several hours in the hope that she would not have to face him this morning. She desperately wanted to forget last night's botched seduction. That was not to be the case, however.

'You asked to see me, my lord?' she asked beneath lowered lashes.

Alex swung around from the window. His chest tightened at the sight of her in her fetching lavender dress. 'Yes, I wanted to speak to you about last night.'

A mantle of rose spread over her cheeks. Her eyes widened and then darted away. 'I see,' she managed to get out.

'I behaved abominably. And I fear have given you a disgust of me.'

'Oh no,' she hastened to reassure him. 'It was quite pleasant actually.' Realizing her incriminating admission, she flushed a deeper shade of red and quickly directed her gaze to the floor.

He smiled, 'Nevertheless, it was little surprise that you turned missish given the way I acted. I promise not to rush you again, my dear. Next time, I shall be mindful of your virginity.'

Her head snapped up. Turned missish! Mindful of her virginity! Of all the arrogant, conceited things to say.

Didn't he listen to a word she had said last night? The man was a heartless rogue, completely devoid of feeling. How could she have the bad taste to believe she actually cared for such a miserable cretin?

'Do not give it another thought, my lord,' she said in a cool, tight voice that underscored her anger. 'As you are unlikely to be in such a position again, I wouldn't let it trouble you overmuch.'

His astonished hazel gaze collided with her frigid blue one. And he stared at her in surprise. For a moment he was rendered speechless. Then he smiled. It was a slow searing smile designed to make her pulse quicken.

'On the contrary, my dear. Given your ardor of last evening,' he drawled, 'I expect we shall be, how did you put it? in that particular position, sooner than you think.'

Color crept into her cheeks as vivid images of last night's intimacy rushed to the forefront of her mind. But she would rather die than let him know he'd shocked her. She crossed her arms over her lovely bosom and fixed him with a chilling gaze,

'Don't hold your breath, my lord. Blue is not your best shade.'

He crossed the room, instantly dissolving the distance between them. 'It won't come to that,' he told her, pulling her into his arms. 'And we both know it.'

Her heart was pounding so hard she felt certain he could hear it. 'It may come as a surprise to you,' she said hotly, her eyes shining with unshed tears. 'But some people require more than physical pleasure to be happy.'

'Devil take it, Kara, I didn't mean – '

'Spare me your empty words of reassurance,' she spat out.

Shoving against his chest, she flew from the room slamming the door with a loud resounding thud.

Alex cringed. Raking his hand through his hair, he swore under his breath. This was more difficult than he had imagined. Sooner or later, her passionate nature would take over. He just hoped it was sooner.

'So, you think there may be a connection?' Daniel asked after listening in earnest to Alex recount Kara's encounter with the Frenchman.

Alex sat back and sipped his port. He shook his head, 'Highly doubtful. Still I do not want my tempestuous wife getting mixed up in all this. It is far too dangerous. If anything happened to her, I'd never forgive myself.'

'I wouldn't worry on that account, if the other evening is any indication, you are as protective as a ferocious watchdog.'

Alex tossed him an irritated glance.

Daniel laughed. 'Come now, Alex. You can hardly blame her for searching out the truth. Admit it, the reason you are so vexed is that she shares many of your qualities.'

Alex looked startled. 'The devil you say!'

'She is intelligent, headstrong and extremely resourceful.'

'And she is flirting with danger,' Alex growled.

'Ah, yes I can see it now. The illustrious Lord Dalton passing up the opportunity to ferret out the truth, especially concerning his own pristine family's past. I think not.'

Alex pondered the idea. 'Perhaps, we are somewhat alike,' he conceded reluctantly. 'But, her unruly nature could get her killed. What the devil was she doing talking to a stranger? Anything might have happened if I hadn't come along.'

'But you did come along,' Daniel countered. 'Don't be so hard on her. Anyone would be inquisitive.'

Alex scowled. 'Why is it, that each time my wife is a topic of discussion, I feel like the oppressor?'

'Because you are, Alex. You are,' Daniel teased.

Unamused. Alex got to his feet and retrieved a map of London from the desk drawer.

'Come look at this,' he said, unrolling the plans for this evening's surveillance across the desk. 'Our man Billy Harper told me that the meeting was going to be held here,' he pointed to St Katharine's Dock in the East End.

'Are you sure you can trust his information?' Daniel asked shaking his head skeptically.

Alex shrugged. 'Probably not. But, it can hardly matter, so long as we find Bouchard I don't give a damn what I have to do.'

Kara opened her eyes and realized it was still night. Something had awakened her. Disoriented and groggy, she glanced over to the opposite side of the four poster bed. It was still empty. Alex had stayed out all night. Again.

She rolled over. Snuggling beneath the warm covers, she tried to block out the recurring image of Alex locked in the arms of another woman. She heard a loud thud as if someone had walked into an object in the dark. Her eyes flew open. Someone was moving around the room! Pushing up on her elbows, she tried to focus in the darkness.

'Aunt, is that you?' she whispered, her voice heavy from sleep.

'No, it is not Henrietta,' came a man's gruff reply.

She sat up. 'Alex?' she asked struggling to make out the figure rustling around in the dark.

'Go back to sleep Kara,' he snapped. At first, she thought from the way he was staggering that he might be drunk. But as her eyes became accustomed to the darkness she saw he was hunched over, holding his stomach.

'Are you ill, my lord?' she asked in concern.

His breathing was ragged as he gritted, 'Go back to sleep.'

But that only served to heighten her curiosity and concern. She lit the taper beside the bed and bounced out of bed.

'What is wrong?' she asked coming over to where he was slumped.

He grimaced in pain. 'Nothing. Go to bed,' he muttered averting his face.

But she was not so easily deterred. She caught a glimpse of his bloodied face and gasped.

'Alex!' She cried in horror. 'Your face is bleeding.' It occurred to her that he had been in a brawl of some sort. 'What has happened to you? And where on earth did you get those filthy clothes?' she asked noticing his old, tattered, dirty shirt.

Alex staggered past her, fumbling in the dimness for a basin of water.

'Here let me,' Kara said, rushing to his side.

Wearily, Alex nodded his head and sank into the chair beside the bed. She poured some water into the basin. Wetting a cloth, she knelt before him and gently attended to the cuts and bruises on his face.

'Who did this to you?' she asked wincing at the condition of his battered face.

He groaned from the pain. 'It is not important,' he told her roughly.

She sighed in frustration. Examining his face with a critical eye, she told him, 'You are badly hurt. I am going to fetch a doctor.'

He caught her by the wrist and held her fast. 'No. It's nothing,' he snapped irritably, 'I have had worse.'

Against her better judgement, she acquiesced, 'Very well, my lord. But at least, let me get some fresh water to clean the cuts.'

He nodded and released her wrist. Sitting forward, he pulled his shirt off. Kara turned around and gasped. His chest was covered with black and blue marks.

'Alex, you must have a doctor,' she insisted rushing to his side. Inspecting his bruised stomach, she shook her head, 'I cannot contend with this.'

Leaning back he let out a long breath and closed his eyes. 'No doctor. I'll be all right,' he grumbled. 'Just go to bed.'

She shook her head. 'I am going for some help,' she stated firmly and grabbed her chintz wrap from the end of the bed. 'You are seriously injured and might have broken bones.'

Stumbling to his feet, he grabbed her arm and pulled her against him.

'No,' he said sliding his arm around her waist and holding her tightly against his bare chest. 'I do not want a doctor,' he told her breathlessly. 'I just need some rest.'

The warmth of his breath brushed against her cheek and he felt her quiver in his arms. Mesmerized by her fathomless blue depths, he was suddenly acutely aware of the alluring woman in his arms and thin fabric of her nightgown. It barely concealed her breasts. He could feel them peak against his bare chest. And her soft, inviting lips were only inches from his own, practically begging for his touch. One kiss and he'd be lost forever.

Having all this soft, warm femininity pressed against him was more than he could resist. He felt a tightening in his groin and cursed Bouchard. He was in no condition to make love to this delectable little beauty.

'Fetch me some brandy from the study,' he said pushing her away.

Kara shook her head, 'Not until you tell me what has happened.'

Alex stared at her. Did she have any idea what effect she was having on him? Or how close he was to devoting the remainder of the night to making love to her regardless of his damned bruises? She looked splendid standing there in her white night-gown, her long, thick hair falling softly over her shoulders.

'Kara, just get me the brandy,' he said in a weak voice as he slumped into the chair. Swallowing, he leaned his head back and closed his eyes. And tried not to think of her silky legs wrapped around his hips.

'Only if you agree to tell me who did this, and why,' she told him with characteristic implacability.

His spirited minx would pick a time like this to argue! 'I am not going to bargain with you,' he growled.

'Very well,' she said raising her chin defiantly and crossing her arms beneath her lovely breasts. 'Get the brandy yourself.'

He glared at her. 'You uppity little hellion! When I am feeling myself again, remind me to beat you soundly,' he said swallowing back the pain, 'Now get me the brandy, you little sorceress. And I'll tell you what you wish to know.'

Beaming from ear to ear, she hurried from the room, and returned a moment later with a large decanter of brandy and a glass. Setting the decanter on the bedside table, she hastily poured him a glass which he drank down in one gulp.

Shivering, she rubbed her arms and scurried over to the fireplace to add more logs to the dying fire. Arms outstretched, she stood before the flames warming herself, unwittingly affording her husband's hungry eyes an excellent view of her delightful shapely hips and narrow waist. Tearing his gaze from the enticing sight, he poured himself another glass of brandy. And tried to think of anything but her luscious little body beneath his.

As if sensing his intense scrutiny, she turned to look at him over her shoulder and smiled. He looked away again and quickly downed the rest of his brandy. Hell, he thought with a hard swallow as he watched her cross the room and kneel in front of him. The one night he would finally manage to crawl between the sheets with his bride and he was in no condition to make love to her!

'Well?' she asked, tucking her feet beneath her.

He smiled faintly at the bewitching sight before him and winced from the cut on his lip. 'I was attacked by a gang of thieves,' he explained and closed his eyes to rest.

'I do not believe you,' she declared tartly. 'In the first place, your clothes are not your own. In the second place, this is not the first time you have done this and – '

His eyes flew open. 'How the devil do you know that?' he growled.

'I am assuming that, as before, you were planning to stay out most of the night only something, or someone, prevented you.'

He grunted, impressed with her intelligence. Of all the bad luck, he'd married a hellion *and* a bluestocking.

'You have an active imagination,' he quipped. 'A few days ago, you were positive I had a mistress, now you are convinced I roam the streets.'

A faint blush touched her cheek. 'As to that, I will admit, I was in error. Aunt Henrietta told me you are finished with Jenny Carrington. And I now believe she was right.'

Alex sat bolt upright and grimaced in pain.

'The devil you say!' He was absolutely stunned. How could Henrietta know about Jenny? They certainly did not move in the same circles. It was true that he had not bothered to scan the society gossip pages, but neither would any respectable person.

'Devil take it!' he muttered under his breath as he dragged his hand through his hair. Jenny Carrington was the very last thing he wished to explain to Kara.

'While I may have misjudged you in that regard,' she went on to say, 'I was not mistaken about your nocturnal activities. You are up to something, my lord. And I should very much like to know what.'

He shot her a murderous glance. He felt like hell! If his ribs weren't broken they ought to be.

'It's late and I am very tired. Go to bed Kara,' he said brusquely.

Squaring her shoulders, she told him firmly, 'I will not. We had an agreement, my lord, do not try to renege.'

'You are a fine one to speak of agreements,' he gibed downing another helping of brandy. 'Or have you forgotten how you chased me to London?'

Her lips pursed with displeasure. 'I did nothing of the sort,' she imparted briskly.

'Ah, yes, it was the sightseeing, I remember now,' he muttered with sarcasm.

'You were telling me about tonight, my lord.'

He sighed. 'Very well, I had an altercation with an old friend. He and a few of his nasty associates decided to spar a few rounds. At least, I think it was him. Unfortunately,' he said gingerly checking for missing teeth, 'I need some more boxing practice at Jackson's.'

'He attacked you? Why? Whatever for? Alex, if you are in some sort of a fix, you must tell me everything,' she advised and settled more comfortably at his feet. Her blue eyes fairly sparkled with anticipation. 'I will help you, if I can. I am an excellent fighter and fiercely loyal.'

He shook his head and chuckled at the idea of his delicate little bride rescuing him from danger. 'I am sure you are all that and much more. But I can handle my own affairs.'

Arching a delicate brow she asked dryly, 'Is that so? Well, my lord, from the look of things, I'd say you need all the help you can get.'

He fixed her with a cool gaze. 'I am far too worn out to discuss this tonight,' he muttered and attempted to stand.

Her mouth twisted with displeasure. 'I've a feeling you are evading the issue,' she sighed, 'but you do look a sight.'

'Thank you,' he grumbled. 'Would it be too much to ask you to lend a hand?'

Putting her arm around him, she helped him to

bed. 'Well, one good thing came out of this evening.'

'And what was that?' he asked leaning heavily on her narrow shoulders.

Pulling back the bed linen she helped him recline, 'At least I know you have been honest with me. Whatever you've been doing, you obviously haven't been unfaithful.'

'Kara,' he muttered grimacing from the effort it took to lie down. 'It would have been a lot easier if you'd just taken my word for it.' He winced and shifted on the bed. 'And a good deal less painful.'

'Yes, well, I can see your point. Nonetheless, I am glad to know you are trustworthy.'

'Thank you so much,' he drawled out.

Kara glanced at his half clothed body and frowned. Faced with a rather awkward situation, she bit her lip and debated what to do. He could not sleep in his clothes. But she was too bashful to undress him.

On the other hand, he might not mind sleeping with his britches on. Perchance, he could remove them by himself. She decided to take his boots off. Dropping each boot on the floor she glanced at his face, he looked almost asleep. She went to pull the covers over him, but he stopped her.

He smiled at his adorable little vixen blushing profusely at the prospect of undressing her husband.

'Kara,' he said enjoying her discomfort immensely. 'I have no wish to sleep in these disgusting britches. I assure you,' he told her smoothly, 'you are perfectly safe. Under the current conditions, I do not think I am capable of much.'

Scowling at him, she hastily undid his britches. He almost laughed out loud, but bit back the urge. Yanking off the offending garment, she threw it on the floor and tossed the covers at him. He laughed and caught the blankets with one hand.

'Goodnight,' she barked and turned her back on his smug face.

His eyes swept over her provocative body silhouetted against the firelight. Once again, he felt a rising impulse to grab his adorable wife, drag her to bed and make mad passionate love to her. But he quelled the urge.

Blast! He was more annoyed than ever with those stupid idiots who had waylaid him. It would be a few days before he would be in any condition to take her to bed. That fact, however, did nothing to diminish his desire for her. Heaven knew, he wanted her now more than ever. And it caused him a good deal of physical discomfort. He couldn't remember the last time he'd been without a woman this long. What was more, he had taken a sound thrashing for nothing. Bouchard was still at large.

He closed his eyes and tried to ignore his aching body. Opening one eye, he glanced at his highly desirable wife. So close and yet so far away, he thought ruefully.

'Aren't you coming to bed?' he asked his voice harsh with emotion. 'Or do you intend to sleep standing up?'

Just thinking about his naked body lying beneath the sheets made her feel warm all over. 'I-in a few minutes,' she mumbled. 'I wouldn't want to disturb you.'

'It's a bit too late for that,' he said under his breath.

She swung around to face him. 'What?'

'Nothing.' He tucked his arm under his head and closed his eyes to sleep. 'You wouldn't understand.'

Oh, wouldn't I just, Kara thought with a sigh.

CHAPTER 11

The next morning Kara awoke to find her arms and legs intertwined with warm, hard flesh that was decidedly male. It was Alex!

His arm was wrapped tightly around her waist pinioning her against the taut length of him. Her heart tripped over itself for he looked as if he never wanted to let her go.

His chest rose and fell softly beneath her cheek. He was still sleeping, soundly, thank goodness. If he awoke to find her draped across his chest, she'd die, simply die, of humiliation. Gingerly, she lifted his imprisoning arm from around her waist and extricated herself from his blanketing warmth. She wondered who had discovered whom during the night. He'd not slept most of the night and it was several tense hours before she found sleep. Her last conscious recollection was having been glued to the edge of the bed, desperately trying to avoid any contact with his glorious nakedness.

Easing herself quietly from the bed she donned her wrap and gazed down at her sleeping husband.

His face looked appalling in the light of day. She *should* have sent for the physician last evening.

His jet black hair fell haphazardly across his forehead making him look almost boyish. Quelling the urge to run her fingers through his raven locks, her admiring gaze slid over his broad muscular chest and down to his narrow tapered hips barely covered by the blankets. She sighed with appreciation and reached out to tuck the blankets around his shoulders. He stirred in his sleep, throwing his arm across the cold empty bed in search of her.

Smiling to herself, she glanced at the bright light creeping through the curtains, and tore herself away from the fetching sight of her sleeping husband. If she was to visit Mr Briston this morning and return home undiscovered, she'd best hurry.

Kara was amazed, this detective work was remarkably easy. She was becoming quite adept at hailing hackneys. And sneaking out of the house was becoming an art. Her stomach was in knots, however, for in a very short time she'd arrive at St James's Palace. Finally, she'd learn the truth about her father's past.

Glancing out the back window, she noticed a mysteriously shrouded black carriage following her. A shiver ran up her spine for she'd seen that carriage once before. It was with Alex outside Madame Jourdan's establishment. In all of London, no two such ominous black carriages could exist. It could not be a coincidence. She was being followed. But why? And by whom?

As the hackney stopped at St James's Palace, Kara leaned out the window in search of the eerie looking black carriage. But it was nowhere in sight. Whoever it was must have turned off onto a side street.

Shrugging off her trepidation, she dismounted from the cab and paid the driver. Her meeting with that bizarre little Frenchman had her imagining all manner of ridiculous things!

Searching the area for her ignoble associate, she wondered if her initial opinion of poor Mr Briston might have been hasty. But as the portly, slovenly dressed man came into view, bumbling towards her, she knew she had been kind to regard him as merely coarse. She only hoped his powers of observation were better than his tailor.

'Milady,' he slobbered tipping his scruffy hat.

Kara inclined her head, instinctively taking a step backward. 'Good afternoon, Mr Briston. What have you discovered?'

'Well,' he said scratching his scruffy unshaven cheek. 'I found out a bit o' news. First, I'll 'ave me money if you please.'

'Oh yes, of course,' Kara said searching through her reticule. 'Here,' she said thrusting the funds into his grimy paws. He took time to count it before shoving it into his torn pantaloons pocket.

'Let me tell you, there is something fishy 'bout this whole thing,' he said as he began his tale, looking around in the most conspicuous manner. ''Tis true that Eden was killed in an accident in 1804 like you said, but so was the wife and child.'

Kara shook her head. 'That is not possible.' Her patience was wearing thin. '*I* am his daughter. My mother and I went to America when I was three years old.' Obviously, this was a complete waste of time. 'I would know if I were dead,' she snapped, clearly skeptical of this man's capabilities. Sighing, she thought she might at least get her money's worth. 'Pray continue with your explanation, Mr Briston.'

He shook his head, 'T'ain't no record o' no journey like you says to Boston. No record t'all of any Simpson mother and daughter. I checked thoroughly. No Eden neither. It's like I told you, you all died in th' carriage accident accordin' to the death certificates.'

Kara was seriously questioning the merit of ever employing this imbecile. It was obvious he had no idea what he was doing.

'That is ludicrous!' she said sharply. 'There must have been a record of a mother and a daughter traveling by ship to America. I have lived there for the last fifteen years. I know I am alive. And I know my mother did not perish in that accident.'

'Ah. But you were supposed to 'ave. That's me point,' he said with a toothy smile.

Agog, Kara stared at him. 'What are you saying?'

'I asks meself, why would someone go to the trouble of forging these documents? 'Cause I know y'are alive and I believes ya story.'

'How keen you are to deduce the obvious,' Kara muttered, rapidly growing weary of his pungent odor and inaccurate information.

'Well, the only people who coulda done the forgin' is someone in service to the Crown. So, I done a bit o' checking and your father worked for the war department, best as I can make out.'

Kara furrowed her brow. 'The war department?'

''Tweren't called that then, but it amounts to the same thing. He was, as you said, involved with them Frenchies. As best as I can tell, he done something dangerous and must 'ave needed to get you and your mother out of the country right quick.'

Kara bristled. 'What are you suggesting?' she asked defensively. 'That my father arranged a fake accident then had our death certificates forged and whisked his wife and child to America?'

'Well, no not exactly. It coulda been that he died in the accident an' someone else forged them documents. I'm not sure 'bout the details. 'Tis obvious that you and your mother survived. I am still workin' it out and o' course I 'ave more details to look into.'

Kara frowned thoroughly disappointed. 'This was not at all what I had expected,' she mumbled. 'Tell me Mr Briston, on what do you base this outlandish supposition?'

'Well, a bit of experience and the facts,' he remarked.

'I have paid you well. And so far, you have given me no facts, only conjecture,' she declared hotly.

'Now hold on a minute. 'Tis a fact that someone wanted, or may still want you dead. Don't you think that is worth your money?'

Remembering the words her mother had written, *The danger, in England, I pray is passed, it has been fifteen years*, Kara shivered. 'You think someone killed my father, then?' she asked timidly.

Mr Briston shrugged, 'Could be.'

Utterly dejected, Kara bit her lip. What did all this mean? 'Thank you for this information,' she muttered thoughtfully. 'I shall of course, be grateful for whatever else you may be able to ascertain.'

He nodded. 'Next week then?' he asked.

Still reeling from the wealth of information he had imparted, Kara slowly nodded her head in agreement. Tipping his worn hat, Mr Briston took his leave.

Wandering aimlessly through the crowded city streets, Kara's heart sank as the gravity of the information Mr Briston had disclosed began to sink in. What was the danger fifteen years ago that everyone kept referring to? Someone may have murdered her father, she thought with a shudder. But how? And why? And then she closed her eyes with revulsion. It was too gruesome to contemplate.

Perhaps, he too was living somewhere under a new identity? But that made little sense. He certainly would have contacted her mother.

It was quite disheartening to learn she was supposed to be dead. And legally was! But who had fixed the death certificates?

Suddenly, it hit her. She stopped in her tracks. What had her mother written? *I know she is in good hands, your hands. As Harry left me to you; so I now leave Karina.* Uncle Charles! Of course, it had to be. He had been involved with the same work as her father. And he was a duke. He must have connections to the Crown. Oh, yes, his grace could have easily arranged for the forged documents.

Well, Kara thought with a doleful sigh, she had no other choice. She must discuss her findings with Alex. She cringed just thinking of his reaction when he learned about the Runner. He was not going to like it.

Her active imagination wreaked havoc with her nerves. She could see it all now. He'd be furious when he learned that she'd crept out without an escort to clandestine meetings. Not to mention the salient fact that she'd broken her word to him. Heavens! she thought biting her lip, she was turning into the most dreadfully deceitful person, almost as bad as Uncle Charles.

But how upset could Alex be? After all, wasn't he the one who had promised to help her? He'd understand once she explained her need to discover the truth. Wouldn't he? She hoped so.

Regardless of his reaction, he was the only viable link to her father's past. At least, the only communicative link. And this time, she would not be put off. One way or another, she would get to the bottom of this quagmire.

Kara arrived back at the town house and was relieved to hear from Violet that his lordship had

265

not yet stirred from bed. Thankfully, her early exit had gone unnoticed.

Creeping into the darkened room, she tiptoed over to the side of the bed and leaned down. He looked so peaceful she hated to wake him. Softly, she whispered his name. He stirred restlessly and mumbled something unintelligible, but he did not wake.

Frowning, she reached out her hand and shook him by the shoulder, 'Alex, wake up.'

His eyes flew open and he looked startled until he focused on her face. And then he smiled. Reaching out he caressed her cheek with the back of his hand. 'You're a lovely sight to wake up to, my dear,' he said softly, his searing grin warming her heart.

Flushing, she lowered her lashes.

'What time is it?' he asked sleepily.

'Noonish.'

'Hell and damnation!' he growled, pushing himself up against the headboard, wincing at the pain. 'Why the devil didn't you wake me?' he asked leaning against the pillows with a groan.

Kara shrugged one delicate shoulder and tried not to stare at his bare muscular chest completely exposed in all its male glory. 'I-I thought you might need your rest,' she stammered nervously.

He smiled at her. 'Forgive me, my dear,' he said instantly contrite for his cross manner. 'That was thoughtful of you. I cannot remember when I last slept so well. Or for so long. Do you suppose you had anything to do with that?' he asked, his eyes gleaming wickedly.

Truth be told, he'd never slept with a woman. He always made a point of returning to his own bed after finding his pleasure. Somehow spending the night was too personal. But he was glad he'd slept with his wife. It felt right to lie beside her.

She bowed her head. 'I shouldn't think so,' she mumbled, nervously fidgeting with the blankets.

'Well, then,' he told her softly, his long, lean finger lifting her chin to look at him, 'you'd be wrong.'

Mesmerized by the warm affectionate glow shining in his hazel eyes, she searched his handsome, slightly marred face. Confide in him! Trust him! A voice inside her head urged.

'My lord,' she said wetting her lips. 'I wish to speak to you.'

Leaning forward he took her gently by the shoulders. 'Indeed,' he murmured, his eyes darkened with passion as he bent his head ever so slowly to kiss her lips.

His lips descended on hers in a soft, achingly tender caress and she was lost. Leaning into him, her lips trembled beneath his gentle persuasion and with a sigh, parted for his sweet invasion.

Unbidden doubts clouded her mind. He'd deceived her before. And last night was proof that he was keeping something from her. Dare she confide in him only to discover that he was not trustworthy? No. It was too great a risk. She was too close to uncovering the truth.

'My lord,' she said pushing away from him. She was amazed at how calm she sounded for she was trembling all over. 'We will be late for luncheon.'

Alex lifted his head. 'What?' he asked blankly. 'Oh yes, the lamentable luncheon.' He added with a frown. 'Is it that time already?' he asked dragging a tired hand through his raven hair.

'Yes, very nearly,' she mumbled stepping back from the bed.

Battling with the overwhelming urge to scream at him and demand a full explanation, she was finding it excruciatingly difficult to maintain her cool facade. In truth, she wanted him to dispel all her doubts and hold her in his arms.

'I wish you hadn't accepted that damned woman's invitation,' Alex grumbled with a painful yawn.

'It is not my fault that she cornered us,' she countered defensively. 'What could I say? You were dreadfully rude to her, Alex.'

He shrugged a careless shoulder. 'She hates me anyway.' Throwing back the covers, he swung his endless legs over the side of the bed.

Kara's eyes widened in shocked dismay. 'Oh!' she squeaked and abruptly turned her back.

He chuckled at her modesty and donned his burgundy satin brocade robe. Examining his disfigured visage in the mirror he frowned.

'I look worse than even I imagined. In fact, I look deuced awful! I only hope my nose is not broken,' he said testing the protrusion for movement. 'Well, my dear,' he said wiggling his molars. 'I do believe I have retained all my teeth, at least.'

Thoroughly depressed, Kara plopped down on the bed. As she reviewed her present untenable predicament, her shoulders slumped.

Alex caught her eye in the mirror and smiled. 'It's not as bad as it looks.'

'What? Oh yes,' she muttered. 'That is good news.' If only that were true! she thought ruefully.

After a solemn curricle ride the two arrived at Aunt Eugenia's stylish town house and were met by a decrepit-looking butler who showed them into the ornate drawing room.

Aunt Eugenia got to her feet and kissed Kara's cheek. 'Welcome, my dear.' She shot a disapproving glance in Alex's direction. 'What on earth happened to your face?' she muttered eyeing him with her quizzing glass.

'I ran into a door,' Alex said amicably.

'Humph, more like a jealous husband,' she clucked and threaded her arm through Kara's. 'Men, they are all alike. And none of them worth a good woman. It is the children that make marriage bearable, my dear. Remember that.'

'I shall try, Aunt,' Kara replied shooting a desperate look over her shoulder in Alex's direction.

He smiled mildly and, clasping his hands behind his back, meekly trailed behind the brittle old woman.

For the remainder of the intimate luncheon, Aunt Eugenia prattled endlessly, imparting juicy pieces of gossip about every member of the ton. Kara found, to her absolute delight, that all she need do to continue the one sided conversation was nod her head and emit the occasional grunt of interest.

Alex took no end of delight in tormenting his aunt by interjecting the odd inflammatory remark which set the old woman off in a tizzy and won a stern look from his wife.

By the time the lemon pudding was served, Kara was yawning from boredom and tired of forcing a smile to her weary lips. Clearing his throat rather loudly, Alex managed to interrupt Aunt Eugenia's diatribe on the deficiencies of London's chimney sweeps.

'I am afraid the hour grows late, Aunt. We really should be going,' he said getting to his feet and tossing the crisp white linen napkin on the table.

'Never say you are leaving! And so soon?' Aunt Eugenia asked. 'You haven't seen my art collection.'

'I am afraid we really must be on our way,' Alex replied firmly. 'Perhaps, next time.'

'Ah well, newly weds,' the old woman said with a note of resignation in her voice.

Kara's heart went out to the lonely, albeit obnoxious, woman. Her next remark, however, instantly cured Kara's sympathetic heart.

'I say, my dear,' Aunt Eugenia said quizzically, 'what were you doing at St James's Palace with that vulgar man this morning?'

Kara froze. Panic ripped through her. Deny it! A voice inside her head screamed amid the deafening sound of blood pounding in her ears.

'I-I beg your pardon?' she sputtered. 'I was not at St James's Palace.'

'Fustian! I am sure I saw you. I tried to get your attention, but then I noticed that disgusting little man and kept my distance. Who was he?' she asked, clearly horrified that a Dalton would consort with such a tawdry person.

Kara felt the color drain from her face. Of all the times to be noticed, and of all the people in London who might recognize her, why did it have to be Aunt Eugenia!

'I assure you,' Kara told the meddling old woman curtly, 'you are mistaken.'

Desperate to get out of this hot stuffy room and away from Aunt Eugenia's probing eyes, she added quickly, 'We really must be going. Thank you for your kind invitation.'

'Kind, pah!' Aunt Eugenia burst out, 'I just wanted to get another look at you.'

Alex slid his hand possessively around Kara's waist. He bowed to his aunt and politely bid her good afternoon. As soon as they were out of earshot, however, his hand closed around Kara's arm in a vice grip.

She flinched in pain. 'Please my lord. You will break my arm!' she cried.

'Nonsense,' he whispered in a low, deadly voice, 'it is your neck I am after.'

* * *

271

Safely ensconced in the privacy of the Dalton curricle, he said between his teeth, 'You deliberately broke your word to me.'

'Alex, I – '

'Be silent!' he thundered, fuming that the little baggage had duped him. Hell! That damned elusive Frenchman or even Bouchard himself, might have made their move at any time while she was out aimlessly wandering the streets of London. 'I was a fool to trust you would keep your word,' he growled.

'Alex!' Kara cried, desperate to explain, but he cut her off.

'We will discuss this at home. Believe me, I am most anxious to learn exactly who you were meeting at St James's Palace, my sweet,' he said acidly.

A large painful lump grew in Kara's throat. In one day, she had learned that she was legally dead and completely alienated her husband. What else could possibly go wrong?

Aunt Henrietta met the returning couple in the front hall with Violet close on her heels. 'Did you two enjoy your luncheon?' Aunt Henrietta chortled.

'Yes, it was . . . pleasant,' Kara muttered removing her bonnet.

'A pile of invitations arrived while you were gone, I took the liberty of – '

'Not now, mother,' Alex snapped.

Aunt Henrietta paled considerably. 'Oh,' she muttered, her pudgy fingers clutching the pearls around her neck.

Thankful for this reprieve, Kara tried to escape upstairs. But Alex's hated voice halted her. 'I would have a word with you, *my lady*, if you please,' he said tugging off his gloves.

Slowly, Kara turned around and descended the stairs. His hand closed none too gently around her arm and he propelled her toward the library. Aunt Henrietta gasped in dismay.

'Do you think he'll beat her, ma'am?' Violet asked aghast.

'Heavens no! Daltons do not beat their wives. They simply, er, reprimand them, for whatever reason,' her voice trailed off.

Rubbing her arm, Kara took a seat before the fire. She did not dare venture a glance in her husband's direction as he poured himself a stiff brandy and downed it.

'Well?' he snapped, slamming the crystal glass down on the silver tray.

'Well, what?' she asked, staring into the fire and clutching her knees with her ice-cold fingers.

'You made a promise to me. And you broke it. I expect an explanation and I expect it now,' he bit out.

Kara shuddered at the harshness of his voice. If he was trying to intimidate her, he was succeeding. Clearing her throat she assured him, 'It is not what you think.'

He slumped into the chair across from hers. 'You have no idea what I think,' he growled.

Kara swallowed, flexing her hands in her lap. 'I did not exactly break my word – '

273

Galled by her temerity, he countered harshly, 'That is not how I see it.'

'No,' she said licking her lips, 'I can see that,' I did not meet the Frenchman, if that is what you are concerned about.'

If that was what he was worried about? He was shaking just thinking of what might have happened to his tempestuous wife traipsing around London.

Struggling to control his temper, he got to his feet. 'I have had enough,' he said quietly, clearly controlling his rage as he paced the room. 'I am not a harsh man by nature. But you have driven me to the end of my tether.'

Kara nodded her head. 'I will explain everything if you promise not to shout at me.'

He leaned his elbow on the mantle. 'Very well,' he said with a deceptive calm. 'I am waiting to hear your explanation. And it had better be good,' he added with a contemptuous lift of his brows.

'Well,' she said taking a deep breath, 'everything started at Grantly. As you know, I discovered some things about Uncle Charles. More specifically, his relationship with my father. Naturally I was, well, curious. You see, I had no idea who the Daltons were. That is, until my mother died and the solicitors told me I was to come to England. So, I decided to, well, to, ah, investigate.' Seeing his ferocious scowl, she took a deep breath and rushed on, 'I was confident your father was hiding something from me and I was determined to know exactly what,' she hesitated, glancing at him beneath lowered lashes to see if he was still listening.

'Go on,' he barked. 'And try telling me something I don't already know,' he added with a chilling smile.

She swallowed. 'You already know that I listened at the door of his study and overheard you say that I had the right to know. I also heard Uncle Charles say something about my not knowing. Anyway, after you left I, ah, well, I fell upon some clues in the study.' Alex raised an eyebrow. 'I found a ledger that proved Uncle Charles had been supporting my mother and me, for the last fifteen years. I also found a letter from my mother. She spoke of her illness, the past relationship with your father and some danger in England. Even more disturbing was the allusion to revenge. Don't you see? I had to find out more. Why is Uncle Charles lying to me? I know my father was involved in France, you accidentally supplied that information, but Uncle Charles was less than cooperative. He would never knowingly impart any information to me. So, I had no choice but to use subversive methods.'

'Kara – '

She held up her hand a tacit command for silence. 'Oh, yes, I know, it is for my own good. But it isn't! If I am supposed to be dead, I think I have the right to know.'

Alex's eyes narrowed. 'What the devil are you getting at?' he demanded roughly.

Gathering all her courage, she announced, 'I hired a Bow Street Runner.' And braced herself for his reaction.

Alex shoved away from the mantle. 'You what?' he exploded, gawking at her in utter disbelief.

Kara grimaced. 'You promised not to shout,' she reminded him, recoiling from his ferocious scowl.

He was pacing again. 'That is the limit!' he roared. 'You went to Bow Street? You actually hired a Runner? Tell me you did not go alone,' he groaned.

Kara looked down at her lap.

He dragged his hand through his hair. 'You actually went to Bow Street? Without an escort? My wife. That tears it!'

'You use them often enough,' she tossed back tartly.

He turned on her. 'How the devil do you know that?' he asked. And then shook his head, 'No. Never mind. I don't want to hear it.' He rubbed his temples. 'Good grief, Kara, do you have any idea of the danger you were in? Whether you realize it or not Bow Street is not, I repeat *not*, where well bred ladies pass their time.'

'Yes, I-I noticed that,' she mumbled lamely.

'Is there more?' he thundered. 'What else have you done behind my back?'

Kara winced. 'You make it sound so horribly underhand. It was not precisely behind your back, well, at least, not intentionally.'

'Forgive me,' he countered with sarcasm, 'if I don't appreciate the difference.'

'If you weren't so difficult to reason with I should never have been forced to go to such drastic lengths,' she spat back.

'*I* am difficult!' he growled. 'What do you suppose you are? Docile? Obedient? On the contrary, you are the most obstinate woman I have ever met. Devil take it! It is most unseemly for you to disobey me.'

'I am sorry if I disobeyed another one of your ridiculous edicts, my lord,' she imparted coolly. 'I only wanted to find out about my family.'

'So you disregarded all common sense and decency? My "edicts", as you call them, are designed to protect you from your own bad judgement. Hell's teeth, you could have been hurt!'

'I realize that now. And I will be more cautious in the future. I only discovered the possible danger to my life this morning.'

Alex stared at her. 'What did you say?' he whispered in a low, deadly voice.

She squirmed on her seat and cleared her throat. 'The Bow Street Runner explained everything to me.'

'Everything?' he echoed with an audible gulp.

'Well, perhaps not everything,' she conceded. 'But I do know that I am supposed to be dead, my death certificate was forged and there is no record of my voyage to America. My father was working for the Crown at the time of his death. I know, or I have deduced, that it was Uncle Charles who helped my mother after my father was killed. If

277

he *was* actually killed in the carriage accident fifteen years ago. What I do not understand is why. But you do. Alex please tell me,' she implored.

Alex studied the outrageous little hoyden sitting before him for a long moment. Shaking his head, he sighed and fell into the chair across from hers. Lord, how he wished he'd never given his father his word!

'I do not know much more than you,' he prevaricated. 'My father did assist your mother after your father's death. And it is true that they worked together during the French Revolution.'

'What you do not know, you could easily discover,' she urged.

He shook his head. 'No, Kara. And neither will you. You will cease this foolishness immediately,' he told her, his voice harsh with command.

'But why?' Kara cried getting to her feet. 'You promised to help me – '

'You are a fine one to mention promises. No, Kara,' he told her sternly. 'You have learned all you need know. I am sorry. But it is too dangerous to pursue it any further.'

'That is absurd!' she snapped. 'I did not purposely break my promise or disobey you intentionally. I had already arranged the meeting prior to our discussion. I couldn't very well cancel my appointment after I'd gone to so much trouble to arrange it. I had to go. Furthermore,' she declared, lifting her chin, 'I am glad I did. I have every right to find out the truth. And I intend to continue my search, whether you like it or not. You go off all night long without so much as an apology, never mind an explanation. I am still not entirely convinced that you are not a brazen adulterer.'

He chose to ignore her comment about his being out all night, he had no intention of explaining his midnight jaunts.

'You,' he growled vaulting to his feet, 'will do as you are told. Or return to Grantly in the morning.'

She gaped up at him looming over her like an ominous giant. 'You cannot pack me off to the country every time we have a disagreement,' she panted hotly.

'True,' he drawled with icy mockery. 'You'd be permanently ensconced there, if that were the case. Nevertheless, you *will* obey me.'

'I will not!' she spat out, craning her neck to boldly meet his furious gaze.

'Good grief,' he breathed. 'You impertinent little chit! How dare you defy me?' he asked pulling her hard against him, crushing her breasts against a hard muscular wall of masculinity, she could feel his large, powerful legs pressing against her thighs.

And then his hands were in her hair holding her head captive as his open mouth came down on hers for a hard, punishing kiss. His hand splayed over her lower back, pressing her against the hard evidence of his desire. Instead of pulling away, her hands went around his neck. Despite her firm resolve to resist him, she kissed him back. Hungrily, desperately, passionately. She pressed her mouth against his, boldly dueling with his tongue as he ravished her willing, eager mouth. Breathless and gasping for air, she tasted, licked and bit at him while his impatient hands explored her burning flesh.

His hands slid over her shapely bottom, her soft hips, up her waist kneading her soft, womanly flesh. And then the warmth of his large hand covered her breast, caressing the soft mound until it peaked, one hard pebble pressing against his gyrating palm. She moaned and strained against him, her soft globe filling his hand completely. The pad of his thumb rubbed against her sensitive flesh while his tongue explored the soft recesses of her mouth. Plunging in and out. Over and over again, each time with ever increasing ardor.

Tearing his mouth away from hers, he whispered her name. It was an aching need. 'Kara . . . Kara.' He kissed her temple, her eyelid, her cheek, her nose and then finally, he took her wet swollen lips in a torrid kiss that was meant to inflame and excite. And it did.

'Oh, Alex,' she moaned threading her fingers through his thick dark hair as his open mouth slid across her cheek to kiss her jaw line, the back of her ear and then her sensitive neck. All the while his masterful hands clutched her round bottom, urging her hips firmly against his. Torturing her with the erotic rocking of his hips until she moved restlessly against him with a will of her own.

'*Alex*,' she cried breathlessly.

Her eyes fluttered open. Gazing into his dark hooded eyes laden with passion, she read the warm invitation written in his sultry gaze. Her body yearned almost painfully for his possession. Even if he didn't love her, for now, this was enough. Her heart was bursting with enough love for both of them.

Dazed with desire and on fire with need, she whispered breathlessly, 'Make love to me Alex, *please*.'

He leaned down and swept her up into his arms. 'This time, my love,' he said kissing the sensitive spot behind her ear as he strode toward the stairs, 'you deserve a bed.'

CHAPTER 12

Ignoring the scandalized gasps of his step-mother, Alex kissed Kara deeply and kicked open the door to their bedroom. As he set her feet down on the ground, she tore her mouth away from his.

'It is broad daylight,' she whispered, breathless with need as she tore at his clothing desperate to feel his magnificent naked body against hers.

'Mmmm,' he said kissing the enticing line of her neck, his impatient hands stripping her luscious little body until she was naked.

'The better to see you, my darling,' he teased capturing her mouth for another torrid kiss. 'You aren't going to turn missish on me again, are you?' he asked, his teeth nibbling on her earlobe.

Mewing with pleasure, she shook her head.

He smiled. 'Good. I'm afraid I'd embarrass myself if you did. I want you too much, my love, to resist your sweet temptation this time.' His hands slid down her waist to caress her round, soft hips. His thumb traced the sensitive hollows of her abdomen until she shuddered with delight.

Feverish with need, her unrestrained response drove him onward. As he rained kisses down her throat to the valley between her breasts, he felt exhilarated. She was so soft, so feminine and she smelled marvelous. Nothing had ever felt so right. He cupped her round supple breast with his palm and dipped his head to sample her luxurious bounty. She tasted like sweet nectar.

Moaning with pleasure, she arched her back and ran her hands through his raven hair clutching his head to her breast. Releasing the hard, rosy bud, he lifted his head and gazed at her delightful face, aglow with desire. Her navy blue eyes were over-flowing with emotion. Her tempting lips were moist and swollen from his ravenous kisses. And he knew he could never have enough of this woman.

She wriggled closer to his warm, strong body, her sensitive nipples rubbing against his hair-roughened chest. 'Oh . . . Alex. I – ' she whispered.

'Hush, my love,' he said, as he framed her face with his hands and devoured her mouth.

And then his hands were moving greedily over her voluptuous shape. Touching every inch of her, boldly exploring her winsome form, sliding his hand over her waist and then cupping her breast. While his other hand savored her soft, round hip kneading her satiny flesh. As he parted her thighs with his hand and stroked her moist tender flesh, she tried to move his hand away. But he would not be deterred.

'Open for me, my love,' he whispered against her mouth.

She relaxed her thighs and his fingers found her soft sensitive spot, tortuously probing her damp softness.

'Alex! Oh . . . Alex,' she moaned digging her nails into his shoulders as she clung to him for support. She had no idea what she wanted, she only knew his touch was driving her mad with pleasure.

He knew. And he wanted to make her ready and willing to accept him. He did not want to hurt her. But her uninhibited response was driving him over the edge of his tenuous control. Desire pulsed through his veins. He knew he must possess her completely. Or die with wanting. Slipping his arm beneath her knees, he carried her to the bed.

Tenderly, he placed her on the bed and leaned over her. Nudging her legs gently apart, he lay on top of her, blanketing her soft, warm body from head to toe. The feel of her soft, warm, incredibly feminine body beneath his was enough to drive him mad with need.

He must go slowly, he reminded himself as he struggled to hold on to the last semblance of control. But that proved virtually impossible for the knowledge that she was entirely and solely his had a heady effect on him. His hard member pushed against her silken sheath seeking entrance to heaven and he knew he was lost. He could wait no more.

With a groan of pleasure he eased himself into her incredible softness being careful not to hurt her more than he could help. She was instantly aware the moment he attained his objective. Her eyes widened and she gasped.

'My,' she said in a tiny voice of mystification, 'you are very . . . large.'

The feel of her soft, wet passage welcoming him was sweet rapture. And he could scarcely think straight.

'And you,' he said huskily, his warm breath tickling her cheek, 'are wonderfully small.' Drunk with desire, he was desperate to lose himself inside her. He covered her mouth with an intoxicating kiss that made her senses reel.

She felt so good. Her warm, moist channel felt like a second skin. He tried to hold himself still, giving her time to accustom herself to their union. But she squirmed beneath him in response to his awesome presence deep inside her.

'Kara, my love,' Alex whispered, his voice harsh with emotion, it was killing him to hold still, she was so tight and slick. With a groan of exquisite surrender, his mouth descended on hers and he kissed her ravenously giving in to his intense need. Slowly withdrawing and then sheathing himself inside her wet, welcoming warmth, each thrust took her closer to heaven.

Her passion was as potent as his which pleased him very much. She kissed him back with such fervor he found it difficult to move slowly. His heart swelled in his chest when she grasped his back clutching him to her, responding with wild abandon to his pleasuring thrusts. She wanted him as much as he wanted her.

'Oh . . . my love, my sweet love,' he groaned and quickened his strokes, driving into her only to withdraw again and plunge deeper. Over and over he loved her at a fevered pitch until they were both swept away by desire, mindless to everything but the joy of their sweet union.

She clung to him, her satin smooth arms wrapped tightly around him and curled her soft, silky legs around his hips, drawing him deeper still. Undulating wildly beneath him, she met his deep strokes with equal hunger, her hips moving almost frantically against his as he took her to undreamed of heights. As he climaxed, pouring his seed into her womb, she strained against him beautifully.

Out of breath and exhausted from their lovemaking, he collapsed on top of her. He felt wonderfully heavy and damp with sweat. The bliss of their union consumed her, and her eyes fluttered shut.

As he turned his face, and whispered her name against her cheek with aching tenderness, a profession of love was on the tip of her tongue. But she bit back the words and kissed him deeply instead. She would wait to hear those words from him first.

Slowly, she descended back to reality from the earth shattering experience. She could feel his heart beating vigorously against hers. And she knew she loved him, completely and without reservation. Their physical union was merely the beautiful confirmation of what she already knew in her heart. It was her fervent hope that he returned some measure of what she felt.

He must care something for her. No one could fake being swept away by their emotions as he had been. Their lovemaking must have affected him in some small way. How he could display such passion without love?

It took several moments for him to catch his breath and collect himself. He lay limply on top of her with his face buried against the side of her neck. Turning his head, he opened his eyes and looked at her.

In the afterglow of their lovemaking, she looked radiant. Her blue eyes sparkled with emotion. Her lips were still moist from his ardent kisses. And her dark, silky hair fanned voluminously on the pillow. She had pleased him so much; he felt his heart might burst with the torrent of these newly discovered emotions.

He pushed up on his elbows and leaned over her. He smiled faintly and brushed her lips with a light kiss.

'Did it hurt you, my love?' he asked in a raw whisper.

She wrinkled up her nose. 'At first.'

'It will get better with time,' he assured her with a grin. Threading his fingers through her silky hair, he kissed her with aching tenderness. 'And we shall have lots of practice, you and I,' he whispered against her mouth.

With an expression of wonderment at the beauty of what they had shared, she reached up and gently caressed his cheek with her palm. His heart turned over and he smiled. Kissing her palm, he placed it around his neck and leaned down to kiss her, lingering over her soft, sweet lips.

He was intensely gratified that their coupling had stirred her as much as him. He'd never experienced such fulfilment before in his life. Making love to Kara was sheer ecstasy. No. It was more than that, much more.

Realizing they were still intimately joined and his weight must be crushing her, he reluctantly withdrew and rolled onto his back. He pulled her into his arms. Cradling her against his chest, he kissed the top of her head and locked his strong arms about her. He never wanted to let her go.

Lazily tracing his fingers along her soft curved back, he reflected on what had just transpired, or more precisely, the impact it was having on him. He'd had sexual liaisons before, but he had never lost complete control. Never. Not like this. It had never been this good. This special. This intense. He'd given as freely and fully as he'd received.

Suddenly, he knew what the difference was, he had never made love before. But he had unquestionably made love to Kara. He had cherished every inch of her. And was completely overwhelmed by his emotions.

Had the little imp who drove him to distraction captured his heart? For some inexplicable reason that worried him. He had never given his heart to anyone. He was not sure the concept was all that appealing. It would make him vulnerable. And that scared him. He'd learned at an early age to be independent. Needing someone the way he needed Kara only led to pain and disappointment.

Perhaps, he was making too much of their coupling. After all, he'd wanted her more than any other woman in his entire life. It stood to reason that the culmination of months of longing would be incredibly sweet.

One thing nagged at him, however. He kept calling her his love. He'd never used that endearment before in his life. And he couldn't think why he should insist upon it now. It just felt right somehow.

Kara moved closer to the soft warmth. Something was tickling her face. Opening her eyes, she realized that she was sleeping in Alex's arms. And the hair on his chest was tickling her nose. Their legs and arms were intertwined like ivy on a tree. She did not want Violet to discover her strewn across her husband's naked chest. It was bad enough that they'd disappeared for the entire afternoon. She tried to ease away from him, but he tightened his arms and stirred in his sleep.

Smiling to herself, she marveled at the feel of his strong arms about her. It was wonderful to be held like this, she thought with a blissful sigh. She was in a glorious mood. It was indisputable, he had made love to her. And it had been wonderful! It was so much more than that. It was incredibly beautiful. He may not love her completely yet, but he needed her tremendously, and her heart was bursting with more than enough love for both of them. Perhaps it took longer for men to admit their feelings. But no matter, she was patient.

She blushed recalling their passionate lovemaking. His need for her was intense. He definitely had strong feelings for her which was a very good sign, deep and abiding love could not be far behind, could it?

Her fingers stroked his chest, absentmindedly tracing circles around the nipple hidden beneath the mass of black hair. Alex grabbed hold of her hand and stilled its movements.

'Is his lordship ticklish?' she teased and lifted her head to see if he was fully awake. Her breath caught in her throat for his dark, piercing eyes were smoldering with passion. His hand slid behind her mass of curls and grasped her head. Drawing her head back, he gazed deeply into her beautiful blue eyes brimming with love. He felt his chest tighten almost painfully. And knew he wanted her again.

'Oh, Kara, my love,' he whispered against her mouth as he rolled her onto her back and pressed her down on the mattress. And then he kissed her with all the savage, unbridled passion he felt inside.

With a blissful sigh, her arms slid around his marvelously broad back and she returned the kiss. His hard, fiery, demanding kisses ignited her passion. And she ached for him to be deep inside her.

Sliding his arms around her, he buried his face in her hair, 'No ill effects from our lovemaking, I hope?'

Blushing profusely, she shook her head. He squeezed her tightly and smiled to himself. She belonged to him. And he liked that very much. It was a new experience for him, one he was more comfortable with than he ever would have dreamed.

'Good,' he mumbled kissing her neck as his hand slid up her thigh to find her soft petals dripping with honeyed nectar.

She was more than ready for him. He lifted her knees and positioned himself at her warm, moist threshold and with one powerful surge, he buried himself inside her. Her eyes fluttered shut and her lips parted slightly with a moan of pleasure as he moved within her, taking her to heaven with the excruciatingly pleasant rhythm of his lovemaking.

She was vaguely aware through the sensual haze that he was breathlessly uttering her name, kissing her face, her neck and her mouth while he worked his magic deep inside her. Bringing her to untold heights of pleasure, again and again. And then at long last, his strokes turned hard and fast, creating a burgeoning ache deep inside her. And she knew he was no longer the maestro, but equally swept away by his emotions. Over and over he drove into her until finally, he shuddered and joined her at the peak of ecstasy.

Kara lay still beneath him, gently stroking his back, thrilled by the feel of him intimately joined to her. After a moment, he turned his face to look at her. Lovingly, she brushed his damp, raven hair away from his face and smiled.

He moved off her. Lying on his back he tried to catch his labored breath. She turned her head to look at her magnificent husband in his naked glory. His arm was resting across his forehead and he seemed occupied by his thoughts. Much to her surprise he was frowning. Hadn't she pleased him?

'What are you thinking about?' she asked, tentatively.

Startled by her question, he turned to look at her. Did she love him? He wondered. He'd dismissed the first time he'd taken her as an aberration. But after the second time, he knew it was not. If possible, it was even better than the first time. It was an earth shattering experience. If she had any inkling of how she moved him she did not show it.

Reaching out his hand he brushed a wisp of hair from her cheek. 'I was thinking about you.'

'And do I make you frown?' she asked timidly, all the love in the world shining in her vivid blue eyes.

The raw emotion on her face made him uncomfortable. It would be so easy to be drawn into loving her more deeply than he ever thought possible. Hell, he was already half in love with her. But he resisted the sentiment. He had to keep his mind on the Bouchard case, he could not allow his feelings to muddle his judgement. As it was, he was having difficultly concentrating on anything for more than a few moments.

He forced a smile to his lips and caressed her cheek with his palm.

'Sometimes,' he told her teasingly, 'you drive me to distraction with your headstrong ways.'

'I rather like this sort of distraction,' she said with a gurgle of laughter as she snuggled under the covers.

He arched a sultry brow. 'Do you indeed?' he asked reaching for her. 'And will you obey me now, little imp?' he asked rolling her onto her back, 'Or do I need to send you packing?' he asked framing her head between his hands and gently kissing her face.

She wrapped her arms around him, and pulled him closer. 'I might require a bit more persuading,' she whispered wickedly.

He laughed and pushed her back against the pillows. Threading his fingers through hers, he pinioned her arms above her head, 'You'll find I'm very a persuasive opponent,' he said as his hips slowly moved against hers.

Her eyes turned limpid with desire. 'I'm counting on it,' she said with a sigh as he entered her.

As the darkened carriage made its way toward the King's Theater, Alex gathered his wife in his arms.

'Kara, my love?' he asked against her hair, 'do you remember our discussion the other day?'

Smiling, she snuggled closer. 'How could I forget?' she asked in a dreamy voice.

His arms tightened around her and his lips brushed against her temple. 'Promise me, you will not continue with your investigating. Leave it to me,' he told her firmly.

She shook her head and pulled away. 'Alex, please don't make me promise.'

'I swear to you,' he said brushing her cheek with the back of his knuckles, 'as soon as this whole mess is cleared up, I'll tell you everything you wish to know. Just be patient.'

She bit her lip and turned her face away. Be patient! She'd been more than patient and still she knew nothing tangible about her father.

He turned her face back to him and gazed deeply into her worried blue eyes, 'Trust me in this one thing.'

When he looked at her with his heart in his eyes, she was helpless to resist him. She was too in love with him.

'Oh, all right,' she sighed, 'but only if you promise the whole truth. No omissions or deletions.'

He smiled and kissed the tip of her nose. 'Agreed,' he murmured as his mouth found hers.

The throng of carriages outside the King's Theater proclaimed the crowd in the lobby, and it took some time for Alex and Kara to weave their way to the Dalton private box.

As Kara gazed around her at the glamorously adorned men and women, her excitement spiraled.

'Now I know why your step-mother loves coming here. All the finery is magnificent! And the performance has not even begun yet,' she said reaching for her husband's hand. He smiled and kissed her cheek.

Her wide eyed enthusiasm for the lavishly decorated theater was contagious. Leaning back, he placed his arm around the back of her red velvet chair and admired his lovely wife. She looked beautiful this evening. Her rich, dark hair softly curled around her cheeks and the nape of her neck. His eyes wandered down the delicate line of her neck to the soft rise and fall of her supple breasts.

Tugging at his collar, he sincerely hoped tonight's performance was going to be short for he was planning a much more intimate performance of his own later on. Over the past four days, it seemed like he'd spent more time in bed than during his entire lifetime. And they had been the best four days of his life.

As the lights dimmed and the curtain rose, Kara felt her husband's hand slide over hers and squeeze affectionately. She smiled at him, the love shining in her blue eyes tugging at his heart. Raising her hand to his lips he pressed a kiss in her palm.

During the performance, his enchanted gaze never left her face. As the lights rose for the intermission and they made their way to the refreshments, Kara was tempted to ask if he even knew the name of the opera, or if he had watched any of the performance on stage. But she thought better of teasing her poor smitten husband and graciously accepted the glass of champagne he offered her instead. The thrill of being adored was going straight to her head.

'I do believe all of London has turned out this evening. I have never seen such a crush,' he commented surveying the large crowd gathered to enjoy their refreshments and discuss the performance.

Lifting the champagne flute to his lips, his face froze,

'Damn!' he bit out under his breath.

'Alex?' Kara asked furrowing her brow at his surly expression. 'What – '

Her inquiry died in her throat as his arm closed painfully over hers and he yanked her about face.

Startled, she searched her husband's furious scowl.

'Is something wrong?' she asked frowning in confusion. Glancing over her shoulder, her eyes searched the crowd to see who, or what, had caused his violent reaction. It was a woman. And she was making her way toward them. 'Why, if it isn't the Marquis of Overfield,' the tall skinny blonde purred in a husky seductive voice.

Alex inclined his head stiffly, a muscle in his cheek throbbing wildly.

'What, no warm reception?' the odious woman demanded. 'Aren't you going to introduce me to the little wife? After all, we were once such *dear* friends, Alex.'

'Who is this woman, Alex?' Kara asked, her guileless eyes searching his granite expression.

'Yes, Alex why don't you introduce us?' the pale faced blonde crooned. 'I am sure your wife would like to hear all about our little interlude.'

Kara glanced at the woman, a look of confusion on her face. The blonde woman smirked knowingly at Kara's artless expression.

'Come now, don't look so shocked,' she told Kara coolly. 'I cannot believe you are *that* naive. Perhaps we could compare notes?'

Whoever she was, she was obviously not a lady. The way she looked at Alex was as though . . . All at once, Kara knew.

Compare notes! She was one of Alex's paramours. He'd obviously shared her bed. And all the same beautiful, intimate experiences which should have been reserved for their lovemaking alone he'd committed with this horrid creature. He'd used this woman, just as he'd used Kara – for a moment's pleasure. And one day he'd discard Kara just as callously. Dear heavens, how many other women had he used as a momentary diversion and then coldly tossed aside?

'I must say,' the smirking blonde remarked, eyeing Kara with disdain. 'You are not at all his type – '

'Shut up,' Alex growled, clutching Kara's arm painfully.

Kara felt as though someone had hit her in the stomach. The room suddenly felt terribly stuffy and it was difficult to draw a breath. Yanking her hand free, she pushed through the crowd desperate to escape that woman's vicious laughter.

'Kara!' she heard Alex cry.

But she did not stop. She had no clear idea where she was going. She only knew she could not go back in there and face that disgusting woman.

Bursting through the theater doors, she took a deep breath of the cool night air and tried to quell her nausea. And then Alex was beside her, pulling her roughly around to face him.

'Let go of me,' she blazed furiously, struggling against his steel grip. But to no avail.

'For God's sake Kara, listen to me,' he beseeched, taking hold of her shoulders.

'Listen to you?' she breathed. 'You are cold and heartless. How could you just toss that girl aside after-after – '

'That girl,' he growled. 'Is a manipulative little bitch.'

She recoiled at his harsh words. 'How can you speak that way about someone you once – '

'Once what? Paid for? Yes, all right. I am not very proud of it, but there it is. She was my mistress. But I was through with her long before I met you. She meant nothing to me, darling. I swear it.'

Hot tears burned her eyes. 'I don't believe you! All those nights you went out you were with her.'

'No.' He snapped the word. 'That is not true.'

'Then where were you?' she demanded hotly.

'Kara, I cannot explain right now – '

'How convenient,' she sneered. 'I can't believe, you shared yourself with her. A virtual stranger, a woman by your own admission you don't even like.

How could you?' she choked out. 'You are despicable. I cannot bear the thought of you touching her, as you have touched me. It's . . . revolting.'

'I had no way of knowing that she'd be here. And I never thought this would happen. Someone must have put her up to it. Good grief Kara, I would never intentionally hurt you. You must believe that,' he implored giving her a hard shake.

'Oh yes, Kara, the stupid little innocent. So easy to manipulate, naive of the ways of the world she will believe anything you tell her!' she spat out. 'How stupid I was to believe in the warmth of your embrace and your torrid kisses. When all the time I was just his lordship's next conquest. Did it amuse you? I suppose you think I am such a romantic little fool that I would even believe that you actually might care for me!'

Reaching out, he tried to put his arms around her, but she shoved him away. 'Don't you dare touch me,' she hissed.

'Have you taken complete leave of your senses?' he growled under his breath.

'Keep your hands off me,' she snapped hotly.

'All right' he replied with a deep sigh, 'I won't touch you. But I don't fancy an audience either,' he said glancing over his shoulder at the interested spectators. 'Let's go home.'

Brushing the tears from her face, she sniffled and nodded her head. His hand pressed against the middle of her back, but she side stepped his gesture. 'I need no help from you,' she snarled.

Alex's jaw tightened and he dropped his hand to his side. Sighing with exasperation, he said with a cool smile, 'After you, my sweet.'

Storming ahead of him, she climbed into the Dalton carriage waiting at the curb. She purposely slammed the door in his face and was rewarded with a grumble of annoyance. It was a childish gesture, but at present, any way she could find to inconvenience his 'pigship' contented her tremendously.

All the way home, Alex tried to explain, but she refused to speak to him. And stared blankly out the window mentally damning his iniquitous soul to hell. He finally gave up. Sitting back, he leaned his head against the velvet squabs and closed his eyes.

He knew he'd hurt her deeply. And he wasn't quite sure what tack to take. She was being foolish of course, completely naive and childish. Jenny was nothing to him. He had not seen her in months. And had no plans to resume the liaison. Wasn't that more than most women could hope for? Of course it was. Most men frequented their mistresses before and *after* their wedding. It was their right. Somehow, though, that didn't make him feel any less wretched.

Tonight's encounter troubled him. No courtesan in her right mind would confront her past or present protector in public. Someone must have paid handsomely for the marquis's public humiliation. And he knew who.

The ride from the King's Theater allowed Kara time to think. Her hurt feelings subsided

300

somewhat and were quickly replaced by raw acrimony. The swine had a nerve! And to think she had entertained thoughts of being in love with him. She actually believed he'd changed his rakish ways. And that he loved her. He hadn't said it in so many words. But she felt it. Especially in those quiet intimate moments together when they'd made love. How could she be such a stupid fool? Obviously, their lovemaking meant nothing to him. How could it?

Hah! Changed by love, that's a joke. She meant nothing more to him than that awful woman at the theater. She almost felt sorry for his jilted mistress. Perhaps she too was foolish enough to believe he cared for her.

The carriage pulled up outside the town house and Alex offered to assist Kara from the carriage, but she yanked her arm free. Gathering her skirts, she stormed up the steps straight past Fowler's dismayed face into the library.

Charging over to the decanter on the table, she sloshed a large quantity of port into a glass and was downing a liberal quantity, when Alex opened the door. She turned around and fixed him with an icy stare.

'Do come in,' she said tartly.

Dismayed by the scene before him, Alex closed the door behind him. She *was* upset! His wife rarely drank, and he knew from experience, she could not hold her liquor. If she kept drinking like that she would be soused in no time.

He frowned. 'I think that will be enough port, my dear,' he said condescendingly as he slipped the empty glass from her unresisting fingers.

'Why?' she asked pointedly, 'would it be wrong? Unbecoming? Or dare I say it, immoral?'

'It would be in bad taste,' he affirmed softly.

'Ah, well, certainly cannot have that now can we? Tell me. I am ignorant on the subject. Just where does becoming tipsy rate on the list of social *faux pas*? Before, or after, having a mistress?' she dared to ask, the port giving her false courage.

He glared at her. By God, he was her husband, and did not need to give her an explanation for anything he did. He was showing her a great kindness having this conversation in the first place. 'You are absurd. I do not have a mistress,' he assured her briskly as he tugged off his gloves and placed them down on the table with a resounding slap.

'Do not hide behind semantics, my lord,' she spat, crossing the room to stand before the fireplace. 'That odious woman was your mistress. Perhaps as recently as last week.'

'So,' Alex said smiling slightly, 'that is what this hysteria is about. You still think I am seeing her? Well, you can rest easy on that account.'

Kara spun around. 'My word you are insufferable. Just imagine for one moment that I am not smitten with your vast array of charms as all the other women in the world appear to be, and perhaps that impenetrably thick skull of yours will comprehend my meaning.'

His jaw tightened as he told her in a steely tone, you are being exceedingly unreasonable.'

'Oh, am I? And just how would you feel, my lord, if I had a lover? Oh, you were very pleased, were you not, that your bride was untarnished, while you, on the other hand, brought a wealth of experience to our marriage bed.'

'You are being ridiculous,' he growled. 'I have told you that I have never broken my marriage vows. And still you persist with this childish diatribe.'

'Very well, since marriage apparently has caused you to become the epitome of propriety. How would you have felt tonight if Jenny had been Jimmy?'

His face darkened. 'I would have called the cad out,' he said in a dangerous snarl. 'The difference between our situations should be obvious even to you.'

'I am quite aware that by virtue of my sex, I must tolerate what you would find unacceptable,' she retorted sharply.

'Hell's teeth! You go too far, madam,' he gritted and closed the distance between them. 'Are you aware that other men keep their mistresses after they are married?' he asked roughly. 'They frequent brothels, gaming hells and a whole host of other ignoble places without discussing it with their wives? You madam, are a most fortunate woman.'

'I see. You would judge yourself against base men to diminish your shortcomings? Or do you perchance believe you have no faults? Are you beyond reproach now that you are a respectable married man?'

'I have one very great fault, my sweet,' he said in a dark chilling voice. 'It is at times like this that I am reminded of it.'

She should have held her tongue. It was unwise to bait him in his current mood. But he'd completely shattered her this evening. Nothing was going to soften her resolve to hate him for the rest of her days. 'Perhaps we have the same flaw in mind?' she offered coolly.

He took a step toward her, and she foolishly held her ground. 'My weakness is in granting you one ounce of understanding. I am far too permissive with you.'

'Permissive!' she gasped, craning her neck to meet his icy gaze. 'You must have confused me with one of your countless trollops, my lord.'

'That tears it, madam,' he roared, every muscle in his face tight with rage. 'I have heard just about enough from you for one evening.' He jerked her hard against his chest. In a pathetic effort to free herself, she pushed against his rock hard body with her palms. But he tightened his hold and pulled her harder against him.

She winced in pain. 'You are hurting me,' she whimpered.

His dark stormy eyes bored into hers. 'There is absolutely no comparison between you and Jenny. My association with her was utterly meaningless. Such arrangements are based on a mutually beneficial situation; convenience for the man and business for the woman. There is no similarity whatsoever to our marriage.'

Too hurt by his words to hold her tongue, she said icily, 'You are wrong. There is one similarity. You've shared both our beds.'

He gave her a gentle shake. 'You are my wife, Kara. We make love together, you and I,' he told her fiercely.

'Do we?' she asked her voice harsh with pain. 'I am convinced you are a heartless rogue, incapable of that emotion.'

He gave her a hard look and set her brusquely away from him.

'I wish to go to bed,' she told him coldly. '*Alone*.'

Inclining his head in mock civility, he bid her goodnight. 'Very well, madam, I shall go out,' he said with chilling detachment that cut her to the bone. In three angry strides, he crossed the room and slammed the door.

CHAPTER 13

Kara passed a restless, miserable night. By the time the first glimmer of sunshine was peeking through the drapes, her eyes were red and swollen from weeping. And she'd blown her nose until it was raw. To make matters worse, she was informed upon venturing downstairs that Alex had still not returned home. Try as she might, she could not help envisaging Alex wrapped in that horrid little blonde's bony arms.

Had she driven her husband away with her foolish jealousy? In the light of day, his past indiscretions seemed less important. After all, she knew when she married him that he was a notorious rake. Fidelity was all she could ask for in any marriage. Regardless of her husband's checkered past, she knew she could never stop loving him. It hurt terribly to realize he did not return the sentiment.

Had he in truth reformed his wicked ways? Or was he in the arms of another woman at this very moment? Thoroughly depressed, she retired to the morning room to sulk.

A knock sounded at the door and her heart leaped to her throat. 'Come in,' she said in a small voice.

The door opened and Fowler appeared. Her heart fell. 'My lady. Lord Rutherford is waiting in the library. I explained that his lordship is not at home. But he has pressing business and asked to wait.'

'We cannot very well leave our guest alone. I shall see him, show him in,' she replied.

What was Daniel doing here at this hour? she wondered as she pulled back the blinds and searched the busy streets for signs of her elusive husband.

Then it struck her, if Daniel was unable to speak to Alex he might impart the pressing news to her. And she might be able to learn something about her husband's nocturnal whereabouts.

She heard the door open behind her and whirled around.

'My lord,' she said smiling sweetly as she extended her hand to receive him. 'I am sorry to say my husband is . . . not at home. Is there something I can do for you?' she asked taking a seat on the settee.

'I hoped I might be able to speak to Alex,' Daniel said reclining beside her.

'What about?' she prodded.

Clearing his throat, Daniel shifted uneasily.

'Come now, my lord,' she said batting her eyelashes in what she hoped was an endearing manner. She'd never tried to flirt with a man before and she wasn't all that sure she was any good at it. But she was desperate to learn more about her husband's mysterious disappearances. 'I am not oblivious. It would appear that you are involved in this business as well.'

'Then Alex told you?' Daniel asked, astonished.

She inclined her head and smiled sweetly.

His shoulders relaxed and he sat back. 'I wondered when he might,' he said with a sly grin. 'Especially after that night at the ball and that damned Frenchman.'

So, the Frenchman was somehow involved. Was Alex pursuing the odd little man? Heavens! Was he the one who attacked Alex? Kara cleared her throat and set about extracting more details.

'I just cannot conceive why this man has proved so,' she searched for the most appropriate word, 'er, slippery?'

Daniel nodded his head. 'Bouchard is a slippery bas- er, sod. But Alex will persevere. When we find him, he will wish he had never been born. I can guarantee you that.'

Bouchard? Was that his name? 'Mmmm,' she said, trying to conceal her bewilderment. 'Alex is certainly aggressive, nothing stops him.' She knew from first hand experience, her husband was as resourceful as the devil. It had not taken him long to seduce her, and she chafed at the memory.

'Bouchard has been a thorn in Alex's side for too long. Believe me, Alex will be doing the world a favor.'

Good Lord! Her husband was preparing to murder this man! Was Alex capable of such a thing? Taking a hard swallow, she tried to conceal her horror.

Daniel glanced at her pale face and sat forward. 'Lady Dalton, have no fear,' he assured her patting her ice-cold hand. 'Alex has emerged the victor thus far. I am sure he will survive to a ripe old age,' he teased trying to lighten her mood.

Nevertheless, Kara was shaken. What did he mean, thus far? How long had Alex known the Frenchman? Who was this Bouchard? And what was the connection to her father? She had never imagined Alex would pursue the Frenchman, much less murder him. He had pretended to know nothing about the man. All the while he was planning murder. Why? What sort of a man was she married to? By heavens, he had a lot of nerve to speak to her of honesty and trust! The man was an unconscionable liar!

'I am sure you are right,' Kara said, quickly regaining her composure. It was a shame Daniel was not her spouse, he was infinitely easier to manipulate. 'There is no telling when Alex may return. And I hate to think of your wasting away your afternoon. Perhaps,' she said with a winning smile, 'you could impart this urgent message to me.'

Daniel frowned and shook his head.

'Of course, if you do not trust me – '

'It is not that,' Daniel hastened to assure her.

'What then?' she asked innocently. He shifted uncomfortably on the sofa and glanced at her sheepishly. 'Come now,' she cajoled, 'certainly, you can tell me. What greater trust is there than between a husband and his wife?'

As soon as the words had slipped off her tongue, she cringed internally. This was the most devious thing she had ever done; searching Uncle Charles's office paled in comparison.

If Alex weren't so obtuse she would not have to resort to deception. Whether or not her husband was indeed a cold-blooded killer, was a rather salient point. It made him decidedly less appealing. Furthermore, she was curious about this Bouchard character. This involved her father, and she had a right to know what the devil was going on.

Daniel let out a heavy sigh, 'Alex will not like this,' he said shaking his head, 'you know how protective he is about you.'

Kara blinked. She did? He was? 'Oh, y-yes,' she agreed. 'Silly isn't it? The way he goes on, you would think I was a mere child,' she laughed. 'But I assure you I can handle myself.'

Daniel smiled, 'Well, I can see no harm in it. After all, Alex has already shared details of his work with you, what difference can it make? And this way, I'll be in time for my meeting with Sir Gilbert.'

Kara furrowed her brow. Sir Gilbert? He is involved as well? Good gracious, who isn't?

'Oh yes, capital idea!' she readily agreed. 'You were saying?' she prodded and hoped she did not appear overly eager as she hung on his every word.

Daniel smiled indulgently at her. 'Yes, well the thing of it is, Bouchard was not among those bas- er, men who attacked Alex. It was as Alex suspected,

310

Bouchard has hired some vagrants to do his dirty work. I believe the Frenchman who accosted you is some pathetic Bonapartist who actually believes in Bouchard's empty promises. I am not clear why he approached you, however. Alex is working on his identity. Did he tell you if he found anything?'

Kara stared blankly at Daniel trying to assimilate the wealth of information he'd just imparted. If Bouchard was not the man who had approached her at the ball, then there were two Frenchmen. Lord, this was confusing!

'Kara, did Alex say if he'd found out his name?' Daniel asked pointedly.

'Hmmm? Oh, no. Just that he was still on the loose,' she hoped that she'd got her terminology correct.

'Damn. I think it is important to find out what that connection might be. Was the attack on you revenge, or an attempt to draw Alex in?'

Her heart stopped. 'Revenge?' she blurted out. Her mother's haunting words rang in her ears, *how can one cling to a vendetta for so long? I would not send Kara to you if I thought you would not forfeit your own life to save her*.

Daniel was too immersed with his own thoughts to notice her concern. 'It is hard to believe that someone could maintain a vendetta for fifteen years,' he said with a sigh as he raked his hand through his blond hair. 'But I suppose it is not beyond the realms of possibility.'

A sense of dread enveloped her as she asked in a small voice, 'Why would someone want to?'

Daniel shrugged. 'Well, your father was a great man. In the process of serving his country he acquired several enemies. Apparently, it was not enough to murder him. They obviously want more.'

Kara drew in her breath. There was no doubt about it, Briston's information was correct. Her father was definitely not living somewhere under an assumed name – he was dead. Murdered. The carriage mishap was no accident. Someone murdered him. It was one thing to suspect it, but quite another to have it confirmed conclusively.

Daniel frowned at her morose expression and quickly added, 'I did not mean to upset you. The country may be safer for you until all this nasty business is cleared up. I'll mention it to Alex, shall I?' he asked squeezing her hand.

Kara's stomach churned. 'S-so, you think this man is after me b-because he killed my father?' she asked with a painful swallow.

'It is a slim possibility. Truly,' he said with a consoling grin, 'nothing for you to fret about. You are in good hands. Believe me, Alex would never lose such a valuable possession,' he quipped in an attempt to lift her spirits.

Clinging to her composure, Kara got to her feet. She needed time to digest all that she'd just heard. 'I am sure he would not,' she replied stiffly.

Daniel quickly rose to his feet. 'Just let Alex know the other night was definitely an attempt on his life.

312

It would appear that Bouchard wants it to look like an accident. The rest can wait until later.'

Kara froze. 'An attempt on his life?' she whispered dully.

Daniel winced. 'It was nothing serious,' he assured her. 'Hazard of the job.'

Kara nodded her head bleakly and walked Daniel to the door. 'Alex is an excellent fighter and an even better marksman. Bravest man I ever met,' he told her in an effort to soothe her worried brow. 'You've absolutely nothing to fret about.'

She smiled wanly. 'But of course, you are right.'

Daniel kissed her hand and hastily took his leave.

Kara was still trying to sort out her troubled thoughts when Aunt Henrietta came clamoring down the stairs,

'Oh, my heavens,' she exclaimed pressing a scented handkerchief to her temple. 'I am quite undone. It isn't safe for decent people to roam the streets.'

Kara looked up and frowned. The very last person she wished to see right now was a clearly overset Aunt Henrietta. 'What are you on about?' Kara snapped.

Aunt Henrietta's eyes widened in horror. 'My dear girl, have you not seen the morning edition of *The Times*?' she asked flinging the paper in Kara's face.

Kara shook her head and snatched the paper from her overexcited aunt who looked ready to swoon.

'I shan't pass another night in this abominable town,' Aunt Henrietta cried clutching her brow. 'It is too much to bear. We simply must return to Grantly post haste, my dear. Wait until Charles hears of this.'

Ignoring her aunt's hysteria, Kara's eyes scanned the page and she read aloud, 'One of Fielding's Bow Street Runners, a Mr James Briston, was found dead this morning, his throat viciously cut.'

Aunt Henrietta cringed and screwed her eyes shut. 'Heavens! It is too shocking. A murder in our fair city!'

It was, according to the paper, one of the most heinous crimes on record in the city of London. And many reformers were calling for the establishment of a real police force. Kara dropped the paper. Her stomach lurched and she felt the room start to sway.

'My dear, are you all right?' Aunt Henrietta asked peering at Kara's ghostly, stricken face.

'Yes, I'm fine,' Kara muttered and sank down on the steps before she fell down.

'I should never have allowed you to read it,' Aunt Henrietta clucked shaking her curly head, 'your constitution is far too weak. Do you need some smelling salts, my dear?'

'No, I'll recover in a minute, it's just a shock, that's all,' Kara mumbled.

'Indeed, it is,' Aunt Henrietta exclaimed waving her handkerchief in the air and sailing toward the kitchen. 'I tell you, I shan't pass another night in this wretched town. The country is the only safe place.'

Kara's head was swimming. Last night. It said he was killed last night. Could this Bouchard be involved? Or . . . Alex? Shivers ran up her spine.

If Mr Briston was murdered because of her investigation then whoever was responsible must have wanted to prevent her from discovering the truth. Which meant that her life was in danger as well. If Daniel was correct, then the Frenchman was seeking revenge.

Clutching her throbbing forehead she closed her eyes. Oh, she thought with a moan, she wanted to go home. How she longed to return to her mundane Bostonian existence! What heaven it would be to forget this horrid little country and all these disturbing occurrences. She'd give anything to escape her insurmountable problems.

What did she have in England? Nothing. Her husband was not in love with her. For all she knew he might even be a murderer. And she had no doubt that he had a handy replacement for her waiting in the wings after she left.

Home. Yes, she wanted to go home. To forget Alex and that horrid little Frenchman. She wished she'd never started the damned investigation in the first place.

Boston was the best solution. It was the only solution. She'd been safe there for the last fifteen years. The problem was, she'd spent most of her money on poor Mr Briston. And she certainly could not get any funds from Alex, at least, not without arousing his suspicion.

How on earth was she going to get the blunt? she wondered chewing on her lip. She had nothing of value to her name. Except . . . her sapphires. She could sell them. They must be worth an absolute fortune.

Her heart sank. Could she actually bring herself to sell her wedding present? What choice did she have? She wasn't about to become this maniacal little Frenchman's victim. And Alex was not in love with her. After last night, he'd probably run straight into the arms of another woman.

'That was very stupid of you, killing that Runner,' Bouchard said as he stroked the black cat in his lap.

'*Mais, je suis* certain the girl would have learned something. And I could not have that,' Philippe replied with an indifferent shrug. 'What else could I do?'

'She would not even know about you if you had not pursued her. I warned you before, Dalton is no imbecile.'

'*Mais*, I grow impatient. When do I kill her?' Philippe asked slamming his fist on the table. '*Quand? Quand?*'

'If you cause me problems with *votre stupidité*!' Bouchard snarled, 'I will kill you myself.'

'But you promised me *ma vengeance*!'

'Have patience!' Bouchard growled. 'You will have your revenge. I too grow weary. Tired of living like this,' he gestured to indicate the decrepit surroundings. 'I think, I will use *la jeune fille* to bait

316

her devoted husband after all.' Throwing his head back he laughed out loud, '*Mais oui*, it is too delicious! The lovesick wag will fall right into our trap. What think you, Philippe?'

Philippe smiled, '*Oui, bien sûr*. It will be *trés facile*. And I will enjoy making her suffer. Her neck is smooth like satin – '

Bouchard waved his hand impatiently. 'Enough about the girl. For now we have more pressing matters to attend to. We must deal with our old friend, Billy Harper,' he said turning his attention to the old man who was cowering in the corner of the decrepit shack, 'We would both have had our revenge if he had not foiled our attempt, you know that of course, Billy?'

'I-I ain't to blame,' Billy cried. 'I gots him to come, like ya asked. I done my part, I did. How's I to know he'd bring his friends? It is his fault!' he declared frantically pointing at Philippe. 'He let him get 'way. 'Cause his lordship is smarter that's what!'

Twisting his moustache, Philippe asked, '*Voulez-vous* I kill him, *maintenant*?'

Bouchard nodded, 'You know what to do.'

'Oh no, guv you canno'. I done like ya told me!' Billy cried backing away from the encroaching Philippe.

'We cannot afford to have *les erreurs*,' Bouchard said popping a chocolate bon bon in his mouth 'You know too much, *mon ami*. And you have a *mauvais* habit of saying what you know to anyone who will pay.'

* * *

As the bell on the door of the small jewelry shop rang out, the short bald man behind the counter looked up. 'Good day, madam, may I help you?' he asked.

'Yes,' Kara replied clutching her reticule to her chest. 'I have some jewels to, er sell.'

The man reached out his hand and hesitantly, she opened her reticule. A pang of guilt ripped through her at the thought of selling her wedding present, but she quickly shook it off and handed the elderly shop owner the jewels.

Examining the sapphires, he shook his head.

'What is it?' she asked, becoming alarmed.

'I cannot offer what these are worth,' he replied with a sigh of regret.

'How much can you give me?' she asked, her heart fluttering wildly in her chest.

He regarded her suspiciously from beneath his wire rimmed spectacles, 'Why would you wish to sell such fine jewels?' he asked rubbing his chin thoughtfully.

'That is hardly your business, sir,' she muttered tartly. 'If you are not capable of handling my business,' she remarked, gathering the sapphires, 'I shall take it elsewhere.'

The jeweler put up his hand in an effort to appease her, 'I did not say that.'

'How much are you offering?' she asked sharply as she flung the enormous jewels down on the counter.

'Understand, I can only offer what the market will support.'

'If you could make your assessment,' she said coolly, her nerves in tatters.

'Jewels like these are rare. Not many can afford them,' he remarked holding the shimmering sapphire necklace up to the light.

She nodded feeling sick to her stomach. His final offer was an insult, but she could not take the time to travel to another jeweler.

'Do you have the cash on hand?' she asked anxiously.

'No, I will give you a promissory note and you can withdraw the amount from my bank.'

Kara closed her eyes in frustration. One more stop to make before she could board her ship and finally be rid of these annoying Brits.

'Fine,' she retorted, tapping her fingers impatiently on the counter while he filled out the draft. She snatched the note and hurried from the shop.

Unfortunately, the bank on King William Street was not within walking distance. And the streets were dreadfully crowded. The encroaching pedestrians all seemed a foot taller than her, making it difficult for her to hail a hackney.

She was certain, as she finally climbed into the back of a hackney that the gods were against her. Never before had she experienced such atrocious bad fortune. She would be glad to see the last of England.

As she reached the bank, her heart seemed to have lodged in her throat. Finally, after what seemed like an eternity, she approached the counter. The clerk counted out the sum and Kara nervously surveyed the bank.

She had no idea what she was looking for. No one could have missed her yet. It wasn't as if she hoped Alex would stop her and profess his undying love on bended knee. Stuffing the money in her reticule, she hurried from the bank. This time, she had wisely remembered to ask the hackney to wait.

'To the docks, East End, as quickly as you can please,' she cried.

The driver raised an eyebrow, 'East End? Are you sure miss?'

'I am,' she said shortly, her patience wearing thin. 'Can you take me, or shall I hail another cab?'

'Oh, no, miss. Anything you say, miss.'

Kara had never been in such a state. Closing her eyes, she rested her head against the black leather seat. Soon she thought, very soon this will all be over. Just a dreadful nightmare in her past.

Except for Alex. Whatever they had once shared, however, it wasn't enduring. That much was patently obvious. He was not in love with her. How she wished their rapport had lasted outside of the bedroom. He was such a kind, considerate lover. But a selfish brute of a husband.

If only he'd expressed a growing closeness toward her. Something. Anything. She'd have bared her soul and begged him to understand. Together they could have faced anything. But that was not to be. And she could not stay. It was too dangerous for herself and those around her.

Boston would not be so terrible. It had been her home as long as she could remember. She could find lodgings and get a job. She was adept with a needle, maybe she could work in a dress shop? Yes, indeed, her future looked very bright. Why then, was she mopping her wet cheeks with her sleeve?

After an interminably long ride through the congested city streets she arrived at the docks. Hastily paying the driver, she gathered her skirts and made her way to the shipping office.

The office door slammed shut behind her causing the mostly toothless occupants to stare at the well-dressed lady who had just entered. Glancing around, at the dingy little office and its offensive residents, she clutched her reticule tightly and approached the ticket window.

'I would like to purchase a one way passage to Boston, if you please.'

The man seated behind the window spat what appeared to be chewing tobacco on the floor and muttered, 'No ship till mornin'.'

Kara recoiled in disgust. 'That cannot be!' she cried. 'You do not understand, I must leave directly. As soon as possible!'

But the repellent man only shook his head. 'That's the best I got.'

Kara took a deep breath, why did everything have to be so incredibly difficult? 'Very well,' she said and digging through her reticule she retrieved the money and counted out the boat fare.

As she slid the money across the counter, a large, obviously male hand slammed down on the currency. Outraged, she was about to turn to wrestle her money from the obnoxious brute when she heard his voice, 'My wife,' he growled 'has changed her mind.'

A jolt of sheer terror ripped through her body. Alex! Thunderstruck, she was frozen to the spot.

Steely fingers closed over her wrist. Pathetic though it was, she lacked the courage to turn around and face him. Before she could open her mouth to speak, he jerked her around and dragged her from the small office, eliciting gales of laughter from the slovenly occupants in the tiny office and bawdy hoots of encouragement.

This was the most mortifying experience of her life which, by comparison to recent developments, was quite a feat. A gust of wind blew her bonnet off her head. She struggled against the giant Colossus to fetch it, but he yanked her arm forcing her to keep up with him.

She lost her precarious footing, 'Alex!' she cried toppling to the ground. His fingers dug into her flesh. He turned to look at her, his dark, stormy eyes brimming with rage.

She'd never experienced this side of the man who loomed above her. He looked ready to kill. And he probably was capable of murder, she reminded herself.

His nostrils flared and the pulse in his cheek throbbed wildly. 'Get up,' he ground out.

She gulped, her breath coming hard and fast. 'Alex – ' she entreated, her heart fluttering like a trapped bird's.

'Get to your feet, madam,' he growled, as he tugged roughly at her arm, 'or shall I drag you all the way to Upper Brook Street?'

She shook her head and managed to get to her feet, 'Alex please – ' she cried breathlessly. 'Ooof,' she gasped as she stumbled behind him striving to keep pace with his brisk gait.

By this time a veritable crowd had gathered to watch the embarrassing episode. Amused by the disgraceful spectacle, they cheered on her brutish husband.

Kara barely had time to catch her breath before Alex opened the carriage door and told her between clenched teeth, 'Get in'. Climbing in after her, he slammed the door.

Surprised her arm was still in its socket, she rubbed her sore wrist and glanced at his chiseled features which were rigid with anger. Trembling uncontrollably, tears of humiliated defeat trickled down her cheeks. She turned her face away from his apocalyptic scowl and buried her face in her hands.

As she began to sob in earnest. Alex uttered an oath under his breath. And snatched his white linen handkerchief from his pocket.

'Do you never carry a handkerchief?' he asked unkindly as he flung it in her direction. 'Considering how often you weep,' he muttered with irritation, 'you might think about investing in a few.'

'I-I am not weeping,' she sobbed into her palm. One hand reached out to retrieve his handkerchief and she blew her nose, noisily.

The carriage pulled up at 10 Upper Brook Street. Alex pushed open the carriage door and jumped down. Not bothering to assist his errant bride, he stormed up the steps.

Fowler bowed respectfully, and helped Kara, between her sniffles, to remove her dirty pelisse. His eyes ran disdainfully over her ladyship's disheveled appearance, but he made no comment.

Alex barreled down the hall and slammed the library door. Nervously wringing her hands, Kara slowly walked to the library. As she opened the door and ventured into his private sanctuary, she saw that he stood poised with his hands in his pockets, obviously attempting to rein in his temper.

Gaining any semblance of control over his emotions was proving exceedingly difficult, however. Devil take it! The little baggage had tried to leave him! He felt like a damned fool. He was certain she was in love with him. And yet, given the first opportunity, she'd run off. How could he have been so wrong about her devotion?

Perhaps, he wasn't. A dull ache settled in his chest. What if the vulgar encounter with Jenny had altered her feelings for him. Permanently. What would he do then? He couldn't bear to lose her love. Although he'd done precious little to keep it. His face was harsh with self-recrimination and rage as he watched her slink into the room.

Creeping over to the nearest chair, she slid into it. As the clock on the mantel underscored the charged minutes passing by, the silence between them became unbearable. She could feel Alex's contemptuous gaze rake over her. Gathering her courage she opened her mouth to speak.

He shot her a venomous look which effectively silenced her. Marching across the room to the drinks table, he poured himself a glass of claret. He gulped it down and smashed the glass down on the tray.

'I realize you are angry with me,' she croaked, glancing at him beneath half closed lashes.

He stood there, ominously tall and angry. 'You have no idea,' he said through clenched teeth.

She took a hard swallow and twisted his now wet hankie through her fingers 'H-how did you find me?' she ventured to ask.

'Henrietta told me you'd gone out,' he retorted sharply. 'And we both know you gave your word to me not to leave the house without an escort,' he added viciously. 'But thankfully, I took the liberty of having the house shadowed.'

'You what?' she screeched jumping to her feet. 'You mean, all this time, after everything we've shared, you never trusted me?'

He chuckled nastily. 'Not a chance. I know you too well, my sweet. It's lucky for me that I didn't trust you,' he muttered unkindly.

'Well,' she said dropping into the chair.

His features contorted with rage. 'You little fool,' he growled. 'What the devil were you about? If you intend to run away after every marital squabble, you'll find yourself living permanently in the country. I haven't the patience for women who fly up in the boughs over the slightest thing. Nor do I intend to allow you to leave me. Ever. Like it or not, you are my wife. I will not tolerate such childish outbursts in the future.'

Her heart swelled with joy. She almost smiled at his fervent declaration. But then she remembered last night and her smile faded.

'I did not fly up into the boughs. And I am not being childish,' she said tartly. Lifting her chin, she met his frigid gaze, 'Last night was no small thing,' she reminded him coolly.

He had the good grace to lower his gaze. She smiled to herself at her minor victory. Apparently, his lordship was not feeling as confident as he appeared.

Alex massaged the taut muscles in the back of his neck. He'd been far too lenient with her from the start. That much was perfectly clear. He should have established his authority more firmly. But like a fool, he'd pitied her. He also desired her more completely than anything else in his life. The mere idea of losing her sent him over the edge. She, on the other hand, could not seem to get away from him fast enough!

'Damn you, Kara,' he lashed out. 'Is this your subtle way of letting me know you find me lacking as a husband?' he asked scathingly. 'A simple rebuke would have sufficed, I assure you.'

She opened her mouth to speak.

But he cut her off, 'What the devil were you going to do when you got to Boston?'

She dropped her eyes to her lap. 'I was planning to seek employment,' she stated meekly.

'Employment? And just what exactly are you qualified to do?' he asked with derision.

'Many things,' she retorted hotly, pricked by his tone.

'And what, pray tell, was I supposed to do?' he asked sharply.

She looked up in surprise, 'Why, I-I imagined you would get an annulment and marry again.' You don't care a wit about me anyway, she thought. 'What difference could it possible make to you who warms your bed?'

'I have told you that divorce is out of the question. And,' he stressed each word succinctly, 'if you recall we consummated our marriage. An annulment would be impossible. Or have you perchance forgotten?'

The memory of their intimacy was clear and ever present in her mind. She had responded to his caresses with total abandon. Even now, she wished she could go to him and feel the warmth and security of his strong embrace.

'No,' she said weakly. 'I have not forgotten.'

'I cannot credit your feeble-mindedness. What if you are with child? Did you think about that?'

No, she hadn't. 'I would have managed.' she replied in a bare whisper. 'It is none of your concern.'

'None of my concern!' he echoed, incredulous. 'It is very much my concern!'

'It can hardly be relevant at present, my lord,' she muttered stiffly, anxious to change the topic of conversation.

'I think it is extremely relevant,' he said obviously nettled. 'Forgive me, if I am not elated to discover that my wife would keep such knowledge from me.'

'I am not keeping anything from you!' she cried. 'It is you who are withholding things from me!'

'I suppose it is my fault for marrying a blasted child,' he muttered tersely.

'I am sorry I do not fulfil the image of your quintessential bride,' she said bitterly, 'If you recall, my lord, this marriage was not my idea. I was coerced, cajoled and finally seduced.'

'You did not seem to object to the latter too strenuously,' he countered coolly.

The color rushed to her cheeks and she lowered her lashes. 'I am well aware that I am trapped in a loveless marriage,' she said in a small voice. A painful lump formed in her throat and she blinked back the tears that threatened to fall.

He dug his hands into his pockets and angrily paced the room. 'Did you honestly believe I would stand by idly while my wife frolicked off to Boston?' he growled over his shoulder.

Her eyes widened in amazement. 'No. I – ' she began defensively.

He shook his head and dragged his hand through his hair. 'Did you think I was so besotted by you?'

She shook her head staring at him in surprise. Was he besotted by her? Lord, she hoped so. 'N-no I – '

But he cut her off again. 'And where the devil did you get the blunt?' he demanded furiously.

She opened her mouth to speak and then snapped it shut. If he was angry now, he'd really be furious when he learned the whole truth. 'If you had me followed by one of your nefarious cohorts,' she said, her voice dripping with insolence, 'you must know.'

He glared at her with burning, reproachful eyes. 'I didn't bother to wait for the entire report. Let me assure you, hearing that my wayward wife had made for the docks was more than enough to send me in hot pursuit. Now, answer me damn it!' he thundered.

Swallowing hard, she shifted on her seat and cleared her throat. 'Well, I um, I-I sold the sapphires,' she said blanching in the face of his furious scowl.

CHAPTER 14

Stunned by her outrageous announcement, Alex stared at Kara for a moment.

'You what?' he asked in a low, dangerous growl.

She feared his deadly calm, controlled tone far more than his raw fury. 'Alex, please let me explain,' she implored, 'I-I *can* explain.'

Fixing her with a cold, icy stare, he leaned back against the large mahogany desk and crossed his arms over his chest. 'I've no doubt you can,' he said in a sardonic tone. 'You might consider the truth, for once.'

Kara's head whipped around. 'That is amusing coming from you, my lord,' she said bitterly.

He closed the distance between them and leaned down, placing one arm on either side of her, effectively trapping her in the chair. Despite her resolve to be strong, she shrank back from his angry, dark scowl.

'Kara I am trying very hard,' he said tightly, 'to control my temper. Do not push me.'

Gulping, she tried to calm the furious beat of her heart. 'It was not my intention to – '

'Be caught?' he interjected maliciously.

Squeezing her eyes shut, she shook her head. 'I had to get away,' she insisted breathlessly. 'I thought that it would be the best for everyone concerned.'

'Very noble, my dear but I do not agree,' came his scathing retort.

'Under the circumstances, what did you – '

'And just what circumstances are those?' he asked caustically.

Utterly perplexed, she gawked at him. How long was he going to maintain this pretense? 'You know very well what circumstances,' she snapped irritably.

'I've already told you that woman meant nothing to me,' he snapped and resumed his predatory pacing. 'I cannot change the past, Kara. All I can offer is my fidelity in future. It was stupid and utterly juvenile to run away in a temper.'

'But I didn't run away because of that,' she told her lap. 'Not entirely.'

He whirled around to face her. 'Then why did you leave me?' he asked.

Her rakehell of a husband sounded like a meek little boy. And her heart skipped a beat.

'Don't you see? I was endangering everyone by staying.'

No, he did not see. 'What are you talking about?' he ground out.

'The Frenchman attacked you because of me.'

'The devil you say! Whatever gave you such a

bizarre idea? I never claimed any such thing,' he barked.

Liar, Kara thought, but she was not going to argue semantics with him at a time like this. 'And when I read about Mr Briston – '

He shook his head in confusion. 'Who the hell is Briston?' he interjected irritably.

She looked at him, aghast. 'You honestly don't know?'

He shook his head. 'Should I?'

'But I thought you . . .' she whispered to herself.

'I what?' he asked stonily.

Shaking her head, she mumbled, 'Nothing.'

'What did you think?' he asked his eyes narrowing with suspicion.

'Briston, the Runner I hired, was murdered,' she said quietly, 'last night.'

Alex's mind pieced everything together with lightning speed and accuracy. 'So,' he drawled, 'you thought I'd murdered him.' He pressed a finger to his chest for emphasis.

She winced and looked away. 'No, not exactly. But you could have been involved,' she offered lamely. It was such a ludicrous conclusion even she had difficulty grasping it.

'For someone who fears her husband you go to great lengths to test my temper.'

'I am not afraid of you.' She told that brazen lie without faltering.

'Well, you ought to be,' he blazed.

Kara's eyes met the force of his furious gaze. 'What are we going to do now?'

'*We* are not going to do anything. *You* are going to learn to behave. But we digress, I have been patiently waiting,' he said in a lethal voice, 'to hear what on earth you thought you were doing.'

Bowing her head, she nervously straightened the folds of her dusty gown as she told him in a horribly small voice, 'After my meeting with Lord Rutherford what else could I do – '

Alex's eyes widened with incredulity. 'You spoke to Daniel?' he growled, ready to wring his best friend's neck. 'What the devil did he say?'

'Enough.'

He gritted his teeth. 'How much, exactly, is enough?'

Kara drew in her breath. 'Let's just say, I put two and two together and realized that more than just my life was in danger. I had to get away. It was all too much to bear,' she choked out, her shoulders slumping.

'Tell me,' he asked crossing his arms over his chest, 'how long did it take your simple little mind to come up with the absurd conclusion to flee to Boston?'

Her head shot up, her eyes blazing with anger. 'How dare you ridicule me? This is all your fault!'

'My fault?' he burst out, utterly amazed. 'You left me as I recollect. Not the other way around.'

Jumping to her feet, she declared, 'If you had told me the truth from the beginning all this could have been avoided,' she insisted, throwing her head back and placing her hands on her narrow hips. 'Instead of deceiving me at every turn – '

Looming over her, he muttered savagely, 'You have a lot of nerve mentioning deceit madam.'

She lifted her chin a notch, unflinchingly meeting his icy stare, 'I have not always intentionally deceived you. If and when I withheld information it was due to your dictatorial nature. You, on the other hand, have lied and misled me from the first. You might have informed me about this Bouchard and the Frenchman.'

'Damn!' he exclaimed and dragged a hand through his hair. What *hadn't* Daniel told her? He was definitely going to throttle him the next time he saw him!

He rubbed the back of his neck and sighed. What was he going to do with her? His life had been utter chaos since they'd met.

Glancing at her, he was once again reminded how incredibly desirable she was. He could not reason effectively when all he wanted was to feel her soft skin against his. To tangle his hands in the thick curly masses of her hair and kiss her enticing rosebud mouth. Feel the delicate round plumpness of her breasts in his large probing hands. And to bury himself deep inside her. He mentally shook himself. The woman had just tried to leave him! She probably despised him.

'I suppose you think you are to be congratulated, my lord. After all, you have successfully retrieved your possession,' she told him, her voice dripping with sarcasm.

He spun around to face her, his dark eyes blazing. Her grit was commendable, but extremely foolhardy at the moment. 'Indeed I have. Lock, stock and barrel, my love. You are mine to do with as I please,' he told her coarsely.

She glared at him. 'So you keep reminding me,' she imparted coolly, insolently holding his gaze.

His angry gaze raked over her with contempt and he uttered a strangled oath. She was a fiery piece! Her temper rivaled his own. He was torn between the urge to take her upstairs and make passionate love to her, and the burning desire to turn her over his knee.

'My dear girl,' he said in a deadly voice, 'it may come as a surprise to you, but most wives do not gallivant all over London.'

'I was not gallivanting,' she retorted hotly.

He fixed her with a steely stare. 'As I was saying, when a gentleman's wife, specifically a marquis's wife,' he stressed, 'behaves like a veritable hoyden it is considered quite scandalous.'

'You are hardly in a position to lecture me on propriety,' she imparted briskly.

'Fine thing for you to say. I am still considering just how I am going to live down the rumors.'

'What rumors?'

'Where should I start? Hmmm?' he asked arching a mocking brow. 'The sapphires you pawned?'

She was acutely penitent about pawning the jewels, but to her chagrin, his lordship did not

seem in the least bit disturbed about their senti-
mental value, only the humiliation their discovery
might cause.

'I,' he remarked with derision, 'for one, am
looking forward to the next social occasion, when
the Dalton sapphires are noticed dangling on some
dowager's neck.'

'Well,' she sputtered, 'can't you get them back?'

His eyebrows shot up. 'You want them now, do
you? It won't be too much of a hardship for you to
wear them? Well then, by all means,' he sneered,
'Anything to please my devoted wife.'

'I only meant that if they will cause *you* anxiety
you should retrieve them,' she countered stiffly.

'I intend to. Unless some other gentleman, with
less of an ingrate for a wife, has already snatched
them up.'

Balling her hands into fists, she fixed him with a
chilling stare. 'I would have cherished those sapphires if they had been given to me in sincerity
rather than deposited at Grantly by your banker!'

'Solicitor,' he corrected coldly.

'What difference does it make?' she screeched at
him, teary eyed. 'Ooh! You are hateful!' she cried
and ran from the room.

Shaking his head, Alex released the air from
his lungs in an angry sigh and sat down. He
crossed his legs across the top of the desk and
leaned back.

Protecting Kara was turning out to be a most
laborious task, never mind attempting to control

her! Daniel was a blasted fool! What did he think he was doing telling Kara about Bouchard?

The door to the library swung open and Alex sat up quickly, half expecting another attack from his diminutive virago. He was surprised when he recognized the intruder as his father.

'Oh, it's you,' Alex said with a sigh of relief as he sat back.

'I say, that has the distinction of being the rudest salutation I have ever received,' the duke replied closing the door.

Alex smiled and sauntered over to the drinks table to pour himself a much needed glass of brandy. 'My apologies,' he said, motioning to his father to accept some libation. 'I was expecting my charming little urchin, not you,' he quipped, sarcastically.

'Ah, yes,' the duke said thoughtfully. 'I saw your wife, scurrying down the hall. She practically flew upstairs, seemed quite beside herself.'

'That would be her,' Alex muttered. He had no intention of discussing his marital squabble with his father. It was humiliating. 'I take it, you received my letter?' he asked, abruptly changing the subject.

'Yes,' the duke said and took a seat before the fire, 'I came as soon as I could. What the devil happened to your face?' he asked, furrowing his brow in concern.

'I came into contact with several large, angry fists.'

The duke frowned. 'I must say, the situation is exceedingly troublesome.'

Alex sat down across from his father. 'You could say that,' he concurred dryly.

'I have heard something of Kara's escapades from Henrietta. And I can see you have had your hands full,' his father said mirthfully. 'Did she really try to run away?'

'Mmmm,' Alex mumbled.

'Why in heaven's name? Kara seems like such a sensible girl, something must have driven her to such drastic measures.'

Alex shrugged. It was a terrible blow to his ego that his wife had tried to leave him. But to have to make up excuses for his father was beyond the pale.

'I don't know. I believe it has something to do with her father. I do not need to remind you that she is extremely resourceful. And deuced difficult when she wants to be. I have never met such a headstrong creature in all my life,' he muttered with a sigh of frustration.

The duke smiled, 'Yes, well, she is young. And of course, eager to learn all she can about her father. It is only natural.'

Alex leaned toward his father, his eyes cold. 'You are taking all of this very lightly.'

The duke shook his head. 'Not at all, that was not my meaning. It is, of course, an extremely serious situation. But Kara does have a valid point.'

'Valid point?' Alex bit out. 'May I remind you that it was your idea to keep her totally in the dark, not mine. Something about protecting her, and it being for her own good,' he snorted derisively.

'Yes, of course, I thought so then, and I still think so now, but I am not blind to the issues.'

Alex sat back. 'And precisely what issues would those be? I should warn you father, I am not in the mood for any more double talk. I am at my wit's end.'

'Yes,' the duke agreed, 'I can see that. Henrietta seems to feel that you perhaps have mistreated Kara and that is why she – '

'Mistreated her!' Alex exploded, jumping to his feet. 'Is that what Kara said?'

'Not exactly – ' The duke tried to explain, but Alex was too busy ranting and raving to listen.

The duke shook his head. 'Such passion, Alex, cannot be healthy for a person. You must learn to control yourself. And calm down, my boy.' His suggestion fell on deaf ears.

'I should have taken her over my knee weeks ago,' Alex grumbled as he stormed around the room, 'The woman is impossible! There is simply no reasoning with her. You have no idea what she has put me through.'

'I can well imagine,' his father replied struggling to hide his amused grin behind his hand.

Alex had always prided himself on his remarkable, iron clad self-control. 'Don't you dare look smug and amused at my expense,' he snapped. 'Allow me to remind you, this ridiculous arrangement was your brilliant idea. If I survive this blasted marriage it will be a miracle.'

339

'Calm yourself, Alex. Kara is very young. I am sure you will manage quite nicely once she settles down. It could be much worse, you know.'

'I cannot see how,' Alex gritted.

'Well, you could be saddled with an unattractive, undesirable – '

'I get your meaning,' Alex interrupted sharply. He was acutely aware of his wife's fair attributes. Slumping back down in the chair, he crossed his leg over his knee and leaned his aching head in his hand.

'Kara is so much like her mother,' the duke mused, 'I can tell you, had I not been married at the time – '

'I am well aware that my wife is a highly desirable, beautiful woman,' Alex said with irritation, 'now, can we get down to business?' he said tapping impatient fingers on his polished Hessian.

'By all means,' the duke replied, downing his drink in one gulp. 'What else have you discovered about this peculiar Frenchman you wrote to me about?'

'Not a blasted thing,' Alex growled with impatience. 'I am fairly certain he is a cohort of Bouchard. His appearance at the ball could have been a ruse to get to me through Kara.'

'Just the same, I am glad you saw fit to keep me informed. It could well be the madman who accosted Kara's father, Harry. Have you actually seen him?'

Alex shook his head, 'Never in broad daylight.'

'I don't suppose it would help,' the duke admitted, 'I never actually laid eyes on his father. The son was quite young at the time. Could it be?' he whispered thoughtfully and then he shook his head. 'No. It is too farfetched. Fifteen years is too long. I saw to it personally that the link between Kara and Eden remained tenuous, no one would make the connection.'

'Then as far as you are concerned there is no connection?' Alex pressed.

'I don't know,' the duke replied, with a shrug. 'I pray there is none for Kara's sake. In any event, if it is this Bouchard fellow trying to get at you through Kara that will prove sufficiently difficult.'

'That was my assumption as well,' Alex averred with a tired sigh. 'But my willful bride has proved a tad difficult.'

'Has the man tried to contact Kara subsequently?' the duke asked.

'Not to my knowledge.'

The duke frowned. 'What precisely does that mean?'

'Just what it sounds like,' Alex replied with a cool smile.

'I see,' his father muttered thoughtfully.

'There is something else, I have not told you.' Alex lowered his gaze to the floor, 'Kara hired a Runner.'

The duke's eyebrows shot up. 'Indeed?'

'Mmm, I told you she was inventive.'

'I never doubted her intellect,' the duke said with a smile.

Alex dismissed his father's admiration for Kara's headstrong tendencies with a frown. 'Evidently, he was found dead this morning.'

'Dead you say? Interesting,' the duke remarked tapping his chin in thought.

'I was wondering about the possible connection.'

'You mean between the Runner and Bouchard?' Alex nodded.

'Possibly,' the duke said. 'Murder is a dangerous business. If your friend Bouchard is working with this Frenchman, however, I sincerely doubt he would sanction random slaying. It is too dangerous.'

'Of course, Kara may be correct,' Alex said with a grimace, 'he could have been slain due to his investigation.'

'Let's not jump to ridiculous conclusions,' the duke rebuked, 'I would say that the poor fellow was probably investigating a case and rubbed someone up the wrong way, stuck his nose where it did not belong, that's all. These types are frequently getting in trouble for one thing or another. He might have owed money. Anything of the sort.'

'I had a feeling you would say that. But Kara is hell bent on the idea that there is a connection between the murder and her father.'

The duke shook his head. 'A cool head is what you need.'

Alex groaned. He knew what he needed. It had everything to do with Kara, but absolutely nothing to do with a cool head.

'Tell me, what have you done to make Kara so distraught?' his father asked.

Getting to his feet, Alex shoved his hands in his pockets and walked over to the fireplace. He placed his foot on the grate and gazed at the flickering flames.

'I wasn't aware you were overseeing my marriage. Isn't Henrietta enough?' he asked coolly.

The duke sighed. 'If you don't wish to discuss it, than just say so. I must say, I cannot abide the way you bristle about uncomfortable topics. All I'm asking is if you are quite certain Kara is happy? After all, you dragged her back here didn't you? How content can she be?'

Alex opened his mouth to issue a scathing retort when a knock sounded at the door, 'Come in,' he growled.

Fowler entered the room, 'Sir Gilbert, my lord.'

It was rare indeed to receive a visit from Sir Gilbert, especially at this hour. 'Very well, show him in,' Alex muttered. He was in the mood for an update on their dwindling investigation.

Sir Gilbert rushed into the room. 'Alex! Thank God you are home.'

Alex looked over at Fowler who stood obediently at the door, 'That will be all Fowler.'

Fowler bowed, 'As you wish my lord.'

'What has happened?' Alex demanded when they were alone.

'It's Daniel,' Sir Gilbert said, ominously.

The duke looked stricken, 'He isn't . . . dead, is he?'

'Very nearly, he was shot.' Alex poured Sir Gilbert a drink which he gratefully accepted. 'We are still not sure who it was. Apparently, he went down to the docks to investigate some old houses there and some blackguard shot him.'

The duke glanced at his son, 'What are you thinking?'

'I am not sure yet,' Alex said slowly. 'Where was this house?'

Sir Gilbert shrugged, 'I have not the slightest idea. Daniel passed out shortly after the doctor arrived. Nasty business that. Took him some time to dig the bullet out.'

Alex flinched. He'd been shot once or twice himself. The first time there had been no laudanum. He still broke out in a cold sweat when he recalled the agonizing pain.

'You are not planning to go down there yourself, Alex, are you?' the duke asked tentatively.

Alex shook his head, 'No, not this evening. I will wait until Daniel is conscious. I want to know more details before I go snooping about.' Alex glanced at the relieved faces of his two companions and smiled slightly. 'I may be hotheaded. But I am not a fool. If Bouchard is behind it, I want to be well prepared to face him. I am no good to his majesty dead.'

Sir Gilbert nodded, 'I agree. If Daniel does not pull through – '

'He'll make it,' Alex said confidently.

'In any event' Gilbert said with a sigh, 'I will send someone round first thing. Or before then if . . .

344

well, if there is any change. Otherwise, drop by to see him tomorrow morning. I must be off.'

Alex showed him to the door. Sir Gilbert shook the duke's hand, 'Good to see you Charles, I am only sorry it wasn't under better circumstances.'

The duke nodded his head. 'Never fear, if I know Rutherford, he'll survive. He is healthy as an ox.'

Sir Gilbert turned a concerned eye in Alex's direction. 'Whatever the outcome, this is not a personal vendetta. It is Crown business. For King and country, Alex, no matter what the cad has done. I don't want you losing your perspective.'

Alex bristled. 'You do not need to remind me of my duty, sir,' he said opening the front door.

Sir Gilbert hesitated momentarily, looking from father to son. 'I've seen him like this before. There is no reasoning with him Charles. See if you can keep him rational for at least the next few days.' With that, he descended the steps and climbed into his carriage.

When they were alone, the duke said to his son, 'He is right you know.'

Alex walked silently past his father.

The duke followed him down the hall, 'What are you planning to do?' he asked sharply.

'I am going to see Daniel,' Alex replied shrugging on his great coat.

'Don't be absurd,' the duke rebuked, 'Alex, he'll be unconscious for hours yet. Wait till the morning. Everything will be clearer then. There is no point in going now.'

'Are you suggesting that I let my friend die?' Alex asked with a snarl.

'I am not aware that there is anything you could do at the moment. You are not a doctor. He has had a physician. It is in God's hands now,' the duke said calmly. 'Unless you intend to take this matter into your own hands, which you promised Gilbert you would not.'

Alex scowled. The devil take Gilbert! Daniel was lying near death and Bouchard was responsible. 'If Daniel dies it will be my fault. Another name to add to the list of innocent people who perished at Bouchard's hands thanks to me.'

'Going after him now won't solve anything. You are not thinking straight. Overwrought like this – '

'How the hell should I be?' he snorted. 'I cannot live with another innocent man's death on my conscience.'

'You must stop blaming yourself for something that evil, sadistic Bouchard perpetrated years ago. If he had not manipulated you it would have been someone else. Those British men would have died regardless,' the duke insisted.

'But it was me. I gave him the information. I caused those deaths. If Daniel dies, it will be my fault as well.'

'How? Did you pull the trigger?'

'No. I did something even worse. I selfishly talked him into helping me with the case. He is one of the best and I needed his assistance to catch

Bouchard. It was my obsession that led to this,' Alex said fiercely.

'Alex, Daniel would be working on another case if not this one. He knew the dangers when he signed on.'

Alex shook his head. 'Why couldn't it have been me?'

The duke placed his hand on his son's shoulder. 'At times like this it is best to cleave to those we love. Find solace with your wife.'

Alex shook his head, 'No!'

'I have confidence in your judgement. I am sure you will come to the right decision. And if you go out that door in the state you're in, you won't be helping Daniel.'

Alex nodded his head and sighed. Kara! Always Kara! Hell's teeth! What an enigmatic creature she was! Why couldn't she be more like those women he met at ton functions . . . those incredibly vapid, stupid, outrageously dull women he could not abide? No. Thank heaven she was not a simpering idiot. He could not tolerate a clinging vine for a wife, but Kara went too far.

What a day! First his wife leaves him. And then his best friend gets shot. For the moment, however, there was not a damned thing he could do about either situation.

His father was right, Daniel would be asleep for hours yet. There was nothing to do but wait. Alex shrugged off his coat. He needed a drink.

CHAPTER 15

The following morning, Violet knocked once and opened the master's bedroom door. 'Mornin' milady,' she said bobbing up and down.

Kara emerged from beneath the blankets, stretching like a warm, contented kitten. And then the memory of yesterday's escapade came crashing down on her. She threw the covers over her head and groaned. For a moment she thought she might have dreamed the whole miserable affair. But she had only to glance at the cold, empty side of the bed to know it was all true.

'Is it a good morning, Violet?' Kara asked dolefully rising from her restless slumber.

'I am sure I donno, milady,' Violet muttered straightening the bed clothes. 'May I draw ya bath then milady?'

'Hmmm?' Kara asked distracted by her troubled thoughts. 'Oh yes, please do.'

'Just like his lordship this mornin', absent minded he was,' Violet commented.

Kara turned to look at Violet in surprise. 'Was he?' she asked softly.

'And in a fine temper, what with sleeping in the library 'n all.'

Kara was too surprised to do more than nod. So, he hadn't gone out after all. Her heart soared.

'What can he expect? Working like he does. A man needs a proper bed to sleep in. Beggin' y'pardon, milady.'

Stains of scarlet appeared on Kara's cheeks and she quickly looked away. 'Yes, indeed,' she mumbled.

'He barely touched his breakfast. Cook fixed it nice 'n' special fer him,' Violet remarked on a sigh. 'Just the way he likes.'

Kara smiled wanly. 'Yes, well, I expect he had other things on his mind.' Like arranging a trip to the country for his errant bride, she thought unhappily.

'Don't I know it. He tore out of 'ere in a hurry, he did.'

Kara furrowed her brow. 'Where did he go?'

'I'm sure I don' know, milady.'

'Was anything wrong?' Kara asked anxiously.

'He never tells me nothin' milady.'

Kara bit her lip. 'Very well, that will be all, Violet. Hurry with my bath, if you please.'

Kara wished she could somehow retrieve those blasted sapphires. Alex would probably never forgive her for selling them. Or for running away. And then of course, there was her ridiculous assumption that her husband was a dangerous killer. She sank down on the bed and buried her face in her hands.

Why did she have to be such an open book? He only had to look into her expressive eyes to know that she was deeply, madly in love with him. And he did not care a fig for her.

Violet hesitated at the threshold. 'I – I almost forgot, milady,' she said. Biting her lip, she turned from the door to face Kara. 'His lordship left a message for you,' she said, retrieving the crisp white parchment from her apron pocket.

'For me?' Kara echoed dully.

Violet nodded her head and shoved the note at Kara. She frowned in surprise and accepted the missive with a shaky hand.

The way she was feeling presently, she dearly hoped the note was not a divorce decree. She broke the Dalton seal and unfolded the heavy white paper. She had to re-read the note several times to be sure she had understood it correctly,

'*My darling, Kara,*' she read softly to herself. Well, at least that was a step in the right direction. He obviously wasn't shipping her off to Botany Bay.

'*I deeply regret our disagreement. And hope that you will accept my most humble apology. I propose a truce. More than that, my dearest, I wish to start over. Will you give this rakehell of a husband a second chance? If you can find it in your heart to forgive me, meet me at the address below. I realize this is short notice and sincerely hope you will not be terribly vexed with me. But I am impatient to see you and cannot wait to begin anew. Please come my sweet, as soon as you are able. All my love to you, Alex.*'

She read the note again and again. He loves me! She hugged the note to her heart. He loves me! She had never been so happy in her life. He'd pledged his undying devotion and she, in return, loved him more completely than she ever thought possible. The two were truly as one.

All this time. She had been waiting for a declaration of his feelings. Hoping that he might return her affections. And it had finally come. Naturally, she would have preferred it in person, but for now, the note would suffice. Everything was going to be all right! Today was the most splendid day of her life. It was the start of her future with Alex.

Kara was still humming merrily to herself, basking in the glory of her revelation when Aunt Henrietta met her in the front hallway barely an hour later.

'My dear, you look positively radiant.'

Kara smiled and tugged on her gloves, 'I feel radiant.'

'I am glad to hear it,' Aunt Henrietta chortled.

'Have the carriage brought round will you, Fowler?' Kara asked cheerfully.

Clearing his throat, Fowler tugged at his collar and glanced helplessly at the duchess. Then he walked uncertainly away.

'Where are you off to in such a hurry, my dear?' Aunt Henrietta inquired nervously.

'Alex has sent for me,' Kara exclaimed waving the note in the air.

Aunt Henrietta looked confused, 'But Alex left express instructions for you to remain at home,' she said wringing her hands anxiously, 'Y-yes, I-I am sure that Charles explained before he left for Hyde Park – '

Kara smiled and patted the agitated duchess's flushed cheek. 'It is all right. Believe me, I am not running off again,' she assured her as she hurried toward the door, 'I really must go, I don't want to keep him waiting.'

'I don't think you ought to – ' Aunt Henrietta insisted.

'I am sure we won't be long,' Kara said kindly. A little concern was natural given her flight of yesterday, but this was ridiculous. Prying her clothing loose from her aunt's pudgy fingers. Kara smiled at the poor woman's tortured face. Glancing at Fowler standing stiffly, beside the door, she realized he was entrenched on the duchess's side. Sighing with frustration she yanked open the door.

'Please, do not worry,' she tossed over her shoulder as she glided down the marble steps out into the bright sunshine.

Undaunted, Aunt Henrietta waddled after her, 'Kara wait, my dear please, wait! You must wait. Charles will be furious with me if you get into any more trouble. I gave my word.'

'Never mind that now, Aunt,' Kara called out as she settled in the carriage.

Gasping for air, Aunt Henrietta raced after Kara. 'Alex is with Lord Rutherford. I cannot imagine why he would have sent you a note to join him,' she cried breathlessly.

Kara smiled and shrugged her shoulders, 'Well, perhaps Daniel is going to be joining us.'

Mopping her moist brow with the back of her hand, Aunt Henrietta looked more doubtful than ever. 'But my dear that simply is not possible – '

'Then Alex will meet me by himself,' Kara cut in, becoming annoyed. 'Now, please, I really am going to be late.'

But Aunt Henrietta's round fat fingers clutched at the side of the black carriage. 'Oh, no, my dear, you must not go.'

Kara sighed. 'If you do not believe me, you may read this,' she snapped thrusting her most cherished note at her irritating aunt. 'Alex and I shall see you this evening,' Kara said stiffly and with that she signaled the carriage to be on its way.

She could still hear Aunt Henrietta calling to her as the conveyance turned the corner. The woman is nothing if not persistent, Kara thought with a laugh. She sighed and smiled to herself, bursting with joy at the thought that Alex loved her. And she was desperately in love with him. Nothing else in the world mattered.

As the carriage wound its way through the city streets, Kara was tossed back and forth on the seat. She'd asked the driver to hurry, but this was outrageous! Clutching the side of the carriage to keep from toppling onto the floor, she called to the driver to slow down. Apparently, her rigorous objections fell on deaf ears for when the carriage finally came to a halt, she was dislodged from her seat and landed in an indelicate heap on the floor. Mumbling to herself about the dreadful driving, she climbed back onto the seat, and straightened her gown.

She peered out the window. And frowned. This decrepit town house could not possibly be the spot her husband intended for a warm reunion. It looked completely deserted. Furthermore, the neighborhood looked distinctly questionable.

'This cannot be right!' she exclaimed, thoroughly annoyed. Not only was she thrown from her seat by this idiot driver, but now she would be late for her meeting with Alex. All because of an incompetent fool who clearly did not know his way around London.

She leaned out the window. 'Are you sure this is the right location?' she demanded. But the driver uttered no reply.

'I said,' she shouted in a louder, more irritated tone, 'are you certain this is the proper address?' And still, the driver remained silent.

Sighing in frustration she jumped down and strode to the head of the carriage. 'I believe you have made a mistake,' she muttered tersely.

As she rounded the carriage, she saw the driver. He was slumped over the seat, covered in blood. A scream escaped her throat and she covered her mouth in horror. Someone had stabbed him. Icy fear twisted around her heart.

'Oh my God,' she whispered, suppressing the bile that rose in her throat. She began to quiver as fearful images built in her mind and sheer horror set in. Her stomach lurched with the realization that Alex was not going to be meeting her. He had obviously not sent the note. Someone had lured her here. The same someone who murdered poor Mr Briston. And now they would kill her. Backing away she practically stumbled over her own two feet as she turned to run. But there was no place to go.

She was trapped. She shivered with panic as her eyes darted around her, frantically searching for an escape route. The buildings surrounding the town house all looked equally deserted. Some of the houses were burned out, there was very little chance that anyone would happen by here to rescue her. Not in this part of town. If they did, robbery or murder would be their objective. Assisting a damsel in distress, a clearly wealthy lady, would not be first on their agenda.

A hand came from behind and clamped over her mouth. Struggling to free herself, she tried to scream, but her protests were stifled by the powerful hand pushing hard against her mouth.

She did not have to see him to realize who it was.

His macabre voice rang in her ears, 'At last we meet *encore, chérie*. I have been waiting a long time for this. And I am not a patient man, *ma petite*.'

A shiver of terror ran up her spine. Wrenching her mouth free, she screamed and wriggled against his iron grip. She kicked at his shins trying to escape him, but he tightened his hold and jerked her head back.

'*Silence!*' he hissed in her ear. 'There is no one to hear you.'

'Let me go!' she cried out. But he only laughed and hauled her away from the carriage. As he dragged her, kicking and screaming into the nearby town house, tears of fear streamed down her face.

The dilapidated house was completely dark. Rotten beams and timbers were scattered everywhere. Kara squirmed violently in a futile effort to break free, but his hands were like vices clamped over her mouth and digging painfully into her waist. When he closed the door his grip loosened, and seeing her opportunity, she sank her teeth into his palm.

'*Alors!*' he exclaimed and immediately released her.

She ran toward the door. But he was right behind her. As she reached for the doorknob, he grabbed a fistful of her hair and yanked her back. Screaming in agony, she fell backwards.

He pulled her roughly against him, '*Maintenant chérie*, do not try to run from me. Or I will break your lovely little neck, *n'est pas?*'

Shaking her head, she fought him, clawing at his face. He captured her flailing hands with his fists. Bending her head, she bit him as hard as she could, drawing blood.

He shouted in pain and struck her brutally across the face.

356

She went flying across the room from the force of his blow and landed with a thud on something cold and hard. Pushing against the floor with her palms, she tried to get to her feet. But her head was throbbing and something thick and wet was trickling down the side of her face.

Run! She had to run, but she was unable to move. Get up! a voice in her head screamed as she tried to inch along the floor. She could no longer see the door clearly. The house was too dim. And her eyes wouldn't focus. Desperately, she tried to crawl across the floor, but the room started to spin. It was no use, she could feel herself slipping away.

Several hours passed before Kara regained consciousness. She was aware of her body aching and slowly became familiar with her environment. Lifting her head, she winced. The pain was excruciating. She reached up and felt her forehead. Something sticky covered the side of her face. To her horror, her fingertips were red. It was blood! Her blood! She licked her dry sore lips and tasted the blood there as well. Touching her mouth she realized it was swollen and her bottom lip had a deep, painful gash.

She was lying on a settee in the condemned town house. A fire was blazing in the hearth casting a some light across the dark, musty room. Trying to orient herself, she sat up. The Frenchman had lured her here. And it was *not* for a romantic interlude. He intended to kill her!

Panic like she'd never known before welled inside her. She had to find a way out of this place. But how? She wasn't even sure where she was. She had to clear her head. To think. But her mind was terribly fuzzy.

No one would come for her. No one knew that she was here . . . except Aunt Henrietta. Please God! Let her read the note and tell Alex.

'So,' a dark, heavily accented voice drawled from across the room.

Kara's heart jumped in her chest. Gasping with fear, she started and looked over at the smartly dressed man seated before the hearth, with the Frenchman standing behind him.

'You are the Lady Dalton, *n'est pas?*'

Kara stared mutely at him. She may be a captive, but she did not have to cooperate with these brutes.

He steepled his fingers under his chin as his gaze slid over her face and settled on her heaving bosom. Kara crossed her arms over her chest and leaned away from the repellent man. But she could not control her spasmodic trembling.

He chuckled softly. 'I see that reports of your beauty are not exaggerated. How like *mon ami* Alex to wed the most *belle femme* in London.'

Obviously, this was Bouchard. Alex's nemesis. Stark, black fright swept over her. It all came together now. All this time that fetid Frenchman was working with Bouchard to get to Alex. And she was the bait. Like a lovesick fool, she had blindly walked into their trap. Had Alex received a similar fallacious note? she wondered. What had it said? *Oh, please Alex, be clever enough to piece it together*!

Her husband would never have written such a note. The profession of love should have alerted her to the trap. She had been so exhilarated by the beautiful declaration that she acted on impulse. She should have known better, Alex would never have penned such endearments. He was not in love with her. It revolted her to think of Bouchard luring her to this horrid place with empty words of affection.

'Don't cry *ma chérie, votre amour* will come to your rescue.'

Kara shook her head and wiped the tears from her face. 'You are a fool,' she hissed, 'he will not come for me.'

He arched an amused brow, '*Pour-quoi pas?*'

'He will be happy to be rid of me. He does not love me. Your trap will not work. You are wasting your time. You've gone to a great deal of trouble for nothing.'

The Frenchman's hands clutched the back of Bouchard's chair, '*Ce n'est pas possible!*' he burst out excitedly. 'You said he would come!'

Bouchard raised his hand, instantly quelling his co-conspirator's excitement, '*Un moment mon ami.*'

Rising from his chair, Bouchard walked over to Kara. She recoiled from him. But he caught her chin with his palm and roughly lifted her tear streaked face.

'You are very brave, *et je pense* clever. But I know the eminent Lord Dalton would not misplace such a lovely bride, *c'est vrai, n'est pas?*' he asked tilting her head back to look at him. Kara jerked her face away from him in revulsion.

'Oh Lady Dalton, you disappoint me, you see, I know your husband well. *Votre amour* is an honorable man. He will come for you *chérie. Tiens,* when he comes – '

'If he comes. He will kill you,' she spat out viciously.

Bouchard shook his head, a slow smile spreading across his face. '*Non, non chérie,* I shall kill him,' he assured her with an evil chuckle. 'You are fickle, are you not? He does not love you, but he will kill to save you?'

'I did not say he'd kill to save me. I said, he will kill you,' she snarled.

Bouchard turned his attention from Kara and addressed the Frenchman, '*Madame Dalton est trés belle, peut-être* I should sample a morsel of what *mon bon ami,* Alex has enjoyed.' He laughed. 'What say you, *chérie?*' he asked Kara. 'Shall we pass the time more pleasantly?'

Her pulse beat erratically at his threatening, ominous tone. Shaking her head, she leaned back on the settee.

'No!' she cried. Desperate to escape this odious man and his nefarious cohort, her eyes darted to the door and she inched along the musty, torn settee. But Bouchard's arm snaked out and he wrenched her to her feet.

'You disgust me,' Kara cried, struggling against his iron grip. 'I would rather die than let you touch me!' she hissed scratching at his hateful face.

'*Ma belle* has claws,' Bouchard said with a smile as he wiped the blood from his cheek. He leaned his face very close to hers, 'Your death has been arranged *ma petite*. Shall I give you to Philippe before your husband arrives?'

Kara closed her eyes blocking out his vile face. He laughed and pushed her back down on the settee.

Her head was pounding. She was petrified and she could not stop trembling. Think, she told herself, and forced herself to calm down and stop crying. She wiped the blood and tears from her face with the back of her trembling hand. The two men had their backs to her and were speaking in low voices before the fireplace. Her eyes flitted around the room, blind panic rioting through her mind.

Seeing a chance to escape, she got up and with her back pressed against the wall, slowly crept toward the door

'Going so soon my sweet?' Bouchard's hated voice asked from behind.

Kara bolted for the door, but Philippe was beside her. He grabbed her by the arm and twisted it behind her back. She wriggled against him trying to loosen her arm, but he squeezed her arm harder. And she cried out in pain as he pushed her down on her knees.

'When can I kill her Bouchard?' he drooled, his eyes frenzied.

Kara screamed in agony for he was breaking her arm.

'*Patience!*' Bouchard exclaimed. 'Dalton will come soon.'

'Please . . .' she wailed, breathing in shallow, quick gasps, 'make him stop!'

'*C'est tout!*' Bouchard snapped, 'she is no good to us with broken bones.'

Philippe released her, tossing her on the floor in a crumpled heap.

'Help me!' she sobbed. 'Someone please help me!' But she knew that no one would come. She was going to die at the hands of these evil men.

'Hush,' Bouchard hissed.

Drying her eyes she sniffled and stumbled to her feet. Was it her imagination or had she heard something? Her heart leaped to her throat. Alex! He had come for her! And then a wave of apprehension rushed over her. But no. He must not come in here. They will kill him!

'Alex!' she cried and started for the door desperate to warn him. Bouchard took her by the arm and covered her mouth with his palm. She struggled against him, but to no avail. He easily subdued her. Dragging her to the chair before the fire, he tossed her into it.

He pulled out his pistol and pressed it against her temple. 'Say nothing, *ma petite*,' he warned her against her ear.

She nodded her head, a cold knot of dread forming in her stomach.

He moved behind the chair. 'Remember,' he whispered 'not a word.'

CHAPTER 16

Kara could hear Alex's Hessians click along the bare wooden floor. The hollow sound battered her already shattered nerves. She closed her eyes. Please God, don't let him come in here! The footsteps came towards the door. Kara's heart thudded painfully against her rib cage. The footsteps stopped and the door slowly creaked opened.

Squirming in her seat, she bit down on her knuckles to keep from screaming. She was helpless to find a way to warn Alex. Clutching at the arms of the chair, she whimpered in desperation. But as she felt the pistol against her ribs, she went still.

'*Silence, ma chérie*. I care not if I kill you now or later,' Bouchard whispered fiercely from behind.

She nodded her head and sniffled.

The Frenchman crept up behind the door, his pistol primed and ready to fire.

'Kara?' Alex whispered. The flames from the fire flickered, illuminating her bloodied, tear stained face. Eyes wide, she shook her head, trying to warn him of the impending danger. But Alex stepped into the room.

'Kara –' he cried, in concern, rushing toward her, not seeing Bouchard in the shadows.

The door slammed shut and the Frenchman moved from behind the door. Cocking his pistol, he aimed it at Alex's head. Alex stopped in his tracks and stiffened as he raised his hands signaling his surrender.

'We meet again *monsieur*,' the Frenchman remarked giving Alex a shove, 'you survived our last meeting, but you will not be so lucky this time.'

Bouchard emerged from behind Kara's chair. 'Pleasant company you keep Bouchard. The son of an assassin, no less,' Alex said sardonically, 'You are moving up in the world.'

'Alex. It has been a long time,' Bouchard drawled casually, 'I am so pleased that you could join us. Your bride had some doubts, I fear. But then she does not know you as I do.'

'Why did you come?' Kara burst out, the tears pouring down her cheeks, 'They are going to kill you!'

Bouchard jerked Kara from the chair and pulled her against him. Watching Alex's malevolent expression, Bouchard ran the tip of his pistol up her waist, along her breast and her neck. Squeezing her eyes shut, she turned away in disgust.

The muscle in Alex's cheek throbbed dangerously and his mouth became a tight line of vengeance.

'She is very beautiful, Alex,' Bouchard said, as he tugged her head around to face him. His foul mouth covered hers and she uttered a stifled protest. Twisting her head vigorously she pummeled his chest with her fists.

Alex lunged for Bouchard. The Frenchman shoved his pistol against Alex's head, '*Monsieur*, you can die *maintenant* or later, it makes no difference to *moi*.' Alex stopped short.

Kara's teeth bit down as hard as she could on Bouchard's lip. With a yelp of pain, he lifted his foul mouth from hers. She spat at him. He stared at her, surprised by her temerity. He touched his lip, and seeing the blood on his finger he laughed.

'She is a tiger this one, eh Alex?' he chuckled. And then he slapped her face. Kara's head swung back and she cried out in pain.

Alex wanted to tear Bouchard limb from limb with his bare hands. But he restrained himself. He was no good to her dead. Watching Bouchard abuse her was driving him mad, however.

This woman meant more to him than his own life. He couldn't live without her. He'd save her or die trying. After all what was his life worth without the woman he loved by his side? Clenching his fists at his side, he forced himself to bide his time and remain calm. Bouchard wiped his mouth with a handkerchief.

'Let her go Bouchard, you've got what you wanted. She has nothing to do with this,' Alex said, in a voice that sounded remarkably calm to Kara's terrified ears.

'Oh, but she does,' Bouchard replied.

Alex looked momentarily confused before realization dawned. 'I will never let you kill her. You cannot honestly expect to get away with this. Even if your frothing lunatic friend here has other ideas. If I die,' he said with a cool smile, 'you know I'll take both of you with me.'

Astounded, Kara's eyes widened in amazement. He was unbelievably courageous. He was also seriously outnumbered. It was a gallant effort, but they were going to die, just the same. She would never live to tell him how very much she loved him. She turned her face away and bit back the tears for she could not bear to watch.

Bouchard laughed. 'You think so?'

'Enough of this,' Philippe cried growing agitated. 'I will have my revenge!' He waved his pistol in the air.

'What a stroke of luck, *n'est pas*, Alex?' Bouchard remarked, proud of his acumen, 'Who would have thought it? You must know that your bride is Eden's daughter. *Et mon ami Philippe*,' he said clapping him on the back, 'has been waiting a long, long time.'

'*Oui*,' Philippe said, 'for fifteen years I have wanted my revenge. And now, I shall have it. I will avenge *mon père*,' he said clenching his fist in the air.

'Yes, you would like that wouldn't you? Like father like son?' Alex muttered with sarcasm. 'Two insane murderers. Nice family.'

'That is not true! *Mon père* was a hero!'

'He was a cold-blooded executioner,' Alex countered coolly.

'Non! He killed the Duke of Englien for his country and Napoleon!'

Alex shook his head. 'You're insane,' he ground out.

Bouchard smiled, well pleased with himself. 'It is perfect is it not? Philippe will kill the girl and satisfy his lust for revenge for his father's untimely demise at the hands of Eden. And I get the pleasure of killing you.'

'You are a genius,' Alex spat out. 'You have a natural talent for attracting murdering friends like yourself.'

'Oh, but Alex,' Bouchard mocked, 'we were once so close. It breaks my heart to hear you say such cruel things.'

'There is a special place for vermin like you. And I am longing to send you there,' Alex sneered.

'I would not make idle threats if I were you,' Bouchard said gruffly. 'You are the one in grave peril. You are an intrepid adversary, but your temper will be the death of you. I will never forget how ferocious you were after those men were slaughtered. A few useless soldiers. What difference did it make? We could have been great partners, you and I.'

'Never. You led those men to their deaths for your own gain,' Alex said through his teeth. 'Think about it Bouchard. You caused hundreds of men to die, their deaths are on your soul. I am ready to die. Are you?'

Bouchard sighed, 'You were always difficult Alex. Arrogant to the last. This time,' he said tugging Kara hard against his side, 'I may do something you would regret more than losing your life.'

Alex stared at Bouchard, his steely eyes blazing with hatred.

'How would you like that Alex?' Bouchard asked laughing at his old friend's enraged face, 'She and I are going to become intimate friends. And you will watch.'

'Please,' Kara beseeched, 'I-if you let him go, I . . . I'll do whatever you want,' she swallowed back the nausea welling in her throat at the mere thought of this disgusting man touching her. 'Please, just let him go.'

'Kara no!' Alex growled and took a step towards her. But Philippe's pistol collided with his chest, stopping him.

Bouchard smiled grimly, 'Such devotion is touching. Do you love him so much?'

'You will kill me anyway what difference does it make?' she replied, utterly despondent.

'Don't be a fool, Kara – ' Alex snapped.

But Philippe cut him off, 'I will kill her now Bouchard!' he bellowed.

Bouchard shot him a quelling look. 'When I say and not before, Philippe,' he commanded.

Philippe shook his head, '*Non!* I was robbed of the pleasure fifteen years ago. She must die for her

369

father's sins. I will wipe the seed of Eden from this earth!'

'No!' Bouchard gritted. 'You will do as you are told!'

'He is never going to let you have her,' Alex said in a low voice. 'He thinks you are insane. He told me so. He'll kill me. And then you. He wants her for himself. He never cared about your cause. He was just using you to get to me.'

Agitated and confused, Philippe looked from Bouchard to Alex.

'It is true, you can see that can't you?' Alex said, egging him on. 'Ask him if you don't believe me. Of course, he is liar. But you know that already, don't you? Think. What promises has he ever kept?'

'Don't listen to him!' Bouchard exclaimed. 'He would say anything to save his precious bride. You and I are comrades. We want the same things,' he cajoled.

Philippe shook his head, '*Non!* He is right. You do not care about my cause. My father died at Eden's hand. But all you ever wanted was Dalton. And now you think to deprive me of my revenge!'

'That is not true!' Bouchard growled.

But Philippe was no longer listening, his eyes had glazed over as if he was reliving the events of fifteen years ago. 'I was only fourteen, I had never killed anyone before. But I knew I had to avenge my father's death. My hands were sweating as I waited

370

for Eden on that road. The carriage rounded the bend and I took my shot, killing the driver.' He smiled slightly, 'They thought they were being robbed, but it was only *le petit Philippe* seeking his revenge. I opened the carriage door and saw the three of them. I had not expected that. I remember you were there *chérie, avec votre mère,*' he said to Kara. 'I thought, what a shame to kill such a pretty little girl, but that did not matter, you were Eden's daughter. You had to die. You both had to die! I told Eden I was going to slaughter his family for the evil he had brought upon me. Eden lurched out of the carriage to wrestle the pistol from me, he thought to overpower me, but I took my shot. He fell on top of me, I labored against his weight. It was then I realized he was dead. When I scrambled to my feet the carriage was gone. Ever since then I have been waiting. Waiting for you *chérie*. To kill you.'

'But why?' Kara burst out, hysterically. 'Why? My mother and I did nothing to you. I could not have been more than three at the time.'

'I swore to blot out *votre père* and his name forever! My father's legacy ends with me. And so shall Eden's.'

'Then it was you who murdered poor Mr Briston,' Kara mumbled, piecing everything together in her mind.

Philippe nodded his head. 'I knew that dirty little man was telling you things. You might have learned too much.'

'So, you killed him,' Kara whispered with a shudder, 'in cold blood.'

'*Bien sûr*, I could not take the chance. I would not lose my opportunity for revenge. I thought never to find you again. But now I have, and I will not fail this time!'

Kara stared at the maniacal little man. He was quite deranged. One way or the other, she was going to die. She could not help herself, but she must try to save Alex.

'Y-you seek revenge for your father's death,' she stammered nervously, 'I see now, that-that you are right. I must die. But Dalton is not your enemy.'

'Kara –' Alex cried in an attempt to silence her.

She turned her teary eyes to his, her heart aching. 'This way, only one of us must die, my love,' she whispered softly.

'For God's sake, Kara – ' Alex barked.

'She is right Bouchard,' Philippe declared. 'I want her. I don't care what happens to Dalton. He is your affair.'

'But I do care!' Bouchard exploded hotly. 'I have been stalked like an animal long enough.'

'Well then, I've good news for you,' Alex snorted with contempt. 'Your wait is over. You are going to die. One way or another. Trust me, I am not as faint-hearted as you. I do not care if I live or die so long as you come with me.'

Eyes wild, Philippe looked about frantically. 'I will not die for your cause Bouchard,' he declared excitedly. 'Give me the girl!'

'Never! Not till he has been forced to watch me degrade her, it will be my final insult before he dies,' Bouchard hissed.

'*Non!* You will not speak to me of *patience*. I will wait no longer,' Philippe cried and lunged toward Bouchard.

Taken unawares, Bouchard released his grip on Kara to grapple with Philippe for the pistol. As the two fell to the ground in a death struggle, Alex grabbed Kara by the arm. Pulling her after him, the two ran from the room. She stumbled and fell just outside the door.

'Come on, Kara!' he snapped. Uttering an oath, he picked her up and hurried outside into the light of day.

Kara's mouth dropped open for the once deserted street was crawling with men. Several armed men waited to invade the town house. Sir Gilbert and Uncle Charles were among them.

'You took your own sweet time!' Alex growled as he strode past them with his wife safely tucked in his arms. 'What the devil were you waiting for? The first shot?'

'My goodness,' Uncle Charles exclaimed, as he noticed Kara's bloodied face, 'is she all right?'

'She will be. No thanks to you two,' Alex muttered gruffly, snuggling Kara in his arms as he crossed the lawn to the carriage.

He set her down on the velvet carriage seat and framed her swollen, bloodied face between his hands. 'Are you all right?'

Too stunned to speak, Kara blinked at him.

He gave her shoulders a slight shake. 'Are you all right?' he asked again, his voice rough with concern.

'I-I . . . y-yes,' she managed to reply with a hard swallow. She looked dazed and confused.

'Nothing broken?'

She shook her head. 'No. I don't think so.'

'Thank heaven for that. If you ever again offer yourself to another man, I'll kill you myself,' Alex muttered.

Nonplused. Her eyes widened and she stared blankly at him. 'I was trying to save you!'

He grimaced. 'A stalwart effort, my love, but completely unnecessary.'

'What?' she shrieked. 'In case you hadn't noticed, they were going to kill us! I was trying to save one of our lives.'

'Do you honestly think,' he said condescendingly, 'I would have walked into a trap like that totally unprepared?'

Her head started to spin. 'Are you telling me . . .' she said breathlessly as the earth moved beneath her, 'that all these men were here the entire time?'

Alex smiled and turned away to observe the fireworks playing out in the nearby town house. Kara grabbed his velvet lapel and pulled him around to face her.

He smiled and covered her hands with his own. 'Darling, you are perfectly safe now. You mustn't be frightened. I've got you.'

'Now! W-what about before?'

'Then too, my sweet,' he affirmed caressing her cheek affectionately.

'You-you mean to tell me, you let me go on and on for nothing!' she gasped in shocked disbelief.

'If you recall, I tried to silence you,' he countered with a roguish grin, 'but as usual, in your head-strong way, that I have grown deuced fond of – Kara!' he exclaimed in concern as she went limp in his arms. 'Are you all right? Darling, talk to me.' It was no use, she'd fainted.

'Not again!' he muttered and gathered her close. It was dashed annoying the way his little minx fainted at the most inopportune moments. This time, however, he was just glad she was alive. He pressed a kiss on her cheek and held her fast.

Kara could hear voices. They were talking about her. But she was too tired to open her eyes. She clung to the last vestiges of sleep.

'She should sleep for a bit longer,' someone was saying. 'When she wakes, give her another dose of laudanum, it will help her sleep. It is important that she get plenty of rest. Other than the cuts and bruises she is fine.'

'Thank you Doctor,' a voice that sounded remarkably like her husband's replied.

Kara heard the door close and she rolled over onto her back.

'Kara?' someone was calling her.

'Hmmm?' she mumbled wishing they would just go away.

'Are you awake darling?'

It was Alex. And he called her darling. Her eyes flew open and she stared blankly at his smiling face.

'It is really me, my love. Are you awake?' he asked, lovingly brushing her hair back from her forehead. She looked down and saw his hand was holding hers.

'What happened?' she asked, groggy from sleep.

He leaned down and pressed a kiss on her forehead. 'You fainted. I hope you don't plan to faint every time I rescue you,' he teased.

Was she dreaming? No she could not be. Her head ached terribly And her entire body was throbbing.

Her eyes fluttered shut. 'I am so very tired,' she moaned softly.

'We will talk later. Go back to sleep, my love,' he whispered and gently kissed her lips, 'I will be here when you wake. I can wait a few more hours. After all, we have all the time in the world together now, you and I.'

Kara wanted to ask him to kiss her again and say those nice things to her until she grew tired of hearing them. But she was too exhausted. She tried to tell him how much she loved him, but sleep overtook her and she mumbled something unintelligible.

Several hours later, when Kara opened her eyes and looked around the room, Alex was sound asleep, slumped in the chair beside the bed. From the look

376

of his unshaven face and disheveled clothing, he had spent some time in that chair.

Trying to push herself up to lean against the headboard. She winced from the pain in her arms. She looked down and saw the black and blue marks on her wrists. Well, at least her head had ceased its throbbing.

She sighed deeply, the horrid events at the town house invading her thoughts. It was beyond comprehension. If she could not feel the cuts and bruises on her body she would have believed it had all been a grotesque nightmare.

That demented man wanted to murder her. He had shot her father in front of her mother's eyes! No wonder Uncle Charles wanted Kara shielded from the truth. Her mother must have been enormously relieved when Kara had no recollection. Obviously, she'd hoped to spare her daughter the harsh reality of her father's death.

Uncle Charles must have decided to send them away for their own protection. If it had not been for that villain Bouchard, Uncle Charles's plan would have been successful. Of course, if her mother had not died, Kara might never have come to England. Strange, how life is full of bizarre coincidences.

'So, you are awake at long last,' she heard Alex say, as he came over to the bed. Kara tried to smile at her remarkable husband, but winced and gingerly fingered her sore mouth.

'Hurts?' he asked, his finger lightly caressing her jaw.

She nodded.

'How are you feeling otherwise?' he asked, his dark brows drawn together in concern.

'Fine,' she said brightly. 'Very glad to be alive.'

He brushed stray tendrils of hair away from her face. 'That makes two of us,' he said beaming down at her.

'Alex,' she said, her voice harsh with emotion, 'that man . . . killed my father. And he would have killed me.'

'I know my darling, try not to think of it,' he said gathering her in his arms. 'It is all over now.' He kissed the top of her head and held her close. 'You're safe.'

'I cannot seem to get it out of my mind,' she whispered, brushing the tears from her cheeks.

He smoothed her hair with his hand. 'I know, my love. It will take time for you to forget, to heal.'

'How did you know where I was?' she asked basking in the feel of her husband's strong, protective arms around her.

'Henrietta gave me the note.'

'T-then you read it?' she asked tentatively, feeling embarrassed that she had fallen for such a blatant ploy.

'Mmmm. Of course, she recognized it as a fake the moment she saw it,' Alex remarked.

Kara swallowed uncomfortably. 'Yes, well I – '

He squeezed her tightly. 'She knows my handwriting, Kara,' he said softly.

Suddenly, she remembered that she had only seen his writing once. As she recalled, it was virtually illegible. It was on their wedding night when she had searched his desk. That seemed like a lifetime ago. So much had changed since that fateful night.

'Then who gave the note to Violet?'

'Bouchard, of course. Poor Violet was his innocent victim. He threatened to kill her if she didn't do as she was told. But as soon as you'd gone, she confessed Bouchard's little scheme, weeping copiously.'

'Poor Violet. She must have been terrified of that brute.'

'Mmm. I received a ransom note when I returned from Daniel's sick bed.'

'Daniel's sick?'

'In a matter of speaking. He was shot. By Bouchard or Philippe, I am not sure which one. It doesn't really matter now.'

'Shot!' Kara exclaimed pushing away from him. 'How can you be so calm about it?'

He grinned at her and drew her against him. 'He is fine. He will be up and about in no time. I knew the moment I saw the note that Bouchard had lured you to the same place Daniel had stumbled upon last evening. Bouchard obviously could not wait. He must have known I would put the two incidents together and come after him. So he decided to make the first move.'

'Why did Philippe kill my father?' Kara asked, 'and who was that man, Englien, anyway?'

Alex rubbed her back soothingly and recounted the details of her father's past. 'As your mercurial mind sorted out,' he said teasingly, 'your father was working for the Crown during the French Revolution. Shortly after the Revolution, Napoleon came into power. Relations between England and France became strained, and England was threatened with a possible invasion from Boulogne. The French discovered the conspiracy against the first consul and the Duke of Englein was executed for his involvement. Eden, I mean your father, was sent on a counter espionage mission to kill the executioner – '

'So that was Philippe's father,' Kara mumbled thoughtfully.

'Yes. Your father completed his mission successfully. What he never guessed, was that the only surviving son of his victim would seek revenge clear across the Channel.'

'I cannot believe it,' Kara whispered, 'I witnessed my own father's murder and have absolutely no recollection.'

'Thank heaven you don't. Philippe was bent on revenge for his father's murder. I think his hatred drove him mad in the end.'

'It was Uncle Charles who had the death certificates forged and sent us to America wasn't it?'

'Yes. If your mother had not taken ill you would still be there. Of course, it was a fluke that Bouchard and the deranged Philippe joined forces. I had an inkling that there might be some connection. Bouchard played on Philippe's hatred of the English He pretended to believe in Philippe's cause. And he created that ridiculous conspiracy to lure me. That is where I was all those late nights, at the docks conducting my investigation.'

'Then our marriage came as a surprise? He did not know?'

Alex shook his head. 'He had no idea. Naturally, the coincidence worked in Bouchard's favor.'

Kara lay quietly in the comfort of Alex's arms for a long, long time digesting everything. It did not seem possible.

'Philippe murdered poor Mr Briston. And I am responsible, if I had not – '

'Kara, Runners know the danger. He knew the risks when he took the job. You are not responsible for the actions of a madman,' he told her, gently caressing her cheek with his palm.

'What did Bouchard mean? You weren't actually a friend of his, were you?'

Alex sighed. 'During the war, I knew him. He was a double agent. He was spying for the French. I inadvertently provided him with some information. Information that cost lives,' he said gruffly, his voice riddled with guilt.

'You cannot believe you are responsible for those deaths? How could you have known he was a spy? He was an evil man,' Kara said, in an effort to comfort him.

'I know that now. I am just glad he didn't hurt you.'

'Speaking of that. You scared me to death. You might have told me that there was help on the way. All that time I thought we were going to die. You let me go on believing that we were doomed. I cannot believe you did not even try to tell me – '

'Kara,' he said pressing his finger to her lips, 'are you actually admonishing me for saving your life?' he asked softly.

'Well, I was frightened. If you knew that we would be saved, you might have told me.'

'Just how could I do that without enlightening our charming companions?' he said.

'I suppose there was no way, but I still wish you had stopped me from blubbering on uncontrollably.'

He chuckled, 'I tried to silence you. But far be it for me to tell my headstrong wife what to do,' he teased.

Kara shot him a reproachful look.

'Besides,' he said, a wicked glint in his eye. 'I rather enjoyed your little speech.'

Kara looked away. 'I am sure I do not know what you mean,' she said stiffly.

'Fortunately for us both,' he said, tenderly cupping her chin with his palm and turning her face toward him, 'I have excellent hearing and an even better memory.'

Lowering her lashes, she fidgeted with the sheets. 'What else should I have done? I thought they were going to kill you, Alex.'

'Look at me,' he commanded softly.

Tentatively, she lifted her eyes to his.

'You were extraordinarily brave. I was quite impressed,' he said staring deeply into her eyes.

Kara smiled shyly, 'I was scared to death.'

'I must say, your declaration of undying devotion took me by surprise. You know, they say to offer one's life in return for another is the greatest possible demonstration of love.'

Squirming uncomfortably, Kara tried to change the subject, 'What will happen to those awful men?'

'I expect they will be buried,' he replied dryly.

'What do you mean?' she asked blankly.

'Ah, yes,' Alex recalled, 'that is right, you fainted. They killed each other before they could be apprehended.'

Kara shivered. 'I still cannot believe it all really happened.'

'It did. But you are safe now,' he said rubbing the small of her back. 'You must know I love you, Kara and I would never let anything happen to you,' he said with aching tenderness.

Kara nodded. Then it hit her, I love you! She pushed away from him.

'What did you say?' she asked in a mere whisper, her vivid blue eyes searching his face.

'I said, I would never let anything happen to you,' he replied brushing her cheek, it was quite a lovely cheek he thought to himself. 'I could not bear to lose you,' he said softly, his thumb gently caressing her cheekbone.

'No,' she snapped shaking her head, 'before that.'

'Oh that,' he said nonchalantly, 'I said I love you.'

'Are you in earnest?' she asked searching his face. She couldn't bear it if he were teasing her.

'Very much so,' he told her, his voice tight with emotion.

Kara stared at him, awestruck.

He laughed. 'I certainly hope you are not disappointed.

'Oh Alex!' she cried throwing herself in his arms. 'How could I be disappointed when you know how very much I love you?'

'I can't think,' he murmured and his mouth covered hers, devouring her lips in a passionate embrace. She did not seem to notice the cut on her swollen lip. In fact, she forgot everything but him; his mouth on hers, his hands caressing her body and the feel of him deep inside her. She wanted only to love and be loved by him.

Afterwards, they lay in each other's arms reveling in their new found joy.

'Alex?' she asked quietly.

'Mmmm?' he replied, lazily.

'When did you know?'

'Know what?' he asked yawning hugely.

'When you loved me, of course,' she said, dreamily.

'Oh that,' he teased. 'Now, let me think, it is difficult to know precisely when. It was certainly not when you hired that Runner. And most definitely not when you ran away. Hmmm, let me see.'

'Be serious,' she censured and pushed up on his bare chest to look at his face, 'it is important.'

He smiled at her and threaded his fingers through her hair, tenderly framing her face between his palms. 'It is difficult to remember when I did not love you,' he told her softly. His dark eyes brimming with emotion.

'You certainly have a strange way of showing it,' she said skeptically.

He laughed. 'Why do you think I went berserk every time you did something foolish?'

She laid her cheek against his chest. 'I knew I loved you the moment you kissed me,' she said with a sigh of joy. 'It was the most wonderful day of my life.'

'Kara,' Alex whispered, rubbing the curve of her lovely little back, 'you hated me!'

'I never hated you,' she countered firmly.

'Madam, I beg to differ – '

'My lord,' she said sliding up his chest to place a kiss on his lips, 'are you actually arguing with me as to when I fell in love with you?' she asked in a soft, seductive tone.

'I might be,' he whispered kissing her cheek, 'provided, of course, that we make up.'

Kara laughed. 'As you wish, my lord,' she said kissing his inviting mouth.

Kara was feeling much better the next morning, but Alex decreed that the couple were not to be disturbed until further notice. He informed cook, in

385

deference to Kara's injuries, that they intended to take all their meals in their bedroom until further notice.

Breakfast arrived on a silver platter. Stretching like a contented kitten, Kara sat up in bed and listened to her husband read *The Times*'s explanation of the Bouchard case.

Munching on a piece of bacon, 'There is no mention of you!' she cried, clearly outraged by the omission.

Alex shrugged nonchalantly and dropped the paper to grab his wife. He pulled her into his arms and kissed her deeply.

'Alex,' she scolded, when she came up for air, 'you kept me up all night. I am famished!'

He groaned and reluctantly let her go. Laughing at him over her shoulder, she hopped out of bed and flitted over to the breakfast tray. Alex leaned back and watched her heap eggs, bacon and toast onto a plate for them to share.

'Kara,' he said in a dark, silky voice.

'Yes, my love,' she replied cheerfully, 'what is it? Henceforth, I am going to be the most obedient wife you could ever wish for. Your every wish is my command.'

'Then come here,' he ordered in a sensual voice.

Kara spun around, munching on a piece of toast, smiled and brought the plate of food to the bed, 'Aren't you hungry?' she asked, climbing onto the bed.

'Mmmm,' he replied his eyes twinkling suggestively as his hand crept around her waist.

'I meant for food!' she cried, slapping his hand away.

'That too,' he teased, picking up her half eaten piece of toast. He kissed her on the mouth and resumed his perusal of the morning paper, reading aloud,

'Rare sapphires, which are supposed to have once belonged to the Lady Dalton sold for – '

Kara dropped her fork. 'Please, Alex,' she whispered, 'I'd rather not hear . . .' she mumbled looking down at her plate.

'No? I think it quite a fascinating story,' he said dryly.

Kara stared at him, incredulously. She knew it was too much to hope that he would ever forgive her, but did he have to rub it in?

Alex smiled at her doleful expression and patted her cheek affectionately. 'Don't worry love, in the end the lucky man did not pay a penny for them.'

Kara frowned, how could he joke at a time like this? Dropping her gaze to her lap, she smoothed out the blankets and mumbled, 'Really?'

'Hmmm, you see the jeweler happens to be a married man himself. He agreed to a simple exchange; the sapphires in return for the tidy sum he paid for them. He understood when I explained about my headstrong wife.'

Her head snapped up. 'You what?' she cried.

Alex laughed and reached into the bedside table drawer to retrieve the sapphires.

'Why you!' she scolded pounding his chest playfully with her fists.

Alex laughed and pulled his tempestuous wife into his arms.

It was hard to believe it was possible to improve on heaven, but she and Alex apparently had managed it. She had never felt such complete contentment

'You are awfully good to me Alex. I wish you had told me! You know how wretched I felt.'

'Mmmm, but this is a much, much better way to find out,' he murmured, as he rolled over on top of her. His mouth came down on hers in a passionate, breathtaking kiss.

Yes, Kara thought, as her arms slipped around his back, it is.

THE EXCITING NEW NAME IN WOMEN'S FICTION!

PLEASE HELP ME TO HELP YOU!

Dear *Scarlet* Reader,

As Editor of *Scarlet* Books I want to make sure that the books I offer you every month are up to the high standards *Scarlet* readers expect. And to do that I need to know a little more about you and your reading likes and dislikes. So please spare a few minutes to fill in the short questionnaire on the following pages and send it to me.

Looking forward to hearing from you,

Sally Cooper

Editor-in-Chief, *Scarlet*

QUESTIONNAIRE

Please tick the appropriate boxes to indicate your answers

1 Where did you get this Scarlet title?
Bought in supermarket □
Bought at my local bookstore □ Bought at chain bookstore □
Bought at book exchange or used bookstore □
Borrowed from a friend □
Other (please indicate) _____

2 Did you enjoy reading it?
A lot □　　A little □　　Not at all □

3 What did you particularly like about this book?
Believable characters □　　Easy to read □
Good value for money □　　Enjoyable locations □
Interesting story □　　Modern setting □
Other _____

4 What did you particularly dislike about this book?
_____

5 Would you buy another Scarlet book?
Yes □　　No □

6 What other kinds of book do you enjoy reading?
Horror □　　Puzzle books □　　Historical fiction □
General fiction □　　Crime/Detective □　　Cookery □
Other (please indicate) _____

7 Which magazines do you enjoy reading?
　1. _____
　2. _____
　3. _____

And now a little about you –
8 How old are you?
Under 25 □　　25–34 □　　35–44 □
45–54 □　　55–64 □　　over 65 □

cont.

9 What is your marital status?
Single ☐   Married/living with partner ☐
Widowed ☐   Separated/divorced ☐

10 What is your current occupation?
Employed full-time ☐   Employed part-time ☐
Student ☐   Housewife full-time ☐
Unemployed ☐   Retired ☐

11 Do you have children? If so, how many and how old are they?
_____
_____

12 What is your annual household income?

under $15,000	☐	or	£10,000	☐
$15–25,000	☐	or	£10–20,000	☐
$25–35,000	☐	or	£20–30,000	☐
$35–50,000	☐	or	£30–40,000	☐
over $50,000	☐	or	£40,000	☐

Miss/Mrs/Ms _____
Address _____
_____
_____

Thank you for completing this questionnaire. Now tear it out – put it in an envelope and send it, before 28 February 1998, to:

Sally Cooper, Editor-in-Chief

USA/Can. address
SCARLET c/o London Bridge
85 River Rock Drive
Suite 202
Buffalo
NY 14207
USA

UK address/No stamp required
SCARLET
FREEPOST LON 3335
LONDON W8 4BR
Please use block capitals for address

ERBR1/8/97

***Scarlet* titles coming next month:**

DEADLY ALLURE   Laura Bradley

After her sister's murder Britt Reeve refuses to let detective Grant Collins write the death off as an accident. Britt suspects that the murderer could be someone with family ties, and soon she and Grant find themselves passionate allies in a race against time . . .

WILD FIRE   Liz Fielding

Don't miss Part Three of **The Beaumont Brides** trilogy! Melanie Beaumont's tired of her dizzy blonde image. She's determined to show everyone that she can hold down a proper job. And if that means bringing arrogant Jack Wolfe to his knees . . . so much the better!

FORGOTTEN   Jill Sheldon

What will happen if Clayton Slater remembers who he is and that he's never seen Hope Broderick before in his life? And Hope has another problem . . . she's fallen in love with this stranger she's claimed as her lover!

GIRLS ON THE RUN   Talia Lyon

Three girls, three guys . . . three romances?
Take three girls: Cathy, Lisa and Elaine. Match them with three very different guys: Greg, Philip and Marcus. When the girls stop running, will their holiday romances last forever?